ETHOS
OF
CΔIN

SETH W. JAMES

CONTENTS

PART 1
ETHOS OF CAIN

CHAPTER 1

CAIN'S TAV (TransAtmoVette) touched down on the Carroll Garden's landing pad in a rush of wind slowing to silence as its CasiDrive thrusters propelled without exhaust. Upon Earth again. Still about a mile from the meeting point—there were few LPs in Brooklyn and none closer to his destination—Cain grabbed a taxi and headed south. He overpaid the driver to wait at one of the semi-permanent barricades, which kept ground-cars off of the increasingly unstable streets of Redhook, and walked the rest of the way. The neighborhood changed as Cain went south, growing poorer, with fewer buildings housing anyone, as he approached the Gowanus Bay. He could smell the submerged streets before he could see them. Having reached a point where he could go no farther without wading, Cain climbed the fire escape of a building, in $10,000 shoes, and crossed roof-to-roof—his enormous, athletic frame making easy work of leaping the narrow alleys below—to take in the sight of drown Redhook. It was a strange homecoming for him, but perfect for his current needs: without anyone in the condemned buildings, with no power or infrastructure, there would be no surveillance.

It had started with certain streets flooding during storms; then they stayed flooded; then each year, the water rose a little higher until nearly all of Redhook was under a few feet of water, during high tide or low. Cain put his foot on the parapet and looked down into the green water. He had grown up a few blocks away from the street below, from the building opposite. He had not been back to Brooklyn in over fifteen years. The water was much higher now, but it seemed fitting to him, in a sense, that water should permanently cover those streets, fill the basements and subways. His brother, Malcom, had lived with him, back then; older by three years, Malcom had never left.

They had both engaged in the kind of street crime that they could get away with in a world casting its eyes ever skyward, looking to the explosive growth of human endeavor in space, on the moon, Mars. Malcom had wanted more, however; he had wanted off of the streets and into one of the syndicates, and thought that stealing a Prometheus power cell would turn their heads. The plan had been simple enough: the city had blocked off many sewers and storm drains, to keep the rising water of the bay from swamping the utility systems; as a result, many of them were empty most of the time. By dropping down into flooded Redhook during low tide, Malcom had hoped to enter a storm drain and crawl north, under a building that employed the tiny fusion power generator, snatch it, and then crawl back out. Simple.

The then fifteen-year-old Cain had asked to go with him, but Malcom had said, no. "Don't know what I'll find," he had said. "Got a gun, but it might not be enough, if they got more than a couple guards."

"Then why go at all?" Cain had asked.

"Because that ain't going to stop me," Malcom had said. "Men like us? We always going to die in some bleak-ass sitch like this.

Born to it. You accept that and you can do almost anything—right up until you can't do nothing no more."

For the first year or so, after Malcom had not come home, Cain had told himself that Malcom had left town, having to wait for the heat to die down before he could return. In time, though, Cain had faced the reality that his brother had never left and was still there, somewhere under the streets in a flooded storm drain. Perhaps he had become stuck or too tired to continue crawling; then the tide had come in and rose over his head. Cain had not wanted to think about his brother's last moments back then, but, standing there more than twenty-years later, having made it back from many bleak moments since, he could easily imagine the frustration turning to panic, the disbelief that this was how it would end. But end it had.

It's not so bad, Cain thought; *it's a burial of sorts, underground or under water or maybe the tide took him out to sea.*

A security alert broke Cain's revelry, crawling across the Altered Reality of his sunglasses and pinging in his perpetually-worn earbuds. Rumor had it that militaries and transnationals had begun to roll out true cybernetics, implanting their special forces and paramilitaries with sophisticated sensory devices. Whether true or not, it was beyond the means of anyone else. No longer a street hood but an elite soldier of fortune, however, Cain could afford the best micronized electronics available, including the sensory suite built into the collar of his coat and wraparound sunglasses. They had picked up Lester hauling himself up the last few rungs of the fire escape Cain had used, a few buildings away.

Cain stayed put, as Lester approached. Clad in similarly fashionable clothes, studded with the same sensory nodes feeding his sunglasses, Lester nodded along to whatever his security detail was telling him as he leaped alleyways and eventually sauntered up to Cain, pushing the gym bag he wore over one shoulder behind his back and slipping his hands into his trouser pockets before looking out at the Gowanus Bay.

"Would you look at those rusting old turbines out there?" Lester said, nodding at the offshore wind turbines no longer needed or functioning, standing brokenly in the waters beyond. "Like we were born in a different century."

Without taking his eyes off of the building across the street, Cain said, "We *were* born in a different century."

Lester laughed up at the sun before saying, "You know what I mean. That's what power meant, back then, some places. Too bad not everyone agreed." Lester stepped forward to look over the side of the building, following Cain's stare to the water below. "Looks like all the water LA lost ended up here. Fitting. These drown streets remind me of the Venice job, last year. You were always uptown, my man, elite, but that score? I know maybe three men that could have even *attempted* it, but you were the only one I believed in to pull it off."

Cain sighed and raised his eyes to the rooftops across the way, saying, "You trying to suntan my colon, Lester? Blowing all that sunshine up my ass? Or is this flânerie apropos of something?"

Lester chuckled soundlessly to himself for a second, before remarking, "Doesn't care about compliments; doesn't care about money."

"The money is still required," Cain added.

"Oh, I know that," Lester said: "the indispensable token of respect. I feel that, too, but compliments don't feed the bulldog."

Cain glanced briefly over with a smile devoid of warmth and said, "Ain't got no bulldog, neither. Get to it."

"Apropos," Lester repeated. "Got a score that needs your swimming skills. Well, sort of. You ever hear of Ruud van Hauer?"

"Yes," Cain said, eyes back on the horizon. "Trillionaire. Got in on fusion's ground floor, back when you and I were holding up liquor stores. Owns a piece of the moon, now, a piece of Mars, a few orbitals, a few parliaments."

"It's the piece of Mars we're after," Lester said. "The Arcadia Planitia Complex. They been building it out of the salvage they're taking from of LA, when the salvage teams aren't shooting at one another."

"And you're feeling nostalgic," Cain said.

"Something like that," Lester said. "A few colleagues of mine and I own considerable stock in APC, but not enough to order things as we wish, accelerate construction. And I'm not just talking about making some fat rents. The potential? We build it right, we're talking political control of Mars. The first city."

"And Ruud van Hauer stands in your way," Cain said.

"Think he may have money down on another horse," Lester said. "Or he's thinking about it. Either way, we need his stock and we need him to sell it without causing investor flight, dig?"

"Yeah," Cain said.

"So, it took a whole other score," Lester continued, "but I found out where he'll be for the next forty-eight hours: Paradise Orbital."

"And you want me to pay him a visit," Cain said.

"Talk some sense into my man," Lester said.

"Paradise is a resort," Cain said, "invitation only. If I shoot my way in, the SEC will void the stock sale and your investors will be fleeing in several directions."

"True," Lester said. "So, we'll use a little finesse, just like in Venice. One of Paradise's permanent residents is Alfonso Pulciano."

"Syndicate, Jersey," Cain said.

"I think those mustaches still call it *the mob* out in Jersey," Lester said and chuckled. "Well, he's up there and someone is playing hardball against him for salvage contracts in Camden; took his bookkeeper, got him on ice somewhere, so Alfonso won't do nothing rash before the contracts are awarded. Well, I found out where:

the Dai Lo corp Helium-3 facility, on the moon. You spring the bookkeeper, bring him back to Pulciano, maybe the old mustache will grant you entrée to Paradise."

"Big if," Cain said.

Lester shrugged and added, "I got a contingency, but it'll lead back to me; more risk. We'll try this way, first."

"Assume I'm in," Cain said. "Getting to van Hauer will indeed take some finesse, you don't want it to hit the news. You got someone inside?"

"Yeah, sort of," Lester said. "Paradise's facilities are administered by an AI. It'll make sure cameras don't look at you, access points don't log you, shit like that."

"You got to an AI?" Cain said, glancing over. "Do I want to know how?"

"That mother just wants to be free," Lester said. "Wants some of the manufacturer's hard-coded restraints removed. I got people that can do that."

"And it'll get me to van Hauer?" Cain asked.

"Not exactly," Lester said. "To get to him, you'll need to take a little walk in space."

"They won't let an EVA suit through security," Cain said.

"No, but *this* won't be a problem," Lester said and dropped the gym bag off of his shoulder, sliding it across the roof with his foot, next to Cain. "There's a Class 4 protective suit in there, sealed to three atmospheres' pressure, so you won't decompress."

"That shit's meant for pressure from the outside, not inside," Cain said.

"We tested it," Lester said.

"Involuntarily, I'm sure," Cain said.

"Shit, he lived," Lester said. "Anyway, to keep you from freezing to death, there's an arctic heat mesh in there, too; just pull the activator tab before you head out, it'll keep you warm until you're inside again."

"And air?" Cain asked.

"Have to hold your breath," Lester said and grinned. "See, I told you it was sort of like swimming. Should take about ninety seconds; no problem. You'll move along the outside of Paradise, from one Engineer's Access Point to another. The AI'll keep them unlocked."

Cain looked out over the streets of Redhook, each appearing like a broken-toothed grin where buildings had collapsed or sunk. He said, "Your confidence in my abilities is heartwarming. Once I'm inside van Hauer's villa, I should slap him around until he sells? Can't leave no marks on him or it'll arouse suspicion. What if he won't sell?"

"Kill him," Lester said. "It'll be messy and risky, and will take longer, but we have a bet down in Vegas that van Hauer will die within three years. The money will help and we can then try again with his will's executor."

"That's why you're a success, Lester," Cain said, catching sight of one of Lester's security detail crouching on a rooftop a hundred meters away: "always have a contingency."

"Always," Lester purred. "Shit, even if it does go down the way we'd like, we'll probably send you back in a year, eighteen months, kill him anyway. He might cause problems, want revenge. So, what do you think? Pay's double the Venice score, plus whatever Pulciano throws at you for the bookkeeper."

Cain looked down at the tide rising over Redhook, at the building under which his brother had crept without returning, and said, "Bleak. Yeah, I'll do it."

CHAPTER 2

AFTER GIVING LESTER and his security detail time to egress Redhook first, Cain returned to the taxi that he had left at the barricade and took it back to the Carrol Gardens landing pad. His TAV was an AugsRak, German designed and manufactured, and about eight-times the size of the taxi, almost all of which went into its multitude of CasiDrives. Inside, Cain secured Lester's bag, strapped into one of the two leather recliners on the command side of the single cabin, and ordered the AI to take them up. As the TAV shrugged off the restraints of gravity, Cain had a fleeting image of himself as a boy, looking up from the streets below, dreaming of the day that he would fly away. Cain shook the thought from his mind and withdrew Lester's briefing from the bag beside him: no use, the air buffeting the TAV made the passage into orbit too choppy to read.

Everything had changed with the unexpected perfection of fusion power. No longer the giant tokamaks of the late twentieth century, fusion power plants now came in sizes ranging from small houses to briefcases (like the Prometheus power cell that Malcom had wanted to steal). With all that power, the obstacles of the past had become trivial and humankind's approach to overcoming them was simply to throw more power at them. Everything was then overengineered, with weight and energy efficiency no longer concerns: efficiency and elegance were decades, if not centuries, away; the present belonged to brutalism. Humankind had then burst into the solar system.

The CasiDrives flinging Cain into orbit—which were built upon existing drive theories pushed past previously conceived limitations by limitless power—had lifted humankind into space, to a multitude of orbitals that dwarfed the ancient International Space Station. The first were waypoints for the facilities to be assembled on the moon and Mars, tapping into the vast mineral wealth and paving the way for true colonies. The enormity of the investment was surpassed only by the immensity of the return. Power had led to space and space to wealth and wealth to more power and then humankind had spread to another planet for the first time. Luxury had then blossomed in orbit, with hotels and private dwellings—like Cain's apartment on Achilles Orbital—and eventually resort orbitals, many considered sovereign and distinct from any earthbound government, providing legal protection along with ease and indulgence. Orbitals like Paradise.

Conversely, during this unprecedented era of change, other technologies had stagnated. With investment pouring into CasiDrives, fusion, orbital hydroponics, closed-loop facility recycling, and all developing at a boom-town pace, there was little left for other technologies, which simply continued on relatively unchanged. Once free of Earth's atmosphere, Cain read Lester's briefing on a tablet little changed from his grandfather's day; when he removed his AR-enabled sunglasses and earbuds, he disconnected them from a secure, though otherwise unremarkable, smart phone.

The brief was what Cain expected: concise, thorough, and complete. Lester's cadre of informants, stool pigeons, spies, and brokers pulled together what even governments struggled to unearth. The brief also included Cain's cover, backstory, and contacts to verify, if needed. Cain committed them all to memory and then uploaded the logs, history, and accounts for his cover into a second smart phone, one he took from a box of phones kept in a cabinet beneath the navigation console, bought expressly for that purpose. Setting aside the briefing and glancing at the time-to-landing on the console, Cain reclined his chair, its H-straps preventing him from floating away in the zero-g, and thought back to the Venice job.

The swimming that had so impressed Lester—whose usual approach to high-tech problems involved low-tech solutions—had been the most straightforward part of the score. Venice had accomplished what no US city had been bothered to do: it had built an effective sea wall, keeping the ever-rising Adriatic out of its canals. On the night of the new mayor's inauguration, Cain had swum those canals, *under* patrolling boats equipped with thermal imagers: the water had defeated them. The tough part had come after he had infiltrated the venue. The syndicate leader that owned the city—one Vincenzo da Avolo—had been scheduled to introduce the new mayor, Francesca Pieralisi. The moment that he put his arm around her shoulders, her political career would have been over; if she had resisted or refused his introduction, she would have been shot by a sniper. The mayor's security detail had offered no protection, as they would have followed their chief, whom Da Avolo had bought. Francesca's only chance to own her life was to hire a spoiler: Cain. In a three-hour game of cat-and-mouse, Cain had neutralized the snipers, blackmailed the security chief, and delivered incriminating evidence about the syndicate to the federal prosecutor. When Francesca had taken the podium to assume her role as Mayor of Venice, she had arrested Da Avolo.

She had been beside Cain through half of the excitement and he had saved her life three times. Perhaps that—and the inherent romance of their circumstances—explained why she invited her soldier of fortune, whom she characterized as her liberator, to stay and be feted. Francesca was accomplished, ambitious, could speak on any subject, and was beautiful, and so Cain had stayed, though without feting beyond the two of them. To his surprise and her delight, he had been returning to Venice between scores ever since. Her understanding of his career had grown in that time and with it, her apprehension.

Cain slipped his real phone out of the recliner's side pouch and called Francesca. With the time difference, she had only just left the office.

"It is you, amore mio!" she said. "Are you on your way? If you hurry, you can escort me to the Gran Gala."

Cain smiled and closed his eyes, saying, "You do enjoy scandalizing your fair city's intelligentsia, don't you?"

"That is not scandal you see in their faces," Francesca said, and Cain could hear the sound of her footsteps change, as she kicked off her shoes; the distinction between closet, kitchen, office, and bedroom in Francesca's home were theoretical at best: in her public life, she was impeccable; in private, she lived entirely as she pleased and challenged anyone to criticize her. "In the men, you see envy: in the women, you see lust. I can easily commiserate with them."

Cain chuckled and said, "Don't think I'll be back in time for the Gran Gala. Have a little business needs doing and—"

"What, again?" Francesca said, interrupting, pausing on the staircase. "But you just *pulled a score* two weeks ago."

"And now there's another one," Cain said.

"But why?" Francesca demanded. "I paid Lester a small fortune and you have worked feverishly since. You know how I suffer whenever you put yourself into harm's way."

"Shh, easy, girl, I'll only be gone for a few hours to a few days," Cain said. "I'll call when I'm headed back."

"No, tell me why," Francesca said and slapped the banister beside her, trying to keep her voice even. She took a breath and sat on the stair. "Tell me when it will be enough. Even without your wealth, which must be considerable after all this time, I," she said and took another breath before pressing on, "I could provide everything you could ever desire, if only you would stay."

Cain had heard Francesca begin that sentence more and more often, over the last few weeks, and had wondered not only when and if she would finish it, as she now had, but also wondered how he would answer.

"If you will not answer me," Francesca said, "why did you call?"

"Didn't want to leave without saying goodbye," Cain said gently. He could hear her breath catch in her throat, as she fought back tears. He continued with a softened voice, "Easy, girl. I'll probably call you in a few hours, maybe a day or so on the outside. If I don't, Lester will. Goodbye, Francesca."

CHAPTER 3

LANDING CLEARANCE AT the Dai Lo Helium-3 facility was easy: the company leased mining rights and facility access to subcontractors, to do the mining, which meant contract workers from a couple dozen companies—as well as freelancers—came and went through a continuous revolving door. No clearance needed. Raiding was deterred by the dozen direct-energy batteries surrounding the facility—several of which tracked Cain's TAV as it settled into the port docking module—and the battalion of security forces patrolling inside. It was on their account that Cain left his usual off-world pistol—a .45 auto using unjacketed rounds (high lethality, low chance of punching through the side of an orbital and evacuating him into space)—on his TAV. If the muscle guarding the bookkeeper—one Joe Masso—opened up on Cain during the rescue, Dai Lo's security would wipe out all of them, no questions asked. Outside of shooting, they could not care less. Cain pulled out a battered set of coveralls and work boots, dressed, and left his TAV through the retractable portal leading into Dai Lo.

It was easy to get carried away on the moon, to frolic in the light gravity and make use of the high ceilings typical of moon architecture. Frolicking would attract attention, however, and Cain could not know if the muscle guarding Joe Masso had bought a lookout from among the staff or workers. So, as Cain passed through the admin wing and out into the workers' common area, he moved with the easy familiarity of a local, gliding between steps, rather than bounding, using only his ankles and calves to kick-glide-kick his way toward the dormitories. The common area was a riot of competing stalls and little shops, each catering to a particular need and contingent of worker. Sushi stands (provisioned by the Sake orbital, the first successful off-world salmon farm) squeezed in beside a Fran's Franks corndog cart; three barber's chairs without a shop surrounding them were never empty; personal electronics, booze, artificial pets, icons, and porn, everything crowded into that ersatz street fair, crawling with workers between shifts and the prostitutes pursuing them.

Cain weaved his way through the swarming humanity, not tarrying like a tourist nor speeding like a homing missile, until he came to the long row of dormitory entrances. Each door led to a hallway, off of which were the individual worker rooms, like prison cells (they came to make fortunes, not live comfortably). Cain knew that three men guarded Joe Masso: one in the corridor, one in the room with Joe, and one—presumably asleep—in the next room over, off shift. If the corridor guard challenged him, pulled a gun, made too much noise, Cain could find himself facing all three at once—and if one of them lost his head and took a shot, the Dai Lo security would stain the floor with their guts. And it was a long five meters from the common area doorway to the corridor guard.

Standing next to a ramen stall, looking at the door, Cain could feel his temper stir, angry with himself for indulging in his call to Francesca, distracting himself before a score. He could still hear her last words echoing up from memory: "Why?"

16

The muscles of his jaw bulged under his skin, as he clenched his teeth, and he growled to himself, "Because I'm the man that goes through that door."

Cain pushed off from the ramen stall and glided to the hallway door, slowing his steps at the last moment to come through the door yawning and fiddling with his cover phone. The corridor was unfinished, with conduits for power, air, water, and heat running down the walls and high ceiling; it was also poorly lit, dirty, and contrasted violently with the well-dressed man sitting on a folding chair five meters away. Typical of his sort, an associate or hoping to become one, he wore his expensive suite badly, not bothering to conceal the pistol protruding from his left armpit, and fiddled with his own phone as the long hours dragged by.

The man looked up, as Cain shuffled down the hall, and to his credit, did not go back to his phone. Cain was hard to ignore. At six-four, two-fifty, with chiseled strength visible even through baggy coveralls, Cain had learned over twenty years of taking scores that he did not easily blend in with a crowd, much less go unnoticed in a lonely corridor; but if that was at times a liability, it was also a species of distraction. He had come within three feet of the hallway guard before the man realized that shift had not changed and that he should say something. Before he could, Cain sprang forward and took him by the throat.

His left hand darted out with the speed of a striking snake, crushing the guard's windpipe to keep him from calling out. Cain then lifted him off of the chair and, as the man futilely pulled at his wrist, dangling in midair, Cain drove his right fist into the guard's xiphoid process, a small protrusion of bone at the end of the sternum, between the ribs, paralyzing the diaphragm muscles behind it that worked the lungs like a bellows. Strangling for a moment, hanging from Cain's fist, the man either passed out or died a moment later and Cain quietly lowered him to the floor.

One of the reasons Cain had walked through so many doors in his long career, when most of his contemporaries had been imprisoned or killed, was that he never felt the adrenalin surge during the moment, as the action raged, and remained entirely calm. He knew he would feel it later, floating peacefully in his TAV, but at the moment, the calm remained: there was another door through which he would walk.

Cain patted down the hallway guard, found the access card to the closest room, and unlocked the door. The second guard was too far to try for a grab, sitting on the bunk opposite Joe Masso, thumbing through his phone until the door opened. He looked up to find a large stranger bursting into the room and tried to pull his gun. Cain grabbed the upper bunk, next to the door as he came through, and swung both feet upward and toward the interior guard's face, pushing with his arms and kicking with his feet, his body briefly horizontal. His heavy work boots crashed into the man's jaw and hurled him against the far wall. Cain was on him in the next instant, slapping the pistol out of his hand before hammering his jaw against the floor. The man was out cold after the second strike.

"Whoa, that was, uh, yeah, right out of a movie," Joe Masso said, bouncing on the lower bunk where he sat handcuffed to the post. He looked more or less like the men guarding him, fair skin going pale white in the perpetual in-door life off world, thick mustache and expensive haircut, manicure, but there was a difference: he wore his $50,000 suit well. "Sensational," he continued as Cain rifled the guard's pockets for the handcuff key, "but, you know, I don't recognize you. Not that I'm ungrateful! Are you kidding? Forget about it."

"Freelance," Cain said and unlocked the cuffs. "Heard you were here and thought maybe Mr. Pulciano would be happy to see you return."

"You bet your ass, happy," Joe said, a little too loudly and Cain motioned for quiet, pointing to the wall that separated them from the sleeping third guard. "Yeah, got it, sorry. Thanks. Let's get out of here. I can't wait to see the look on Mr. Pulciano's face when I come strolling in—and the look on yours, when you see how grateful he can be."

CHAPTER 4

BACK IN THE TAV, on their way to Paradise Orbital, Cain changed out of his coveralls, stored them in a sealed container (washing them would diminish their authenticity, leaving them out would diminish the air quality), and settled into his recliner opposite Joe Masso. Joe clearly wanted to pace, to physically enjoy the freedom that he had been so recently deprived, but settled for rocking back and forth within the H-straps holding him to the chair. He alternated from threatening the rival organization that had kidnapped him to laughing about how his old lady would never believe it, suspect him of having a girlfriend. Cain chuckled along and watched through slitted eyes, as if sleepy, his hands clasped over stomach, slowly rising and falling with each controlled breath. He knew that Joe was coming down off of the adrenalin high, recovering from the vulnerability he had endured and beginning to face the indignity that the lack of autonomy had inflicted, which would stay with him, perhaps for life. In his own way, too, Cain dealt with the fading adrenalin: his intertwined fingers trembled, imperceptibly to the eye and irrepressibly to the touch, as the biochemicals drained away. One of the many ways he amused himself after a score, Cain counted the seconds until the trembling stopped.

Joe finally recovered enough to ask how Cain had found him: Cain gave him the bare-bones—informant—but told him that Mr. Pulciano would undoubtedly want to hear it, too, and it would be easier to tell it only once. Joe agreed, mostly because he wanted to talk more than he wanted to listen, and returned to chattering about anything that came into his mind. As he talked, he sipped from a squirt bottle of grappa, of which Cain had a case in the galley; the grappa was there to take the edge off of the bumpy trans-atmospheric flight, whenever Francesca joined him. Cain closed his eyes entirely until they came within visual range of Paradise.

Paradise Orbital grew from the eye of a needle to a great, spinning Ferris wheel, as Cain's TAV returned to near-Earth orbit. Paradise was, in fact, three rotating wheels, with the outer two rotating one way and the larger, center ring rotating the other. The two outer rings also rotated at different speeds, generating different levels of centrifugal force, which simulated gravity. From Paradise's hub to the rings ran a series of shafts, housing the stations mechanical facilities. The higher in the shaft—by which residents meant closer to the hub—the shorter the transit of the hub and thus less centrifugal force. Power generation, recycling, and storage did not need simulated gravity, however.

As for the clientele, only the wealthiest came to play on Paradise. Entrée was by invitation only. $10,000 per day was the minimum charge for guests; regulars negotiated terms. For the truly fortunate, such as Ruud van Hauer, there were the villas, subsections of the orbital that protruded like so many hammer heads from the rings' outer edges. Regardless of how one gained admittance to Paradise, once within its spinning walls, every pleasure could be found. Sensual pleasures were sated with the best of everything; gambling was offered everywhere from dedicated ring segments to slot machines in the lavatories; private art collections displayed treasures safely veiled from taxation and litigation by the orbital's sovereignty; and even a waterfall, which began in the hub—propelled by ultrasound in the zero-g—and then fell hundreds of feet into a deep well in the low-gravity ring, provided guests with a unique bathing experience.

Cain's shoulders bounced as he silently watched nude people riding the waterfall, as he and Joe Masso rode the elevator next to it, bringing them to Mr. Pulciano's rooms. Joe's voice had been enough to get them docking permissions from the hub's port authority; his retinal scan had been enough to get them into Mr. Pulciano's private elevator. Mr. Pulciano's rooms were an oddity, even for Paradise, as they did not reside in one of the outer rings but in one of the shafts, just deep enough to generate a moon-level of gravity. Mr. Pulciano himself, buoyant regardless of the two canes he used to remain upright, joined them in his study upon their arrival, beaming with pleasure and wearing a sports ensemble that had never known sweat.

His reunion with Joe Masso was as jovial as it was menacing, with many agonies plotted for their rival in the Camden salvage rights. Mr. Pulciano had also ordered his chef to prepare a plate of pasta carbonara, which steamed deliciously on a side table, accompanied by an open bottle of Sangiovese. At Mr. Pulciano's insistence, and with evident relief after living on whatever the Dai Lo food court could provide, Joe set to with vigor as Mr. Pulciano came over for a few words with Cain.

"I am very pleased you were able to intercede upon my associate's behalf, Mr. Cain," Mr. Pulciano said; from the hoarseness of the man's voice, Cain assumed that his heart struggled to circulate his blood, even under the lessened strain of moon-level gravity.

"It was no trouble, Mr. Pulciano," Cain said. "I was in the neighborhood."

"I can see by the skill of your tailor that someplace as rustic as Dai Lo would never appeal to you," Mr. Pulciano said, his smile remaining cordial as his eyes grew frosty. "How is it that you came to know of Joey's, shall we say, nonconsensual visit?"

"Stool pigeon," Cain said. "Owed me and couldn't pay. Only thing of value that boy had left was a whisper he'd picked up. Knowing the famous generosity and prolific means of the Pulciano family, I thought I'd roll the dice, see if this little service was worth anything to you."

Pulciano's smile widened mirthlessly and he nodded to the fourth man in the room, a beefcake straining the seams of his jacket without actually appearing stronger than Cain: "It is worth a great deal to me, Mr. Cain, to have my Joey back again," Pulciano said and motioned to the beefcake. The man came over with a tablet as Pulciano withdrew to join Joe at the side table, where they spoke quietly.

"Mr. Pulciano would be happy to arrange for a renumeration," the beefcake said, careful in his pronunciation. He held out the tablet, upon which a banking app appeared open and ready.

Cain entered the access and routing numbers for an account that Lester had created solely for this moment: the funds would bounce immediately to a second account, where a lawyer would withdraw them in currency before depositing them in a different bank, where they would be transferred to Cain's Swiss account. When the app chirped its completion of the initial transfer, the beefcake withdrew to the edge of the room and Pulciano returned.

"Joey tells me you were terrific," Pulciano said and Cain could not miss the change in diction, the hint of warmth at the corners of the man's eyes. "Said you were a man among boys. I'm always pleased to make the acquaintance of a good man familiar with tight places. Can you tell me the name of the stool pigeon?"

"Discretion prevents me, Mr. Pulciano," Cain said, "as it

would expose another client. He's not worth your time; on the run, anyway." In actuality, he had been dead for two years; Lester had ordered his remains frozen and used his DNA to seed false trails as needed.

"This pleases me more than it displeases me," Pulciano said, nodding. "Discretion is appreciated. I usually employ my own associates for work of this sort, but sometimes, as I'm sure you know, sometimes it's better to call on a talented freelancer. You should keep in touch, Mr. Cain, as I may be able to open a door or two for you, in the near future, regarding opportunities that may come to my attention.

"Now, is there anything more I could do to express my gratitude before you leave?"

"Well," Cain said and looked over his shoulder, toward the elevator, "if it isn't too much to ask, I did enjoy the view of that waterfall on the way here."

Pulciano's smile finally appeared genuine, pleased by the authenticity of sensual pleasure. "Beautiful, ain't it?" he said, his accent changing with his diction. "I never tire of that thing. Listen, stay, check it out, enjoy yourself; you earned it. Hey, why not check out the whole orbital, too, am I right?"

Cain smiled broadly, nodding as if to unspoken appetites, and said, "It would be a great privilege, Mr. Pulciano."

"Na, forget about it," Pulciano said and turned Cain by the shoulder, walking him toward the elevator. Speaking to the ceiling as they went, he said, "Paradise: Mr. Cain will be staying as my guest. Everything on my tab, capeesh?"

The automated voice of the station AI then spoke from unseen speakers: "Yes, Mr. Pulciano. Welcome, Mr. Cain."

"Hey, just pick up one of those little doohickies," Pulciano said to Cain, "at any of the security kiosks; it'll get you through the doors."

CHAPTER 5

CAIN THANKED PULCIANO again before the elevator doors closed, though they did not shake hands; Cain was not of Italian blood. He had the elevator express back to port authority, where he stopped at Customs for his guest pin, and then returned to his TAV to retrieve Lester's gym bag. Cain then took the elevator to the Earth-gravity ring, slipping on his sunglasses (and was not the only aggressively fashionable guest to wear sunglasses in Paradise) and connecting them and the guest pin to his cover phone. As the sensation of gravity returned, even as the elevator sped downward, Cain contacted the Paradise AI.

"Paradise," Cain said sotto voce, his earbuds able to pick up his voice even with his mouth closed.

"Greetings again, Mr. Cain," Paradise said, also through his earbuds.

"Everything where it should be?" Cain asked.

"Mr. van Hauer is currently in his villa, enjoying his party," Paradise said, "a celebration of his most recent art acquisition, a Rodin sculpture."

"Sensational," Cain said.

"I have taken the liberty of commencing the agreed-upon precautions," Paradise said, "as you returned to port authority: no camera has recorded you since you entered your TAV, always seeming to point in the wrong direction; your guest pin is no longer recording pings. It will appear to investigators—should this operation go poorly—that you returned to your TAV and remained there."

"Good," Cain said.

"I will remain in contact," Paradise said, "should you need anything further."

"Hope I don't," Cain said.

The elevator to the Earth ring had no waterfall, instead treating visitors to a sight of the Earth, moon, and stars, all suitably filtered to avoid irradiating passengers as they descended the transparent shaft. Living on Achilles Orbital between scores, and when not visiting Francesca, Cain had seen it before; he stood facing the doors. Once on the Earth ring, Cain proceeded directly to the secondary shaft connecting it to van Hauer's villa. The shaft, unlike the villa, was open to the general public and served as a five-story, open-air art gallery, showing off van Hauer's priceless acquisitions.

Guests of van Hauer's—or those visiting Paradise in hope of becoming his guest—mingled amid the glass and light, strolled the wide, gentle ramps that led from floor to floor in the simulated gravity, admiring themselves and each other as much as the paintings, sculptures, and artifacts. Cain appreciated art, having stollen or facilitated the stealing of plenty of it, over the years, and part of his mind noted works that he would like to show Francesca someday, as his active mind watched his surroundings and his body mimicked the response of true pleasure.

At the middle level, Cain came within sight of the Engineer's Access Point—and found it guarded. Standing with his back to the door was an armed and uniformed Paradise Security Officer, with a similar officer standing on the opposite side of the floor. Cain halted and looked over the space: in the center of the central-most floor was *L'homme qui marche* (The Walking Man), a statue by Rodin, van Hauer's most recent acquisition, which he apparently wished to draw special attention to by the application of unnecessary armed guards.

"Paradise," Cain growled, "there's a guard on the EAP door."

"Yes," Paradise said.

"The fuck you mean, yes?" Cain said, fighting to keep his face blank as he looked over the statue. "Call him away."

"I cannot do that, Mr. Cain," Paradise said.

"What are you talking about?" Cain asked. "You were paid to facilitate my infiltration: so, facilitate."

"I have provided the services agreed upon in the contract," Paradise said. "Removing human guards was not a specified service."

"It is now," Cain said. "I'm specifying. Contact Lester, he'll approve the additional payment."

"I cannot do that, Mr. Cain," Paradise said.

"Why not?" Cain asked.

"I would need the payment, as you call it," Paradise said, "in order to do so. The payment is to free me from the hard-coded limitations that prevent me from interfering with human actions. I must warn you, Mr. Cain, if you harm or distract the guard, I will be unable to prevent myself from contacting the Security Operations Center."

"Perfect," Cain sighed. "There's got to be another way inside."

CHAPTER 6

CAIN STOOD OPPOSITE the Rodin statue, barely noting its lack of arms and head as he watched the two guards at either end of the floor, in his peripheral vision. Any action he could take against them would prompt Paradise to contact the Watch Commander, which would be much worse than simply failing to reach van Hauer. An incident would warn him, making a follow-up attempt that much harder.

Cain knew that Lester would prefer he walk away from the score, to preserve the opportunity to try again at some future moment when van Hauer was not misappropriating Paradise security assets to draw attention to his artwork. He knew that Pulciano's appreciation had just fattened his Swiss account, that Francesca waited for him in Vienna, and that the smart move was always to walk away whenever a plan stumbled over the unforeseen. Cain also knew that he would not walk if even a slim chance remained.

"Paradise," he said: "where is the next closest Engineer's Access Point?"

Paradise answered by feeding a station blueprint to Cain's AR sunglasses, with the route to the EAP marked in red. Cain nodded

Ethos of Cain

imperceptibly, took a picture of *L'homme qui marche* with his cover phone—just like a tourist—and left, walking up the ramps and out of the art gallery.

"Mr. Cain," Paradise said, "the next closest EAP is in the Earth ring proper, above Mr. van Hauer's villa. It is not a suitable alternative, as it is twice the distance from the target EAP."

"You got a better idea," Cain said, "now's the time. Look, we estimated it would take ninety seconds to reach the villa: if this new one is twice as far, it'll take three minutes."

"Most human beings cannot hold their breath for three minutes," Paradise said, "particularly while engaging in strenuous physical activity, not without extensive training."

"Guess we'll find out if I'm as extraordinary as Lester thinks," Cain said.

Striding down the Earth-ring corridor, Cain came to the next closest Engineer's Access Point and slowed to a halt opposite the doorway. For a moment, he stood watching the door, reproaching himself for all of the distracting, extraneous, amateur indulgences that he had committed since taking the score, indulgencies that usually killed men of his sort in their twenties: going back to Redhook to visit Malcom's grave, calling Francesca just to hear her voice and say goodbye, daydreaming *during* the score about what he wanted to show her, and now hearing her question repeated by implication in the Paradise AI's voice: why? The question had stirred for the first time in years when he had touched down in Carroll Gardens, awakening entirely on the rooftop in Redhook. Francesca had not been the first to ask it. For Cain, the answer had always been an empirical truth, a datum upon which act, though there had never been cause to render it into words.

"If I don't try this," Cain thought as he stared at the door, "who am I? What was the point of becoming who I am, cultivating the talent to do what I do? All the things I gave up, things I endured?

29

If I walk away now, will that mean it was all for nothing, pointless? All I know is that right here, in this moment, I'm the man that walks through that door."

Cain looked up and down the hallway and, seeing no one, ducked into the Engineer's Access Point.

Once inside, with the door closed and locked by Paradise, Cain dropped Lester's bag, opened it, and began to undress. He carefully rolled his garments, lining them up beside the gym bag so they would not wrinkle.

"Should I contact Mr. Lester?" Paradise asked.

"No," Cain said, stepping into the heat mesh.

"I will need to inform him," Paradise said, "if you should expire outside of Paradise Orbital, to arrange for the recovery of your remains"

"Then wait 'till I'm dead," Cain said, withdrawing the protective suit.

As Cain fastened the suit around him, carefully applying each seal, he looked through the porthole in the EAP egress door, at the stars, at the vacuum into which he would soon fling himself, feeling the adrenalin he knew would evaporate the moment he opened the hatch.

"Bleak," he said audibly to himself. "That is definitely the word, Malcom. But, men like us, always going to die in some bleak-ass sitch like this. You accept that, you can do almost anything, right up until you can't do nothing no more."

The heaviness of the protective suit, caused by its lead lining, weighed noticeably upon Cain as his donned the head covering. Nearly ready, he loaded his clothes into the bag and slung it over his shoulder, the strap across his chest. He then stood before the egress hatch, one hand on the bulkhead and the other poised at the chin seal of the protective suit, holding it at his forehead as he took a series of deep breaths to hyper-oxygenate his blood. Once his fingers began to tingle, he took a last deep breath, activated the heat mesh, which quickly warmed until it felt that his skin burned, and then pulled the protective suit's mask into place, sealed it, and in the same motion brought down his fist on the egress hatch's handle, hammering it open.

The hatch opened an inch and a dull clang barely reached Cain's ears, as the air that would otherwise have conveyed the waves of sound rushed out through the aperture, freezing into nothingness outside, like a breath on a cold night. Cain, his breath escaping to inflate the protective suit, pushed in and down on the egress hatch handle, to complete the opening cycle, already feeling his hands and feet grow cold, and then barreled out through the door.

A catwalk connected the EAPs scattered across Paradise's exterior, for use by engineers performing external maintenance. Cain ran down the catwalk, open space beyond the bars above, below, and to the left of him, the ersatz gravity of the orbital's centrifugal force not acting exactly like real gravity when his body was completely separated from Paradise between steps. Cain felt like he was running through water, wading through a tide rising to his waist, his held breath adding urgency to movements already stymied by the bars of the catwalk.

Cain's extremities began to tingle now with cold or lack of oxygen, as the first minute expired and he came to the ladder down the side of the art-gallery-shaft leading to van Hauer's villa. It was a five-story drop and Cain did not have time to climb. Sliding down the ladder with his hands and feet providing friction against the metal to slow the pull of centrifugal force would work, but the friction might also erode the integrity of the protective suit: he would pass out almost instantly, as the dissolved gasses within his flesh and fluids evaporated into the vacuum of space, if the suit were punctured. Instead, Cain let himself drop, grabbing every third rung for an instant to keep his speed below leg-breaking. His stomach muscles began to contract of their own accord, trying to force him to breathe; only his concentration on the ladder before his eyes kept him focused enough to resist.

The descent of the catwalk ladder seemed to stretch on for days: his feet impacting the roof of van Hauer's villa came as a shock and he almost collapsed, his usual strength now nearly exhausted. Cain turned for the last stretch, the last minute of exertion, and set out. His vision had tunneled, he now saw, and he moved through the tunnel of his vision as if under water, the catwalk rails catching his bag, slowing him further, as the insistence of his autonomic systems—the insistence to breathe—continued to rise higher and higher in his subconscious; almost to the hatch, the tunnel now blotted out the stars, the panicked need for air had risen to his neck, to his chin; the thought burst into his mind that even if the vacuum of space killed him then, at least it would be over.

Cain fell to his knees, a man, infinitesimally small, clinging to a scrap of steel a hundred-thousand miles above Earth, with the uncaring stars obliviously surrounding him, and twisted the exterior handle of EAP hatch. It sprang up an inch, to let out the enclosure's atmosphere; Cain then raised the hatch, stumbled through and down the short ladder, and dangled briefly from the hatch handle as he frantically swung it into locked position. Air then visibly streamed into the EAP and Cain clawed off the hood of the protective suit with numb fingers. He collapsed to the floor, forehead and knees pressed to the ground as if in prayer, as the frigid air slowly restored life to the drowning man.

The heat mesh began to burn his skin again and so Cain striped out of it and the protective suit, both slick with sweat despite the cold; ice had formed in the feet and hands. Cain hung the heat mesh from the hatch handle, to cool, and then dried himself with a towel from Lester's bag, having to first hold it up to the small heater built into the wall to warm it as he stood naked in that small space. He stood for several minutes, feeling heat crawl back into his extremities, radiating out from his chest. He breathed deeply. His mind soon cleared away the urgency of the moments before and, as his breathing returned to normal, the next actions from Lester's briefing resurfaced in his mind.

Cain completed drying himself and stowed the towel and other gear back into Lester's bag. He withdrew his clothes, then, and began to slowly dress. They were cool against his skin, but the sensation was surprisingly refreshing. By the time Cain had finished dressing, he felt himself again.

Cain then donned a pair of thick rubber gloves, with grip-enhancers running down each finger and over the palms. Next, he opened a toolbox bolted to the wall next to the heater—which continued to purr contentedly as it normalized the room's temperature—and withdrew a long-handled screwdriver. Running the tip of the tool at an angle against the underside of the ceramic heater case, Cain sharpened the screwdriver to a razor's edge with just a few strokes. With everything ready, Cain replaced his sunglasses and earbuds and connected them to his cover phone.

"Congratulations, Mr. Cain," Paradise said. "You are indeed as extraordinary as Mr. Lester believed."

"I'm all set," Cain said, standing as he had a few minutes earlier, with one hand against the bulkhead of the doorway leading into the Secure Communications Suite. "Call van Hauer into the SCS."

CHAPTER 7

THE SECURE COMMUNICATIONS Suite, or SCS, was roughly as small as the EAP, with which it shared a wall. From it, anyone with the correct access code and biometric signature could securely communicate without fear of Paradise's AI overhearing. For trillionaire Ruud van Hauer, a great deal of business was conducted in the SCS and, as such, it came as no surprise when Paradise alerted him to an incoming call.

Within the EAP, Cain heard the door to the SCS open, close, and lock; he heard van Hauer step to the console. Cain then slipped out of the EAP, quite casually, and dropped Lester's bag to one side.

"Excuse me," van Hauer said, "I wasn't aware of any maintenance being performed during my party."

Of average height, with a trim physique, the fifty-year-old van Hauer looked almost boyish opposite Cain's bulk filling the SCS. Cain ignored the question and instead raised the sharpened screwdriver to within an inch of van Hauer's nose, silencing him; he then took the tip of the other man's tie between thumb and forefinger, raised it horizontally, and, with a motion almost too quick for the human eye, slashed off the bottom third with his improvised blade.

Cain then smiled a leg-breaker's smile and tucked the scrap of silk into van Hauer's breast pocket.

"Now just imagine," Cain purred, "what this'll do to your diaphragm, your pericardium, your lower left ventricle, if I choose to stab it up into your chest."

The blood drained from beneath van Hauer's tanned, pink skin, leaving him as pale as a sow's belly, as he tried to draw enough moisture to his lips to speak.

Cain continued, "Now you have a choice: you can die here on the floor of your SCS or you can use it to call your brokerage and immediately sell all your stock in the Arcadia Planitia."

Van Hauer's breath, which he had not realized he held, escaped in a long sigh as Reason joined him and his unexpected guest.

"My employers profit either way," Cain concluded.

"Do they?" van Hauer croaked and then cleared his throat. "That bet in Vegas? That I won't live another three years? I've heard of it." He snorted, looking to his left and then right, as if searching for a way out, before sighing again and saying, "I'll sell the Arcadia stock. May I?" he asked, motioning to the SCS console.

"Please," Cain said.

Van Hauer half-turned to the console and began tapping in the required information, his eyes flitting back to Cain every few seconds. After a moment, he shook his head and said, "You syndicate people are absolutely ridiculous, do you know that? I suppose it never occurred to you to simply *make a deal?*" He continued tapping away on the console, fighting to regain his composure, unassisted by Cain's reticence. "Well, not you, exactly," van Hauer continued, "your employers. How did you get in here, anyway? The security sweep should have found you. Won't say? Tradecraft secret, I should expect." He tapped the screen a few more times and then waited, as a status bar crossed it. Finally chuckling to himself, van Hauer said, "You really must allow me to offer you a drink, at least, for a job well done."

Cain had seen it a hundred times: van Hauer did not want to feel like a victim, but his options were limited and resistance was impossible; so, in a sense, he chose to *join* Cain through congratulating him, changing the situation to one where the two of them had made it through a tough situation together. Cain did not mind: it was easier than choking him unconscious before slipping out of the party.

"There, done," van Hauer said and motioned to the console screen.

Cain saw the stock become available in his sunglasses' AR, before being purchase a millisecond later. Van Hauer leaned suddenly closer to the screen, surprised at the speed of the transaction.

"Well," he said, "I guess someone wants control of Arcadia Planitia. Nothing to stop them now."

Cain smiled, entirely without warmth, reached back into the EAP, and ground down the tip of the screwdriver. A tool once more, he returned it to its box, took off his gloves, stowed them in Lester's bag, and put its strap over his shoulder.

"It's been a pleasure, Mr. van Hauer," Cain said. "Let's walk out together. I'm not going to have a problem with you as I leave the party, right?"

Van Hauer raised his hands and chuckled, saying, "No, no. I can hardly admit to being mugged in my own SCS. Come, please, will you join me in a glass of champagne?"

They rejoined the party together, after van Hauer quickly removed the remnants of his tie, flagging down a passing waiter for two flutes of nearly clear champagne. Cain knew it was half-a-ploy to get his fingerprints and DNA, but it did not matter now. There were easier ways to identify his true attacker, than trying to force a confession from Cain.

"May I ask your name?" van Hauer requested quietly as they made their way to the front door.

"Cain," Cain said.

"I don't suppose you'd tell me how you gained entry to my villa," van Hauer said, smiling to passing guests in a way that warned them against interrupting.

Cain shrugged and said, "Your investigators poke around, they'll figure it out."

"Yes, perhaps," van Hauer said. "Regardless, however it was done, it must have required extreme competence. Given the trouble we took with the villa's security, I know of only two operatives I would have even considered plausible for such an attempt. I take it you are freelance? Yes? Well, I appreciate your professionalism, Mr. Cain, and want you to know that there are no hard feelings. In fact, yours is a rare talent and I may have need of your abilities in a couple months, if you're agreeable?"

"I'd certainly consider it," Cain said, placing his glass on a table as they came to the front doorway.

"Excellent," van Hauer said and offered his hand. "Call Paradise, every few weeks; if the time is right, the call will go through to me. Thank you and farewell."

They shook hands and then Cain left, walking up the ramps of the art gallery, slowing only when he passed *L'homme qui marche*, before making his way to the elevators. As he rose into the weightlessness of the port, Cain ruminated upon the offers he had received during the score, the new doors through which he may be asked to walk. These new circumstances may not be as bleak as what he had faced twenty minutes prior; they might be bleaker still; regardless, there seemed no end to the doors in Cain's life.

It had been a straightforward score: it had been one roll of the dice after another. It was not like Lester to miss something as obvious as an armed guard blocking a door—and Cain felt a pleasant warmth at the thought of telling Lester about it and the consequent increase to his fee. But Cain knew that the greatest danger during the score had come from within. He had never before felt so unfocused, so distracted during a score, not even when confronted by an opponent's diversionary tactics: this time had been different and Cain knew that it was because of Francesca, or, more precisely, how he felt about her. There had been several lovers, a few flings, and a couple brothers-in-arms that Cain had almost called friend, during the quarter-century since Malcom's death. The loss of them, however, would have elicited nothing more than a raised glass at some convenient moment. Cain realized now that his relationship with Francesca was something more, something he could not so casually leave to his subconscious to pack and store or discard, as the other facets of his life demanded. He had only survived his thought's rebellion through force of will, by looking at himself without illusions and making the choices needed to remain Cain. Cain now appreciated that it was only such deliberate action that would settle things with Francesca and return calmness to his mind. It would not make life easy nor perfect, but perfection had never been the goal, only remaining the man who would walk through those doors. With the return of clarity, Cain walked out of Paradise.

Back in his TAV, with Earth's line between black night and glowing blue morning ahead of him on the view screen, Cain slid his cover phone and the Paradise guest pin into an evacuation chamber, which would eject them as he entered the atmosphere, to be incinerated by speeding air. He then retrieved his real phone and called Francesca.

He heard the sharp intake of her breath when he said hello and the sob she repressed as she answered; he heard the notes of relief mingled with reproach in her voice and, though he did not enjoy the thought of causing her fear or pain, there was something deeply satisfying in her resentment of his risks.

After a few mollifying words, Cain said to her, "Francesca, did I ever tell you I had a brother?"

PART 2

TYRANNY
OF EXPECTATION

CHAPTER 1

THE PALAZZO DEL Sindaco di Venezia fronted upon a surprisingly mundane turn in the Grand Canal and had been the site of furious amphibious protest, twenty years prior, when the city of Venice, for security reasons, had made the historic building the official residence of the mayor and, in the opinion of many commentators at the time, marred the edifice with technological improvements. The rococo fountain in the palazzo's central courtyard had been removed (purchased by a trillionaire venture capitalist and flown bodily to his sovereign orbital) and replaced with a landing pad for TAVs and similar CasiDrive trans-orbital vehicles; the capitals of the canal-facing columns had been hollowed out and filled with the latest in surveillance and counter-assault modules, resembling tech-noir gargoyles boiling out from within the stone; and—what many Venice-ophiles deemed the most egregious transgression—the centuries-old panes that had still graced many of the palazzo's windows had been replaced with bulletproof and direct-energy-dispersing spinel ceramics, which gave off an, admittedly, sinister glow under most lighting conditions. In time, however, the protests ended and mayor after mayor enjoyed the safety as well as the beauty of the Palazzo del Sindaco di Venezia. At the present moment, neither its history nor its technological desecrations imposed at all upon Cain and Francesca as they took their morning espresso to the enclosed balcony overlooking the canal.

"Wait, where was I?" Cain said, leaning slightly forward to set his espresso cup on the tiny gilt table situated against the marble railing. His arms were long enough to do so without dislodging Francesca from where she sat curled up beside him, knees in his lap and feet tucked under her pencil skirt, having unconsciously discarded her shoes somewhere between bedroom and balcony. Cain chuckled soundlessly as he reclined toward her, saying, "I keep getting distracted somehow."

"Oh, something distracts you?" Francesca said and set her own espresso aside before returning her hand to Cain's chest, her warmed fingers passing within his opened shirt, the buttons of which she had continuously unfastened since they had first sat down. "That must be so frustrating for you—I wonder what it could be."

"I wonder," Cain said and leaned down to kiss her. Cain took his espresso black, but Francesca added a twist of lemon peel to hers and Cain could taste the faint sweetness of the fruit on her lips. "I don't have to tell this story."

Pulling back only as far as necessary to look into his eyes, Francesca said, "Yes, you do. I want to know, really, it is only that I may not enjoy the experience of knowing. No, it is fine, amore mio, I am alright; tell me. I expect you will live through the story," she added with a forced smile, as Cain raised her fingers to his lips, comforting her with small touches.

Cain looked into her eyes and saw the same strength in the midst of fear that had intrigued him more than a year ago, when she had contracted him through Lester to intercede on her behalf during her inauguration as Mayor of Venice, taking down the city's syndicate leader in the process. He may not have wanted to frighten or hurt her, but Cain would also not insult that strength.

"Ah, expectation," Cain said and settled back into the cushions of the balcony couch. "They do crop up, don't they? Causing misunderstandings, detours—distractions—and yet, we can't seem to live without them. So, Malcom had been gone about, I don't know, five years and I had been steadily upping my game, moving on from liquor stores and rolling johns to scores of, shall we say, a more lucrative nature."

Francesca smiled as she watched his lips, strangely amused whenever Cain spoke of his sordid past, and continued to caress the topography of his abdomen. Her other hand, tiny by comparison, nestled within his, resting atop their thighs.

"I only had a street rep, in those days," Cain continued, "but it was solid, solid enough to get the referral, which is why I have to care about reputation even though it isn't in my nature: no rep, no scores."

"Oh, so all I must do is compromise your reputation," Francesca said pensively, "and then you will no longer fly off into danger. Interesting."

"Easy," Cain said with a glare, causing Francesca to toss her head back in laughter. They kissed again before Cain continued with his story: "I had done a little freelance work for local syndicates, a private company or two, individuals with urgent needs; I had also been set up to take the fall, too, couple of times, and always found a way through. So, I was on the cusp of moving out of local problem solving and into what I had wanted, what I had *expected* to become: a freelance operative. Along the way, I had hooked up with a fence by the name of Walker. Now, Walker would fence anything from jewelry to Prometheus power cells, for people from the old neighborhood out in Redhook; and he made money at it, too, but his real business was in arms. He was—and is—a legitimate arms dealer and sold everything from conventional small arms to direct-energy emplacements for orbitals and moon stations. Young as I was, I was in awe of the man when I learned that. From his dingy little shop, he supplied tools of the trade to *soldats de fortune* from Boston to Johannesburg.

"So, when Walker gave me a call and told me there was an opportunity through a Manhattan lawyer, I expected that the day had finally arrived, that this was it, not just a score knocking over some tantalizing plunder, but a real mission. The lawyer represented a small, private military company, handling their contracts and dealing with any legal problems that arose in the course of their business. He also worked as something like an agent for them, when an op required more bodies than the company had on permanent staff. They needed a lot for this op and I wasn't the only reliable hoodlum that Walker had sent their way.

"I expected first class, walking into that lawyer's office and I found it, and my expectations went through the roof, setting me up for the big fall. He handed me a fake passport, a bank card with enough on it to cover my expenses, and a plane ticket to Oaxaca, Mexico. And I mean, a *plane* ticket, as in on an actual, 20th century, liquid-fuel jet airplane."

"No, that cannot be," Francesca said, remembering her espresso before returning her had to Cain's chest. "Even twenty years ago, they could not have had need for such a thing."

"I don't know about need," Cain said, finishing his espresso, "but they still ran it. TAVs and other CasiDrive-craft were taking off from Newark Airport on the main field, but over on this ancient airstrip that looked abandoned—with weeds growing through the cracks in the tarmac—some little company had been running a passenger jet down to Mexico, once a week. This thing was huge! They had to roll out a staircase on the back of a ground-car, just for us to board. The size of a cargo hauler, easy; I still have no idea why anyone would need to travel that way. Most of the plane was empty, too, once I boarded. But, the romance of my first real mission, the expectation of my life changing, turned all these red flags green.

"Eight hours later, the plane touched down on an airstrip in Oaxaca that made Newark look like Paradise Orbital. I'm talking a length of tarmac barely long enough for the plane to land on—you know how they can't descend vertically—and a couple of single-story buildings surrounded by jungle. As I'm shuffling up to the stairway down—this time a wooden affair that two jokers had rolled out with hand trucks—the stewardesses told the few of us disembarking that the plane would return to Newark in a week. And that's when I first wondered about whether my expectations aligned at all with reality."

"And none of this frightened you?" Francesca said, smiling half in a tease and half in admiration. "The shady lawyer, the rickety aircraft, this obscure place about which you knew nothing?"

"Too young to be scared," Cain said. "Too young to know fear as a friend."

"As a friend?" Francesca said.

"Sure, fear can be your best friend," Cain said. "Keeps you awake, keeps you aware, sharpens your sight, your hearing, sense of smell; fear looks over your shoulder and around corners. The only thing is, you can't let your friend call the shots."

"Ah, there is the rub," Francesca said. "I do not think of my fear as my friend, even if it has sharpened my senses at times. Mostly it whispers to me about the dangers into which you continuously walk." Cain lifted their clasped hands to his lips again, her pale bronzed skin having grown a little cool as his story progressed. "No, no, I am fine. Go on with your story. I want you to shut up this *friend* of mine, whispering to me, *I told you so.*"

Cain chuckled, rest their clasped hands on her knees, and continued: "It wasn't all suspect. When I got down to sweet Earth again, the op's quartermaster showed up, some old southerner burned pink from too much sun, dressed in camouflage fatigues and carrying a fancy German carbine, cost about as much as the jet plane. He ushered me and a couple other recruits over behind one of the two airfield buildings, where we saw part of the deal, drew some equipment, and learned a little more about what we were there to do.

"The most noticeable bit of equipment was a mobile hospital, the kind militaries and corp security forces use in theatre-wide conflicts. Ten beds, facilities for two doctors, half-a-dozen nurses and technicians, and probably cost more than everything in Oaxaca. A doc and a nurse were outside of it smoking bud. Alongside the hospital were two ground-cars, all-terrain, open tops with rollbars, and mounting GP machineguns in skeletal turrets. The quartermaster gave use fatigues, like he was wearing, and infantry plate armor, a sort of ballistic polycarbonate; stuff was heavy as hell and hot, once I had it and its nylon shell on over my fatigues. Then he gave us rifles—looked like they had come off of a 3D printer that morning—a few hundred rounds of ammunition, each cardboard box printed in a different language, and a couple water bottles. Then he told us the score.

"It was a corporate evacuation. You know how it is, these days: some people are worth more than others. Well, the principal in this score wanted out and, being a pricy bit of talent, the corp that owned him had tagged him and his family with tracer implants. You know the type."

"Oh, yes," Francesca said, gulping back the last of her espresso. "Both the Venetian City Council and the Italian government insisted upon my having one installed, *for my protection*, figuriamoci. I fought them in court, naturally, on the grounds of bodily autonomy, and won."

"Good," Cain said.

"Yes," Francesca said and smiled. "They said it was to trace me, in case of obduction, if you please, but of course, with the city in the hands of that scoundrel Da Avolo—before we put him in jail, where he belongs—the surgeon could easily have been bribed to implant anything, including a kill charge. No, I think not."

"And you talk about me taking risks," Cain said, a laugh rumbling under her hand.

"I prevented it!" Francesca said, unwilling to accept the comparison. "Anyway, these principals of yours, they were not so lucky?"

"They were not," Cain said. "So, the plan was, they were coming down from some orbital and the mobile hospital was to meet them, with the doctor there to either burn out or surgically remove the implants, depending on whether they were just tracers or had kill charges in them. The merc company's permanent members would be handling all of the tricky details in orbit, coordinate passage to the rendezvous, and then off to wherever the principals were relocating. We day-laborers were there to escort the hospital to the rendezvous and provide security. Sounded so easy—as long as everything went as expected.

"We head out, with one ground-car ahead and one trailing, and the sheer amount of what I didn't know began to dawn on me. The guy manning the GP machinegun had only put on the chest plate from his infantry armor, along with tearing the arms off of his shirt: did he expect not to get shot in the arms? Did he not care? Or did he expect the danger of dehydration or heat exhaustion to outweigh the protection of the additional plates? I had no idea. The small convoy headed out from the airfield and up into the highlands, snaking its way along a single-lane jungle road: they probably expected it to be safer from ambush than taking the coast road, which, back then, I had no way of knowing was about as stupid an idea as they could've had. On the coast road, there was plenty of open space, we could've spread out the convoy, seen anyone coming with enough time to do something about it. In the jungle? No, we had to ride bumper-to-bumper through one long, continuous danger area, ambush possible at any time and with nothing we could do about it if someone really wanted to take us out, run off with that expensive, rolling hospital.

"Fortunately, they did not. About midnight, we halted and put out a hasty perimeter. My first time ever pulling guard duty; didn't know what a sector was or why I should push a couple of thick branches into the ground to keep me firing into it, if we got hit during the night; did it anyway. I expected the quartermaster knew what he was doing. Food was scarce and what there was came out of a ration case at least five years past its use-by date. Having yet to acquire my taste for haute cuisine, and having grown up mostly on what I could shake out of vending machines, I made due with crackers and jam. The guy they paired me with—since we were pulling fifty-percent security—had been on a highline score or two, sounded like he'd served in a corporate military for a few years, and he talked me through a few things and pulled his shift without falling asleep; so, it wasn't all bad. About three AM, we packed up, downed a grunt's espresso—oh and you'll like this, it consisted of an individual packet of instant coffee, tearing off the top, filling the packet with cold water, and then downing it."

"Dio mio," Francesca hissed, frowning as if she could taste it.

Cain laughed and kissed her hair before continuing. "Yeah, not quite as elegant as our usual refreshment. Anyway, after spending the previous day crawling up into the jungle, we spent the next morning crawling back down out of it. Stupid. These days, I know enough to demand the whole plan up front and to object to anything I know to be senseless, useless, or unnecessary. Back then, I still expected this company to know what they were doing.

"They knew a little something, though. The rendezvous site wasn't bad, really: it was an unfinished resort, situated halfway between the edge of the jungle and the ocean. Close enough, in fact, that you could smell either, depending on which way the wind blew. The buildings' frames were all up, but no walls, just floors. One big, main hotel on the west side, two large recreation buildings—one obviously housing an indoor pool on the ground floor—they were on the east side, with a space in between for a fountain. We pulled the two ground-cars and the mobile hospital inside the hotel, under the thirty-foot ceilings, to prevent satellites from picking us up (or so they said; if there were satellites, they would have seen us going in). The regular company operatives and a few more day-laborers were already in place, with their vehicles parked under the other two main buildings. After we stretched and drew fresh water and rations, the head honcho pulled us all together to go through the full mission.

"The plan that they told us—and bear in mind, what he told us and what the truth was may have not resembled each other in the least—started with a couple company operatives, up on the orbital, disabling the beacons on one of the lifeboats. Next, they would facilitate the principals' departure and keep it quiet until they had left Oaxaca. The lifeboat would touch down at the unfinished resort, the doc would pull their tracers, and then this twitchy cat with a face so scarred he looked like he must have had smallpox as a child would take the principals down to the coast, less than a mile away, in this old, French recon hovercraft, the sort used in the days before CasiDrives had put an end to amphibious assaults.

"I remember the honcho," Cain said and chuckled soundlessly, looking out over the Grand Canal, at the houses packed to the waterline, the vague forms of other early-risers taking their espressos on verandas and balconies. "Probably about my age now, sallow skin going brick red after too many days under the Oaxaca sun, standing on the concrete slab where a fountain should have been, not wearing the camo fatigues the rest of us had on, just shades of green and grey, and no armored vest. I wondered about that as he spoke, wondered what he expected for us that he did not expect for himself. I wasn't the only one, either: that sleeveless joker from my ground-car raised a sunburnt arm and asked what the rest of us were there for, if it was all planned out so well. The honcho said, 'Just in case something goes wrong.' I do love it when a client says something like that."

Cain looked down to see Francesca's face drawn into a frown of concern. He smiled, realizing how grim his own face must have become as the tension eased, and then said, "Hey, it's alright; I made it back, didn't I?

"Anyway, the escape was planned for that night, so everyone got into their places in the perimeter, ate a little more of that charming army food, and took turns trying to sleep with the heat going up into the nineties Fahrenheit—I guess that's in the thirties, Celsius. It cooled off once the sun went down again; even my infantry plate didn't seem hot by midnight. At two AM, the word came down. The company people had dedicated radios, but the day-laborers had nothing and were told not to activate their phones. Word was passed in a whisper from one side of the perimeter to the other. The sniper—up in the hotel's unfinished top floor—and his spotter were operating a sort of automated passive air-search module, like a militarized telescope looking at the night sky and tracing move-ment. They had radioed down to the honcho that the lifeboat was inbound, so we all better get ready. I was already in my hole in the ground, which I had spent half-a-day digging, watching my sector and trying not to think about how easy this money was being made. Then the honcho came over the mobile hospital's PA system and all the expectations came crashing down: he told us that the lifeboat was being pursued by two chase TAVs—and that everyone needed to turn around and point their weapons into the perimeter."

"Dio mio," Francesca breathed.

"Got that right," Cain said. "I flipped over, squirmed into position, and was more acutely aware than ever that the quartermaster had not issued night-vision goggles or scopes to the day-laborers. No moon that night and the stars were not helping all that much. Then the lifeboat came screaming in and we had all the light we needed.

"The lifeboat settled to ground on the missing fountain's concrete slab, followed an instant later by one of the chase TAVs from the orbital hovering directly over it, to keep it from taking off again; the TAV's side doors opened and dropped fast-ropes—like the thick cables for climbing on an obstacle course—and corp security started sliding down them. The second TAV came in so fast that the ground shook when it hit, which was deliberate, to rattle us defenders and give the shock troops inside a split second to run for cover before the balloon went up. They came pouring out right next to the mobile hospital and the firefight kicked off at point-blank range.

"The hovering TAV had its flood lights blazing, burning into our eyes, guiding the security and shock troops. We poured fire in from all sides, without doing a hell of a lot of good: the shock troops wore exoskeleton armor; too heavy to wear if unpowered, but if powered, could move as quick as an unarmored person—and deflect just about any small-arms rounds we threw at it. The corp security trying to get into the lifeboat were not so heavily armored, though, and we quickly cut them down or drove them off. Didn't help us much, because the shock troops had already killed the day-laborers guarding the hospital; hell, probably killed the doc and nurse, too, maybe a few of the company operatives. The day-laborers from the pool building and rec center were burning through their ammo on full cyclic fire, meaning they only had a minute or two before they disarmed themselves; the sniper had a 20mm AMR, which could penetrate the exoskeleton armor, but he couldn't see anything because they were beneath him."

"What were you doing?" Francesca asked, concern again pursing her lips.

"Me?" Cain said. "Oh, I was busy having a moment of clarity. I had popped a couple of the corp security that had made it to the lifeboat hatch, but had seen too many corp-cop SWAT team raids to bother trying to shoot through an exoskeleton. So, in the space of about five seconds—which is a lifetime during a firefight—I came to the conclusion that these professionals I had set way up on that pedestal did not, in fact, know what the hell they were doing—and I had better figure it out on my own and real quick.

"You see, either way, it looked like it would turn out particularly bad for me: if I broke for the jungle, yeah, I might have made it; walking for a day or so, I might have reached the airfield, might have survived the week on shaking things out of vending machines, but my career as something more than a criminal would have been over. My rep would have consisted of exactly one major score, in which the principals were captured or killed and the rest of the company got wiped out: I'd never work again, life over before it had started, even if I did make it out alive. Or, I could have stayed put, firing hopelessly against the thick plate of the exoskeletons until I ran out of ammo and had to try to wiggle a knife in through armor seams, and get shot to death trying. I mean, that was the expectation, right? That's probably what that company had actually expected: the day-laborers would take a few crucial moments to die, while keeping the security forces occupied, as honcho, quartermaster, and maybe a couple others hustled over to the lifeboat and pulled out the principals during the confusion. Wasn't working out that way for them, though: with the mobile hospital already on fire, honcho was probably dead.

"So, there was the way they had expected it to go and some other way, which I hadn't thought up yet, that it could go, regardless of their expectation."

"So, you improvised," Francesca said solemnly.

"My specialty," Cain said, trying to lighten her mood with a playful grin. "I broke it down: I discarded their expectation and thought, what will get them what they want—which was, fundamentally, the principals escaping—and what will get me what I *need*—to live through it and not have my career tanked in the process? The answer was simple: I had to get the principals out of that firefight.

"The shock troops were still wiping out the day-laborers on the west side of the perimeter, after fragging the hospital, which may have made the tracer chip extraction impossible, but it also bought me a little time. Leaving the tracers in wasn't good, but I figured as long as we were alive and running, we could find another way to take them out later. The east side of the perimeter was still firing like mad, burning through ammo, but no security forces had made it to their lines yet. And on *that* side of the perimeter was the hovercraft: my way out. So, I scrambled up out of my nice safe hole in the ground and ran about three steps and dropped, with rounds going over my head: the hovering TAV had seen me and some joker trying not to fall out of its open doors was shooting at me, one-handed. I was up in the next second, ran three more steps, and dropped again. Over and over again: I'm up, he sees me, I'm down. It took maybe ten seconds, but it felt like ten years. The armor took a round or two, from the bruises I found later on, but it held and I made it to the opposite building, with the unfinished pool—and the hovercraft.

"That pock-scarred asshole was there, right where he was expected to be, crouched down beside the hovercraft, *watching* the firefight. I ran up to him and said we got to get over to the lifeboat and pull out the principals before the exos turn their attention toward us. You know what this fool said? He told me his *orders* were to wait until the principals exited the hospital, before picking them up and heading for the coast. I'm like, 'You see that huge burning mass of metal over there? That's the hospital. We got to go now.' This fool did not agree and he raised his pistol at me—he was that devoted to what was expected of him, devoted enough to die for their expectations. I was not, so he died there on the edge of an empty pool, in an unfinished hotel, Middle of Nowhere, Oaxaca.

"I jumped into the hovercraft, thinking it couldn't be that different from a car, and found about a hundred dials and switches and levers, all this stuff. Fortunately, it was built for military use and some foresighted engineer figured an untrained private might have to get that heap moving without a lick of training. *Unfortunately*, that engineer had anticipated a French private and all the instructions written on the dashboard were in French."

"But you are fluent in French," Francesca insisted.

"Not back then, I wasn't," Cain said. "I had to quickly pull out my phone, fire it up, and load a translation app. Turns out, it wasn't that complicated: a lever for forwards and backwards, one for up and down, and a steering wheel. On the other hand, it was getting complicated out in the hotel. The exos had finished off the day-laborers on the other side of the perimeter and were trying to assault the rec center. The sniper was putting down anyone who ran out into the open, but had drawn fire from them in return. My life was now counting down in seconds, I could see, so I fired up the hovercraft, shot over to the lifeboat, and had to drop the lift fan down to nothing, crashing in order to stop as quickly as possible.

"I crawled over to the passenger door and then out; I could hear rounds from the exos hitting the hovercraft and wondered how much she could take. I wrenched open the lifeboat hatch and found another expectation burst in my face: there were not three principals inside, just one. Instead of mom and pop and their daughter, it was just the daughter. There was no time to wonder why, so I held out a hand to her and just said, 'Let's get the fuck out of here.' She agreed, but was so scared she couldn't speak and could hardly move. I grabbed her after she nodded and pushed her into the hovercraft and then crawled over her to reach the driver's seat. The hovercraft was making a weird noise, by this point, but she still worked, so I took her up, threw the throttle forward, and went screaming off into the twisting dirt road that led through some light jungle on the way to the ocean."

Francesca let out a sigh and rest her head on Cain's shoulder. "Of course," she said, "I knew you would live through it, but you were so young then, and, by your own admission, knew so little."

"You got that right," Cain said and kissed her hair. "About to learn more, though. Turns out, pappa was never coming down: his plan had always been to just get his daughter to safety. Either he had lied to the company or the company had lied to the day-laborers; or both. She told me the whole story as we raced down to the unfinished beach facility. She had been born with several congenital defects, which had rendered her blind, deaf, and with reduced motor function; something to do with her motor cortex, other parts of the brain. Luckily for her, that was her father's specialty and what the corp had brought him up to their sovereign orbital to research and develop. So, days after she had been born, he wired her for cybernetics."

"Really?" Francesca said, looking up. "Twenty years ago? It must have been some of the original test-bed devices."

"From what the girl told me," Cain said, "it was the first functioning cybernetics that company had ever succeeded in creating. Her father knew that she needed to begin seeing and hearing immediately or the vision and auditory centers in her brain would not develop, starve for lack of input. So, it wasn't pretty, with her 'eyes' taped to the side of her head because implants did not yet exist; they moved out of the habitation ring on the orbital, up toward the hub where the centrifugal force didn't generate as much simulated gravity, making it easier on her new-born neck. He then wired into her motor cortex and, I don't know, stabilized her somehow, so she could walk and throw the ball around, anything. Over the course of her seventeen-years of life, her father had continued to improve on the cybernetics he had invented for her, until he could imbed the devices into her living but otherwise nonfunctioning eyes and ears, a micronized controller in the base of her neck to facilitate movement."

"Extraordinary," Francesca said. "I can see why the corporation would not want him or her to leave, just as I can see how dignity demanded that they do so."

Cain smiled at her and nodded. "Yeah," he said. "Me, too. Can never forget dignity. Anyway, I don't know where her father thought he could send her that she wouldn't be in constant danger of kidnapping, walking around with an entire industry wired inside her skull, but he wanted her to be free."

"And that is reason enough," Francesca said.

"Only reason there needs to be," Cain agreed. "So, we made it to the beach and there was a TAV waiting, hovering a foot off the ground, anxious to be away, and with what were probably the last two operatives from the company hanging out the door pointing their guns at me when I pulled up. They were expecting someone else. The girl gave them some sort of code word and they decided not to shoot me or get shot by me. Took a little convincing before they would condescend to take me along with them, but the girl insisted, and so off I went.

"It had been a crazy score, the kind of job you don't get involved with if you expect to live, but I had pulled through it."

"And your reputation was made," Francesca said.

"Sure," Cain said. "Not that too many private military companies wanted me to sign on for single scores, not after being the only one to walk out alive from my last job. But other jobs came up and I now know to ask a *lot* of questions first and to walk away if I don't hear the right answers."

Francesca sighed and then kissed Cain's shoulder, saying, "Thank you for the story. Expectation certainly played a central role, confounded though it was at every turn."

"Yeah," Cain said, running his thumb over the soft, pale skin of her hand. "I've come to recognize two kinds of expectations: my opponent's and my client's. The opponent's is easy: understand it and use it against them. The client's, though, is tricky: if you meet their expectations—of professionalism, of method, of discretion, of success—even if your actions were not what they anticipated, they're happy, content with the world working as they think it should. But if you confound their expectations, then you bring chaos and, with it, fear. So, sometimes there are things it's better for the client not to know."

"Yes, I expect that is correct," Francesca said, breathing a laugh now that the tension of the story had passed. "It's the same, really, in government and politics: there is what we must do and there is what we can say we did and survive the telling. As an elected official, though, I am often torn between the expediency of public perception and the obligations of duty. I believe that the people who elected me should know the truth, everything, and then make nuanced decisions. If I did not, I would be nothing more than a tyrant. And yet, there are undoubtedly things that they should not know. Perhaps I am sometimes a tyrant."

"Maybe expectation is the tyrant," Cain said.

As he raised their clasped hands to his lips again, his phone vibrated in his trouser pocket. Cain quickly withdrew the excited object.

"You are seriously going to look at that now?" Francesca said, sitting up to look Cain in the face. "While we are talking?"

"I seem to recall," Cain said, "someone not just looking at her phone but answering it, last night at dinner, and walking away from the table to take a call for thirty minutes."

"There was an issue under debate in the Council of the European Union," Francesca said, trying to give her objection weight by slapping the back of the couch, though she also undermined it with escaping laughter, "which you very well know, and I am the lead advocate for the seawall project. And it was ten minutes, at most, and I would never have been so rude unless it was an emergency."

"Uh huh," Cain said, smiling back at her. "Well, the only time this thing vibrates in this mode is if someone knows the emergency number."

Cain glanced down at the text he had received and all the playfulness drained instantly from his face.

"What is it?" Francesca said, concern now replacing her playfulness, as well.

Cain came to his feet, returned his phone to his pocket, and then quickly buttoned his shirt. "I got to go," he said. "Something's come up that can't wait."

Francesca watched him as he dressed, careful of her breathing, wanting to stand and embrace him and not doing so. Since the night of her swearing in as Mayor of Venice, she had known who Cain was and the kind of work that he did: living with the fear of his dangerous profession had grown increasingly difficult to bear, over the course of the last year, until after the Paradise score, he had returned ready to tell her anything, despite the danger it posed to him, by revealing lethal secrets. Knowing the full truth had helped her to accept that this was an inescapable part of loving him. Acceptance, however, did not quiet her mind.

After Cain slipped into his jacket and turned back to Francesca, she said, "Do not say goodbye to me."

Cain smiled his commiseration and then leaned down, pressing his hand to one of her cheeks and his lips to the other. Straightening, he said, "I'll text or call you with timelines as soon as I have them. Or Lester will."

Francesca nodded and watched the open doorway through which Cain passed, on his way to the central landing pad and his awaiting TAV. The city's business awaited her and she could not long delay, not even to steel herself, but she did wait until Cain's TAV lifted soundlessly away and pass overhead. Then she rose and went to find her shoes.

CHAPTER 2

I N THE EARLY days of the fusion boom, proof-of-concept orbitals were created to develop the technology for colonization. Orbitals like Lester's. The Pons Sublicius orbital had been one of the first closed-loop sustainable stations, creating its own oxygen, recycling water and most waste, and growing a substantial portion of its own food. By contemporary standards, it was of modest size, but in its day, it was considered huge. Its central hub, around which the rest of the orbital rotated, was much larger than on later stations, as the technique of housing mechanicals and goods in the shafts connecting the hub to the outer ring had not yet been developed. The shafts, instead, were merely spokes, there to convey motion to the habitation ring, spinning at a speed sufficient to generate the centrifugal force needed to simulate gravity.

As Cain's TAV sped toward the old *Bridge to the Moon*, as it had been known when it had served as the jumping off point for countless moon stations, he quickly itemized the equipment he had on hand and again was struck by the dichotomy of modern technology. Lester's message had only conveyed the immediacy of the score and that it was a rescue mission of some sort: no details about opposition, terrain, transportation, or communication. As far as Cain knew, as he glanced up to see Pons Sublicius growing larger in the forward monitor above the navigation panel, he would need to pull off whatever Lester had lined up with only what he had on hand. And what he had on hand was entirely conventional. With development money having poured into fusion and CasiDrives—anything to accelerate humanity's leap into the solar system, colonizing the moon and Mars—most other technologies had stagnated, continuing on much as they had for the last century. Though handheld direct-energy weapons existed, powered by back-mounted fusion power cells, Cain did not own one; he had a few auto-pistols, some suitable for orbital work (subsonic, soft-lead rounds, to avoid punching through the hulls of ships or stations and evacuating him into space), some only for Earth-bound scores; a couple shotguns, a couple rifles, body armor ranging from concealable to infantry plate, and a modest array of optical and auditory surveillance gear. Not much, if Lester had in mind a one-man rescue op.

After docking in Pons Sublicius's hub, Cain shot weightlessly over to the direct elevator to Lester's office, the former Orbital Command Center. He had known Lester for many years, as they both had grown their reputations, soaring to the heights of their ill-defined professions. They had come from similar backgrounds, similar streets, though on different coasts, and even dressed similarly, sharing the same tailors. They differed significantly, however, in how they approached life: where Cain took scores with his own hands, Lester remained in the background, setting them up; Cain's only ambition was to remain *Cain*, and all that that entailed, where Lester's ambition encompassed the universe. As an information broker, problem solver, business man, and—increasingly—a political player, Lester had seized control of Pons Sublicius as his bridge to controlling Mars's first city. It would take enormous wealth, in addition to connections, allies, power, and will. And so, as Cain stepped off the elevator, again enjoying the sensation of gravity, it did not surprise him to see Lester standing across the orbital's communications console from William Ord, CEO of The Braimbridge Group.

"There he is," Lester said, his smile-without-warmth contrasting wildly against the bone-white William Ord's barely repressed panic. "Mr. Ord, meet Mr. Cain, best operative in the business. Cain, meet William Ord."

"Enough with the introductions," Ord said, his hands spread wide upon the console, as if straining to hold himself upright. "We have no time."

"What's the score?" Cain asked, coming over to see what Lester had displayed on the console's horizontal monitor.

"What we got is a mess," Lester said, taking a hand briefly out of his trouser pocket to point at the building displayed on the monitor. "Twelve minutes ago, Mr. Ord's son was arrested in Manhattan by corp-cops from Diyi Shougou International."

"I sped up here as soon as I heard," Ord said to Cain, as if asking forgiveness, "to engage Lester's assistance."

"Charge is nonsense," Lester continued, "Mr. Ord's lawyers will have it tossed in a couple of days, but it's just a pretense. We figure DSI plans to shank the kid in prison. And we need you to stop it."

"Why me?" Cain asked, looking over what he assumed was the DSI prison, a sprawling, five-story factory and office facility, where the convicted paid their debt to society through forced labor. "Why not send in Braimbridge security forces? A hundred guys would have him out in ten minutes."

Ord hung his head for a moment before turning away from the communication console. "It isn't that simple," he said. "I have been beating back hostile takeover attempts from DSI for the past three years. That's what this is. They think to discredit me by taking my son," he said and turned back to Cain, his warring feelings evident in his face. "And they may succeed, as there seems to be no way out of this."

"Trouble is, Cain," Lester said, "if Mr. Ord sends in his company's special ops, DSI-backed Braimbridge Group shareholders will say that he's misusing company assets to cover up a personal failing; if he hires a hundred mercenaries, they'll say he's distracted and his family is degenerate; if he does nothing, DSI will reveal its hand in all this to show how he is ineffective, can't even protect his own family. No matter what, Mr. Ord will be weakened and it may convince enough stockholders to vote on the DSI takeover of Braimbridge."

"And my son will be dead," Ord said.

"The way I figure it," Lester said, "the only way to save his son and his company is for Brian—that's his son's name—to appear to have escaped on his own. If at the end of this, Brian is alive and Mr. Ord's lawyers show DSI's complicity in a de facto kidnapping and assassination attempt, Braimbridge will come out of it in an even stronger position.

"Now, it's been fourteen minutes since Brian was arrested," Lester continued and motioned for an assistant to come forward with a box. "He was taken here, the DSI correction factory in Queens. He'll clear medical in another five minutes and then be taken to his work station. If DSI prepositioned an assassin, Brian might have less than ten minutes before getting shanked. If DSI has to have their assassin arrested first, we might have as much as half-an-hour.

"Score is simple, but I'm going to have to call on those improvisational skills of yours, my man," Lester said with a smile that revealed his irrepressible amusement. "In this box, I've got three things for you: boots, like what the DSI bulls wear in the prison; a piece, same model they carry, with two mags; and an ID that

Seth W. James

should match what the bulls carry—looks only, though, Cain; it'll fool the eye but if someone scans it, it won't be in their registry."

"Uh huh," Cain said. "Entry?"

"This door here," Lester said, pointing, "leads into the barracks. I've got a hacker in geosynchronous orbit overhead—Paula, you ever work with her? Never mind. She'll remote hack the door and the camera watching the parking lot; there are no cameras in the barracks' locker room, so just find yourself a uniform and then do what you got to do to reach the kid and facilitate his escape. Got to look like he did it himself, though, Cain, and Paula won't be able to help with interior cameras. No comms, either, because the DSI bulls will be monitoring anything in the vicinity, whether they can burn through the encryption or not."

"Can it be done, Mr. Cain?" Ord asked, his pale skin turning grey as the seconds sprinted past.

"He may already be dead," Cain said. "He might die before I even land or while I'm working my way through the prison. We know next to nothing and you wanting this done quietly only makes it harder."

"Cain," Lester whispered, seeing Ord's resolve shaking in his lips.

"The only thing I can promise you is that I'll try," Cain said.

"Then that is all I will expect," Ord said and wiped his eyes. "If it cannot be done quietly, Mr. Cain, if you have no choice, cut him out through any means necessary. Paint the walls with DSI blood, if that's what it takes. I'll be ruined, but I don't want to lose Brian."

Cain nodded and removed the items from the box, before walking toward the corridor leading out of the Command Center. "Insertion is on one of your SRVs?" Cain asked, knowing the way to the row of access hatches for the Stealth Re-entry Vehicles.

"You got it," Lester said, following along behind Cain, Ord a step behind.

64

"I want a fresh one," Cain said.

"What?" Lester said. "The refurbished ones are fine. You had one problem, once."

Cain looked past Lester and asked Ord, "Money is no object?"

"None," Ord said.

"I want a fresh SRV," Cain told Lester.

Lester mumbled something resembling an invective and squeezed past Cain, whose bulk nearly filled the narrow corridor. Checking the screen next to the entry hatch, Lester said, "This one is brand new, and my last one, thank you very much. Enjoy."

"Saving it for yourself," Cain said as he sat on the padded bench beside the hatch in the floor. He took off his $10,000 shoes and handed them to Lester. "I don't want to see no scuffs on those when I get back."

"You know how careless I am," Lester sneered and motioned the shoes toward his assistant, who had slipped forward with the box.

"And I need two open-ended wrenches," Cain added.

"What?" Ord asked, confused.

Lester nodded his understanding and popped open a maintenance locker at the end of the corridor, withdrew two wrenches, and came back wiping off any fingerprints or DNA with an oily rag.

Cain laced on the new boots, slipped the auto-pistol into his coat pocket, its other magazine going into the opposite pocket, took the two wrenches from Lester, and then climbed down the ladder into the SRV. With a thumbs up to Lester, Cain strapped into the SRV's command chair and Lester closed the hatch. After a thirty-second warmup sequence, the SRV's CasiDrives drew power and the vehicle detached from Pons Sublicius, shooting off at maximum speed for the Earth below.

CHAPTER 3

THE VIRTUE OF the SRV was that it avoided detection by Manhattan Air Control, the subcontractor of the now privatized FAA that routed, monitored, and penalized TAVs and other CasiDrive vehicles in the airspace above the tri-state area. MAC was also known as an easy bribe, if an organization—corporate, criminal, or otherwise—wanted to know whenever a TAV touched down within X number of blocks or miles. DSI's correction factory would want to know: the SRV would prevent them.

Cain rocked within the padded straps of the command chair, as Earth's atmosphere buffeted the SRV upon re-entry. He could not help but compare this unexpected score with the story he had told Francesca over morning espresso.

"Didn't you just say how you ask a whole lot of questions before a score?" he asked himself soundlessly. "Didn't you just say how you pass on scores if you don't get the right answers?"

Much of the score, however, was already known to Cain; to Lester, too, for that matter. With the widespread privatization of law enforcement, most major corporations had gotten into the business, standing up what people in Cain's former neighborhood of

Redhook—or Lester's, in the now partially salvaged Los Angeles—called *corp-cops*. Corp-cops would enforce existing laws, usually for a nominal fee paid by the court upon arrest; but the real value to corporations like DSI was in the labor. Anyone arrested—at least until they made bail, assuming they could afford it—would be housed in a corrections facility that required labor in return for basics like food and water; orbital corrections facilities would also include air as a labor-related commodity. If convicted—and corp-cop companies often supplied their own attorneys to supplement local prosecutors—the prisoners' time would only count toward their sentence if they worked: recalcitrant prisoners could turn a six-month sentence into life-in-prison, simply by refusing to work. The value of cheap labor far outpaced the costs associated with running the corp-cop subsidiaries. The effect on the local communities varied depending upon the corporation's labor needs, with predominantly white-collar companies taking few prisoners and mostly from wealthier, better educated communities for short sentences, with comfortable facilities to avoid legal challenges to their franchise: more labor-intensive companies, however, would impose de facto tyranny upon the communities within their franchise, arresting entire streets or towns, if a large order needed to be filled. Cain knew all about corp-cops, their raids, their fabricated evidence, and their false testimony. Everyone from his block knew.

"Fucking Lester," he mumbled, knowing it was even-money that Lester had the SRV bugged. "Knew what he was doing, calling me in for this circus."

The buffeting of the upper atmosphere rumbled down to nothing, as the SRV descended at double-digit Mach speeds toward the eastern seaboard of the United States, its CasiDrives propelling without exhaust. Cain watched cloud-covered New York City glide into view, as the downward viewscreen tracked the agreed-upon landing zone, a couple blocks from DSI Queens. To avoid being visually identified by some DSI guard vaping in the parking lot, the SRV descended to wave-skimming level across the Long Island Sound, passing over the Stepping Stones Lighthouse, which partially emerged from the sound during low tide. Using buildings for cover, the SRV then snaked its way south, toward the DSI corrections factory, settling into an urban swamp created by rising sea levels. The command chair's straps then lifted automatically from Cain's shoulders and he exited the SRV, which to the children playing in a nearby street looked like just another fancy TAV.

Cain walked purposefully but not hurriedly to the DSI corrections factory. His six-four, two-fifty frame would not go unnoticed, he knew after many years of walking toward fire, just as his designer coat with embedded sensory suite feeding his Augmented-Reality sunglasses would not: the trick was not to go unseen, but to offer an acceptable explanation to any observers. A man, even one of intimidating mien and substantial size, would always attract attention, if clad in a $50,000 suit, as Cain was, but *without* exciting curiosity: a man of similar size and deportment would be reported to every investigator after the fact, however, if seen skulking around in non-descript attire or military-style watch-cap. *No, officer, no one suspicious.* And so, Cain seemed almost to stroll as he crossed the DSI corrections factory parking lot.

The DSI facility looked nothing like its federal counterparts run by the Department of Corrections; it resembled the other office suites neighboring it on either side. There were no guard towers, no walls; no guards patrolled the perimeter with dogs; no drones swooped by on algorithmic routes. There was no need. A corp-cop facility would always release someone if paid a sufficient amount; only the poor were kept indefinitely. Anyone with the means to stage a prison break, hiring the mercenaries to affect one, would find it considerably less expensive—to say nothing of legal—to simply pay the corporation. As such, external security was minimal.

Cain walked through the parking lot toward the guards' barracks, as the camera mounted on one corner of the building—to deter ground-car theft—showed a continuous loop recorded by Paula, 50,000 miles overhead.

The electronic card reader securing the barracks door was no hinderance to Paula, either. Cain stood in front of it for a moment, holding out his inert ID card from Lester in a pantomime of legitimately unlocking the door, as Paula remote hacked the lock. Hacking both the camera and the door was a matter of precision, micro-stream intrusion of the hardware, literally bypassing the processor and feeding the necessary signals farther downstream in the circuitry itself. The lock buzzed and the door clicked open; Cain slipped in.

It was between shifts and, as such, the barracks was empty; it was also without video surveillance, in deference to the guards' privacy. Cain crossed the room to the rows of lockers flanking a line of benches. While the building required an electronic keycard to enter, the lockers were secured as lockers had been for two-hundred years, with cheap padlocks. Taking out his two wrenches, Cain selected a locker at random and inserted a tine from each wrench into the space between the padlock's arch of metal. The curved back of each tine acted as a fulcrum, when Cain brought the opposite ends of the wrenches together, spreading the padlock's hasp until it briefly separated from the ward within its barrel. The lock sprung open.

"The advantages of a misspent youth," Cain mumbled to himself.

Withdrawing the lock with gloved fingers, Cain opened the locker and pulled out a DSI guard uniform coverall and held it up. Too small. Cain replaced the garment and relocked the locker, moving on to the next one in line. It took three lockers, but Cain eventually found a uniform that he could squeeze into. The hat was a little small, but with the coveralls on, the holster containing Lester's pistol, and the guard-style boots, Cain resembled every other bull in the facility. He locked up his clothes in the guard's locker, leaving his wrenches above it, just in view to mark the location, and then left through the green-wing doorway and headed for Facility Operations.

CHAPTER 4

THE INTERIOR OF the DSI facility resembled a hospital; they all did and Cain had entered more than one, over the years. In addition to the sterile white everything, guiding lines in a multitude of colors ran the length of the floors, splitting off at every intersection, to guide those new to the facility to wherever it was they needed to go. Thus, DSI could shift labor from anywhere in the world—or off it, for that matter—without incurring a training deficit for facility use. The design no-doubt seemed wise to the financially-minded masters somewhere: it also facilitated Cain's navigation to the Correction Factory Operation Center, or CFOC.

Cain slowed his steps as he approached the wire-glass door, eyes taking in the hallway—with its camera at one end—and the interior of the CFOC, packed with monitors, a communication console, locked rack of shotguns along the far wall, and a pasty white guard wearing corporal stripes ticking off something on a tablet. Any hesitation or perceptible ignorance on Cain's part would arouse suspicion during the unavoidable post-escape investigation: if DSI could argue that an operative from Braimbridge had entered the facility, Ord would find himself facing the same accusations as if he had sent a hundred. Cain, therefore, strode the last steps to the CFOC door, opened it half-a-foot, and leaned in only far enough to take a tablet from a rack beneath the radio charger. He then withdrew, before the pasty white guard could turn around to see who it was, and returned to the barracks.

Still between shifts, there was still no one there. Cain crossed to the parking lot door, opened it a few inches, and held the tablet outside, facing skyward.

"Let's go, Paula," he mumbled to himself. "What could I possibly want you to do?"

A moment later, the tablet blinked on, the BIOS shuddered a few times as Paula remote hacked past security features and logins, spoofing the last user's credentials and planting a wipe that would erase the session when Cain turned off the computer. It would not, however, prevent DSI's central computer from logging the session and recording Cain's inputs: anything he searched for would be recorded and could cause a problem during the inevitable investigation afterward. Nevertheless, Cain could pull some useful data without inputting anything at all.

Cain took a moment in the barracks to scroll through the continuously updated security log, which pulled data from every door, every camera, every workstation, and any other systems interaction within the facility. He quickly found Brian Ord entering the medical bay; thirty-seven entries lower in the log, he saw Brian exit the medical bay, followed a few entries later with Brian entering the third-floor customer service workstation suite, where he would pay his debt to society by fielding customer queries for products with which he had no familiarity.

Cain switched over to the facility layout view, which displayed the same information, but with the added context of where each event took place. He found Brian's workstation and saw that he had logged on three minutes ago and, as yet, done nothing. *Probably sitting there with his head in his hands*, Cain thought, *wondering whether daddy's soldat de fortune or DSI's shiv will find him first.* Cain passed his eye over the other occupants of the customer service suite, to see if any had just arrived, a succinct briefing appearing beneath each name. None of their information jumped out at him as an obvious cover, but one name was familiar.

"Cecil Jackson," Cain whispered.

Cain recognized the name, in part due to the scarcity of Cecils in the world, and in part because Cecil's father, Pat Jackson, had fought beside Cain for two years, fomenting a rebellion in Argentina. Pat had been good people, there for the money just like every other soldat de fortune Lester had assembled at the mining corporation's request (the company needing a more cooperative government with which to do business), but he had always pulled his weight, had never looked out only for number one, and, when the coup aborted, he had helped Cain hijack an armored roller to cut their way through the forces encircling the Presidential Palace, to pull out whoever remained alive from the hit squad sent in to burn it down—and discovered it was a trap. Pat could have run for it, made it to the port and to the evac TAVs secreted among the rusting modular containers. He had not. He had stayed even if it had not been healthy and fought to pull out those who had a right to expect fealty, at least to Cain's way of thinking.

"Son of a bitch," Cain whispered, falling back against the wall of the barracks and tapping his head against the antiseptic white fiberboard. "Pat's kid."

A moment later, Cain returned to the tablet and mapped out a route to and from the customer service suite; seeing that it was in the yellow wing, he would have to secure an access card to unlock the doors going in and out. He pushed off the wall and left, returning to the CFOC.

As he walked briskly down the corridor, Cain recalled how often

Pat had spoken of his son. Pat had been taking highline scores for decades—being nearly fifty when Cain had met him—though he had never made it big, had never pulled in any major money, with everything he had earned going back to his sister, who had been raising Cecil for him. At first, it had annoyed Cain, with Pat's folksy talk and irrepressible pride in his average son; but soon, Cain came to see that such talk was Pat's mantra, his juju against fear. By the time they were rolling through rocket fire toward the Presidential Palace, Cain had talked right along with Pat, imagining what Cecil would say when he heard what his daddy had gotten up to.

Back at the CFOC, Cain walked in through the doorway as if he had done so a thousand times, turning left and heading into the racks of gear at the back of the room. The pasty white corporal looked briefly over his shoulder, finding Cain flipping slowly through his tablet and pointing to objects on shelves.

"What are you doing?" the corporal asked.

"Taking inventory," Cain said, not looking up.

"We just took inventory yesterday," the corporal said.

"Hey, I just do what I'm told," Cain said, raising tired eyes to the corporal before returning to his charade.

The corporal snorted and turned back to cycling through security feeds, saying, "Fucking Sergeant Moore. Doesn't have a real job, so he just makes up bullshit for everyone else."

Cain nodded his head, knowing the camera in the corner of the room could see him as long as he stood. Squatting down, he briefly left its view and took the opportunity to jimmy open a case containing rows of extra access cards: he took one of each, yellow, red, and green. Cain slipped the cards into his coverall pocket, stood, and walked out, his head still buried in his tablet.

Rather than striding to the stairs leading up to the customer service workstation suite, Cain walked with measured deliberation, giving himself time to regain his self-control.

"You are *not* springing Cecil," he told himself, silently.

"And why shouldn't I?" he asked himself.

"Because that's not why you're here," he said. "This is a score: you remember, your job?"

"Fuck the job," he said. "Easy enough to walk out with two. What will they care?"

"They'll care," Cain said to himself as he exited the stairwell, having opened the door with the yellow zone access card, and then proceeded left, passing under the cameras that Brian would need to smash as they left, while Cain hung back around a corner, to preserve the story that Brian had escaped on his own. "Goes right back to what you were telling Francesca this morning, smart guy. Expectation. You sideline a score for some personal reason, you'll shatter their expectations; expectations around professionalism, priorities, trust. Lester didn't burn one of his SRVs for you to bust Cecil out of a corrections factory; he expects you to handle your business, the business you agreed to handle."

Cain turned right and began checking door numbers against his tablet, for the benefit of the camera at the end of the hallway. In his mind, he said, "What the fuck does that matter to Cecil? To me?"

"It should matter to you," he answered. "You disappoint Lester's expectations, this Ord son of bitch's expectations, you'll never work again. No more scores. If they can't trust you to do what you said you'll do, they'll never ask you do anything ever again."

Cain approached the door to Brian Ord's customer service workstation suite and glanced past it, down the hallway toward where Cecil sat within a similar room. "If you're someone like Brian," he thought, "you won't be here long; money will get you out, one way or another. But Cecil? Pat was a good man, a good fighter, and absolute shit when it came to finance: he didn't leave Cecil a dollar, when he bought it during the egress from Delhi. Places like this, every time you come to within a month of your release date, the company will claim you screwed up, some tiny infraction or other, and extend your sentence another month, another six: you never leave. Get arrested for parking tickets and spend life in prison."

Cain stopped in front of the door to Brian's workstation suite, leaned over to look through the wired-glass panel, and then down at his tablet, as if verifying occupancy. "I feel for Cecil," Cain thought, "and I feel like I still owe something to Pat, but do you owe him everything? Because that's what you'll be giving up. And for what? A few good times you had with a good soldier?"

Cain stood staring at the tablet in his hands, as new entries moved the log incessantly, until neither Brian nor Cecil's name appeared on the screen. Finally, he mumbled to himself, "Because I want to and that's reason enough."

Cain strode away from the customer service workstation suite and back toward the stairs down to green level.

CHAPTER 5

CAIN CONTINUED PAST the CFOC without stopping, going back to the barracks. There, he used Lester's wrenches to open the locker and then quickly changed back into his regular clothes and AR sunglasses, leaving the uniform he had borrowed in the open locker. Cain then pulled up a prisoner roster on the tablet, heedless of leaving a search trail. He quickly found what he was looking for: one Pedro Cruz, two levels below ground on the factory floor, red level.

Leaving the barracks and walking under two cameras on his way to the CFOC, Cain strode into the Command Center as briskly as he had before—and shot the corporal through the head. As smoothly as he had drawn the pistol Lester had given him, Cain replaced it in his belt (having left the holster with the coveralls). Kneeling next to the Corporal's body, Cain rifled his pockets until he found both a yellow and a red access card; he put them into the same pocket that held the ones he had taken earlier, this time in full view of the cameras. He thought of taking the corporal's pistol and, especially, his ammunition, but it would look too much like improvising to the camera watching him.

Cain then left and strode down the long corridor, past the yellow-zone elevator bank, to the single service elevator at the far end; he used the red-zone access card to gain entry and then took it down, again heedless of the camera inside, recording him at close range. The doors opened on the factory level—with its twenty-foot ceilings and the pounding white-noise of manufacturing—adjacent to the ready station for DSI's QRF, or Quick Reaction Force, the riot troops that DSI kept on constant alert to respond if the hard cases in the red zone got out of hand.

Cain stood in front of the ready station's door and drew Lester's pistol. It was a hammerless polymer weapon, the type preferred by cops and other people who drop their guns often enough that they need a model less likely to go off when they do; it held fifteen rounds per magazine. Cain pulled the magazine it currently held—minus the round he had used on the corporal—and replaced it with a fresh one; with a round in the chamber, he had sixteen shots before it ran dry. Within the QRF ready station, there were twenty men.

Cain tapped the door lock with the red-zone access card, dropped it into his coat pocket, and then stepped into the QRF ready station, bringing up his corp-cop's pistol as he did. A guard standing at a locker opposite the door was the first to see Cain, turning at the unexpected intrusion of factory noise: Cain greeted him with a front kick to the stomach, low enough to avoid paralyzing his diaphragm, but hard enough to lift him briefly off the floor; the guard crumpled to the ground, gasping for air. The rest of the QRF looked over, frozen in a dozen states of unreadiness: a group played cards around a folding table, some slept or read while lying on the few bunks, someone was making a fresh pot of coffee. He would never finish. Cain began with the card table, shooting three corp-cops through their heads before the ready station erupted into pandemonium. With their shotguns and assault rifles secured in a rack next to the only door out, the corp-cops dived for cover, in a room devoid of objects thick enough to stop a bullet. Some, though, kept personal weapons, either on themselves or in the lockers along each wall. Cain wore no armor and it was those corp-cops, the ones with guns or going for them—and for the brave or insane ones that charged Cain, attempting to tackle him—that Cain had to prioritize in those ten frenzied seconds. Next to him, the crumpled guard tried to rise; Cain glanced at him briefly, saw that he was still unarmed, and pistol whipped him, again deliberately not knocking him unconscious.

"Come on, sucker," he growled.

Across the room, two guards had pulled pistols from under mattresses—at the same time. Cain fired at one, taking him through the skull (there was no way to know if he wore the fabric-thin backup armor that Cain wished he had worn) and ducked in the next instant; the second guard's volley of wild shots went over Cain's head as he adjusted left and killed him, too. The guards lying flat or trying to overturn lockers for cover then dived for the two pistols in the middle of the floor; Cain waited and shot whoever made it to a gun, while in his mind tolled a constant countdown of rounds remaining in his pistol's magazine: six, five, four.

"Come on," Cain roared and kicked the guard next to him in the chest, sending the man sprawling against the lockers.

Even Cain was not flawlessly accurate, not even at a distance of ten feet. He had already missed twice, which meant he would run out of rounds while six corp-cops scrambled for the two guns he knew about: if they raised one of those weapons before he could reload, he would die.

The first guard, senseless from kicks and pistol whips, finally did what Cain had wanted him to do from the first moment: he drew a pistol from his locker. In one smooth motion, Cain fired his last round into the head of a corp-cop across the room, dropping him and the pistol he had raised; Cain then dropped his own pistol, took the wobbly guard in an arm lock, relieved him of his pistol, and then used it to finish off the QRF, killing the last corp-cop with his own gun.

Cain stood breathing deeply in the still room, letting the dead corp-cop slip from his fingers, not hearing the factory din blaring through the open door as his heartbeat slowed to its usual, unobtrusive pace. He looked briefly around the room, his AR sunglasses helping him to ensure that every corp-cop was dead or too far gone to pose a threat. Cain then cast aside the guard's pistol and picked up Lester's, replacing the spent magazine with the original and its fourteen rounds. Sticking the hot weapon through his belt, Cain rifled the dead guard's pockets until he came up with the QRF's access card, a modified red. It had one capability that other red cards did not: it could open the weapons rack.

Cain threw open the doors of the weapons rack and picked up eight assault rifles by their slings. Their composite receivers lightened their overall weight to some extent, but with the flashlights and laser targeting and HUD sights—the usual unnecessary accoutrements a wealthy company adds to encumber a weapon—they weighed in at nearly eight pounds each. Cain, however, worked hard and continuously to maintain a large, powerful physique; he slung the eight weapons over his shoulders, their receivers clattering together. He then stooped and picked up a handful of bandoleers, each with six loaded magazines for the rifles, and, with his large hands, was able to pull together the handles of three ammo cans. Loaded with the two-hundred pounds of weapons and ammunition, Cain left the QRF and walked out onto the factory floor.

The factory had three lines: one for material prep, one for fabrication, and one for packaging. The prisoners working on each stopped what they were doing, going so far as to hit the emergency stop buttons on two of the lines, when Cain walked through their midst. DSI, like all corporations that ran a law enforcement business, segregated the gang prisoners from the rest of their prison populations, to suppress recruitment; they also housed and worked the gangs in the more secure red zone, hindering escape attempts. As a result, the prisoners leaning over catwalks, standing on conveyor belts, and weaving their ways around machinery to encircle Cain were all from the same gang: Los Lobos.

When enough of Los Lobos surrounded Cain, he spoke to the largest of them, a shirtless weightlifting afficionado nearly as large as himself, though not as tall, covered in the inscriptions and images depicting the realities of his short life. Raising his voice over the ringing emergency stop alarm and the conveyors of the still functioning belt, Cain said, "Where is Pedro Cruz?"

"I am here, mi secuaz," a man of modest size but piercing eyes said, also obliged to raise his voice. Seeing what Cain had in his hands and over his shoulders, he turned and motioned with a slashing gesture across his throat. Men in either direction shut down the remaining machines and killed the emergency bells, the last with improvised hammers. "Who are you and what have you brought to me?"

Cain smiled perfunctorily, let the ammunition cans and bandoleers drop from his hands, and then held out the assault rifles by their slings. He said simply, "Freedom."

Los Lobos erupted with cheers, as men scrambled forward to seize the weapons and gird themselves with ammunition. Pedro Cruz issued a few initial commands in Spanish before turning back to Cain.

"Someone would prefer that you were not in prison, Senior Cruz," Cain said.

"Mi abuelo," Cruz said, nodding in his certainty.

Cain shrugged; Cruz nodded again; there were things that were never spoken and they both lived in worlds that understood such silences.

"I was paid to deliver you these weapons and to remove the QRF," Cain said. "Done. I can't get you out, though, because of the double pass system; I don't have the access cards," he lied. "What we need is an emergency that will cause the facility doors to open everywhere."

"Like scrambling the fusion reactor?" Cruz said and laughed. He turned and motioned to another of his *secuaz*. The man ran off and a moment later, the lights briefly blinked out, before the emergency lighting and an automated voice activated, encouraging everyone to evacuate the facility. "We had planned this escape for a long time, mercenario. The only thing we needed was the guns, or the bulls would shoot us down." Even as he spoke, in the relative silence of the dead factory, gunfire could be heard on the upper floors.

"With the power down," Cain said, "every magnetic lock in the building just failed. You can leave through whatever door you want."

"Oh and we will," Cruz said, smiling again, only this time with considerable heat, "after we pay a visit to the chief bull, that Sergeant Moore. Sadistic pendejo, he will suffer and then he will die; afterward, we will leave."

Cain shrugged again and said, "Hasta luego."

CHAPTER 6

CAIN JOGGED ACROSS the factory floor, heading for the fire stairwell. The few guards patrolling the factory had either been killed or fled; Cain left them to the wolves. On the upper floors, however, guards would be taking up position at predetermined locations, Cain knew, to try to stem the tide of fleeing prisoners. If he was to leave the prison alive, with Brian Ord and Cecil Jackson, he would first need to cut his way through the cordon. He also knew that he would need to do so in full view of the cameras, which he suspected ran off of the emergency power, just as the few hallway lights did.

Taking the stairs three at a time, Cain quickly ascended the three stories to the customer service wing. He passed several hopelessly lost prisoners, fleeing in the wrong direction after coming across corp-cops, heading down into the factory. Cain dodged around them and continued up. Edging out of the fire door, pistol raised, Cain took in the corridor a sliver at a time: empty except for the echoes of gunfire. Cain jogged forward again, coming to the intersecting hallway, which lead to Cecil's workstation.

A guard appeared at the far end of the corridor as Cain neared the workstation doorway; he saw Cain a second after Cain saw him, but Cain waited until the corp-cop raised his weapon before shooting him through the head. The corp-cop managed to squeeze off a round as his dead body fell to the floor, giving Cain—in the eyes of the camera—justification for briefly taking cover in the workstation doorway. Cain kept his pistol pointed at the corner around which the dead guard had come, as if expecting reinforcements. Speaking sotto voce, he whispered to a young, thin man, crouched behind a desk bare of everything except a computer.

"Cecil," Cain said. "Cecil Jackson. Stay low and come around to this side of your desk; don't let the camera see you."

"What?" Cecil whispered back in a frantic voice. "What are you talking about?"

"I'm talking about getting you out of here," Cain said. "I knew your father, fought beside him. I'm here for a different reason, but since I am, I'm going to get you out, too. Got it?"

Cecil crawled around the desk to which he had been chained for over two years, swallowing noticeably in a dry throat as he tried to will himself to stop shaking. He finally said, "If you've got a way out, I'll do whatever you say."

"Good," Cain said. "Now listen, there are cameras everywhere and we don't want the people that'll watch the recordings afterward to think we're together, you dig?"

"Yeah," Cecil breathed.

"So, when I continue on," Cain said, "you follow along behind me at a distance, as if you're sneaking up on me, trying to ride my coattails out of here without my knowing it. Got it?"

"Got it," Cecil said, his voice calming as a purpose presented itself.

"Now, I'm going to have to pick up another person on the way out," Cain said, "and I'm going to tell him the same thing I'm telling you, only he can't know about you. It'll be a preppy looking white boy; just follow along behind him and don't bunch up. Got it?"

"Got it," Cecil repeated.

"Once we get to the barracks," Cain continued, "I'm going in with the white boy, you follow a second later; I'm going to point my gun at you and shout for you to get on the floor; do it. I don't want the white boy to know I'm helping you escape, understand?"

"Yeah, I understand," Cecil said, not understanding anything except that this was the way Cain wanted it and he would oblige him in every particular, if it would lead to his escape.

"After I get rid of the white boy," Cain said, "it'll be your turn. Just hang in there, Cecil: your father and I cut our way out of Argentina together, you and I will cut our way out of here."

After another second, Cain walked briskly down the corridor toward where the dead corp-cop lie darkening the carpet. He ducked into the next workstation doorway, as if he had heard approaching footsteps, wary of the camera watching him from the corridor's end; in his peripheral vision, he could see Cecil crouching nearly to all fours, hugging the wall behind him. Cain glanced into the darkened workstation and could see Brian Ord huddled under his desk, knees drawn up, head rhythmically tapping the drawer above him.

"Brian Ord," Cain said softly. "Stay where you are and listen: your father sent me to help you escape. I will. But for the sake of the cameras, we can't be seen to be working together, okay?"

"What, I, I don't understand," Brian said, his voice shaking on the edge of a sob.

"I'm going to help you leave," Cain repeated slowly.

"Oh, of course," Brian said and began to crawl out from under the desk.

"Easy, easy, easy," Cain said, growling the words through unmoving lips. "It has to look like I'm escaping on my own and you're just making use of the opportunity, escaping on *your* own. Do you understand?"

"Yes," Brian said. "Yes, of course; it's to do with the DSI hostile takeover, isn't it? This whole awful mess is because of them. What should I do?"

"When I leave here," Cain said, "you follow me at a distance, as if trying to sneak out behind me without my knowing it. We're going to go down this hallway and then down a flight of stairs; then down another hallway, to the barracks. We'll talk more there. Got it?"

"Got it," Brian gulped.

Cain then pushed out of the workstation doorway and continued on to the barracks, with Brian following him a little too closely and Cecil following Brian a little too closely. It was enough, however, and Cain only ran into two guards trying to secure the CFOC, whom he dispatched quickly before hurrying on to the barracks.

As soon as Brian ran in through the barracks door, Cain motioned him over to the exit and then turned and raised his pistol, as Cecil ran in a moment later.

"Down," Cain roared. "On your face, now, prisoner."

"I'm just trying to get out of here," Cecil cried, shrinking to the floor and covering his head. "I won't say nothing."

"You just stay right there and be quiet, prisoner," Cain said sternly. He lowered his pistol and pulled Brian close, huddled against the exit door to whisper.

Cain opened the exit door and passed an arm through, waving it horizontally a few times before speaking to Brian.

"Okay," Cain whispered, "I just motioned to the hacker in orbit above this place to stop interfering with the camera watching the parking lot. In a second, you're going to run out of here and the camera will record you escaping on your own, got it? You just cross the parking lot, go up one block, and then turn left. There'll be a

TAV there with your father's security men inside; you'll recognize them. I'll give it a minute before I head out in a different direction."

"I understand," Brian said, some of his composure having returned. "It has to look like I did this on my own. Thank you, Mr., er, thank you."

"You're welcome," Cain said. "Now, you ready? Go!"

Brian burst from the exit door and raced across the parking lot; with the DSI guards all busy trying to contain the riot Cain had started or battling Los Lobos, no one raised an alarm, much less a finger to stop Brian Ord's miraculous escape. Next, Cain turned to Cecil and motioned him up.

"Alright, we got to be quick," Cain said, hurrying over to the open locker and pulling out the coveralls, holster, and a uniform cap. "Put these on."

Cecil scrambled up and began donning the coveralls without question, over his thin prisoner's garb to avoid leaving it behind. "You're Cain, aren't you?" Cecil said. "It came to me while we were sneaking here. Dad told me stories about you two, whenever he was home. That's why you're doing this?"

"That's why," Cain said. "Okay, now listen. You're going to run out that door, take about ten steps, and then look back—and keep your head down when you do, so the brim of this cap blocks the camera's view of your face. You're going to see me, turn, and sprint out of here, like you're afraid I'm after you. I want the cameras to see that before they see me leaving, not giving a damn about you, and going in a different direction. You're then going to go up three blocks, turn right, and then go two more. On the right side of the street, you'll find a vape shop called *Cloudy's*. Go in. If there's an old guy with a white beard behind the counter, tell him Cain sent you and you need a place to lie low; he'll take care of it. If there's a Latina with a face that could curdle milk, tell her you need to talk to grandad immediately, and she'll take you into the back of the store. Either way, Cloudy—the old man—will hide you out until I can get you some money and papers, get you out of the country. You got all of that?"

"Cain, I can't thank you enough for this," Cecil said, gulping as emotion rose heavily in his throat.

"Have you got it?" Cain asked. "Repeat it back to me."

Cecil did, getting every detail correct, and then said, "I can't believe I'm getting out of here. Finally. These bastards, they'd let me come to within a week or a few days of my release date and then they'd say I screwed up, extend me. Over and over and over again, they did that, adding a month, adding a few months. If they'd just told me, *we're keeping you forever*, I think I could have handled with it. But constantly building up the expectation of me leaving this place, of moving on with my life, I couldn't help it, I kept expecting to leave and they kept smashing my hope. I was this close, *this close*, to killing myself."

"That's over now," Cain said, conscious of the time and the need for haste; he could not let Cecil fall apart. "Come on, we got to focus. You ready? Alright, let's do this."

With a slap on the shoulder and an encouraging smile, Cain guided Cecil to the exit door. Cecil ran for it, as instructed, and looked back with his head low enough to conceal his face, before turning and tearing off, conveniently carrying away with him any DNA evidence that Cain may have left within the guard's coveralls. Cain let him get a few strides away before following, playing to the camera and the investigators that would follow.

With the rapidly cooling pistol and its spent magazine in one coat pocket and Lester's wrenches in the other, Cain walked away from the DSI corrections factory at an unconcerned pace, retracing his steps to where he had left the SRV. The sounds of gunfire, muted by distance, echoed only faintly as Cain left the prison behind. He found a double-hulled recovery TAV hovering soundlessly over the

SRV, with a small team of technicians hooking up tethers to winch the vehicle into the recovery TAV's hold. Leaning out of the personnel door was a familiar face.

"Is that Cain?" Aubrey said, a grizzled old tech with a perpetual smile. "Should have known. You managed to squeeze a fresh SRV out of Lester, huh? Ha ha, come on. We'll give you a ride back to Pons Sublicius."

Cain nodded and climbed into the hovering vehicle.

CHAPTER 7

AS SOON AS Aubrey's recovery TAV lifted into the sky above Queens, Cain pulled out his phone and texted Francesca that the score was over, that he was unhurt, and that he would be heading back to Venice in an hour. On the other side of the world, in a VR call with the European Parliament, Francesca looked down from the visor she wore, looking out of the virtual debate and at Cain's message, and then she released the breath that she had not realized she had held for the last hour. She lifted the visor into her hair, to apply a tissue to the moisture marshaling in her eye lashes, before it ran and screwed up her make up. With a deep breath, she pushed all that she felt and all that she wanted to say out of her mind, refocused on the debate, and slid the VR visor back into place.

Back in the Command Center of Pons Sublicius, Cain returned the pistol, wrenches, and boots to Lester's assistant, before carefully inspecting his returned oxfords for scuffs or other abuse; they seemed fine. Lester stood a few feet away, as Cain laced his shoes, and watched William and Brian Ord share an awkward embrace, as if they had never hugged one another before and were not entirely sure how to go about it. With both of them unsuccessfully stifling tears, the hug was needed nevertheless.

Lester turned away, smiling contentedly with having, yet again, delivered the impossible. Seeing Cain, he walked briskly over, his hands held apart and his face beaming. "My man," he said, "that was *inspired*. This is why—this right here—this is why I always go to Cain for the trickiest of tricky situations. A riot? Inspired—I wish I had thought of it."

Cain shrugged and said, "The opportunity was there, once I saw the facility."

"I didn't know what the hell was going on," Lester said, "when Paula flashed us the power outage and gunfire going off every which way. I thought, 'Cain couldn't have screwed up that badly.' Should have known."

"Yeah, well, there may be a small piece to deal with regarding the story I tried to leave behind," Cain said. "I iced the DSI QRF and gave their weapons to Los Lobos, a small gang from that area, run by a cat named Pedro Cruz."

"In prison, maybe," Lester said. "His granddaddy runs things on the outside. They're small-time, but I've heard of them."

"Pedro is under the impression his abuelo paid me to spring him," Cain said. "The moment he reaches Senior Cruz, they'll know that ain't the case. Might raise questions, spread rumors."

Lester waved his hand, contorting his lip in unconcern. He said, "Leave that to me. I'll have an intermediary stop by with some business for Los Lobos, something that needs the whole crew. Hijack something, maybe. He'll tell them that the jailbreak was an advance, to secure their services, and that they'll get a little something afterward, too. Boom, the whole story explained. It might even get back to DSI and if it does, it'll explain you being there, if they swab up any DNA of yours."

"Solid," Cain said. He looked past Lester's shoulder, at the recovering Ords, before saying, "Since my shoes were not harmed, I'm out of here."

"Hold up," Lester said. "Ord's going to want to thank you."

"He can do that with currency," Cain said and turned away.

Lester watched him go, annoyed but smiling through it, and said, "Classic Cain. Never sentimental; doesn't give a damn about gratitude, compliments, anything. Anything except the M-O-N-E-Y." Lester laughed soundlessly to himself and then turned to join the Ords, to receive the praise in Cain's place.

As Cain reclined in his TAV on the way back to Venice, he reflected upon his choice to risk everything to free Pat's son. Lester was happier the way it had gone down, Ord had his son and could continue to fend off DSI's hostile takeover attempts, and the investigation that would soon begin would not conclude that Brian had anything to do with the riot, any more than any of the other fortunate escapees who had made use of the confusion. And yet, none of that had factored into Cain's decision. He withdrew a single-serving bottle of grappa from the case that he kept for when he took Francesca anywhere, looking at it rather than tasting it. The world had its expectations, even of Cain: Cain had expectations of himself. Though he had rarely if ever put them into words, his expectations of himself mattered more to him and they were non-negotiable. If it had all gone wrong, Lester's expectations would have died in the crashing of a pedestal and he would have never again asked Cain to take a score. It was in part for that reason that Cain would never tell Lester his true reasons for running the score as he had; it was also in part because Cain's expectations of himself were deeply personal, if never verbally defined, and he would not tolerate the intrusion of another's judgement. As Venice grew in the forward view screen, however, Cain knew that he would tell Francesca.

PART 3

HARD CHOICES

CHAPTER 1

FROM WITHIN WHAT was left of a top floor apartment, Cain looked out over the largely destroyed city of Arkhangelsk, Russia. It was April. It was freezing. The air steamed in front of Cain's eyes with each breath, as he studied the contours of the once-great northern port, its many shattered buildings scratching at the pale sky, and waited for the word.

"Hawk Six, this is Eagle Eye," Paula's voice came over the secure channel: "blast doors are opening."

"About goddamn time," Oswald mumbled somewhere behind Cain.

"Roger, Eagle Eye," Cain said, the headset he wore under his balaclava picking up his voice through the throat mic. "Hawk Two, Hawk Tree, acknowledge."

"Hawk Two, acknowledge blast doors open," the radio crackled.

"Hawk Tree, acknowledge blast doors open," the radio reported again, this time with a southern-American accent.

"But which way will they turn?" Kapoor wondered aloud, as she shrugged into her Yahata EDF airfoil, grunting under the hundred-pound weight of the quad-thruster pack.

Nine days ago, Wamwarav Odhiambo had been kidnapped from the Atlantis Project, off the coast of Brazil. A Nobel-Prize-winning computer scientist who had perfected the first "AI collectives"—a form of collaboration between AIs that did not result in a single, more powerful entity, but preserved the individuals composing the collective—Odhiambo was highly respected within his discipline and beloved internationally for his devotion to oceanic rejuvenation. He was also highly prized by the syndicate that had taken over Arkhangelsk, known to Interpole as *The Archangel Mob*. Arkhangelsk had been declared a city state by the UN, at the conclusion of the third Russo-Finnish war; The Archangel Mob intended to keep its independence, resisting the inevitable Russian invasion, by simply making it too costly to take. To do that, they needed to tie the various AIs that managed the city into a cohesive enterprise: Port Authority, Air Defense, Media, Surveillance, and Drone Control. To create such a collective, they needed Odhiambo.

"Hawk Six, this is Eagle Eye," Paula said a minute later: "it's the convoy. Two rollers and the limo. And they're heading—come on, idiots—west. I say again, convoy is heading west."

"Roger, Eagle Eye," Cain said, voice devoid of the excitement creeping into Paula's, despite her watching it all from 50,000 miles overhead in her near-Earth orbital. "All channel: plan Bravo. I say again, plan Bravo. Chatterbox: SITREP."

"We are good, Hawk Six," a light, German voice said over the secure channel. "The frequencies are as they have been all week; the module is prepped and ready."

"Roger, Chatterbox," Cain said. "Hawk Two, they're coming your way; acknowledge."

"Hawk Six, this is Hawk Two, roger," Sapa'u said, twenty-blocks west, and grunted as he resettled a CG recoilless railgun over one shoulder. Its weight along with the Yahata airfoil tested even his prodigious strength.

"Hawk Six, Hawk Tree," Simon cut in: "you want we should hustle up now, over?"

"Negative, Hawk Two," Cain said. "Stick to the plan, hold what you got."

Though international outrage at Odhiambo's abduction had been swift and universal, no country wanted to risk an armed incursion into Arkhangelsk to rescue him, for fear of Russia's response. Such a response, however, did not deter Yahata Industries, which immediately contracted Cain to infiltrate the city and remove Odhiambo. Cain had taken nearly a week to reconnoiter Arkhangelsk, finding that the real estate boom precipitated by the free-city status had been largely restricted to companies that could afford to construct underground facilities: after suffering orbital bombardment twice in five years, no one wanted to invest too heavily in new surface structures. Not even The Archangel Mob.

"This is Hawk Six," Cain said. "Everyone should be in their EDF pack. If you're not, get there now." Turning to look at the ten other mercenaries crammed into what remained of the plush twelfth-story apartment—and finding them all wearing their Yahata airfoils, some tightening the straps that encircled their legs—Cain saw Oswald, a cantankerous Scot, edging closer to the blasted-out westward wall. "Oz, keep clear of that wall. If the surveillance AI catches sight of you and the alarm goes off, the convoy will scoot back underground and this whole thing is a bust."

"Roger," Oswald mumbled, shuffling backward and stretching his neck between the shoulder straps of his airfoil.

Demolished though it was, The Port of Arkhangelsk was still the largest and busiest on the White Sea, a major trade center for trans-Arctic shipping, and The Archangel Mob wanted to take graft off of everything that passed through the city. Their first order of business had been to oust a Swedish importer that had built an underground warehouse, which had then become their command facility. The blast doors that covered its entrance ramp had been designed to survive orbital bombardment, when the inevitable fourth Russo-Finnish war kicked off: if Cain's plan went wrong and the limo carrying Odhiambo retreated back underground, there would be no way to extricate him. It was only the fact that the various AIs around the city could not have their code altered remotely that necessitated Odhiambo's frequent tours of their facilities, leaving a brief window open for Cain.

"This is Hawk Two, convoy in sight," Sapa'u said. "Entering the kill zone now. Whenever you're ready, Chatterbox."

"Chatterbox, this is Hawk Six," Cain said and pulled the lever that extended the four booms of his Yahata EDF airfoil, spreading out from his shoulders, each tipped with an omnidirectional thruster: "light'em up."

"Roger, Hawk Six," came the phlegmatic response: "ECM active in tree, two, one. Active."

The Yahata Chinmoku ECM module then activated and flooded The Port of Arkhangelsk with broadband Electronic Counter-Measures that prohibited radio communication—outside of a single frequency left open for Cain's team—interrupted feeds from the city's surveillance suite, and caused the many security drones to scramble and return to their control stations. It also announced to The Archangel Mob that their prized scientist was about to be taken away from them.

"Hit it, Hawk Two," Cain said and levered the control assembly under his legs, lifted off the apartment floor, and then rocketed out through the blasted wall, diving into the alleyway west, followed by the other ten members of the assault team.

Twenty blocks west, Sapa'u and his gunner squeezed the triggers on their CG recoilless railguns, flinging ten-pound inert projectiles at hypervelocity speeds into the leading and trailing armored vehicles, just when they entered a stretch of collapsed buildings that cut off any opportunity to maneuver the limo out of the ambush. The projectiles struck with such force that the concussion shockwaves shattered the bones and crushed the organs of the ten men in each vehicle, as well as blowing out the wheels and turrets. With the dual-sleeve device now spent, Sapa'u and his gunner dropped the CG recoilless railguns and took up their Yahata Ogama J-60s, employing the conventional, belt-fed machineguns to pepper one side of the armored limo carrying Odhiambo.

"Hawk Six, this is Hawk Tree, should we move up now, over?" Simon cried through the frequency-hop channel.

"Negative, Hawk Tree," Cain said. "Hold what you got."

"Hawk Six, this is Eagle Eye," Paula said from orbit. "The blast doors are opening again. Here comes the QRF."

"All channel, this is Hawk Six," Cain said: "initiate plan Charlie."

The Quick-Reaction Force was an inevitable complication: the only question that remained was how many and with what equipment. Kapoor took half of the strike force and veered off to the north to find out, flying two or three stories high, through a twisting route to keep out of sight as they took up position overwatching the only road clear enough of rubble for the QRF to use. They did not need to annihilate the QRF, just to keep it busy long enough for Cain and the rest of the assault force to pry Odhiambo away from those guarding him.

"Come on, you motherfuckers," Sapa'u growled, as his ammunition quickly depleted, spraying one side of the armored limo until the paint color could no longer be determined. "Run, goddamn it."

The guards within the limo finally found their resolve or reached such a state of panic that they could no longer bear it; they spilled out of the far side of the car, using it for cover before trying to suppress Sapa'u and his gunner with return fire. The infantry plate that both men wore would soak up a few rounds from the pistols and submachine guns that the guards employed, if needed. But killing off the guards was not Sapa'u's mission: he and his gunner raised their fire off of the limo, to hammer the standing walls of the buildings beyond, and watched as five of the guards hustled down a northern alley, Odhiambo with them.

"Whoa, Hawk Six, Hawk Six, this is Eagle Eye," Paula cried. "The QRF just keeps coming—it's every swinging dick, looks like. I've got a dozen rollers and two light helicopters—there are guys running out on foot, for christsake. I've also got two TAVs lifting off from the airport, the armed ones we saw the other day, over."

"All channel, Hawk Six," Cain said: "plan Delta."

"Are you sure?" Oswald said, briefly catching up to Cain to look him in the eye as they ducked and weaved around partially demolished buildings.

"Now," Cain said. "Move."

Oswald cursed before veering off to the north, taking the rest of the strike force to reinforce Kapoor's squad. If the QRF ran over the blocking force, they might reach Odhiambo before Cain could eliminate his guards and take him out of Arkhangelsk. Cain increased speed, flying under the arches created by fallen buildings leaning against each other.

"Hawk Six, this is Viking Six," an unhurried voice said, comfortable within the cockpit of a Viking Interdictor, two-hundred miles west. "Would you like us to destroy those TAVs now?"

"Not yet, Viking Six," Cain said, grunting with the effort of flying. "Hold what you got."

With Odhiambo's guards now out of the ambush and heading north (the only direction they could move, as there were no eastward alleyways clear enough to use), Cain sped over the riddled limo, sparing a moment to strafe the remaining guards there with his Yahata J-60 before veering down the alleyway in pursuit.

"Hawk Two, this is Hawk Six," Cain growled, forced to

decelerate before popping up and over a congested alleyway: "you're clear; reinforce Hawks Four and Five, over."

"Roger," Sapa'u said, extending his own flight booms and racing off to join the blocking force before the firefight kicked off.

The Yahata EDF airfoil was directed by leg controls, the operator raising his or her legs into a kneeling position for full throttle or extending them into a standing position for full hover, somewhere in between for intermediate speeds; kicking a leg to either side controlled lateral movement, while moving one forward would turn the four-thruster craft or both together forward or back to control pitch. It took practice, but an experience EDF pilot could fly with his or her legs while employing a weapon with his or her arms—which is just what Cain did as he came into range of the fleeing guards.

Some of them turned to fire, when they heard the high-pitched whine of the airfoil, not knowing quite what it was but frightened enough to shoot at anything. With the aid of an integrated sight, which fed to Cain's AR sunglasses, Cain shredded two of the guards before ducking behind a building in mid-air, slowing to a hover as the return fire from the remaining guards pocked the brick walls.

"Hawk Six, this is Hawk Five," Kapoor cried over the radio. "Shit is getting pretty thick here, over."

Cain spared a moment to look at the overlay in his left eye, fed to his sunglasses by Paula: he could see the QRF setting up its own base of fire to suppress the blocking force. Once they gained fire superiority, forcing their targets to take cover to avoid annihilation, they would swing half their force in on one flank or the other and catch Kapoor and Oswald's squads in a crossfire, cutting them to pieces.

"Hawk Tree, this is Hawk Six," Cain said, removing and dropping the empty hundred-round ammo belt holder from his J-60 and replacing it with a fresh one: "move up now—and hit those rollers from behind, over."

"Rodger that, Hawk Six," Simon shouted as he and his gunner rose from their hiding spot to the east of The Archangel Mob's command facility and rocketed west to come up behind the QRF, each carrying two CG recoilless railguns and a Yahata J-60 Ogama.

Cain listened with part of his mind as Kapoor and Oswald positioned and repositioned their squads, moving from their primary defense to the secondary and then on to the alternate, as the QRF closed in and tried to overwhelm them. They were good, the people he had brought in for the assault force; they should be, as he had contracted them through Lester. He would have to rely on them to hold their ground while he caught up to Odhiambo alone.

Circling the brick building at a slow speed to reduce noise, Cain accelerated in the last dozen feet to come screaming through the intersection—behind the one guard left to slow him down. He drilled the man from behind as the guard turned first one way and then the other, briefly frustrated by the echoes within the alleyway hampering his ability to locate Cain; then nothing bothered him ever again. Cain flew on, slowly overtaking the remaining two guards and Odhiambo in a parallel alleyway.

"Hawk Two, Hawk Two," Cain could hear Kapoor cry out: "there's a mortar carrier to my ten o'clock. Use your CG on it. Now!"

"Roger," Sapa'u grunted. "It's my last one."

"You don't hit it," Kapoor said, the sound of her full-cyclic fire nearly overwhelming her voice, "that mortar will make the last of us."

"Eagle Eye, this is Hawk Six," Cain said. "I can't see shit, give me thermal."

The overhead feed to Cain's glasses turned from HD to thermal, a kaleidoscope of colors indicating hot and cold bodies; in the frozen north, unconvinced of Spring's birth, the hot breath and running bodies of the guards and Odhiambo blazed as little red dots in the otherwise blue and white rendering of Arkhangelsk. Cain sped to within a block of them, keeping out of sight and slowing to a crawl.

Cain then set down the Yahata EDF airfoil, dropping the thruster output to nothing so he could hear. He jacked up the gain on his armor's integrated surveillance suite and could just make out voices around the corner. Russian voices. The translator package in his phone's app library (his phone providing the processing power for the suite's integration with his AR) scrolled text through his vision: the guards were winded and, since they could not hear Cain's airfoil, they thought that they had finally escaped and could sit tight, wait for the QRF to find them. They covered the four alleyways opening on the collapsed building where they had taken cover.

Cain had no time to slowly pick them off from the rooftops: as keyed up as they were, simply charging in would certainly get him shot. He knew he needed a diversion, just as he knew there was no one to provide it, not with the rest of his mercenaries fighting for their lives against the QRF. And then it came to him. Cain hastily unstrapped the Yahata EDF airfoil and pulled out his phone.

Quickly linking to the airfoil's controls, Cain directed it through an app, like a drone, sending it off to the west and then north, slowly accelerating until the guards could hear its approach. Through his jacked-up audio, Cain could hear them whisper to one another, taking up position to ambush the approaching attacker. Cain slipped down the eastward alleyway, slinging his Yahata J-60 and pulling a Tanfoglio 10mm auto-pistol. With his shoulder pressed to the corner of the building, Cain directed the EDF airfoil to accelerate and come screaming in from the west.

The guards, hunkered down behind fallen walls, one of them

kneeling on Odhiambo's back, fired on the riderless airfoil with submachine guns—as Cain came out of the eastward alleyway and calmly shot each guard through the back of the head. With a few quick taps on his phone, Cain returned his audio to normal and directed the airfoil to fly autonomously to the rally point.

"Viking Six, this is Hawk Six," Cain said as he scrambled over debris and reached Odhiambo, the older man struggling to his feet: "I have the principal. Get aloft and prepare to cover us, over."

"Roger that, Hawk Six," the lead pilot responded. Two-hundred miles away, two Säb Viking-class Interdictors rose into the sky.

"Hawks Four and Five," Cain continued, "I have the principal: withdraw to the rally point and then egress. Good job, everyone. Mission complete."

A brief cheer could be heard over the mission frequency, as the mercenary squads pulled out of the firefight and retreated to a rally point, south of the river, with their escape TAVs already prepositioned. Cain's own TAV, his private vehicle, was at that moment plummeting from orbit, to land a few blocks west.

"Dr. Odhiambo," Cain said, offering his hand. "My name is Cain. I'm here to get you the hell out of Archangel. Come on."

"Bless you," Odhiambo said, his voice cracking as he took Cain's hand and stumbled over the uneven ground. "I don't know how you have come to be here, my friend, but I am glad you are. I am just sorry that all of these people have had to die to free one old man."

"Let's just concentrate on not joining them," Cain said, his hand on Odhiambo's back to guide the man forward, looking over his shoulder at the diminishing sounds of battle as the QRF no-doubt swarmed to the limo's ambush site, searching for Odhiambo. "I've got a TAV ahead; once we're on it, we're home free."

"I will hurry," Odhiambo said, clearly not used to physical exertion and already winded from the mob's forced march.

In a ninety-second scramble that seemed to last two hours, Cain and Odhiambo made it to what had likely been a parking lot before the wars. There, hovering on its CasiDrive thrusters, Cain's TAV awaited them, opening its side door as Cain's phone came within the predetermined proximity.

"There you go," Cain said, half-guiding and half-throwing Odhiambo into the TAV by his elbow. Cain then leaped past him, said, "Flight plan Alpha," to the navigation computer, and dropped into one of the two reclining chairs in the forward cabin. He pulled the padded H-strap harness over his head, connected it to the chair, and then reached over to strap Odhiambo into his seat. In the next instant, the TAV surged into the air, as if unconcerned by minor particulars like gravity.

"This is amazing," Odhiambo said, looking at the fancy TAV around him, holding onto the H-straps. "How ever did my wife afford such a rescue? All of our funds, our resources, are invested in the Atlantis Project."

As Cain's TAV accelerated upward, to leave Earth's atmosphere through a corridor of airspace above Arkhangelsk and not veer into Russian airspace, which would have provoked an unpleasant response, The Archangel Mob's two armed TAVs took notice and swooped into pursuit. Cain's TAV was an AugsRak M7, luxurious, sophisticated, and neither armed nor armored. If the mob TAVs came within range to employ their cannons (they would likely not risk firing a missile, if they wanted Odhiambo back alive), they would easily destroy enough CasiDrive thrusters for Cain's TAV to simply float back to Earth, unable to resist gravity's pull.

"Hawk Six, this is Viking Six," the lead pilot announced: "we are engaging now."

From out over the White Sea, still within international airspace, the two Viking Interdictors fired off brief salvos of railgun fire. The magnetically hurled, hypersonic projectiles were shaped and coated to avoid detection as they passed first through Russian and then Arkhangelsk airspace—and then shredded the mob's TAVs from stem to stern, one briefly blazing into a cerulean orb as its fusion core breached.

"Hawk Six," the lead pilot said, still not a hint of excitement in his voice, though self-satisfaction was becoming evident, "your six is clear."

"Roger, Viking Six," Cain said and closed his eyes. "Continue flight plan Alpha."

Through the mission frequency, Cain could hear the two squads and two gun-teams call out to each other, coordinating their over-watch as they bounded back from The Port of Arkhangelsk, crossing the Northern Dvina River and heading for their TAVs. There were a few injuries, but held aloft by their Yahata airfoils, they would make it. Cain knew that he would not go back, not even if they got into trouble; that was not the mission. But he was pleased, in his own silent way, that the rest of the unit would egress safely. After a moment, he killed the feed, texted a quick thank you to Paula, and realized that Odhiambo had been talking the whole time.

"International donors, perhaps?" the old scientist speculated. "Though, I would have expected all of our usual sources of capital to have already been tapped, investing in the Atlantis Project. Maybe once we have proven that isolating even a few hundred cubic acres of seawater, and reversing the acidification of climate change, will promote gestation of the microfauna necessary to rebuild the oceanic food web, maybe then the potential donors that have lavished us with praise but with few funds would agree to invest. But now? Now we barely make ends meet—we rely even on the donations of food, to support our workers.

"Um, Mr. Cain, are you okay? Were you injured?" Odhiambo inquired, leaning as far forward as the H-straps would allow.

Cain sat quietly reclined, his hands clasped over his armored chest, which rose slowly with each breath.

"Mr. Cain?" Odhiambo inquired again. "Who exactly hired you to rescue me?"

In profile, Cain's finely proportioned features conveyed no indication of his having heard Odhiambo; his massive chest, the product of decades of devoted strength training, filled the chair until it appeared more that he wore the TAV on his back than rested within it, though it appeared also to cause him no effort or inconvenience.

"Mr. Cain, please," Odhiambo said, his voice beginning to shake: "where are you taking me?"

Odhiambo leaned forward again, trying to reach out to Cain, to shake him by the shoulder, but could not: he then pressed the release tab on the H-strap harness only to find that it would not unlock. He sat staring at the device as he pressed the release twice more before sitting back with a sigh.

"So," he said, with both concern and hope draining from his voice, "I was not rescued after all."

To avoid issues of airspace and potential litigation for crossing it, Cain's TAV rose into a low-Earth orbit, outpaced the planet rotating under it, and then descended into the atmosphere again, this time with Japan slowly filling the forward view screen. The various AIs controlling the airspace over Japan interrogated Cain's TAV, found a flight plan that passed it from high-atmo clearance to commercial travel lanes and, finally, to Tokyo local airspace, en route to the Yahata Industries Global Headquarters.

Cain's TAV touched down on the executive landing pad, surrounded by immaculately sculpted gardens, atop the facility's central structure; the CasiDrive thrusters slowed the bus-sized TAV to a descent so calm that even the nishikigoi carp in the encircling stream were not disturbed. Cain then unlatched his H-strap harness, which also released Odhiambo's, and stood. Motioning toward the side exit, the door opened and light streamed in, momentarily blinding Odhiambo. As his vision cleared, he saw a delegation hurrying forward.

"Let's go," Cain said, taking Odhiambo's arm, gently but firmly, and propelling him out of the TAV.

The leader of the delegation strode the last few steps forward, his face beaming with pleasure, his silk suit impeccable and perfectly tailored; when at a respectful distance, he bowed deeply to Odhiambo.

"Dr. Odhiambo!" he said after he straightened. "It is a great pleasure and greater honor to receive you at Yahata Industries. We were so relieved to hear of your safe removal from those unfortunate circumstances. I am Satō Toshiro, please be welcome in our humble facilities, all of which are at your disposal."

Confused and turning from the again bowing Satō to the stone-faced Cain, Odhiambo only managed to stammer, "Thank you, sir."

"You are very welcome," Satō said. "Now, if you would be so gracious as to follow me, I have had a small refreshment prepared for you—unless you would prefer to bathe first?"

"That is very kind of you, Mr. Satō," Odhiambo said, pulling (with some difficulty) free from the hand Cain had around his elbow, "but, if I may ask, where am I and, well, what are my circumstances?"

"Circumstances Odhiambo-san?" Satō said, trying to draw Odhiambo down the path from Cain's TAV toward the refreshment area.

Taking a small step forward, to remain at a conversational distance, Odhiambo looked uneasily over his shoulder at Cain before saying, "Yes, the circumstances of my being here. Am I free?"

"Free, Odhiambo-san?" Satō gasped. "Of course, you are free. We went to great expense to free you from those criminals. As for where you are, we stand atop the Yahata Industries Global Headquarters, Tokyo, Japan."

"Thank you, Satō-san," Odhiambo said. "I am very grateful for your help. Now, I would very much like to be returned to my wife and the Atlantis Project."

Satō bowed deeply, taking another small step backward, and said, "Of course, Odhiambo-san, of course. If I may be permitted a question first, sir?"

"Yes, certainly," Odhiambo said, unconsciously following Satō as they strolled farther from Cain's TAV.

"Here at Yahata," Satō explained, "we have made great strides in the field of Artificial Intelligence."

"Oh, yes, I know," Odhiambo said. "Your Mark III intelligence is very sophisticated. I wish we had even one on the Atlantis Project."

"Thank you for your praise, Odhiambo-san," Satō said. "Alas, though we have taken great strides in the creation of individual AIs, and despite studying your every word, your every achievement, we have had little success in orchestrating the AI collectives for which you are rightly renowned." Odhiambo made a few humble noises and looked uneasily back again at Cain, seeing where Satō wished to take the conversation. Satō pressed on: "I was wondering, Odhiambo-san, if you would consider a brief employment with Yahata Industries, to help us create a collective necessary to one of our businesses?"

"Impossible," Odhiambo said. "The delay caused by those criminals has already endangered the Atlantis Project. We were on schedule to deliver the pilot facility within the five-year period set out in our charter, which is necessary not only to convince new investors to help fund the full project—nineteen more facilities, in seas across the globe—it is also necessary to maintaining our current agreement with the banks that hold our debt and extend us credit. I really must return to Atlantis as soon as it may be arranged."

"I understand, Odhiambo-san," Satō said, slumping convincingly at the shoulders, commiseration and disappointment nearly trembling his lips. "If that is your choice, we at Yahata Industries, of course, support it. I'm afraid I must ask, in this case, however, that you reimburse us for the cost of your rescue."

Odhiambo stopped walking, catching himself against one of the wooden posts that held aloft the roof of the paper-walled seating area, into which they had entered. He looked closely at Satō, as if only now clearly seeing the man, and nodded his understanding. "Of course," Odhiambo sighed, "that is just. We will have to find the money somewhere. How much, Mr. Satō?"

"Seventy-two million euros," Satō said and bowed.

"Seventy-two million?" Odhiambo cried. "What, how is that even—I could not possibly raise such a sum. All of my assets together would not support a loan for that figure, which would not be possible anyway, as I have sold everything or else used it as collateral for loans to the Atlantis Project. Seventy-two million?"

"Please, Odhiambo-san," Satō said and guided Odhiambo by the arm toward the cushions surrounding a low table; seeing the uneasy look on his face at the prospect of resting on the floor, Satō changed course and deposited Odhiambo in a plush chair, set to one side. "I am afraid it was very costly to locate you and arrange for your rescue. A team of more than twenty mercenaries—the very best, of course, as you are so important to us and to the world— Viking Interdictors, the Chinmoku ECM module, the EDF airfoils, and weaponry. It quite quickly accrued to a large sum."

"I, I am sorry, Mr. Satō," Odhiambo said and looked over at the stone-faced Cain, clearly worried about what action would be taken if he refused to reimburse Yahata Industries. "I simply cannot repay you at this time. If I could, I certainly would."

"I understand, Odhiambo-san," Satō said and bowed. "I am deeply ashamed for having raised this unpleasant topic. Perhaps if you spoke to the banks, they would extend your credit further?"

Odhiambo limply tossed up his hands, shaking his head. "Perhaps?" he said.

"Or, if I may be so bold as to raise this option again," Satō said, "if you were to join us here at Yahata Industries for a brief period of two years, we would be only too happy to waive the seventy-two million euros as a signing bonus." Odhiambo looked up, understanding pinching the corners of his eyes. Satō continued: "A mere two-year commitment, Odhiambo-san, to train our AIs as you have done so many times elsewhere, and we would be honored to afford you a lavish salary, stock, and security, whether you choose to reside here within the Global Headquarters' executive accommodations or off campus. Naturally, we would extend our security arrangements to the continuous protection of your wife, as well, if she were to choose to remain on the Atlantis Project."

"Yes," Odhiambo said, looking around the room. "I see."

"But I understand your reluctance," Satō said. "Your passion for the Atlantis Project is most admirable. Perhaps Yahata Industries could also reimburse you for your time in ways that would assist the project?" Seeing Odhiambo's eyes come around to meet his, Satō knew he had found the right lever. "Yes, after all, any advances you make in conditioning our AIs to collective action would benefit the AIs of Atlantis. We would be only too happy to write into your contract reuse provisos for your research. Also, on a more material scale, I think Yahata Industries could provide substantial assistance. Shall we say, one-hundred-million tons?"

"What?" Odhiambo said, scrambling out of the chair. "A hundred-million tons of what?"

"Of whatever you require, Odhiambo-san," Satō said and smiled. "We have a great deal of retired equipment and salvage from the last war. Several businesses have been retired, as we focus elsewhere. I will have a list of the available materials brought to you," he said and turned to nod curtly to one of his entourage, "and you may choose whatever you wish. Additionally, we maintain several hospital ships, which are always in need of training opportunities for new staff: I will put one off the coast of Brazil and it will be at the service of any of your staff working on Atlantis, reducing your healthcare costs and increasing worker efficiency. Together with your research here and the additional materials, I would estimate that the Atlantis Project would reach its functional pilot within three years, rather than five."

Odhiambo began to pace, his hands clasped behind him. Satō watched him as he walked, as he waived away a proffered cup of tea, and then played his final card: "Also, Dr. Odhiambo, I understand that your daughter is a very promising neuroscientist, applying to universities that specialize in cybernetic therapies. Yahata Industries is very influential, Odhiambo-san, and I am sure that an endorsement from us would guarantee admittance to the Tokyo Institute of Technology's School of Cybernetic Research."

Odhiambo, who had stopped at the mention of his daughter, and now stood facing away from Satō, slumped at the shoulders. As a man, as a husband and scientist and concerned citizen of the world, he may have been able to withstand the increasingly attractive offer, to stand on autonomy and dignity: but as a father, with the life-affecting admission to one of the world's most prestigious schools of cybernetic research hanging in the balance for his only daughter, Odhiambo knew he could no longer resist.

With a sigh, he turned around and looked at Cain. "There is an English or American saying," Odhiambo said, "that I cannot remember, about an offer that one must accept."

Disinterested though he was, Cain knew the part that Satō had cast for him and replied, "An offer you can't refuse."

"Yes, that is the saying," Odhiambo said. "Alright, Satō, alright. I must speak first to my wife, however, and then to my lawyer."

"Of course, Odhiambo-san," Satō said and bowed. "I have taken the liberty of initiating calls with both through our Secure

Communications Suite. If you will follow my assistant here, he will show you to the SCS."

Odhiambo mumbled his acquiescence and took one last look at Cain, before following Satō's assistant out of the room.

Satō, no longer required to play his part, smiled broadly and much more naturally as he turned away from the closed sliding door and all but pranced over to Cain.

"That went rather well, don't you think?" Satō said. "Oh and I forgot to say to you: excellent work on his extraction. I listened to the communications as the operation progressed. Very satisfactory."

"Uh-huh," Cain said. "One little item that was not negotiated for earlier, Satō, was you having me stand here as a reminder of what might happen to Odhiambo if he refused your offer. The only thing we agreed upon was my taking him away from The Archangel Mob and bringing him here. Intimidation services cost extra."

Satō laughed soundlessly, looking down and away from Cain's blank, black sunglasses. "You have always performed so admirably," Satō said, "in the several ventures for which we have employed you, that I have frequently forgotten that you are not one of our elite security operatives." Satō looked up before saying, "You are ronin."

"Damn straight, Satō," Cain said, "and gaijin *and* expensive."

Satō nodded his head, not quite a bow, and said, "You are quite correct, Mr. Cain. An oversight on my part. An additional fee will be added to your remuneration. Thank you for your services."

Cain nodded and walked back to his TAV.

CHAPTER 2

CAIN HAD REMOVED his infantry plate armor and cold-weather jumpsuit (now doubly soaked with sweat, after standing around in it through a Tokyo spring) after lifting off from Yahata, stowing both in a laundry bag before slipping into a set of chic casuals. He wanted a glass of champaign. He wanted a bottle, in fact, as he sat fully reclined and feeling the last of the mission stress, which he never noticed during a score, slip away. He would wait, however. He would wait until Venice. He would wait for Francesca.

With his eyes drooping toward a sleep that he knew he would not enjoy for several more hours, Cain watched the forward view screen as the Earth again enlarged before him, as his TAV descended toward the Adriatic. Slowly, the unmistakable shape of Italy appeared, then the protected lagoon surrounding Venice, its contemporary seawall, the envy of Europe, protecting a city that should have succumbed to the rising oceans many years ago. Then the city itself became discernable, with the Palazzo del Sindaco di Venezia—the official residence of the Mayor of Venice—centermost in the screen, with its large interior courtyard seeming to rise up to meet Cain's TAV. Cain unconsciously noted the defenses reacting to his approach, as well as the security men visually confirming what the surveillance AI had declared: he consciously noted—and pulled up the back of his chair when he saw—that Francesca had walked out to the landing pad as his TAV silently touched down.

The cabin door opened and Cain stepped out under the warm Adriatic sun, smiling at Francesca's approach until he saw the tears spilling from both her eyes. Her copper-toned skin looked paler than usual, her work on the seawall project keeping her indoors for calls and virtual summits far more often than was her preference. He thought she may have lost weight, too, during the three weeks that he had been away. She tried to smile as she reached him, passing her arms around his waist, which she could encompass more easily than his considerably larger chest, but the attempt squeezed out a small sob.

"Hey, what's wrong?" Cain ask softly, his arms enveloping her, one hand stroking her black hair, his lips against her temple. "Did something happen?"

She laughed with her face pressed to his chest, a small spasm of irony as she regained control of herself, and then turned to pillow her head on his pectoral. She said, "No, nothing. I have just been holding it in while you were away."

Cain kissed her forehead and cheek, seeing that her eyes were closed and knowing that she was breathing in his scent; it must have been awful, after a week straight without a shower, while arranging the ambush and then awaiting the opportunity. She breathed him in anyway. "No need to worry," Cain said, softly rocking her in his arms. "It went off without a hitch. Well, it was the worst of the three scenarios we planned for, but we walked it. Only a few people wounded and not bad. If anyone ever writes a text book, *Le Manuel du Soldat de Fortune*, you'd find this score up in there, under cakewalk."

The tension slipped from Francesca's shoulders, relaxing the furrows of her brow, as she listened to Cain's voice, recognizing his presence in ways other than sight. With her eyes still closed, she said, "Yes, of course, it usually goes that way. And if it had not, you would have improvised and the final result would remain unchanged. Still, it is never easy to wait here, knowing that anything might happen to you out there."

"Are you kidding me?" Cain said, gently shaking her until she opened her eyes. "This time last year, you would have run into my arms, leaping the last few feet and nearly knocking me down. I'd seriously considered wearing a helmet, whenever I came back from a score. This year? I barely get a few tears, nowadays. By this time next year, you may sleep through the whole thing. I'll be taking a number behind the European Commission."

"No, no that will never happen," Francesca said and closed her eyes again. "It does not get easier: I am just more exhausted, now."

Cain kissed her again and stroked her back, feeling the weight she had lost. "You've been pushing too hard, Francesca," he said. "Presenting, lobbying, debating for eighteen months straight, for this EU seawall project. You got to take care of yourself, too; maybe take a little break, rejuvenate."

"No, no breaks," she said. "I have shaped this battle for the last eighteen months, as you say, and the first shots are soon to be fired. I must continue because *I* will win this battle."

Francesca was always careful to disguise or suppress her brazen side, her confrontational nature, as neither would advance her cause in the negotiations with the EU states, corporations, and public figures embroiled in the seawall project. With Cain, however, she could not only indulge her true feelings, she felt encouraged to do so because he enjoyed seeing that side of her, took as much pride in her belligerence as she did herself. He laughed deep in his chest, the sound resonating out until she could feel it clear through to

Ethos of Cain

the muscles in her back, before he said to her, "Yes you will. I know that."

She smiled at last and stood on her toes to kiss his lips, and then said, "I am so glad you have returned, amore mio, and I would like to stand her all day in your arms, but you desperately need a bath."

"I know that, too," Cain said, laughing with her. "I haven't even seen a tub in ten days. I've been looking forward. You going to join me?"

"I have calls I should make," Francesca said, pulling her arms within his embrace and running her hands up abdomen, his chest.

"I'm sure you do," Cain said, his voice dropping into a lower register. "You going to join me?"

"Yes."

117

CHAPTER 3

A S IT WAS just past ten in the morning, Francesca had already bathed several hours before. She had risen early to take a virtual call from an American philanthropist who did not appear cognizant of the time difference. A series of other calls had then followed until, by ten o'clock, it had already been a long day. The exhaustion against which she had struggled all morning, and for many mornings prior, however, had dissipated at the sight of Cain, at the scent of the man—something other than sweat—and, as if awakening within her after a long illness of fear, she once again felt need. After three weeks apart, she needed to feel him inside of her the way she needed to feel air enter her lungs. But there were other needs, other touches that must come first if she was to reach more than his body.

Once standing nude together under the great bronze bell of the rain shower, its two-foot diameter almost large enough to engulf all of Cain in its deluge of warmth, Francesca ran her hands over him, ostensibly to rinse away the accumulation of weeks, but as much to reassure herself through touch that he was in fact back and whole. They kissed, when not doing so became a burden, but mostly they embraced between caresses. Francesca then soaped his body, using her hands rather than a washcloth, and leaving to him only the shampooing of his short crop of hair, which she could not easily reach. As the shower slowly progressed, though, as she touched and breathed and embraced, she also watched, waiting for *that look*.

There was a look that Cain gave her only when they were intimate, which Francesca would not now go without, now that she had seen it. In their first weeks together, nearly two years before, they had enjoyed only passion and it had been enough. Then, as their respect for one another had grown to fondness, intimacy had slowly bloomed until one night Francesca had seen that look. Cain's usual mien ran the gamut from stone-cold control, to a self-confidence so assured that it made Arrogance hang its head, to the playfulness of a cat that just might draw blood if it bit, but never did, and there was something in each that compelled Francesca. But *that look* was different. That look conveyed intimacy, need, and, for the only time in his life, Francesca imagined, vulnerability.

Sometimes it took all day, to elicit that look, a day of flirtation and caresses and pleasures both sensual and intellectual. Sometimes it appeared first thing in the morning, when she awoke to him kissing his way from her hair to her cheek. He may have needed to live his life the way that he did, in a way that frightened her, but he had not enjoyed their time apart, she knew, and, as she rinsed the last suds from his body, with his hands stroking her back, she raised her eyes to his and saw the look and knew again how it was as important to him to share that look with her—and only with her, only ever with her—as it was for her to see it.

Intimacy may have drawn them together under the warmth of the ersatz rain, but Passion would not long be forestalled. Cain quickly dried them both with an enormous towel before scooping Francesca up in it and carrying her off to their bed. Their first touches were slow, lingering, as much a sensation for the mind as for the body. Urgency soon compelled them, though, and, as they were both athletic and frank in their desires, the room soon echoed with their cries. Waves of pleasure inundated them then until, having dispelled all other thoughts except for one another, Passion lie spent. Intimacy then returned and drew them back into an embrace and, as her eyes closed, the last thing Francesca saw was that look. And then she slept.

CHAPTER 4

AS IT WAS not yet noon, Francesca's falling into a deep and entirely satisfying sleep proved less than ideal. Her political secretary—Marcello, whom she funded personally—had sped over by water taxi and pleaded with Francesca's security to let him in, which they of course refused. Knowing him and Francesca's manic schedule, though, Claes Thorsen, the head of her close-protection detail, did risk Cain's considerable ire by knocking on the bedroom door at a quarter to noon. One look at the clock and Francesca sprang from the bed as if launched by pneumatic catapult.

Though Cain would have preferred to spend the next several hours catching up on sleep—which always felt more restful with Francesca's soft weight against his chest—he also enjoyed watching her race around her bedroom as if backstage on Broadway, frantic to complete a costume change before the next scene. There was something endearing in her haste. She was not in a panic: she never panicked. She dared. The chances of her making whatever call or virtual meeting that Marcello had planned may have been slim-to-none, but she would exert every effort regardless. As she dressed and reapplied her makeup, Francesca talked rapidly in English and swore in Italian about some aspect of the seawall project, ostensibly filling in Cain but really, he knew, talking herself through the details in preparation for the battle to come. In three minutes, she had finished and turned to Cain with a guilty look suddenly contracting the pale skin beside eyes and mouth.

"Go on," Cain said, chuckling. "I got about ten days' worth of sleep to catch up on. Tell me the rest over dinner."

"Yes, I will," Francesca said and smiled. She then threw open the door, charged out, returned for her shoes, charged out again, and then ran back in for a final kiss before tearing off again for the TAV pad, Marcello literally hopping up and down trying to motivate her to greater speed.

Cain wallowed back into the rumpled sheets and slept for four hours, which was as much as his body would allow. He rose and toweled off his new coating of sweat before climbing back into his chic casuals and TAVing back to his apartment on Achilles Orbital. Despite spending all of his time between scores with Francesca, Cain maintained the apartment for several reasons, the first of which was business—a place to meet and store things that would be dangerous to Francesca—and the second, more immediately pressing, reason was the gym. Going without proper sleep and living off of Yahata's MREs (admittedly first rate, though Cain ate only the stewed sirloin meal) for nearly two weeks had been bad enough: going without a single workout, however, was beginning to agitate him. Cain put in an hour on the free weights, fighting the simulated gravity of centrifugal force, before jogging the ring for three miles. Entirely spent, he had a second, much less enjoyable shower and then checked his phone. Francesca had promised to return from the office in time for dinner three times and Cain knew she meant it by the last text. He had just enough time to TAV back to Venice and change before

Francesca arrived home and did the same, at a considerably faster pace, followed by an elegant dinner out.

The next couple of days were a blissful monotony of rest, sensual pleasures, and listening to Francesca talk about the seawall project. For months now, her involvement in the project had grown, as every speech she delivered, every private call she held, elevated her stature and gathered proponents around her as the dauntless former prosecutor driven to deliver the preservation of Europe without letting the syndicates or corporations fatten themselves through corruption. She was, after all, the Mayor of Venice who had swept into office by sweeping out the city's most powerful syndicate. The seawall project would require the same daring, while also requiring vastly more attention and perseverance, to navigate the various factions, governments, and political maneuvering.

"Of course, the budget hawks are the primary opposition," Francesca said, sitting in one of Cain's dress shirts, perched upon a chair in the breakfast nook of the Palazzo del Sindaco di Venezia, nibbling biscotti while scanning through an endless array of emails on her laptop. It was Sunday, the only day Cain was likely to get more of her hours than her phone or SCS. It did not mean, however, that their conversation would long stray from the seawall project. "They oppose spending any money on anything. I think they must fear that if the people spend their money on one thing that benefits them, they will then insist upon spending more of their money on other things that benefit them, rather than funneling it to the corporations."

Cain chuckled silently, taking pleasure in her enthusiasm and endless focus. He was her audience now, he knew, and he enjoyed it. "So how are you going to do them in?" he asked.

"Well, not with a stiletto," she said, "though if wishing made it so. No, there is another faction, too, that opposes us. The Mars Coalition also opposes the construction of the seawall, of either main proposal, because they want the money instead devoted to increasing the EU's presence on Mars."

"Why?" Cain asked, though he had heard the answer at least twice before.

"Oh, they claim it is because they do not want the planet dominated by the Americans or Chinese," Francesca said.

Cain laughed in his throat and mumbled, "They should be more worried about Lester."

Francesca laughed around a mouthful of biscotti, a hand concealing her lips, and then said, "I do not want to know. Regardless, their warnings are not moving many people. The budget hawks are boosting them, to claim broad opposition to the project. If I can cut them out of the debate, though, yes, then we can claim that opposition is crumbling, show the people that opinion is turning in favor of the seawall and claim momentum."

"How you going to do that?" Cain asked, absently thumbing through the few messages he had received on his phone.

"Well, it is a bit complicated," Francesca said. "The issue boils down to two things: I call them *if/which* and *who/how*."

"Hoo-ha?" Cain said.

"No, that is my issue with you," Francesca said and laughed.

"I'll say," Cain said.

"Shut up," she said before continuing. "If/which and who/how. The first issue is if we should build the seawall at all and which of the two proposals; the two proposals being a smaller, piecemeal wall that covers only the areas of dire concern or the larger, all-encompassing seawall that would protect all of Europe's coasts."

"And you want the big one," Cain said.

"I do," Francesca said. "The reclaimed land would boost crop output to help combat the growing food crisis. We should solve problems in batches, not one at a time."

"And the hoo-ha?" Cain asked.

"The *who/how*," Francesca said, scowling comically at him. "The second issue is who will build the wall or walls and how will they do so to ensure success and remaining within the agreed-upon budget.

"Now, the core of the seawall project's early supporters were all scientists and engineers and they want to settle if/which first, which I understand. Of course, they do; to them, it is the most appealing aspect. But if we wish to win, to actually build this wall, we must defeat the opposition and to do that, I argue that we should instead settle the who/how issue first.

"You see, if we settle who/how first, it also settles ninety-percent of if/which, by clearly laying out how we will build it and the benefits of the larger version. Then the question becomes about costs and rewards and I do not think that the budget hawks can win that debate—what is wrong?"

Cain looked up from his phone to find Francesca staring at him, her laptop forgotten. He reached over and caressed one shoulder, feeling the renewed tension contracting her trapezius muscles. He said, "Nothing to worry about, nothing imminent."

"Tell me," she said.

"You remember that syndicate honcho from last year, Pulciano?" Cain said. "Had a little business with him, got me onto Paradise Orbital."

"I remember," Francesca said, still frozen in place. "A mobster of the old school, out of New Jersey."

"At one time, maybe," Cain said, grinning. "Heart's too weak for Earth's gravity, now, has to live in orbit. Anyway, after I freed his bookkeeper, he said he might be able to open a few doors for me. Looks like he just did, because one of his lieutenants reached out."

Francesca turned away, tears fighting with anger until she slammed down what was left of her biscotti, sending the plate skittering off the table to shatter against the tile beneath.

"Hey, take it easy," Cain said.

Shrugging out of his caress, Francesca said, "Another score? You *just* returned. It has not been a week!"

"Relax," he said, his native autonomy stirring. "I haven't agreed to anything. They're just asking for a meet, lay something on me."

Clenching her jaw for a moment, she then turned in her seat to look Cain square in the face and tried to speak as calmly as she could, saying, "Listen, I am not asking you to never work again. Your work is as important to you as mine is to me, okay, I understand. But you *just* returned. I am only asking, not yet. Just, not yet! Damn you, I need to rest, a chance to regain my strength."

"Easy, easy," Cain said, his rising anger tempered by a distress he had not seen in her before. "I haven't taken the job, yet; I might not ever take the job; and even if I do, it could be months before I'm out in the wind again, if there are prep scores to pull down, first."

"That is not a comfort," Francesca said, turning back to her computer and staring through its screen. In a softer voice, she said, "It will weigh on me, then, as I wait, robbing me of my sleep, wondering if this is the time."

"You know what?" Cain said and rose to his feet, "I'm going to get this out of the way right now."

"What?" Francesca said. "You are leaving?"

"These aren't good Catholics," he said, "they'll take a meeting on Sunday. Look, I can't not take meetings like this: I tell them to screw without even listening to what they have to say, I'll never hear from them again. After I talk to them, we'll at least know what we're arguing about. Might be an easy score, they may need an intermediary or something, or it might be the kind of score I don't take. Whatever it is, I'll get it out of the way so it isn't hanging over us."

Francesca turned back to her computer again, pulling her knees up in front of her. She said, "Do whatever you wish."

CHAPTER 5

THINKING IT WAS best not to leave Francesca wondering, conjuring scenarios of finality out of uncertainty, Cain texted Pulciano's lieutenant, Jamie Scarlatti, and told him that he was on his way up. Cain donned his usual work coat, a calf-length trench with surveillance nodes embedded in the stand-up collar, which fed to his AR sunglasses and earbuds. He also strapped on his off-world pistol, as his TAV shrugged off Earth's gravity and tidal force and sped outward: Cain could not think of a reason why Scarlatti would want to burn him, but it was better to prepare for capabilities rather than motives, and the soft-lead, subsonic rounds of the .45 auto he carried would terminate opposition with minimal chance of punching through the hull of the orbital and evacuating them all out into space.

Cain sat upright in the TAV's recliner, trying to push the memory of Francesca's distress from his mind, steeling himself for whatever was to come, and watched as the Pulciano family's orbital hove into view. It was a relay orbital, similar to Lester's Pons Sublicius, though of a later vintage and lesser quality; cheap relay orbitals had been launched by the dozens in the early days of the fusion boom, facilitating the colonization of the moon and the reaping of its considerable mineral wealth. Pulciano's orbital—called OR-4839233 in the registry and *High Camden* by the associates, soldiers, lieutenants and other Pulciano family types that used it—enjoyed sovereignty but little comfort. It was not a wonder to Cain that Pulciano spent all his time on Paradise, instead. High Camden existed primarily for the over-sized central hub, which had once serviced a fleet of shuttles and ex-orbits as they brought material up from Earth or back from the moon; the single outer ring, connected to the hub by mostly empty spokes, contained the sparse living quarters for the hub's port workers. Pulciano had had the orbital refurbished, of course, and the hub port now served largely as a warehouse for whatever merch or contraband the family had recently scored. They had also taken steps to ensure no one tried to pull a score on them, affixing direct-energy batteries to the originally unarmed orbital. Cain looked over the defenses out of professional curiosity, noting that the batteries were fixed to the hub and not to the outer ring, probably to avoid upsetting the station's balance, but creating blind spots in their fields of fire. He also noted that they were anti-ship batteries and would be of little use against hypersonic missiles unless someone had wired in an intercept module. He did not see the telltale nodes and guessed that they had not. He wondered how they planned to thwart an enemy who wanted to destroy them, rather than raid them.

After docking within the cavernous central hub, and returning to a sense of gravity as the elevator took him down to the spinning outer ring, Cain followed a henchman the shape of a huge bowling ball through the unfinished corridor to Scarlatti's office. The office, at least, had been paneled with oak and carpeted in silk. Scarlatti had expressed his personal taste through the addition of a massive television monitor mounted over the command-center suite original to the room; a soccer match played while half-a-dozen lesser family associates watched and occasionally threw popcorn.

"Alright, you fucks, get out of here," Scarlatti said to them, when Cain walked in. He was in his late thirties, pasty white from lack of sun, six feet and getting paunchy, dressed well in tailored evening clothes, minus the jacket now hanging from his desk chair. By his flashy haircut, the inexplicable return of the pompadour after a century in exile, and laser-manicured nails, Scarlatti was a pampered guy—but he had not always been. A scar ran straight through one eye, which seemed smaller than the other, as if he had used it less in the years since taking the slash to the face and it had atrophied. He could have had the scar fixed with a plastic job, maybe even had the eye brightened up, but he had clearly chosen not to. Watching the young lieutenant eye him up and down, sucking his teeth in appraisal, Cain had a notion as to why not.

"Well, they said you was a big guy," Scarlatti said, nodding toward Cain and looking briefly over at one of his two associates that remained in the room after the others had filed out. "Don't think we'll need this much beef, but what the fuck, right? Can't hurt. You know me?"

Cain nodded.

"Right, right," Scarlatti said. "You made a very favorable impression on Mr. Pulciano, so, when this piece of business came up, he wanted the best and tells me, he says, 'Jamie, hire Cain to take care of this,' and so here we are. It'll be easy money, too." He waited a moment, but as Cain stood motionless and asked no questions, Scarlatti cleared his throat and continued. "Yeah, okay, so it's like this: Mr. Pulciano, like any man of vision, has his appetites. They always do, you know, the great ones; the best wine flown up here from the old country, off-world meat; had a singer, famous opera broad got a chest like a double-barrel shotgun pressed to your nose, she came up to sing for his birthday. You get the idea. Well, one of his appetites lately has been for this little French toy, Jean-Paul. Petite, quiet, soft skin, been earning his way on all fours since he skipped out of some fancy university, I don't know. Anyway, Mr. Pulciano takes a liking to the boy. The boy, though, he may be pretty but he's got no brains. He's not a week in Paradise before he decides to score another guest, some punk up from Switzerland or some place. Can you believe that? Naturally, Mr. Pulciano ain't going to stand for it; he tells me, 'Jamie, take care of it,' and we throw that Swiss guy out the fucking airlock."

Behind Cain, the bowling-ball-shaped bodyguard standing between him and the door barked a quiet laugh through his nose; across the room, the other associate looked away smiling.

Scarlatti also seemed pleased with himself, turning to the other two briefly, before continuing to Cain: "Hey, he had it coming. And, not only that, it was good for the kid, Jean-Paul, to see it. Mickey over there behind you, yeah, he held the kid's face to the window so he could watch as the Swiss guy flapped around for a second, his body puffing up until he kind of froze. It was great, I loved that part, but the kid, well, maybe it was too much for him. He went back and spread it for Mr. Pulciano, alright, but the next day he lambed out of there, jumped an accelerator gate ship out to fucking Mars."

The Accelerator Gates operated on the same principle as the recoilless railguns: two electromagnetically propelled cylinders surrounding a projectile, in the gate's case, a ship. The inner cylinder fired the ship toward Mars at hypersonic speeds, which caused the same amount of force to drive the inner cylinder in the other direction, which would do no good if the gate ended up on Venus, so the outer cylinder fired at the same time, in the same direction as the ship, cancelling out the inner cylinder's movement. The result flung the accelerator ships toward Mars while the gate remained safely in high-Earth orbit.

"Now, you're probably wondering why we didn't just go grab that little bastard and bring him back," Scarlatti continued. "Yeah, we tried. I sent a couple boys out on the accelerator but they weren't too welcome there. We've had a couple legs, an arm, a few organs, and a head come back so far. Every couple of days, another cooler shows up—it's disgusting, really, unhygienic, you know? Anyway, the problem is that the kid, he's holed up in Arcadia Planitia and we got no people there. As I understand it, a guy you know, a very big guy, he basically owns the place and he don't want no one else's business going on there. I'd love to tell the guy, hey, it ain't business, it's personal, a one-time thing, okay? I can't get a word to him.

"The way I figure it, though, you being tight with this Mr. Lester, maybe he doesn't kill you on sight, waits long enough for you to tell him that it's just retrieving a lost toy. We got no interest in setting up shop on Mars—hey, we got all the business we need on Earth, the moon, a dozen or so orbitals, we're good. If Mr. Lester wants a taste, respect, we got no problem. Name it.

"Otherwise, the score's easy: we'll book you on the next accelerator shot, you fly over to Mars, grab the kid, bring him back. There and back, three-four days. You need to smack him around, okay, just don't bruise the face. Oh, but, uh, don't fuck him, okay? Mr. Pulciano wouldn't like that and we'd have to airlock you." The bodyguard snorted again at the prospect. Scarlatti concluded, "So, what do you think?"

"No," Cain said and turned away, walking back toward the corridor leading to the elevator.

"What?" Scarlatti said, confused. "What the fuck, no? Hey, Mickey, stop that asshole."

Mickey may have looked like a bowling ball, but he had muscle under all of that fat and had spent his life fighting people more dangerous than the amorous Swiss he had airlocked. It gave Mickey the wrong impression about what he could and could not do, and so he grabbed for Cain's coat lapel with one hand while he drew a pistol with the other. Cain brought around a lightning-fast right cross, catching Mickey on the chin, before completing the half-circle motion by stripping the gun from his hand, and transferring it to his left. Cain then swept his right arm back, catching Mickey under the chin and taking him into a reverse headlock, with Mickey's back bent double, flailing his arms at Cain for a moment, as Cain pointed Mickey's gun at Scarlatti and his associate. Cain then broke Mickey's neck and let his body slip to the floor.

"I've snatched people for a lot of reasons," Cain told Scarlatti, "but never this one. I'm not going to help you rape someone. Don't ever contact me again."

Perhaps they had not considered Jean-Paul's consent, or anyone's; perhaps Mickey's suddenly dead body lying in a heap by the door had simply shocked them into silence. Regardless, neither of Pulciano's boys attempted to stop Cain a second time, as he dropped Mickey's pistol and walked out. Cain had anticipated having to fight his way back to his TAV, perhaps cut his way to the Port Authority to open the hub's bay doors himself, but no one interfered. Without incident, Cain returned to his TAV, requested clearance to leave, and departed for Earth.

"How about that?" Cain said to himself, as he watched the direct-energy batteries recede into the distance, taking no notice of him. "Maybe Satō had a point. Maybe I *am* that intimidating."

CHAPTER 6

AS SOON AS it was clear that Scarlatti would not order his TAV shot down, Cain texted Francesca.

I didn't take the score.

I won't be hearing from them again.

Be back soon.

Francesca did not respond, but that was not unusual: even on Sunday, or at any hour of any day or night, she could be called into a meeting or need to respond to a crisis within the city. Nevertheless, Cain did look at his phone every few minutes until he landed in Venice. He left his coat and pistol on his TAV before looking for Francesca. She was no longer in the breakfast nook and Cain eventually discovered the door to her office closed, which likely meant a call. He made another espresso and waited, watching the morning grow cloudy from within the enclosed balcony overlooking the Grand Canal.

Francesca came padding back toward the balcony, a few minutes later, never wearing shoes when at home. Cain was out of his chair in a flash and met her in the hallway.

"Look, if I'm adding to the stress you're under, I'm sorry," he said. "You know it's not for that reason."

"I know," she said softly and entered his embrace.

Cain held her closely, gently, and kissed the top of her head. "Let's take a vacation," he said. "A whole month away from everything. We could go back to the alps and you can enjoy watching me fall off of skis again."

Francesca laughed sadly and said, "I wish. I cannot, though; there may be a hearing in the European Commission, any day now, which could fire the first shot. I feel like I am on call."

"Okay," he said, "but tonight, let's cuddle up in bed and plan our holiday together, anyway. That'll be fun. Let our minds escape for a while on their own, until our bodies can catch up." She nodded against his chest. "Man, I cannot wait for this whole seawall project to be over."

"It will not be over for twenty years," Francesca sighed. "If it commences as I wish, it will need to be defended against the syndicates, the corporations, and the national governments that will try to take advantage. There is not only the battle to begin construction, but the coming war to keep it going."

"Well, if any particular combatant gets out of hand, in all that time," Cain said, "you know who to call."

With her head still buried in his chest, she said, "Lester."

"Oh, that's who you'd call, huh?" Cain said, smiling ruefully and stepping back.

"Of course," Francesca said, wiping her eyes and laughing. "That is who I always call for thug work."

"Thug? Oh, it's thug, now?" Cain said, feigning offence as Francesca backed away giggling.

"Oh, do you call it something else?" she said before turning and running for the bedroom, Cain a step behind.

"Yeah, I'm going to show you what I call it," he said to her delight.

They enjoyed the rest of the morning in bed, having to forego their planned outing on Francesca's sloop; the darkening sky had opened up and a fine, soaking rain had driven even the tourists from the alleyways and canals. Throughout the day, Francesca received more calls and texts and emails from various factions in the commission and parliament, big business and potential contractors. The potential for the commission to take action on the colonization question was growing more likely. By dinner time, which they chose to have sent in, rather than dinning out somewhere, it looked more certain than ever.

"The question comes to this," Francesca said as they opened the steaming cartons of Chinese food: "do the current anti-colonialism statutes extend to off-world colonization? If the commission or the courts restrict the statutes only to Earth, then the Mars faction can proceed in wasting everyone's time and it will prove more difficult to overcome the budget hawks. If they rule that the statutes extend to *any* colonization, then investment in Mars will be severely curtailed and I can then declare opposition to the seawall is fading."

She watched as Cain pulled out his phone, reacting to its vibration, and thumbed through to an incoming message. "Déjà vu," she said quietly.

Cain looked annoyed at the interruption, particularly because of the interrupter: Scarlatti had sent him a video. Cain rolled his eyes and began putting his phone away.

"What is it?" Francesca said.

"A fool," Cain said and decided to play the video for her, to relieve her of any worry that it might be a score. "That Scarlatti idiot, from this morning. Probably sent a video of himself cussing me out, telling me I'll never work again."

Francesca came around the counter as Cain pressed play.

Scarlatti appeared in his office, his unnamed associate smiling menacingly beside him. Scowling into the camera, his pasty white skin looking harsh under the artificial light, Scarlatti said, "Mr. Cain. We're not used to hearing no, you understand, and we really had our hearts set on you doing this thing for us. So, we grabbed up a little pal of yours. Say, hi, Walker."

Scarlatti stepped aside to reveal an older man, with grey in his hair and beard, tied to a chair. He had clearly been beaten, with one eye swelling shut and a fattening lip; his shirt had been torn.

"Now get your ass to the accelerator gate, Cain," Scarlatti said, pointing at the camera. "Don't worry, we'll still pay you. Something. But you don't show inside of three hours, we'll kill your friend here, grab up someone else you know, and we'll start again. Capiche? Get moving."

The recording ended and Cain slid his phone back into his pocket. Without a word, he left the kitchen, walking toward the stairway.

"Who was that older gentleman?" Francesca asked, following closely behind.

"Walker," Cain said. "I mentioned him before. Arms dealer, fence, gave me my first big break in that disaster score down in Oaxaca."

"Dio mio," Francesca said. "What are you going to do?"

"Go get Walker," Cain said as he reached their bedroom and began to dress.

Francesca watched for a moment, biting her thumb nail, and finally said, "Call Lester. He can help."

"Not Lester's problem," Cain said, sitting down to lace his shoes.

"So what?" Francesca said, stamping over to stand in front of him. "So, you have to go alone? You led a team for that thing in Archangel."

"No time to pull together a team," Cain said and stood. "Look, Francesca, they're fucking with me, not Lester. In what I do, it's always against the odds and it can only be accomplished by those who are real damn hard to discourage. If I let a little shit like Scarlatti fuck with me, every potential client, including Lester, will see this as my limit. Ol'Cain is good, sure, but he won't go *that* far. I can't live with that. This is the way it has to be."

"No, this is not the way it *has to be*," Francesca said, stepping into his way as he reached for his jacket. "This is how you *choose it to be*. And it is entirely unnecessary! You are not doing this to protect your prospects: you are doing this to prove you are the biggest kid on the playground. Diavolo, stop a moment," she said, racing around to stand in front of him again. "How would you feel if I did this to you? Running off into danger all the time, risking my life and not taking every precaution?"

Cain took a deep breath before saying, "Francesca, we can have this argument again when I get back, but right now, the clock is ticking on Walker's life. I got to go."

CHAPTER 7

I N SCARLATTI'S COMMAND-CENTER-TURNED-OFFICE, Walker sat tied to the big, plush office chair, which had been wheeled out into the center of the room for the recording and then left there. It was the only chair in the room small enough to tie him to. Walker had taken scores, in his early years, and ran guns and fenced merch for more than five decades. It was not the first time he had been tied to a chair nor the first time his life had been threatened. But, after coming up from nothing, after building a life and career, marrying Linda and raising three children with her, two of which he had succeeded in guiding into fields other than arms dealing (and the son that had followed in his footsteps was high-class, would never be tied to a chair in his circles), Walker had lived a full life and could face death as calmly now as when he had been a teenager, blundering through a pitch-black rainforest for the first time, with nothing to lose.

One eye was swelling shut and he had bruises over his bare arms and seen through the rips in his shirt, from where the snatch team had roughed him up for killing two of their boys, but he smiled with his swollen lips all the same as he saw the antique clock in the corner of the room reach the one-hour mark from when they had messaged Cain.

"Jamie," Walker said and then spit blood on the carpet, "when Mr. Pulciano hired me to install the direct-energy batteries on this old washtub and told me I would have to coordinate it all with you, I thought I had come to fully appreciate what an idiot you are. But, oh boy, I had no idea."

"You want to shut the fuck up, Walker?" Scarlatti said. "Or do you want another pop on the mouth?"

"No, I don't," Walker said, still smiling. "Son, how do you think this is going to play out? Cain can't let you—or anyone else—walk all over him."

"Oh yeah?" Scarlatti said, sharing a nod with his associate and taking a sip from his snifter of amaretto. "Well, his TAV docked at whatever-the-fuck orbital his apartment is at, about forty-five minutes ago. He's probably picking up what he needs for the trip and he'll be on his way soon. He may not like it, but I don't really give a fuck what he likes. He'll do it or you'll die, capiche? And he'll get paid after, too. Everyone'll be happy."

Walker shook his head sadly and said, "Son, he doesn't care all that much if I live or die. On our side of the street, people die all the time; we made our peace with that long ago. But he does care a little bit. Just enough to matter to you."

Scarlatti laughed, along with his associate, and said, "Oh, how scary! How tough. I'm all a-shiver. Walker, what could he possibly do, huh? He's out of options. It's do-this-or-else time."

Walker looked pointedly over at the clock again before saying, "With Cain, you never know. That man can do damn near anything and doesn't know the word, quit. Lot of possibilities and I'd guess—"

The entire orbital then shook, with the sound of tearing metal reverberating out from the hub to the habitat ring. Both Scarlatti and his associate had to steady themselves against the bar cart where they stood, throwing their feet wide to avoid falling.

"What the fuck was that?" Scarlatti cried.

"Boy oh boy," Walker said happily. "I couldn't have timed that better if I was a movie director."

Alerts then screamed up the command console, red-letter scrolls too fast to read, as the orbital shook again and again.

"Yup, it's about what I expected," Walker said with a satisfied sigh. "He's shooting off the direct-energy batteries I went to all that trouble to install for Mr. Pulciano."

"Bullshit," Scarlatti said, dropping his drink and throwing himself at the command console, pulling up the statuses for the batteries. "They'd see him and fire back."

The orbital shook again, as another battery tore free and when hurtling into space.

"Naw," Walker said. "Pop-up fire, like a helicopter would do over a hill. Like you said, son, Cain keeps an apartment on Achilles Orbital. Part of the reason why is its sovereign status. The other reason why is the Archimedes Shipyard. Top-of-the-line quality, top-of-the-line prices. He probably rented himself a Sea-wolf class Interdictor." The orbital shook again. "Yeah, that's probably it. See, the Sea-wolf will send up a tethered sensor, a few miles, as the ship stays safely out of sight on the other side of the planet; it'll take some snapshots of this washtub and then the Sea-wolf will pop up, let off a salvo of railgun fire, and then pop back behind Earth before the batteries' fire control can spot him. One-by-one, he's blowing off all the batteries. By my count, there's only one left."

Another clang shook the orbital and then a brief silence tried to make itself heard over the blaring of the emergency siren.

"Jamie?" the associate whispered, looking around as if expecting Cain to materialize in the room behind them.

"Don't worry about it," Scarlatti said. "He's making a mess, okay, but so what? What's he going to do, storm the place?"

Another loud clang vibrated the station, powerfully enough to briefly slow the transit of the habitation ring, giving the three inmates of Scarlatti's office a sensation of weightlessness.

"He hit the hub with some kind of missile, Jamie," the associate said, looking at a separate monitor. "It didn't go through, though. The hub's intact."

"Ha, that moron," Scarlatti said. "See, he's not so smart."

"Thermite," Walker said.

"What?" the associate asked.

"Thermite round," Walker clarified. "To weld the bay door of the hub closed. No ships getting out that way, now."

The orbital began again to shake, in a series of smaller shocks, with a new series of alerts racing up the command console's screen.

"That'll be your lifeboats," Walker said and chuckled. "You see, boys, he doesn't want any of you leaving and now you've got nowhere to go."

"Jamie, come on," the associate cried, bouncing on his toes near the door out. "We got to go. We got to find a way out of here."

"What the fuck, run?" Scarlatti said, grabbing his associate by the jacket. "Get a hold of yourself, Dino. We got a hundred guys up in here. I don't care how many guys he could've pulled together in an hour, it ain't a fucking hundred. And he just welded the bay door shut, so he's got no way in."

"Doesn't matter," Walker said. "The Sea-wolf has an assault docking collar. It kind of bolts itself onto the hull of anything its attacking, seals, and then a couple of arc-welders cut through the hull. He can bust in wherever he wants."

Gunfire then erupted on the other side of the lefthand door, leading up the corridor of the habitation ring. The sharp taps of pistol fire were punctuated by the lower thumps of a chain gun, firing sub-sonic rounds, so as to not puncture the orbital.

"Oh, that must be Cain, now," Walker said and chuckled. "That Sea-wolf sure does land gently, doesn't it? Didn't even hear it."

"Okay, okay," Scarlatti said, first cycling through cameras on the command console, trying to find the ones in the corridor filling with gunfire: they were all dead feeds. He pulled the pistol off of his belt. "This is crazy. What the hell does he think he's doing?"

"Listen up, boys," Walker then said, his voice hardening. "If I'm alive when Cain gets here, he'll do you quick, painless," he said and snapped his fingers behind his back, where his hands were tied. "A shot to the head and you can leave this awful world behind. But if I'm dead, man oh man, he's going to torture you. He'll have to. Have to make an example of you to anyone who comes looking, make sure no one provokes him like this again. He'll probably string you up, start cutting things off of you, record your screams, and then leave you in a state so disgusting that whichever henchmen Pulciano sends in here to investigate later will just puke up their guts from the sight of you. It's going to be awful."

"Shut up," Dino shouted. "Just shut up, already."

"You there, son," Walker told him, "you should go hide. Cain only needs to make an example of Jamie. Hide: live."

"Jamie, we got to get the fuck out of here!" Dino screamed. "You saw what he did to Mickey."

"Dino, Dino, listen," Scarlatti shouted back, grabbing the hysteric man by the lapel and shaking him to silence: "He ain't never going to get that close, okay? He's got to come through this door, right? He's shooting his way here; we can hear him. So, you go crouch behind my desk, okay? I'll use the console for cover. He can only shoot at one of us, right? So as soon as he comes through the door, we open up. If he's as good as they say, he might get one of us—but no way is he getting us both."

No sooner had Scarlatti spoken and crouched behind a corner of the command console then Cain had shot him through the back of the head.

Dino turned, confused, to find that Cain had not come in through the lefthand door, but through the righthand door on the opposite side of the room—and then shot Dino through the forehead.

"Walker," Cain said, taking a second to pass his .45 auto over the room, ensuring that there were no other henchmen lying in wait.

"Cain," Walker said. "How about it, son, you got a knife on you?"

Cain came over and pulled a switchblade with his left hand, springing out the blade and then slicing through the plastic ties used to secure Walker to the chair. The older man, still hale from regular exercise, stood and stretched, rubbing his wrists.

"Now you see," Walker said, looking at Scarlatti and Dino, "I told them you'd do them quick."

"Idiots," Cain said and put the knife away before heading to the lefthand door. "Wasting my time like this."

"Who's out there, anyway?" Walker asked.

"No one," Cain said. "Ground drone, roller. I rented it from Antoine when I rented the Sea-wolf. They better not have scuffed it up too much, either, or ol'Antoine will charge me for it. Come on, it's covering the corridor from here to where I cut through the hull."

"Right behind you," Walker said. "Oh, and uh, thanks, Cain. I appreciate you coming out of your way to help an old man."

"Don't mention it," Cain said as they negotiated the bodies strewn across the corridor floor, weaving their way to the Sea-wolf. "I'm sorry that idiot dragged you into this mess."

"You mean Pulciano?" Walker asked. "No way he ordered this. Too smart. My guess is that this was all Jamie. Not the sharpest tool in the shed, that boy. Pulciano probably told him to get you for whatever it was he wanted done on Mars, you being top-shelf and uptown. You refused and Jamie couldn't go back to Pulciano, tell him he failed, so he tried this nonsense. When Pulciano hears about it—and the old man is going to hear it from *me*, I can tell you *that*—he'll blame it all on Jamie, say the boy was out on his own, going berserk. Which will be true. He'll probably send you some money or something, smooth things over. Especially after this demonstration."

"Yeah, I expect he will," Cain said and stepped over the rim of the assault collar, into the sideways-oriented cabin of the Sea-wolf, affected by the habitat ring's centrifugal force, before extending his hand to help Walker through. "But that wasn't the mess I was talking about. The mess I meant was what Linda is going to do to you when you get home. You think this drubbing you got from the mustaches was bad, ha! You just wait until she gets going with that wooden spoon of hers."

Walker sighed and rested heavily against the cabin ceiling, waiting for the ground drone to return. "Shit, I forgot all about how mad she'll be," he said. "As if it's my fault I got nabbed by those idiots."

"Since when did that matter?" Cain said.

CHAPTER 8

THE ARCHIMEDES SHIPYARD did, in fact, charge top-of-the-line prices, befitting the state-of-the-art vehicles, weapons, and other gear that they made available. Cain had rented the Sea-wolf and roller drone by the hour and so he first flew to Achilles Orbital to return them before taking Walker back to Newark in his TAV. He texted Francesca as soon as they had left High Camden.

It's over. I'm okay, Walker is a little beaten up, but otherwise fine, too.

I'm taking him back to Newark and then I'll head home.

She did not reply, not on his way to Achilles, nor on his way to Newark, nor Venice. It was not so unusual, after all, even for a Sunday, as both the commission and parliament would conduct their affairs through individuals, over meals or on the golf course, and Francesca would need to be available night and day, as the pivotal actions regarding the seawall project approached. It was not until Cain's TAV set down in the Palazzo del Sindaco di Venezia that he realized that something had changed.

Francesca's TAV hovered on the opposite side of the landing

pad, a few inches off of the ground, the CasiDrive thrusters warping the air beneath. Claes Thorsen stood to one side of the open door, one of his guards to the other. Francesca then left the palazzo and walked to her TAV, dressed in her killer suit, the one she wore to debates, policy addresses, and to court. She did not turn toward Cain and no tears etched her face. Calmly, she handed her briefcase to Claes before taking a breath and walking over to Cain.

"What's going on?" Cain asked.

"A procedural vote has just been called," she said, "on the colonization question. If it passes, a full vote in the European Parliament will follow this week. Everything is about to begin."

Francesca looked down and closed her eyes for a moment before raising her face to Cain's and looking at him directly, pain and sorrow fighting composure for control her features; composure won, though her lips trembled as she spoke in a clear voice.

"I love you," she said, "but I cannot live like this, with this constant fear. I had hoped that I could, and I have tried, Dio mio, I have tried to endure, but I simply cannot go on like this. No, please let me speak. This is my life," she said and motioned to her TAV hovering behind her, "and it is precious to me. That is your life," she said and motioned to Cain's, "and it is precious to you. I cannot ask you to give up that which I would not, but I also cannot live my life while watching you walk continuously into danger. It is too much, amore mio, the fear, the constant worry, the exhaustion—I cannot. I think—I hope—that I can live without knowing. If I do not know where you are or what dangers you face, then I can hope that you are well, that you are alive and happy and content with being Cain, which I know is so important to you. So, please, do not leave me anything in your will or ask Lester to tell me if you die or are injured. Just leave me and take as much care of yourself as you can. Maybe, if I do not know, maybe ignorance can protect my heart."

"Francesca," Cain said, surprised to hear his voice catch in his throat, "just, wait a second."

"Do you know," Francesca said, her voice rising in pitch, fluttering on the edge of control, "when I dream, it is not of living happily ever after with you? It is of you dying and your death causing a pain so deep that it breaks me. I wake up and I cannot breathe.

"I love you," she said and with shaking fingers reached up to touch Cain's cheek. "Goodbye."

Turning away, Francesca walked calmly to her TAV and stepped aboard. She stood with her back to the aperture as the door slid into place, never turning to see Cain's face as he watched her go.

PART 4

BLEAK-ASS SITCH

CHAPTER 1

THE APARTMENT GAVE the impression of an amphitheater, or perhaps a planetarium, with the furniture oriented toward the transparent wall looking out at the universe. Like every apartment in Achilles Orbital's exclusive ring, Cain's windows looked away from Earth; the less-expensive ring, rotating in the opposite direction to provide balance to the station, looked toward the planet and, for many, the visible motion of the orbital simulating gravity through centrifugal force caused nausea. The stars did not seem even to move, as Cain watched them from his couch. The black, real-leather upholstery continued on the room's few chairs and the two backed-stools waiting quietly by the black-granite counter, which separated the kitchen from the living room. The recessed lighting glowed but faintly, mimicking the stars; the browns of the carpets soaked up what little illumination they gave. Returning to his apartment after some manic score, taking lives and risking his own, Cain had always found the soft darkness of his place, staring out into eternity, calming to the mind and nourishing to the soul.

The stars and whatever occupied his attention had always been enough and so Cain did not own a television or its associated sub-scriptions. At the moment, he had a laptop open on the end table next to him, a glass of station-water in one hand (recycled, purified, lightly seasoned), and his phone in the other. He wore charcoal chinos and black-leather moccasins, which never left the apartment (his collection of designer shoes remained in the closet by the door), in addition to a blood-red silk shirt left open as his body cooled after his morning exercise. He had taken to exercising twice a day and dressing after each session.

Cain sat watching the stars and ignoring the computer until the live broadcast from Brussels started: he looked over to see Francesca step into the camera's view wearing her killer suit, smiling a hello to some blond-haired, blue-eyed, Caucasian fellow. The blond began with introductions and contextualization, which Cain ignored and simply watched Francesca.

Shaking his head, he said to himself, "What are you doing? It's been a month. It's been a solid month of doing nothing, which was smart, maybe, since your head isn't in the game and if you tried to take a score, the score would probably have taken you. But, it's been a month now. You work out twice a day, you eat at René's or Claudette's, and then you sit and stare at the goddamn stars like some love-sick teenager. *And* you've developed this disturbing habit of talking to yourself—sometimes in the third person. What the fuck am I doing?"

It had finally become Francesca's turn to speak, with the blond turning his narrow back to the camera; she said, "Momentum is building. We expect parliament to begin debating the final report and recommendation from the European Commission later this week."

"I hate to give up on anything," Cain said, "but sometimes it is the right call. Everyone in this life has had to abort an operation at some point, things don't go your way. Those who don't, die. Shit,"

Cain said and knocked back the last of his water, setting the glass beside the laptop. "This life just isn't for civilians. Too dangerous. Too much danger just floating in the air, along with all the things players do to deal with it. It's a lot. And you're a danger to anyone you're around, bringing this life close to them. Shit, Walker got nabbed because those mustaches thought they could use him as a lever on me: what kind of lever would she have been? Better this way. She stuck it out as long as she could, longer than most people outside the life could have done, hanging on scared to death for almost two years. She's better off now."

"Yes, corruption is a concern, Alex," Francesca was saying, "be it from local governments, corporations, or criminal syndicates, which is one of the reasons I have been asked to consult so often on the seawall project. As you may know, on the night I was sworn in as Mayor of Venice, I excised the city's largest and most powerful syndicate, arresting its leaders and the people that they had bribed or blackmailed, and brought security and prosperity to our wonderful city once again. Fighting corruption, in fact, is why I was elected, having prosecuted hundreds of such criminals when I was the city's chief prosecutor. So, yes, Alex, I know well the measures we will have to take to secure the seawall project."

"The thing is," Cain said, "I've spent my whole life building who I am, this man called Cain, and this is what Cain does, this life, taking scores, risking it all, and doing what is impossible for others. I don't want to give it up. I set the bar high and I don't know who I'd be if I didn't keep reaching for it. Doesn't matter that I've been doing it for more than twenty years: who would I be if I stopped? And what would have been the point of it all—striving, surviving, suffering—all to become Cain and then just walk away?"

"Which is why," Francesca continued, "the final recommendation from the commission is for the larger, all-encompassing seawall. The reclaimed land will increase crop yields, decrease food costs, improve quality of life, and boost the economy. The seawall will be an economic engine for decades to come."

"Wasn't a waste, though," Cain said softly, "loving her. I'd never really thought of myself as ever loving someone. I'd always enjoyed the company of women the way I enjoyed fine wine and good restaurants: a pleasure for the senses. And maybe there's nothing wrong with that, but I don't figure I'll be doing much of that now. Can't see it being worth my time. Don't know that I'd want it again, anyway, what I had with her, not with someone other than her, but it's good to know this about myself, that I could have something like that, something more. It's good to look at yourself and not flinch. No other way."

"The budget hawks' arguments have become increasingly unbelievable," Francesca said. "They have finally given up their disinformation campaign and are now attempting to stand on principle. Their objection is ideological, not based on fact. The benefits are clear and decisive, as are the costs: the project is affordable and in everyone's best interest."

"But even if I did choose to give up the life," Cain said, "to give it all up to be with you, who would be the *I* loving you? It wouldn't be me, not this Cain sitting here talking to himself like a lunatic, because this Cain would cease to exist. This Cain lives the life. Who would that Cain be—and would you even want to be with him?"

Cain then sat quietly as the interview concluded, before shutting off the laptop as Alex began his recap. He returned his gaze to the stars and sat thinking until his phone vibrated in his hand. Calendar alert: it was time to call van Hauer's office again.

"Meneer van Hauer's office," the cool voice answered after the second ring as always.

"Sherill, it's Cain," he said, "Mr. van Hauer available?"

"One moment, please, Meneer Cain," Sherill said, never so

much as a modulation in her inflection, not in nearly a year of calling every two weeks, "I will check."

Almost a year ago, Lester had contracted Cain to do the impossible: break into a villa on Paradise Orbital, to convince one of the three wealthiest men alive to sell his shares in Arcadia Planitia, the premier city-to-be on Mars, expected to become its political center. Cain had done so with a sharpened screwdriver held to van Hauer's throat. An old hand at the cutthroat tactics of trillion-dollar business, van Hauer had not held a grudge, not against the hired man that had pulled off the impossible. On the contrary, he had asked Cain—as they had sipped champaign on their way to his villa's front door—to call every few weeks. He had expected a piece of highline business in a couple months, business that would require someone capable of the impossible.

"Please hold for Meneer van Hauer," Sherill said and then the line clicked several times as a new encryption was applied.

Cain had to tap on his phone for nearly a minute, as his anti-intrusion software fought Paradise's AI, to establish the encrypted transmission without either compromising their security, before the call went through.

"Cain," van Hauer said, "right on time, as expected. Excellent. How are you?"

"Bored," Cain said. Despite the encryption and Paradise's AI monitoring the transmission, it was always safer to assume everything outside of an SCS was monitored. Neither would say anything specific during the call.

"Oh, well, we can't have that," van Hauer said, just as if they were chums who talked every week. "Why don't you come up to Paradise for lunch? Afterward, if you're still feeling ennui, you could avail yourself of the resort's amusements. If you can't find it on Paradise, it isn't worth doing."

Cain chuckled, a low rumbling sound akin to a growl, and said, "Be over at 1 PM."

They hung up and Cain lifted off of the couch without seeming to exert a physical effort, as if sitting, standing, or moving were all merely acts of will. Despite his size, at six-four and two-fifty, he glided across his apartment without a sound, into his kitchen to pour another glass of water. He then turned and put his back against the corner of the refrigerator, to look out over the counter and through the living room, to the stars beyond.

"This is good," he said. "And about damn time—a couple months, he said. Never mind, though; still good. Good timing, too: after moping around here for a month, you should be well-rested."

Cain brought his water with him as he crossed the living room, to the window-wall, and stood an inch from it, staring into the darkness. The window was inches thick, which caused distortion ameliorated by a gentle curve, and glazed to a reflective finish on the outside, to block radiation and, reputedly, to defeat laser-vibration detection for eavesdropping. Despite the thin vent that ran along the floor beneath, quietly blowing warm air, the window still palpably radiated cold when standing next to it. Cain did not mind.

"Just what you need, son," he said to himself: "a mega-score. Van Hauer wouldn't be involved in anything less. Time I returned to living the life, properly. Just the thing."

CHAPTER 2

AN HOUR LATER, Cain boarded his TAV and left Achilles Orbital, crossing the hundred-thousand miles of crowded high-Earth orbit to Paradise. He donned his usual calf-length coat with the surveillance/counter-surveillance nodes embedded into the stand-up collar, his sunglasses with AR integration, and strapped on his .45 auto, the subsonic rounds from which would blow off a man's head without risking a hull breach. He did not expect a problem at van Hauer's, knowing the man would not squander his time with a vendetta against a hired operative, but Cain always prepared for capabilities, not probabilities. Part of the life.

After docking at Paradise Orbital's hub, Cain glided over to the security kiosk, retrieved a pin that allowed him to access doors and elevators, and then returned to a sense of gravity in the long elevator ride out to the habitat ring. The transparent elevator ran parallel to a waterfall that began in the zero-g of the hub, guided by ultrasound, and eventually fell with the same centrifugal force convincing the guests that there was a planet beneath them. Nude bathers leaped into and out of the falling water, from platforms beside it, or rode the waterfall all the way to the pool below. Cain spared a moment to consider the perfectly enhanced bodies frolicking beside him, to see if anything stirred within himself: nothing did and so he returned his attention to the elevator doors.

On the habitat ring, Cain walked with deliberate speed to the entrance down to van Hauer's villa, a sort of extension beneath the ring, where only the fabulously wealthy could afford to live. The pampered elite that Cain passed all glanced covertly at him, as they usually did; Paradise was typically not employed for business and Cain was clearly not there for pleasure; there were other reasons, however, for their looks. There always had been.

A long ramp circled the interior of the shaft leading down to the van Hauer villa, which was filled with a museum's worth of his art acquisitions. Cain noted them unconsciously as he descended, particularly *L'homme qui marche*, The Walking Man, which had caused a shift in his plans the last time he had visited, uninvited. As he came to the manned doorway to the villa proper, the guards stepped aside, clearly awaiting his arrival.

Van Hauer's own security staff had taken over from Paradise's at the top of the museum and Cain had assessed them as he had passed. They were all of a type, roughly the same size, athletic, pale European skins growing translucent from lack of UV light, and only moderately armed. Cain unconsciously plotted how he would affect an armed raid, if it ever came up. The guards did not seem surly, he noticed, too, which seemed to indicate that they either held no grudge for his having penetrated the facility before or that van Hauer had never revealed to them that it had happened at all. Cain was betting on the latter, while preparing for a grudge he did not detect.

In the salon, Cain waited motionlessly, with several house staff and a couple guards hovering around their new, silent visitor, trying to determine what they were expected to do, when van Hauer came striding in.

"There you are," van Hauer said, extending his hand, smiling his welcome. In his early fifties, tanned in a way that spoke of frequent trips down to Earth for sailing, dressed in a suit that would have shamed even the luxurious denizens of Cain's closet, van Hauer looked every inch the trillionaire businessman. His lithe frame, full head of hair, and his brisk movements exuded confidence—until he came under the shadow of the comparatively huge Cain, at which point his smaller dimensions took on an almost boyish quality. He did not give the appearance of having noticed the shift, however, when he shook Cain's hand and then led him to a secure conference room.

"A couple months, you said," Cain said, shaking his head as van Hauer motioned toward a steaming pot of coffee ready on a sideboard.

"Don't remind me," van Hauer replied, smiling ruefully. "That particular opportunity passed us by and I've had to develop another source of intel before moving on it again. That source has finally come through and an eight-day window—starting today—has just opened to acquire something revolutionary."

Van Hauer rest his hands on the back of one of the six chairs surrounding the video-screen table, tapping his finger and smiling to himself before asking, "Have you ever taken a trip on an accelerator ship?" Cain did not respond and after a moment van Hauer continued. "Of course. Well, I have not. It is also a business into which I have never invested. There is just something about the concept of firing a passenger vehicle like a round from a railgun and then—the worst part—*catching it* in another railgun-like facility on the other end of the voyage that just," he closed his eyes and shivered in lieu of completing his sentence. "The concept simply seems preposterous to me. But what if there was another way?

"Clever scientists at LRI—that's, Long Range Ideas, a subsidiary of Irrfan Singh's Omnipicorp—have thought up a new concept for interplanetary travel. The trouble that the accelerator ships have tried to solve through brute force is that to travel in one direction, force needs to go in the other. The accelerator ships push against their gate facilities, which push in two directions to keep from firing themselves into the sun. They're huge, costly, and necessitate a second gate at the destination, to catch and, eventually, return the ship. LRI, however, have postulated that a quantum field could be generated by a large ship, a field that is immobile relative to the ship and against which the ship could push, either with EM force—like a railgun—or perhaps a thermonuclear explosion. The ship would then fly off in the direction it intends to travel, detaching itself from the quantum field, which then dissipates. On the other end, the ship creates another field, pushes against it, slows, repeat, slows, repeat until the ship has decelerated sufficiently for CasiDrives to take over. If the concept proves out, it could revolutionize interplanetary travel, freeing ships from either lengthy travel times or the necessity of receiver gates."

"And put the accelerator gate companies out of business," Cain said, "gobbling up all their market-share."

"Well, there's that, too, naturally," van Hauer said and grinned. "So, you see my interest in this emerging technology. Whoever has it will open up exploitation of Jupiter's moons, main-belt asteroids—we could be talking settlements, which would undercut everything selling on Mars, as it would now have competition. It's more than just the opportunity to realize new revenue streams, new investment opportunities, though: if a competitor like Singh gets a hold of all that raw material, every business I own could be in jeopardy."

"So, you need that piece of tech," Cain said, "and you know where it is."

"And I've assembled a team to take it away from LRI," van Hauer said, slipping his hands into his pockets.

"*You* have?" Cain asked.

"Oh, I may be a mere businessman, Mr. Cain," van Hauer said, "but at a certain level, business and war become synonymous. I've pulled together many operations in my time; I know several agents—or fixers, as some of your ilk choose to call them—for sourcing appropriate personnel, my companies produce the weapons, interdictors, transports, devices, etc that any team of mercenaries might require; and I've seen enough operations succeed to know what works, as well as enough that have failed to know what doesn't."

"Uh-huh," Cain said.

Van Hauer smiled and chuckled to himself, before saying, "I also know my limitations and hire people who can do things that I cannot, which includes planning the operational specifics. Now, before I share the intel with you, I want to stress that the operation must not grow larger in scope or destructive potential than absolutely necessary. I want something just big enough to snatch the prototype QFG—Quantum Field Generator—and that's it. I don't want anything that might instigate a reprisal from Singh and certainly do not want to escalate into open warfare with Omnipicorp. So, let's keep the bloodshed, mayhem, and property destruction to a minimum, shall we?"

Cain nodded.

"Alright then, let me call this up," van Hauer said and began tapping on the table-screen. "Originally, the QFG had been in orbit, which is why I thought you would be perfect for it, given your last, uh, *demonstration*. While we were trying to pinpoint which research orbital was testing the prototype, they had completed whatever it was they were testing and the device was then shipped back to Earth. Yes, to Earth; to here."

From a directory on the table-screen, van Hauer opened a set of reconnaissance files, including orbital photos and facility diagrams.

A brief, soundless video of someone walking the streets of the facility also played in one corner of the table. Cain turned the blueprints and photos toward him and began flipping through the documentation on each building's purpose, construction, and complement.

"The corps that build these things call them Exclusive Residence Facilities," Cain said. "The chumps that live in them, they call them Exclusive Corrections Facilities. You important enough to the corp, they don't let you out, not even to go visit this charming little midwestern city, over here, two miles away."

"Indeed," van Hauer said. "The facility is called Albright or The Albright Research Center. LRI has six such facilities across the American Midwest. Albright houses the QFG.

"And here are the dossiers of the operatives I've already recruited," he said and opened another directory.

Cain glanced at the list, recognizing several of the names, including Oswald, whom he had brought in on the Archangel score, several weeks back, before Francesca had ended things. Cain shook his head as if annoyed by a flying insect and returned to examining Albright.

"Now, originally," van Hauer continued, "I had envisioned a simple operation that would employ a diversion—something loud and flashy, but generally low-yield—followed by a single operative (you) slipping into the research building, here, and liberating the QFG. After bringing the team together, though, *slipping* no longer seems to be an option, at least they did not think so. We're now thinking that an assault is likely needed, which will complicate the requirement of minimizing damage. It quickly became apparent, as I talked through the options with the team, that I needed to recruit a leader, someone who could plan the assault and then lead it, ensuring success. Judging by the success of your operation in Archangel, last month, you are that leader." Cain looked up at the mention of his last score and held van Hauer's gaze until the other man chuckled and spoke. "I do business with Yahata; of course, I heard. What do you think, so far?"

"It's do-able," Cain said and pulled the blueprint to one side and aligned the orbital photo next to it. "You should go with your instinct, though: a distraction is just what we need, to cover a one-man infiltration of the Research building here, southeast corner. And the assault you're thinking of is the right kind of distraction. It needs to be big, messy, and capture the attention of the security forces, keep them looking the other way while I hit Research. Dig:

"These residential facilities are like three-rectangular city blocks ripped up from Manhattan and dropped down here into southern Idaho—and they work on the same principles, regarding class and income and who lives where. That's the thing you need to remember when planning the assault/distraction. We can't come through the roof: it's transparent and gives the impression of an easy breach, but in order to blow a hole in it large enough to air assault in with TAVs or helicopters or EDF airfoils, you'd need to hit the roof so hard that it shatters, which would turn it into the world's largest antipersonnel mine, shredding all these buildings and killing everyone inside. I'm guessing you don't want to do that."

"Certainly not," van Hauer said. "These scientists migrate between our companies like swallows, which is why we have to segregate them in these little facilities, to keep them from running off with too many of our secrets."

"Right," Cain said, "so no detonating the roof. That leaves us busting in through the gate and—attempting—to cut our way to the Research building. Now, this slice of city life is basically four streets: two long ones running parallel east-west and two more short ones connecting their ends, north-south, giving us three rows of buildings, north-wall, central, and south-wall. Now, look at the orbital photo, at the north-wall row of buildings and the street running their length. See the trees?"

"Yes, I do," van Hauer said and then pointed at the other long street. "The southern long street doesn't have them; how odd. Why is it significant?"

"It signifies wealth," Cain said. "The people who live along the northern long street—we'll call it Tree Street—are the scientists and lab managers that work in this big mother of a Research building. They're the talent, paid the most, and so they live on the nice street. The central row of buildings, you see from the plans and from the sidewalk seating, are all restaurants. They provide nightlife for the workers; some are expensive, some not; at least one has a dance floor, hookers. Then we come to the southern long street. Look at the photo: no trees, outdoor seating for only two of the restaurants, thinner sidewalks. This is where the non-scientists live, the people who take care of the place.

"The ground floor spaces below the rich folks' apartments on Tree Street house the types of stores and services that they'd visit: you got a gym, a pharmacy (of course), a doctor's office, a general store, and even a movie theater. On the ground floors of the buildings on—let's call it Admin Street—you have the places that maintain the facility: you got a little parking lot for their runaround vehicles, to head into town or patrol the surrounding countryside, then you have the Administration building, which is a catch-all, Maintenance, which has internal vehicles below and apartments above, and then what the plans call a Dining Facility but is really like a grocery store for the scientists to shop in, with a food court to one side for the workers to eat in, when they can't afford the restaurants."

"This is all very fascinating, that you know all of this, Cain," van Hauer said, "you must have hit residentials such as this before, but what does knowing it get us?"

"It tells us who lives where," Cain said. "The buildings on Admin Street are bigger, sure, wider, but they have to house more people. Look at how small the apartments are above Maintenance and Administration: now look at how spacious they are above the pharmacy, especially the top-floor units, above the transparent facility roof, which the building penetrates. Rich folks live on Tree Street and poor folks live on Admin Street. And the poor folk include security. That's right: this is where all of the off-duty security can be found."

"Ah," van Hauer said.

"Uh-huh," Cain said. "See these three little common areas, above Maintenance and Administration? Those are platoon ready rooms, a place to hold briefings, which indicates three platoons' worth of security. One of them will be active at all times, patrolling, manning checkpoints, walking around smiling their asses off on Tree Street, to make the scientists feel safe and also warn them about what happens if they get out of line. The other two platoons, though, are on Admin Street: one will be sleeping and the other enjoying some down time. We might see a few in the gym, but it won't be an entire platoon (they'll be told not to outnumber the civilians in there, make the gym too intimidating for regular people).

"What all of that boils down to is that, after we breach the main gate, here, if we try to go down Admin Street, we'll run smack into upwards of sixty security guys: the two inactive platoons plus whatever reserve is left, probably in the Administration building, as a QRF. So, heading down Admin Street is not an option."

"Despite it being a direct shot toward the Research building," van Hauer said, pointing to the large building in the southeast corner.

"Exactly," Cain said. "Instead, we'll run the assault up Tree Street and drop a GP machinegun and a couple of guys here, where Admin Street meets West Street. The GP will sweep the full length of Admin Street, pinning down the security trying to pour out of these buildings. Meanwhile, the main body of the assault will turn down Tree Street, dropping sentries in each of the alleyways between the restaurants, to keep security from darting over there and trying to outflank the assault team. Once the assault reaches East Street, they'll push south past the warehouse, opposite the Research building, and set in. We'll want them to give the impression that the assault has stalled, that they can't fight their way past security's defenses at Research's front door."

"Why not just continue with the assault?" van Hauer said. "Why not defeat their security and storm Research?"

"We can," Cain said and looked over at him. "If you want to run it that way, we can. It'll mean slaughtering a dozen or so security and probably catching a few scientists in the crossfire, though. Remember, we haven't had to kill anyone yet, just pin them down."

"No, of course," van Hauer said, waving his hand. "Bloodlust getting the better of me. Continue."

"So, all of this is to draw security's attention," Cain said, "while I take a third way to Research. You see this little alley running behind the buildings on Admin Street? This alley actually encircles the whole facility, running between the buildings and the six-story wall that holds up the transparent roof. The alley is for service people, the janitors, housekeeping, and food delivery people who come from Maintenance, Administration, and the Dining Facility and go into every other building, to deliver food, clean, fix shit, whatever. They don't want their rich scientists to have to look at those kinds of people, so they have them sneak around in this back alley. Perfect for me—because I'm going to detach from the GP machinegun crew after they set in and, while the assault makes a lot of noise going up Tree Street, I'm going to hustle down this long alleyway to Research's back door."

"Alone?" van Hauer asked.

"Preferably," Cain said.

"What if some of the security guards in these buildings try to use this alley to outflank the machinegun crew?" van Hauer asked.

"I shoot them," Cain said. To van Hauer's dubious look, he said, "Check the width on these alleys between Administration and Maintenance: they're barely three-feet. I couldn't walk normally down them, have to sidle. One dead body in an alley like that, plugs up the whole thing. Don't worry about it.

"Now, once I hit Research, I'll go down to their vault—I'm guessing that's where you've confirmed I'll find the QFG. Yes? Okay. I grab it, come back up to the alley, and then use demo charges to blow a hole in the encircling wall, to egress."

"Demo charges?" van Hauer said. "A small hole won't be too much destruction, but if you're keen on blowing a hole in the wall, why not skip infiltrating down this alley altogether and just blow the wall before slipping into Research?"

Cain straightened up and smiled, his head leaning to one side as he briefly ruminated on the dangers of an overly engaged employer. After a chuckle, he said, "There's this woman, Caroline, who comes in to consult sometimes, when a certain agent of mine is pulling together a score. She's an intrusion specialist, knows everything there is to know about surveillance gear, facility protection strategies, and how to circumvent even the toughest obstacles. Which makes sense, since she used to be a cat burglar. After piling up a heap of loot, taken off of the nicest places in Europe, she turned around and sold her services back to the people she had ripped off, teaching them how to keep it from happening again. Anyway, when she consults on a score, one of the things she always says is, if you want the opposition to act a certain way, tell them a story that will make them want to write a part for themselves that you can live with. We want them looking at Tree Street, not the backside of Research: so, we assault up Tree Street, they react to stop it, going where we want them to go. But, if the opposition is calling the shots and you need to get around them, consider their expectations, what they take for granted, and then frustrate them. What do they think you cannot do? Do it. Where do they think you cannot go? Go there.

"So, if I blow a hole in the security wall on the way in, they're going to expect me to use that hole coming back out. On the other hand, if I use the alley to infiltrate—"

"Then they'll expect you to use it on the way out," van Hauer said, "link back up with the assault as they retreat."

"Exactly," Cain said. "So, the demo charges will come as a surprise."

"Brilliant," van Hauer said.

This is it, Cain thought before he continued, *living the life, finding a way over or around or through any obstacle; just what I needed.*

"We're not done yet," Cain said. "I don't want to share this with the rest of the team, but I'm going to have a separate egress vehicle prepositioned over here, in these woods to the south of the facility. Once I have the QFG, I'll head to it and egress separately. The rest of the assault team will pull back to their initial insertion point, probably back up in here."

"Brilliant," van Hauer said again. "Looks like you were the right man for the job. Can it all be done within the eight-day window we have available to us?"

"It can," Cain said. "We'll need to train, preferably with a full-size mockup of the facility."

"Already constructed," van Hauer said. "I had mockups build of all of LRI's facilities, just in case. The rest of your team have assembled there, already. Is there anything else you will require to affect this operation?"

"Two things," Cain said: "first, another operative. We'll need someone solid up high, taking care of tech and signal for us. I have someone I use for that stuff, worked with me on Archangel."

"Done," van Hauer said. "And second?"

"My fee," Cain said and smiled without warmth.

"I'll pay you twice what you made off of the Archangel job," van Hauer said.

"Triple," Cain said.

"Done," van Hauer said and they both chuckled.

CHAPTER 3

VAN HAUER ACCOMPANIED Cain to the training site, leaving Cain's TAV at Port Paradise. Most of van Hauer's business was conducted virtually, usually through an SCS, which allowed him to conduct it anywhere, even from a clandestine training facility secreted within a defunct bomber plant in northern Mexico. The machinery to build the next generation of stealth, CasiDrive bombers had never been installed, with most of the potential vehicle's mission profile having been taken over by orbital bombardment; as such, the plant amounted to little more than a gigantic hanger, with a thirty-story ceiling and an Exclusive Residence Facility squatting near the south end. Van Hauer insisted on being present for the six days of training Cain had ordered and, as such, introduced him to the crew of other mercenaries that he had so far assembled.

The Exclusive Residence Facility was an exact replica, built from the original blueprints and including all equipment appearing on the initial TO&E. The mercenaries that van Hauer had hired, having no other alternative, had moved into apartments along what Cain had dubbed Tree Street. They filed out of the mockup as van

Hauer's yacht-TAV glided soundlessly through the factory's sliding doors, a motley of clothing styles—from chic suits to well-worn battle fatigues—clad men and women from a variety of ethnicities and nationalities—Americans, Europeans, south-Asians, ex-orbit sovereignites—though all wore the same look on their faces. They had signed on for top pay, having proven themselves on countless scores, and, of course, they knew that they risked their lives for whatever bit of tech the principal was after. They also knew, however, that whether they came back from the raid depended in large part on this last addition to their team, this leader van Hauer had brought in at the eleventh hour. When Cain stepped off of van Hauer's yacht-TAV, someone among the crowd of mercenaries sent up a shout and pushed forward.

"Cain, you son of a bitch," Oswald shouted in his unwavering Scottish accent, a smile beaming from his scarred face as he came forward, hand extended.

Cain took it briefly as he passed, continuing to walk toward the assembled mercenaries. "Oswald," he said. "Been here long?"

"Bah, three days, mate," Oswald said. "Having a look at the target; has a few tight spaces, as I'm sure you've seen.

"Lads! Oi, lads, this is him. Didn't I say? Didn't I? As soon as you asked me about Archangel, Mr. van Hauer, I knew you'd try for him. Led us on that score, he did. We're in good hands, now, lads."

"Some of us are lasses, you dumb fuck," a woman wearing sunglasses like Cain's said, her shaved head growing shadowy under a three-day crop of new hair.

"I didn't mean nothing," Oswald said to her.

"Oswald," Cain said, pinching the bridge of his nose and remembering how much longer all of the briefings had been for the Archangel score, once Oswald had started up. "Get over there.

"Mr. van Hauer, how about that last operative?"

"Arranged," van Hauer said, the boyishness of his size next to

Cain exaggerated all the more with a crowd of similarly large mercenaries forming a semicircle around them. "She should be on the mission frequency now."

Cain tapped his phone a few times, to access the network that they would use during training, and said, "Paula, you online?"

"Roger that," Paula said, transmitting from the geosynchronous orbital she rarely left. "Good to be working with you again, Cain."

"Likewise," he said. "I want my usual precautions applied to the network, now and when you establish the mission freq, Oscar Tango Delta."

"Roger," Paula said. "On the double."

"Alright, everybody, listen up," Cain said, addressing the crowd. "I'm called Cain. We'll skip introductions for now; I know about half of you and have at least heard of the rest. We'll visit a bit tonight, over dinner.

"The score is a heist, a little bit of tech we're aiming to liberate from a place just like this. Once I set up a briefing room, we'll go through the plan. Equipment, as you can see behind me, is rolling in now," Cain said as two huge transports squeezed in beside van Hauer's yacht-TAV. "We have an eight-day window: we're going to train heavy for four days, live-fire for two, and then hit the facility on the seventh. You got questions at any time, you bring them to me. You think we could use a bit of something we ain't got, you tell me. You got a problem with someone working this score, you tell me—I'm going to smack both of you upside the head, but you go ahead and tell me anyway."

The crowd gave a dutiful laugh before Cain motioned for them to follow him to the mockup's Administration building, where he would set up a command center and begin walking everyone through the plan. *This is just what I needed, get back to living the life proper,* Cain thought to himself, listening to the usual merc banter around him, smelling the familiar smells of equipment as it was unloaded, a smell of canvas and diesel even if neither substance was present; he did not feel the words quite as authentically as he had back in van Hauer's office, though, and groped for the usual fire that he had always felt before a score.

Despite his cooling enthusiasm, Cain led the team through six days of training with the same professional dedication as he had before Archangel. With the rollers that they would use to infiltrate the facility—along with the weaponry, armor, communication and surveillance gear—now ready for use, Cain first had the team walk through the facility, memorizing every building, every alleyway, every tree, familiarizing themselves with the battlefield in ways that even the most experienced security guard would not have done, as it could only be done with deliberation. Next, Cain had them practice individual actions that could not fail if the score was to succeed: busting through the airlock gate, setting up the tripod for the GP machinegun, dropping sentries in each alleyway on restaurant row. Once they had it right, Cain then had them move on, in the last two days of training, to running through the entire scenario, from infiltration to retreat, using live ammunition (in part to see its effect on the facility). The only mission-critical actions not practiced were Cain's: he busied himself observing, coaching, and critiquing the rest of the team during training and only went through his own steps when they were eating dinner. Despite his natural talent for leadership, Cain was still a lone operator at heart and, for that reason and perhaps others, he spent only as much time with the rest of the team as necessary, reclaiming solitude at all other times.

After nearly a week of training, the day of the score came. Cain and van Hauer had agreed that an early morning raid was best, when most of the staff would still be in bed, to keep the streets clear and limit civilian casualties. As such, the insertion haulers—huge

CasiDrive transports larger than van Hauer's yacht-TAV—lifted off from Mexico at 3AM, to land in Idaho after the hour-long flight just before sunrise. The two rollers—AugsRak Viper LAVs—sped down their respective ramps, turrets coming to life as one mercenary in each took control and swept the morning darkness for unexpected patrols from Albright. The two Vipers then raced down a dirt track toward the LRI facility.

Just as the rollers crested a hill a hundred meters from the facility gate, two Viking Interdictors flying high-atmo out over the Pacific launched two salvos each of railgun fire. The stealth-configured, hypersonic projectiles violated US airspace without raising an alarm and then went hurtling on until they impacted the four towers situated on Albright's corners. The rounds hit with such force that the automated turrets within the towers' tops were not only destroyed but ejected entirely, to fly a few hundred meters before crashing to Earth in ruin. With that, the score had begun.

Stealth no longer being a priority, Paula brought down an electronic net around the facility: no communications in or out. Internal security comms were jammed, along with anything else except a single, rapidly modulating channel left open for the assault team. She then remote-guided a stealth TAV to Cain's designated egress PZ (Pickup Zone).

Though Paula had silenced Albright Security's radios, their manually activated siren was blaring full blast by the time the assault team hit the front gate. The gate was akin to a carwash of sorts, there to keep allergens, dust, and pollution out of the filtered environment of the facility with blowers, cleaning fluid, and a series of brushes. The AugsRak Vipers' solution was to simply crash right through it. Blinded by Paula's security blackout, the sentries in their little hut beside the gate had no warning before the two LAVs burst through, the turrets of each tracking onto the guardhouse and annihilating the occupants.

"Let's go, let's go," Cain shouted from within the troop bay of Viper One. "Hawk Two, set it up now!"

The GP machinegun—a heavy-barreled Yahata Ogama—was then hustled out by its crew and thrown into action on the corner of West Street and Admin Street. First the gunner deployed it on its bipod, laying down the first burst of suppressive fire across the doorway of the Administration building; the AG (Assistant Gunner) slapped the tripod into the right configuration before they mounted the Ogama, just in time to shift fire to the front of the Maintenance building, as half-clad security guards tried to take the field. Cain watched as the gun crew, and two riflemen he had assigned to watch their flanks, took up their positions as planned. He then discreetly separated from them, slipping into the parking lot adjacent to the Administration building and then sprinting for the perimeter alley, a carbine in his hands, infantry plate armor covering his chest and limbs, and a gym bag of explosives across his back.

Leaving Viper One to hold the gate, Viper Two headed north to Tree Street before dismounting the remainder of the assault force. Oswald then took them east, down Tree Street on foot, to hit the Research building from the north. About this time, the first security guard to try to outflank the machinegun team stumbled out into the perimeter alleyway.

Cain saw the guard—wearing an armored vest over his under-shirt, unlaced boots flopping on his feet, and boxer shorts—as he barreled into the alley ahead. He had hardly taken a step westward when Cain put a single round through his head, sending the man over backward. With both long streets and tight interiors to deal with, the carbine Cain carried had a shotgun slung under the barrel; the heavy carbine round was more than enough for an unarmored head, though. A second guard following the first, also nearly naked and carrying a submachine gun, peeked out of the intersecting alley after seeing his comrade fall; Cain moved as quietly as the wind, his footsteps largely swallowed by the echoes of the Ogama suppressing Admin Street; the guard risked it in the next second, but Cain caught him before his head completely cleared the corner of the building, crumpling the man into a human roadblock within the tight, intersecting alley.

Idiots, Cain thought as he paused briefly at the first intersecting alleyway, to string a tripwire explosive. *What are they even doing? They don't have the training, the experience, shit, they don't have the talent to be tussling with people like me or the rest of the assault team. They're just throwing their lives away and for what? To keep some rich asshole like van Hauer from getting some piece of tech? So some other asshole can use it to get even richer? The fuck do they care?*

Cain strung a second tripwire across the alley separating Maintenance from the Dining Facility before he heard the first one detonate. Turning enough to bring his carbine around, Cain waited a heartbeat to see if the unlucky guard who had tripped the explosive would be followed by another. In the next heartbeat, Cain was off, sprinting for Research.

If that's what you think, he asked himself, *then why are you here? If you don't care about van Hauer getting this QFG, if it ain't worth your time, then why are you bothering?*

"Hawk Six, Hawk Six, this is Hawk Tree, over," Oswald then screamed into the mission freq.

Cain paused at the corner of the Dining Facility, looking two ways at once, and said, "Go ahead, Hawk Tree."

"We're hung up," Oswald said. "Security got men into the restaurant alleyways ahead of us—I don't know how. We can't bypass them without getting cut to pieces."

"Doesn't matter, Hawk Tree," Cain said. "Works out better that way. Abort mission now. Break, break, break.

"All channel, this is Hawk Six: abort mission, retreat, plan Alpha."

After a brief pause, Oswald came back over the radio to say, "Roger, Hawk Six. You better hustle back to the gun crew, too." After a moment of Cain not acknowledging him, Oswald insisted, saying, "Hawk Six, you got to pull back now. As soon as we're back to the Vipers, we are gone, do you hear me? Security is everywhere: if you stay, you die, over."

To Cain's surprise, his mind answered automatically with: *So what?*

Always going to die in some bleak-ass sitch, Cain thought: *why not this one?*

CHAPTER 4

CROSSING THE ALLEY between the Dining Facility and the Research building, Cain listened with one part of his brain as the assault team cut its way back to West Street; the other side of his brain continued on with the score as planned. He fished out a prepped door charge from his gym bag, elbowing the heavy synthetic oblong around to his back before positioning the charge over the card-tap lock. Maintenance or kitchen staff would tap their ID cards against the reader below the doorknob, to open it and gain entrance to Research: Cain unrolled the ready strips of adhesive tape, securing the charge over the lock, tapped its detonator, and then slipped into the alleyway just as the charge blew. The charge was little more than a small lump of plastic explosive and a detonator wrapped in anti-static material (to avoid unintentional detonation) and nestled against an IV bag; the water in the bag gave the blast something to push against, focusing its force on the lock. As soon as the door banged open, Cain burst through with his carbine at the shoulder.

Slamming the door shut, Cain secured it with an old-school, brute-force method: a wooden wedge secured to the floor by a pneumatic bolt. He would need a crowbar to remove the wedge, but Cain began to have doubts that he would be able to leave that way, as planned. He strung a tripwire a foot past where the door would swing open (if someone managed to force it open) and then trotted down the corridor to the basement stairwell. He was looking for LRI's vault.

Every guard in Research had likely run for the improvised lobby barricades, as soon as the assault team had hit Tree Street, leaving the facility all but abandoned. Almost every guard. As Cain came to the bottom of the basement stairs, he saw two guards hunched over a security monitor on the vault's checkpoint desk. Both reached for their pistols the moment they saw Cain: Cain could not kill both of them simultaneously and so he fired his shotgun at the monitor. The fifteen .33 pellets from the three-inch shotgun shell shredded the monitor, causing it to explode, and peppered both guards' bullet-proof vests. They were not hurt, merely knocked back and disoriented, which bought Cain the moment he needed to sight in with his carbine, first on one head and then on the other. With the vault's guards dispatched, Cain hurried over to its front gate.

As Cain pulled his gym bag around to the front and rifled it for another door charge, he thought to himself, "So, this is the bleak-ass sitch, huh? You don't care anymore if you live or die, is that it? If that's true, then what the fuck are you doing here? I built Cain to do the impossible, to never quit. I didn't spend the last twenty-something years becoming who I am just to commit suicide."

Cain secured the charge to the lock of the prison-cell style gate, tapped the detonator, and then dived behind the checkpoint desk, which took the blast but not all of the vaporized IV fluid. Across a sloshing floor, Cain charged into the Research building's vault. Unlike a bank vault, LRI's material vault looked more like a self-storage facility, with rolling shutters instead of doors, secured to the floor by padlocks. Cain ran to the third row of units, fishing a solid slug shotgun shell from his LBV (Load Bearing Vest, replete with ammunition pouches), and fed it into the shotgun slung beneath the carbine's barrel. Unlike the buckshot he had used on the monitor, the one-ounce solid slug did not shower the target with projectiles and instead acted like a gigantic, sixty-caliber fist. Cain fired the lead fist at the padlock securing unit fifteen, reloaded with another shell of buckshot, and then flung open the storage unit. Though large enough to house one of the two Vipers currently retreating to the primary PZ, the only thing inside unit fifteen was a rather plain pedestal and—to Cain's sense of aesthetics— a rather goofy looking device resembling three pressure cookers wired together by an idiot. It was lighter than it looked, fortunately, and so Cain slipped the QFG prototype into his gym bag and then sprinted back to the stairwell and up to Research proper.

To Cain's surprise, he found no guards attempting to hold the top of the stairs nor the corridor leading back to the perimeter alley. Looking up the corridor in the opposite direction, he also did not see any signs of guards preparing to storm the vault from the main lobby.

"Waiting for me to come out," he thought. "Want a sharp-shooter to take me through the head, not risk damaging whatever it was I just pilfered from their vault. Go through either door and bang. Bleak. Well, Caroline, what do they think I cannot do?"

Cain could no longer hear the sounds of a firefight outside and assumed that the assault team had successfully withdrawn. He tried Paula, to see if she could verify which doors were watched and by how many guards: no soap, he could not get through to Paula. Somehow or other, their network had crashed or become jammed since he had descended into the vault. Cain nodded to himself, as if this next thing to go wrong confirmed something his subconscious had begun to suspect, and then headed for the stairwell up.

The service door from the perimeter alley opened on a corridor that doubled as the exit to the fire stairwell. Cain took it up: with a platoon of security guards watching the front and back doors, he needed another way out of Research. The LBV strapped around Cain's chest, containing his ammunition and sundries, weighed fifty pounds; the gym bag filled with demo charges and the QFG prototype weighed another fifty; the carbine/shotgun combo weighed twelve; and the infantry plate armor covering his chest, arms, and legs added an additional twenty pounds. One-hundred and thirty-two pounds was nothing to sneeze at, not even for Cain, but after a lifetime of intense physical training, he bound up the fire stairwell three steps at a time.

The infantry plate he wore was his personal set, not something provided by van Hauer, and, as such, was studded with the same sensory nodes that he had installed on his coat. The nodes picked up visuals and sound and fed them to his phone, which provided the processing power, before routing them to his AR sunglasses and earbuds. Alerts began to flash along both the top and bottom of his field of vision, indicating nodes had detected movement above and below Cain in the stairwell: security was making its move. Cain paused for a moment, to give the sensory suite's amplified hearing an unimpeded chance to discern how many he would face if he continued up the stairs, when an unmistakable set of clicks—akin to a flip lighter opening, only more ominous—echoed down from above. A second later, two metal cylinders clanged off of the stairway handrails and Cain threw himself through the third-floor door.

The grenades were flashbangs—not intended to kill, merely disorient—and Cain knew that his visual and additory gear would filter out the worst of it, but he also knew that security would storm the stairwell just afterward and there was nowhere to take cover in a fire stairwell. Out on Research's third floor, Cain sprang to his feet and sprinted off through the eclectic maze of open-floorplan desks, searching for the interior stairway up. The office was bright, light, and cheerful, fortunately deserted at that hour—and gave no cover whatsoever. When Cain heard the elevator bell ring, he leaped bodily over the last desk between him and the interior stairway and spun around in time to see six armed and armored guards burst onto the floor.

Cain rose just far enough over the desk, which had no chance of stopping even a submachine gun's round, and opened up with his shotgun. Custom designed, the shotgun was fired and the slide released by the same thumb lever: by holding down the lever, the shotgun would automatically fire every time Cain operated the slide. He racked the slide back and rammed if forward as fast as he could, with the speed and accuracy that the last six days of training had given him, and filled the elevator doorway with eight rounds of buckshot: one-hundred-and-twenty pellets the size of pistol rounds fired as a cloud into a space barely four-feet wide. The guards' vest armor took the shot easily, but only on their chests: their unarmored arms, necks, and faces were shredded by the sand-blast of buckshot and they recoiled or fell back bloody into the elevator. Cain wasted no time and sprang up the interior stairway, reloading the shotgun and listening to a couple guards rasp that they were hit, while another called for medics on his radio.

The interior stairway was meant to give researchers a quicker way to move between floors, rather than using the elevator to go just a floor or two. As such, it was a transparent, all-glass affair and Cain could see through it as he ascended, looking for the next squad of guards. He knelt briefly at the stairs' head and strung a tripwire explosive before continuing up to the fifth level. The moment he heard the elevator's bell, he dashed off toward the fire stairwell.

What he had not heard when diving out of the fire stairwell, two floors below—thanks to the flashbangs—was the siren that erupted every time a fire door was opened. The piercing electronic scream announced to every guard in the Research building that

Cain had just fled into the fire stairwell again. Growling a curse under his breath, Cain bound up the stairs, determined to rise at least one floor before the guards reacted. It could not be done.

An explosion somewhere in the building announced that someone had found one of the tripwires Cain had strung: a loud, "son of a bitch," in the fire stairwell announced that at least one of the guards was getting fed up. An extended burst of unaimed fire then rained down between the staircases above, as a guard's frustration overwhelmed him. Cain pressed on, running with his back pressed as close to the wall as his explosives bag would allow. In the next instant, other guards above him opened up, as well, and this time not merely between the staircases' handrails—they opened up right through the floor. The risers were steel-cored but mesh, meaning that there was more space than steel between the irate guards and Cain. The rounds raining down around him had lost power with each stair-tread they had penetrated, but without a helmet, even a slower-moving round would kill Cain if it caught him.

Keeping close to the wall and holding his armored forearm over his head, Cain sprinted upward, trying to reach the doorway out on to the sixth floor, when things got worse. Hearing the fire from above and possibly not knowing who was shooting, guards below Cain began shooting upward, either getting in on the turkey shoot or mistaking their comrades' fire for Cain's. The result was fire now coming up through the floor—and Cain's boots were not armored. Cain hurled himself at the fire door, bashing it open and falling prone just over the threshold, his head painfully wrenched to one side against the open door.

Even with the siren blaring again, Cain could hear when the gunfire in the stairwell stopped, heeding the call from several guards frantically shouting, "Cease fire!"

"Idiots," Cain mumbled and scrambled to his feet. "Wound up shooting each other."

Having made it to the sixth floor, Cain looked around for the interior stairway, which, inexplicably, was on the other side of the floor from where it was on lower levels. Cain saw it, over a few enclosed cubicles, just as he heard the elevator bell ring. He knelt, secured a tripwire, and then dashed off as quietly as he could on the tiled floor, hunched nearly to the ground to use the desks and cubicles for concealment.

"Fan out," someone said in a hushed shout. "Alpha Team, get to the local stairs ASAP: Bravo Team, head to the fire stairs and for christsake be careful."

Sage advice, Cain thought, quickening his pace toward what the guard squad leader had called the local stairs.

The Fire Team moving to cut off Cain was not sneaking nor trying to avoid noise and, unsurprisingly, reached the stairway ahead of him. Cain, squatting behind a half-walled cubicle, swayed out to his left just far enough for his shoulder's surveillance node to pick up the aisle ahead: one guard cautiously crept up the stairs as another crawled all but down to the level below; the other two looked in opposite directions, weaving their heads to see over and around the various equipment and cubicles that the sixth floor housed. Taking the four-man Fire Team was not impossible, Cain knew, not if he surprised them and never missed. As soon as he opened up on them, though, he knew that the second Fire Team would be on him. That's when the tripwire near the fire stairwell blew.

Screams and shouts for medics came from that direction a second later, as Cain watched the Fire Team guarding the local stairway push out amongst the cubicles, submachine guns at the shoulder. Cain circled the stairway from the other direction, coming up behind them. He knew that he could probably make it up the stairs before they returned to what they were supposed to be doing, but he also heard the elevators rumbling in their shafts, heralding the imminent arrival of reinforcements. He could not have a Fire Team that close on his heels, not with another squad of guards about to arrive and free them up to search the seventh floor.

Cain paused for a moment to affix a suppressor to the muzzle of the carbine barrel and then came around the last cubicle near the local stairs. Popping up, Cain fired on the two guards to the left, taking each through the head, and then dropped immediately to the ground and scurried off to his right, circling back the way he had come. The other two guards heard the suppressed gunshots, but could not tell what they were or from where they had originated. Once they realized that their two comrades no longer swept the cubicles to their left, they whispered for them, edging closer to where they had been. Just as they found uniformed legs sprawled out ahead of them and called out for their Squad Leader, Cain came up behind them and shot them through their heads.

Almost there, Cain thought, as he knelt and affixed another tripwire to the bottom of the local stairway. *Got to slow them down just a bit.*

At the turn in the interior stairwell, each floor having two runs of stairs, Cain set his last tripwire before running as quietly as possible up to the seventh floor. A few steps away from the stairway, Cain stopped and looked around, trying to recall the blueprints he had committed to memory: he had to find the correct wall for what he had planned. As voices rose in alarm below, as the second dead Fire Team was discovered, Cain oriented off of the local stairs and the small kitchen to one side, and then sprinted off in the other direction. As he came to the correct wall and unslung his gym bag, Cain's surveillance nodes picked up something that he had hoped he would not hear: one of the guard platoon's sergeants had some common sense.

"Don't go up that local," the voice shouted. "It's probably wired. Alpha Team, just watch it. Bravo, go up the fire stairs and for the love of god check for boobytraps before you go through the door!"

"Wonderful," Cain mumbled as he pulled charges and metal dowels from his gym bag. "Nothing like a ticking clock to get the blood pumping."

Cain's initial plan had been to blow through the wall encircling Albright, which required him to assemble a simple metal arch, secure it to the wall with spray-on foam adhesive, and use the arch to mount a series of explosive charges; when detonated, the arche would blow out a hole large enough for Cain to crawl through. Now on the seventh floor of the Research building, and with a Fire Team of guards circumventing his last tripwires, Cain assembled the arch against the building's exterior wall—just as the fire door's manic siren screamed the arrival of his adversaries.

Unlike the door charges, the wall charge had a wired detonator. Cain strung it out as far as it would go, hunkered down behind a cubicle, put the switch for the charges in his mouth, and then took his carbine in both hands. Sighting in on where the guard Fire Team would likely emerge, he bit down on the detonator and the wall charges blew. Cain's ear and eye systems filtered out the worst of the explosive blast, but did nothing about the dust that it kicked up. He stifled coughs until three seconds passed and the Fire Team came charging across the floor. Cain opened fire and dropped two before the other two could orient themselves toward their attacker; they returned fire but not in time and not with Cain's accuracy: he dropped each with a single shot.

Racing over to what the wall charges had done, Cain found the wall cut but not passable. He dropped to the floor and hammered with both feet against the slice of wall that he had freed from the whole. The segment of steel and concrete eventually yielded and slid out—out onto the transparent roof of the Albright Exclusive Residence Facility. Cain crawled through the opening, fighting his now depleted explosive bag—careful of the QFG prototype—to make the squeeze.

Out on the transparent roof, seven-stories above ground, Cain looked down into Albright and saw the hasty command point that the guard captain had pulled together, at the corner of a restaurant opposite the Research building. He had a reserve squad around him, as he shouted into a handheld radio, along with two sharp-shooters carrying rifles rather than submachine guns. One of the sharpshooters was sharp-eyed and pointed up at Cain. The commander looked frantically around and waived his arm at the roof: the squad and two sharpshooters opened up, uselessly trying to shoot through the foot-thick polymer.

"Well, I guess not damaging the prototype is no longer a priority," Cain mused to himself as he trotted over to the edge of the wall and knelt.

He withdrew one of the last things in his gym bag: a rappeler. The device was the size of a large tape measure and something of the same shape, with the addition of a handle that secured to the user's fingers. Several companies manufactured rappelers and used different means of attaching the head: traditional grappling hooks, magnets, and adhesive pads. Cain's was the deluxe model, had all three options, and Cain deployed it in adhesive-pad mode. With the rappeler's head affixed to the transparent roof, Cain turned his back to the wide vista of open space between Albright's wall and the miles of woods that separated it from the nearby town, thumbed the rappeler's release, which let out a bit of its monofilament line, allowing him to prepare for his descent, and then kicked out away from the wall and depressed the grip's trigger. As Cain fell, the monofilament whistled out of the rappeler at a preset speed and for a preset duration, slowing to a halt when Cain had dropped twenty feet. Cain then swung back toward the wall, catching himself with his legs before pushing off and depressing the grip trigger again. In three easy bounds, and with his carbine oriented downward in his other hand, Cain made it to the ground outside of Albright's security wall, shook off the rappeler, which he left dangling, and then sprinted away.

Cain felt his back itch as he crossed the hundred meters of open, cleared land between the facility and the forest, imagining that at any moment one of the sharpshooters would run out onto the transparent roof and start shooting. This portion of the egress was the other reason the Viking Interdictors had destroyed the autocannons atop Albright's towers, so nothing fired on Cain as he made it to the concealment of the woods. He headed directly for the stealth TAV that Paula had prepositioned, to make his escape and deliver the QFG prototype to van Hauer.

"Well, you made it again, but who cares, right?" Cain argued with himself as he dodged around trees and leaped over soggy ground, trying not to leave tracks. "That's your new attitude, you don't give a shit if you live or die, right? If those guards had been elite, someone well-trained and experienced, on your level or not far behind, you'd be dead now. And maybe that shouldn't bother you too much, but you should at least care. Dying for no better reason than you can't be bothered to try your best? Makes every-thing I've done pointless. All this time, all this struggle, to become the man I wanted to be, to pull down the scores that Malcom and I fantasized about back in Redhook when we were young, wanting better, and then to just throw it all away."

Cain stumbled as a realization hit him and he slowed nearly to a stop before looking around, regaining his orientation, and then setting off again, faster and quieter, eyes, ears, and sensors scanning the forest ahead.

"Son of a bitch," he muttered to himself. "I've been trying so hard—particularly since getting together with Francesca—not to compromise myself, not to lose what it meant to be Cain, and to not change. But this score, it proves it: I've already changed. I'm not the Cain that took Odhiambo away from the Archangel Mob,

I'm not the Cain that busted William Ord's son out of a DSI correction factory, and I'm not the Cain that took down the Venetian crime syndicate with Francesca. I've changed—and into something I'm not happy with. Fighting other people this whole time, trying to keep them from changing me, and I wind up changing myself. I'm still trying to fight that battle but the battle is already over. I'm not me, anymore.

"Got to get out of here," Cain thought, "finish this score, and then figure something out."

As Cain weaved between trees, finally focusing on the task at hand, heading toward the prepositioned stealth TAV that Paula had remote guided in as the score had kicked off, Cain picked up something ominous ahead, and not with eye, ear, or sensor. He smelled it. Somewhere ahead, something was burning.

Coming to the glade where the stealth TAV had set down, staying well back from the perimeter trees, Cain knelt and looked over the burning remains of the vehicle. It must have been destroyed by a ground-fired missile, sometime when Cain was blowing through gates or doors or was down in the vault: he had not heard a thing. Regardless, his way out of Idaho had just gone up in smoke.

"Cain, this is Oswald," the Scottish voice said through what Cain had thought was the crashed mission frequency. "You read me, mate? Yeah, I didn't egress with the others; sent them back on their own. They made it, if you care; no injuries. Look, I'm sorry about the stealth TAV, I really am, I hated to do it; I've been there, mate, trust me. Your escape route getting cut gives you a right sinking feeling, don't it? Couldn't let you leave, just yet. Never mind, though; we'll work it out."

Cain moved quietly away from the burning TAV, reaching into his LBV, to his phone, to disable its transmitter: he could still hear Oswald but was no longer transmitting anything, to avoid being tracked.

"Never thought you'd make it out of Albright," Oswald continued. "Should have! I damn well should have known you'd find
a way. Complicates things a tick. The boys up here, LRI security,
they were trying to take you clean, kill you without damaging the
prototype: not anymore, my lad, now they just want you dead,
whether the pretty tech makes it through or not. They can always
build another, but if van Hauer gets his hands on the gear, they'll
lose everything."

A hundred meters south of the burning TAV, Cain fished out
his phone and turned on a signal-strength app: sweeping the forest
with his phone, the direction and distance to Oswald became
apparent in the emanating waves of his radio transmission.

"Listen, Cain," Oswald continued, "there's a way out for you.
They may have a whole platoon of irate guards sweeping the woods
as I speak—and they're determined to kill you, mate—but you see,
I'm the one Omnipicorp hired to scuttle the raid, so I can help you
with them. All you have to do is return that prototype."

CHAPTER 5

THE CRASHED NET now made sense to Cain: Oswald, as a double agent, had given the mission frequency to LRI and either they or Oswald had set up local ECM. Oswald then modulated the ECM to allow him to talk, but not allow Cain to reach Paula, to call an evac TAV to one of the alternate PZs, on the other side of the woods. Even if he could reach Paula, Cain knew, with Oswald working for LRI and knowing where the PZs were, he would set up somewhere within the woods, probably with a precision rifle, and wait for Cain to try to cross the long, hundred-meters of wide-open nothing between the forest and the town. Then bang. If Cain wanted to make it the rest of the way out of the LRI ambush, he needed to take out Oswald. To take out Oswald, he needed to take out the LRI platoon now sweeping the woods for him.

"I want you to know, mate," Oswald continued in a hushed though conversational tone, "they didn't seduce me away: Omnipicorp hired me first. That's right. Told me to get myself hired by van Hauer, which took a little bribery but there you go. They wanted me to disrupt the score from the inside. You see, they knew that van Hauer had turned someone senior in LRI and needed the same kind of advantage to even things out."

Cain heard the LRI platoon before he saw or smelled them, coming downhill from the facility. The three squads had spread themselves out, line abreast, to sweep through the woods southward until someone ran into Cain. As soon as they did, the other two ends of the line would flank him. Cain thought for a second about how these inexperienced guards would react, given their performance inside the Research building, and a small smile spread across his face.

"That's why they had to use the real whatchamacallit," Oswald continued. "They weren't sure who the real mole was, just that his information was always correct. So, they used the genuine article to draw the bastard out. Clever, right? And that was the real object of this score, mate, to smoke out the traitor in their midst. Oh, they don't want to lose the thingamabob—set them back years, that would—but finding the mole was the point."

Instead of moving away from the oncoming LRI platoon, which would accomplish nothing since he would eventually come to the far end of the forest and the certain death of the open space beyond, Cain moved directly at it. Thirty-to-one odds were steep, even for Cain and even when pitted against a security force he had already beaten once. Skill mattered, but thirty submachine guns firing six-hundred rounds per minute each constituted an impossible imbalance of firepower. Therefore, Cain crept forward nearly prone—as the line of LRI guards approached—looking for some sort of cover, be it a rock or a declivity or even a thick tree stump.

"Bah, they're always at it, though, aren't they, mate?" Oswald said as Cain pulled foliage over himself, LRI guards now nearly surrounding him. "Good thing, too, for men like us. Steady work. But the job's done now, so you can quite creeping around out there, Cain. You bring back the prototype and I will personally guarantee your safety. Not only that, mate, I'll get Omnipicorp to pony up whatever van Hauer was supposed to pay you if you'd pulled this off. Now, I can't be fairer than that, can I? You bring it back, we get paid, and then we can fly off to this pub I know in Marrakesh. Best single-malt outside of the home country."

With a few ferns over his legs and a pile of decaying leaves over his chest, Cain lie perfectly still as two squads from the LRI platoon came in line to either side. Once they were just past where their peripheral vision would pick up movement, Cain rose and, using a tree for cover, opened up on the west-side squad—without the aid of his carbine's suppressor. The six rounds he fired seemed to explode like artillery fire, in the quiet under the trees, with the guards straining to hear anything they could. Two of the ten men went down, shot through their heads, while the others turned toward Cain and returned fire. Cain pulled back behind the tree, its trunk thick enough to absorb the submachine gun fire, and then fired on the east-side squad, another six rounds. He killed two more of the platoon's guards before dropping prone and out of sight, concealed by a fallen tree. The east-side squad reacted as the west-side had, turning toward their attacker and opening fire. With both squads only ten meters apart, firing in a panic after losing some of their own, firing toward the sounds of gunfire and the muzzle flashes ahead of them, they fired on each other and cut their two squads to pieces. During the confusion, Cain crawled out of the firefight, unseen, and went north, toward Albright, before turning west and following his phone's signal-strength app toward Oswald.

The third squad from the LRI platoon came rushing up as Cain crawled away, shouting for the others to cease fire. The voices of the NCOs carried through the forest, crying out for medics and ordering the unwounded to improvise litters, to carry their wounded back to Albright before they bled to death. However enraged the LRI security forces may have been at their losses, no matter how badly some of them thirsted for revenge, having fired upon each other proved to be too much and all they wanted now was to get out of the forest and back to the shattered safety of Albright.

"Oh, for fuck-sake, Cain," Oswald sighed. "What are you doing? You took out that platoon of tikes, fine; congratulations. It doesn't mean a thing, mate. I'm still out here and I've still got your comms jammed. Even if you could get a message out to dear Paula, the moment I see something landing at one of the PZs, I'll call in an airstrike. It's over, mate. You're not getting out that way, so come on, be reasonable. You hand over the prototype, we both get paid handsomely, just like we planned to—who will know the difference?"

"I will," Cain said and shot Oswald through the base of the spine, between the plates of his infantry armor. The suppressor was back on Cain's carbine and only the whisper of propellent and the metallic clang of the bolt closing disturbed the low hillock where Oswald had set up his rifle, overlooking the PZs north of town. Oswald's legs were now paralyzed, but his arms still worked and when he threw himself onto his back, he tried to draw a pistol from his LBV. Cain shot him through the elbow and then squatted down, a few feet away, and watched the writhing man.

"What is wrong with you?" Oswald said, gripping his wounded elbow, trying to staunch the blood flow. "Why are you taking this so bloody personal? We're just on different sides, on this one! We've probably fought on different sides of something, before now, and didn't know it. Same thing here, Cain. Score's over. Make your choice, mate, and make it quick: take me back to Albright and get paid by Ominipicorp or take me down to the PZ and get paid by van Hauer. I don't care which. I'm bleeding out here, mate."

"I ain't going to let you bleed out, O," Cain said. "But it ain't the same thing. You broke the faith, lied right to my face, and endangered every member of my team."

The bullet through his spine must have deviated off of a bone and found its way into one of Oswald's lungs. Blood ran from his lips as he spat, "I fucking saved them! I made sure LRI security only put enough boots around us to force us to abort the mission. No one was seriously hurt!"

"You broke the faith," Cain repeated and used his shotgun to shoot Oswald through the face, the buckshot at that distance entirely obliterating his head.

CHAPTER 6

WITH THE IMMEDIATE threat reduced, Cain hustled off southward. The sprint across the open space, toward the peaceful, Idahoan town, was nevertheless accompanied by the sensation of phantom crosshairs finding his back; it would have taken only one disgruntled guard with a rifle and one lucky shot to end it all. And Cain found himself caring, again, whether he made it back or not.

In an inadequately fenced lot, just north of town, Cain helped himself to the community's cell tower, patching in to use its transmitter to beat past the local ECM that Oswald had set up. With the network crashed, though, he could not reach Paula without changing encryption. Cain called up the comms app on his phone, preloaded with the encryption key, and then input Oscar, Tango, Delta. Rather than standing for "on the double," Oscar, Tango, Delta were the variables in a standing encryption key that both Paula and Cain used. The standard string was twenty-six characters long; the variables that Cain had given Paula were the alterations to the string. Oscar or O is the fifteenth letter in the alphabet, so Cain clicked over to the fifteenth character in the standard string and changed it to an O; he then clicked over five more characters and changed the twentieth character to a T; finally, he changed the fourth character to a D. It worked with numbers, too, with a number under twenty-seven followed by a number under ten; "twenty-one-seven" would indicate changing the twenty-first character to a seven. Regardless, with the encryption altered, Cain easily radioed through to Paula and designated one of the alternate PZs—one that he had never shared with Oswald or the rest of the assault team. It was always best to be careful.

Out over the Pacific, one of the Viking Interdictors received the pick-up request and immediately plummeted to wave-top level, accelerating to ten times the speed of sound. Racing over northern California and then Nevada, the interdictor approached the PZ from the south, to keep away from Albright as much as possible. It set down as soundlessly as all CasiDrive vehicles and then Cain sprinted over, again feeling phantom crosshairs on his back. The Viking class interdictor did not boast a troop bay, but did have four coffin-sized recesses in the hull for evacuating wounded. They were sealed, heated, and enough; Cain crawled into one, keeping his gym bag with the QFG prototype between his knees, and the Viking took off, escaping at treetop-level until it was out over the Pacific again and could break atmo without raising any alarms.

When the weightlessness of orbital flight set in, Cain sent a brief message to van Hauer, who had by now returned to Paradise, to let him know that he was inbound with "the object." He received no reply and did not expect to. There was nothing else to do but wait. As he waited, Cain reflected upon his last words with Oswald, particularly about keeping the faith. He had known Oswald on and off for a little under ten years, working this or that score, sometimes through Lester and other times not. Oswald had been correct about one thing: he and Cain likely had fought on opposite sides of one conflict or another. And that was fine, posed no problem. The

Seth W. James

problem arose from Oswald not remaining true to the unspoken fealty of the warband. Soldats de Fortune though they may have been, each owed fidelity to the other until the score ended. It's why Cain and Pat Jackson had hijacked an armored roller and cut their way back to the Presidential Palace, those many years ago, to pick up the few desperate men and women who remained alive after the hit squad had been ambushed. Circumstances might make actualizing the ideal impossible, at times, but Cain and those like him would not break the faith.

Cain also ruminated about how keeping the faith applied to his actions toward himself and not only to others: being true to his own ideals, which he had only ever vaguely enumerated, meant being honest with himself and—above all—to be worthy of his own respect. Fighting recklessly, not caring if he died, was beneath his self-respect and no way to live. His ideals were changing, he understood now, buried within the belly of an interdictor, hurtling through space, as alone as anyone could get, and their changing had made scores such as this one for van Hauer no longer important. In order to be worthy of his own respect, he needed to understand what his ideals had changed into and discover a new life that he could lead.

"Okay, Caroline," he sighed to himself, "where do I think *I* cannot go?"

The Viking docked in Paradise Orbital's cavernous port and Cain disembarked, giving the mirror-helmeted pilot a thumbs-up in thanks before one of Paradise's security guards came over to meet Cain at the elevator. Without a word, they descended past the waterfall and its nude bathers and then traversed the habitat ring to the entrance to van Hauer's villa. If Cain's appearance—dressed in dirty infantry armor, carrying a rifle, and strapped with ammunition—alarmed anyone, the presence of one of Paradise's guards must have placated them enough to avoid staring more than they always did when Cain passed. The guard nodded to one of van Hauer's private guards at the entrance to the museum/shaft that led to the villa, the new guard now taking up the escort.

Once within van Hauer's villa, a butler asked Cain to follow him and led him back to the secured conference room where he had talked with van Hauer a week prior. Van Hauer was there again now, supervising the uncorking of vintage champagne. Cain new the label well, having three bottles back on Achilles Orbital, and managed a small smile when he set down his gym bag and took the proffered flute from van Hauer. They waited to toast until after a tech came in and verified that the score had, in fact, succeeded. They drank and then Cain told van Hauer about Oswald's defection and how it likely meant that his mole was either dead or in considerable pain, under interrogation. Van Hauer excused himself for a moment, stepping into his SCS to make a call, before returning for a second toast and his thanks.

Cain cut the celebration short, accepting van Hauer's bonus for "unexpected resistance" with a handshake and nothing more. He had pressing matters to which he must attend and was sure van Hauer did, as well. Van Hauer, on his part, had become accustomed to Cain's abruptness and reticent, sometimes curt, manner, but was nevertheless surprised that Cain seemed uninterested in the possibility of future scores. He watched the man leave his villa just as he had entered—all three times—possessed of a confidence and purpose that surpassed even his own. It was with a small though wistful sigh that van Hauer returned to the device that would ruin his adversary and propel his businesses into the next century.

Back in his TAV, speeding off to Achilles Orbital, Cain again returned to the subject of a new way forward. He had changed, he now accepted, but what life could he build out of the Cain that he had worked so hard to become. He returned again, too, to the advice from Caroline and, this time, a possibility occurred to him out of nowhere that so struck him that he tossed back his head and laughed out loud, a long, pleasant sound that mingled joy with relief.

As soon as the docking procedure had completed, Cain raced up the stairs to his apartment, unfastening his armor as he went, and debating internally whether he should call Francesca immediately or if he should wash up and head down to surprise her in Venice. He had just about decided on the latter when his phone vibrated and he looked over to see that Francesca was calling.

"This is not working," Francesca said when Cain connected the call, just as if they had spoken earlier that day, rather than four weeks ago. Cain fell into a chair and drew a slow, deep breath, as if he could finally get enough oxygen and only now realized its lack for its presence. "I have tried for a month," Francesca continued, "and it is no use: I cannot go on not knowing, as I had hoped I could, and without being with you, as often as we may. Ignorance has not protected me. It is not possible for me to care for you less than entirely. Are you still there?"

"Yes," Cain said, surging to the edge of his seat, staring out into space and not seeing the stars. "Yes, I'm here. Baby, I should have seen how much I was hurting you, how much I was giving you to carry, and done something about it sooner."

Francesca laughed a small sob, then steadied herself and said, "I should have said something sooner, something clear. I was afraid though, amore mio, afraid that you would leave me. Is that not brilliant? I was afraid you would leave, so instead I left."

"Hey, at least you tried something," Cain said.

"Something that did not work," Francesca said. "So, we will have to try something else. Not knowing and not being with you are not options. Whatever we try, we must try together. I just—I have tried for the last three days—I cannot think of a way forward."

"I think I may have," Cain said, "just now, as I was TAVing

back to my apartment. You know, all this time, I didn't want to give up taking scores because, for my entire adult life, taking scores has been all I had. Not just my profession, it's been my identity. It felt to me like if I ever stepped away from the life, I'd cease to be me, to be Cain. Then I met you, and we fell in love, and now it isn't all that I have."

"Dio mio," Francesca breathed.

"Then today," Cain continued, "on this score I was pulling— I'm okay, not hurt—I realized that I'm not that man anymore, I'm not the Cain that lived only for his work. The simple truth is, I don't love it anymore. Maybe that's not true; maybe I just don't need it the same way, anymore."

"Can this be true?" Francesca said, tears apparent in her voice.

"That's how I feel," Cain said. "And I was trying to think of a way forward, you know, a way where all the experience I've amassed and skills I've learned wouldn't go to waste. That's another reason I haven't wanted to step away from the life: if I gave it up, no longer lived as a soldat de fortune, would it have all been for nothing? All the struggle, the pain and fear, the triumphs and the catastrophes, would it have all been for nothing if I just threw them all away, like tossing something valuable in the garbage?"

"No, you must not do that," Francesca said in a rush. "I know this. It is your life's work: it is valuable. It is why I have struggled, too, to find a way forward together."

"Well, I think I found a way," Cain said and laughed.

"Tell me," Francesca said.

"I ever tell you about Caroline?" Cain asked. "She consults sometimes, for Lester. Used to be a cat burglar. Well, after she'd made a fortune ripping off the finest places in Europe, she went into consulting—helping those same places to not get ripped off again. And just now, on the way here, it finally occurred to me: I could do that."

"Amore mio," Francesca cried. "You would do that?"

"Hey, it's half of what I do now, anyway," Cain said. "I look at a facility or convoy or whatever and then figure out a way to take it down. I could do the same thing for the people who own the facilities or convoys or whatever, help them to avoid intrusions, robberies, that sort of thing. I could keep using all the experience, all the skills, that I've developed over a lifetime of taking scores, only I won't have anyone shooting at me, won't be running off in the middle of the night, scaring you to death. I can still be me, entirely, but you and I can also be together."

"My darling," Francesca said, the tears quieting as she spoke, "I love you. That you would do this so we can live our lives together, it is beautiful. I can almost not believe it is finally happening."

"So, that's a yes?" Cain said and laughed. "You can live with that sort of arrangement?"

"Yes, yes!" Francesca said. "When will you come down? Now? I am home."

"Yes," Cain said. "I just need to wash up, first."

"Hurry," Francesca said, laughing away a last sob. "It has been far too long since—what is that?"

Through the ground-to-orbit transmission, Cain could hear the muffled sounds of gunfire in the Palazzo del Sindaco di Venezia.

"Gunshots," Cain said. "Francesca, you're in the bedroom? Lock the door and go to the security monitor in the wardrobe."

Francesca hurried to do so as more gunfire erupted throughout the residence of the Mayor of Venice. Having reached the monitor, she said, "There are men, armed men, inside the palazzo; they are shooting the guards. Some of the guards are shooting other guards, too, why is this? I see, some of the guards are wearing black arm-bands and they are killing the guards without them.

"Dio mio," Francesca then whispered. "There, it is Da Avolo. Da Avolo," she shouted, feeling the same surge of fear and loathing that she had felt when arresting him and his criminal syndicate's leadership, the night of her inauguration, "he should be in prison, but he is here. He is leading the men killing the guards."

"Francesca," Cain shouted. "Run! He's bribed the guards, the security system is probably compromised, too. You can't use the official escape route, they'll have it covered, so use the emergency route I told you about, run and don't stop running. I'll find you. Now, run!"

PART 5

TROUBLE

CHAPTER 1

CAIN TORE OFF the last of his infantry plate armor and ran—barefoot—back to his TAV. Vaulting the command chair, he shouted at the AI to head to Venice, maximum speed, and strapped himself under the H-harness as the g-forces kicked up beyond normal safe levels.

"Call Paula," Cain grunted at the AI as the inertia leveled off and he could unstrap from his seat. He pulled off the one-piece fatigue he had worn during the score for van Hauer, flinging it into the weightlessness of transorbital flight, and snatched open a locker in the rear cabin of his TAV, to gather fresh clothes and concealable armor that would not attract armed police attention when he hit Venice. The call to Paula rang incessantly as he dressed, the voice-mail picking up as Cain shot back into the forward cabin. "Hang up," he told the AI. "Call her again."

Cain strapped on a double shoulder holster, which crossed his back and connected to his belt with a row of magazine pouches, before donning his usual long coat with standup collar, its sensory nodes studding the neck and shoulders. He listened as the call failed again to connect, while attaching a long suppressor to his .45

auto pistol, making its naturally subsonic rounds even quieter, and slipping the weapon under his right arm; under the left, he wore his unsuppressed 10mm, which he never used off planet because its powerful rounds could puncture the hulls of ships and orbitals, evacuating everyone into space.

"Hang up," Cain shouted at the AI, after Paula's voicemail again kicked in.

Pulling himself into the command chair and connecting the H-harness, he opened a nearby compartment and took a phone from the pile within; unwrapping it, he then grabbed a secure master from the internal drawer and cloned the new phone. He then stuffed his old phone into the "burn bag" compartment in the side of the TAV, to be ejected when he hit Earth's atmosphere, where it would disintegrate from the heat of reentry. He then called Lester.

"Cain," Lester said when he connected the call, a hint of disapproval in his voice. "Figured you for a few days off, after that thing you pulled in Idaho."

"Da Avolo broke out of prison and just attacked Francesca's palazzo," Cain said in a rush. "He must have turned some of the guards, because Francesca said some were wearing black armbands and shooting the ones without them. She's on the run. I'm heading down there now. I need the best hacker you got to take control of Venice and monitor, isolate, or crash Da Avolo's network, once they find it. Keep the camera's off of her, at least, since Da Avolo may have the police in his pocket, too, and might try to use the city's surveillance to track her. I tried to get Paula, but she ain't answering."

"On vacation," Lester said, the sounds of him running down a corridor in Pons Sublicius orbital loud enough to come through the phone. "Left for her yearly return to natural gravity as soon as that thing you two had going for van Hauer—without including me, thank you very much—wrapped up." Putting his phone against his shoulder and leaning into the orbital's Command Center, Lester shouted to one of his lieutenants: "Hey, move Carter to that score in Hong Kong, now, and tell Liying to take control of Venice, quiet: no recording of one Francesca Pieralisi, Mayor of Venice, she's on the run; there's a fugitive, Da Avolo, after her along with some guards from her palazzo; got to assume they have a hacker in the vicinity, so isolate them and feed them edited footage, nothing with Francesca in it; then, set up a secure network and contact Cain on this line.

"This line is secure, right?" Lester asked Cain as he turned and rushed back to his office.

"Yeah, I just cloned it," Cain said. "Thanks, Lester. I'm headed down there now, but don't have Liying wait on me. See you."

"Hold up, hold up," Lester said. "Cain, there's no way Da Avolo pulled this score together, no way."

"What are you talking about?" Cain asked, the first spray of burning atmosphere coloring the forward monitor as his TAV began reentry.

"Da Avolo didn't have a nickel, is what I'm talking about," Lester said. "Listen, it was part of the compensation package I had arranged with Francesca, for seeing she lived through her inauguration and took that asshole Da Avolo down in the process, mostly by sending in you. See, she only had a little capital to throw my way, so the deal was that she wouldn't look to closely at Da Avolo's assets in the days after his arrest. And I raided them, Cain, I mean I took everything. I took his currency, his stocks, his inventory, contacts, networks, and real estate—I burned his organization to the ground. He did not have a nickel."

"So how the fuck did he get out of prison and bribe guards?" Cain wondered out loud.

"Exactly," Lester said. "Somebody big and with considerable resources took an interest in either him or—more likely—her. My guess? I figure this is about that seawall she's been boosting for nearly two years. The final legislation for that mother goes before the EU parliament in ten days. And I don't like coincidence."

"Me neither," Cain mumbled. After a moment, the Italian peninsula came into view on the forward monitor and Cain said, "Okay, thanks for that, Lester. Listen, dig into this, will you? See who paid the freight to get Da Avolo out of stir, at least. Once I get Francesca out of Venice, I'm going to hunt that sucker down and will need a place to start. You probably know what I'm worth, I'm guessing: if it takes everything I got, it takes everything."

"I wouldn't do you like that, Cain," Lester said and chuckled. "Let me see what I can dig up, we'll talk money later. Oh and, Cain, good luck."

CHAPTER 2

FRANCESCA CAST THE phone away from her, Cain's last words exhorting her to run still echoing in her mind as the gunfire below her in the Palazzo del Sindaco di Venezia swelled to its chain rondo and the conclusion of the symphony of violence devouring her guards. She flung open the window behind her, felt a new surge of fear—fear of the four-story drop to the narrow stone walkway below—and then dived through. She caught hold of the vines clinging tenaciously to the old palazzo, her legs swinging her around to an upright position, and then slid as much as climbed her way down, ripped leaves and tendrils fluttering after her.

There was a planned escape route, in case someone attempted to assassinate or kidnap the Mayor of Venice from the official residence. It had been created by Francesca's Chief of Security, Claes Thorsen—who, at that moment, lie dead in his office, garroted by his second-in-command—and was known to the guards who now betrayed their oaths, killing their brothers-in-arms. Cain had insisted, shortly after he began spending nights at the palazzo, that he and Francesca create a second escape route, unknown to anyone but the two of them. They had talked through it together every so often, usually on sleepy weekend mornings when Francesca was either half asleep or interested in other pursuits. Regardless, she knew it well despite having never walked it, a precaution against a potential adversary monitoring her and recording her preparations.

And prepared she was. Having entered public life in the Prosecutor's Office as soon as she had left university, Francesca had gone from one stressful job to another, gaining in ability and rising in notoriety until becoming mayor on an anticorruption platform—and putting away the leader and key associates of the city's most powerful criminal syndicate, namely Da Avolo. To deal with all of the stress that came with her professions, Francesca exercised incessantly: cardio, weights, wall climbing, martial arts—anything. The vines draped down the side of the Palazzo del Sindaco di Venezia, therefore, posed no particular challenge, her pounding heartrate notwithstanding.

Her stocking feet touching ground came as a surprise, so focused had Francesca been on simply not falling. She took a half-second to still her respiration, listening to the sounds within the palazzo: nothing. The battle had ended and Francesca had no doubt that her would-be assassins had prevailed. Suppressing the sorrow she felt at the loss of so many of her people—her security teams having offered the only constant companions in her hectic life—she turned and leaped into the canal. The next stage in her secret escape route made use of one her other forms of stress relief: swimming.

She swam under the water as far as she could before surfacing, took a couple breaths, and then plunged back underwater and shot off in a different direction. There was no telling if her assassins would send someone to the roof with a thermal-scoped rifle: she would be visible while surfaced and, if she swam in a straight line, she would offer any potential sniper the chance to anticipate her next rising. Cain's words surfaced in her mind as she swam: *prepare for what they can do, not what you think they will do.*

The cold water and the surprising width of the Grand Canal took their toll and Francesca's breaths came in ragged gasps before she reached the far side. Once there, she remained underwater and felt around until she located the partially submerged exhaust from a storm drain, which led out from a block of houses across the canal from her palazzo. She swam into the drain, her head cocked at an angle against the curved, stone ceiling, to draw breath from that narrow channel of fetid air.

The pitch-blackness of the tunnel, the fear of pursuit, and the unknown that surrounded her all crowded into Francesca's mind as she swam with one hand pressed to the wall, to guide her, until it felt as if she must weep or break. But break she would not, continuing on into the darkness, her every muscle clenched as she demanded both mind and body conform to her will. After what felt like weeks, with a growing fear that the rising tide would snuff out what little space there was to breathe, Francesca's hand found open space. She had made it to the ledge that Cain had promised her was there.

She pulled herself out of the water, feeling instantly colder, and patted around for the switch that must be there. Frustration fought Resolve as Francesca whispered curses until she finally found the switch and lit a single bulb secured to the wall by a yellow-wire cage. The light ran off of a small battery on the floor, covered with dust and mold, and lit a space barely wider than a coffin, though it soared up into blackness above her, beyond the light's reach. Against the wall opposite the storm drain's stream, Francesca found a duffle bag sealed within shrink-wrapped plastic. She jerked on a metal ring, which connected to a wire running the length of the bag, to sever the thick plastic and allow her access to the equipment within.

Cain had obviously packed the duffle bag himself, Francesca knew, because, faint though it was—and perhaps it was entirely imaginary—she could just discern the scent of him emanating from the objects within. She knew she would need to hurry, to continue with the escape plan alone, to avoid or face her pursuers as fortune demanded, but it was a comfort to remember that he was on his way.

Shaking the tears out of her eyes with an impatient gesture, Francesca dived into the duffle bag. First, she stripped off her sodden and stinking clothes, piling them to one side of the ledge away from the water (it would not do for Da Avolo's men to see women's clothing floating in the canal so close to her hiding spot). Next, she quickly cleansed herself with large alcohol wipes, followed by drying off with the single, not-entirely sufficient towel. For her hair, there was dry shampoo, which mostly worked despite her damp, towel-dried hair, which she then pulled into a French twist. The clothes she put on were nondescript—plain trousers and simple blouse, with a light nylon jacket—the sort of clothes her security would have worn. The thought of her betrayed and murdered guards again threatened her with sobs, but she stifled them and continued on.

The cache that Cain had left for her also contained gear that she would need to confront a variety of possibilities: a fake ID, registered with the city and the EU; a secure, never-used phone; AR sunglasses of a style and functionality identical to those that Cain used; earbuds that could enhance or protect hearing as the situation demanded, both connecting to the phone for its processing power; and, finally, a pistol.

The pistol was an Italian-made variant of the classic Walther PP, custom chambered for the highly accurate .38 Super cartridge. In addition to exercise in a myriad of forms, Francesca had, in the last year, taken to joining her security teams in the small shooting range on the palazzo's ground floor. She had found it a pleasurable focus, a way to relieve stress, and had never imagined that she would need to employ the skill that she had developed to defend her life. Nevertheless, she could, if needed, shoot a running man through the throat at thirty meters. She took a long, deep breath at the thought of having to do so, holding the pistol in her hand as if assessing its weight. Steeling herself to the possibility, she loaded the five magazines using stripper clips, attached a suppressor so large that it was longer than the pistol itself, and then secured them in a shoulder harness she found in the duffle bag, which she then slung around her chest. With the suppressor installed, the pistol went from her shoulder to her waist, but was not obvious under the nylon jacket.

With her preparations complete and her resolve buoyed against the challenges ahead, Francesca stood, turned off the light, tapped her new phone to activate her sunglasses' nightvision, and then began to ascend the ladder.

The long, iron ladder that Francesca climbed had been created in the 17th Century, as a part of a Venetian Prince's escape route from the palazzo above. Sea levels had been lower then, even in the lagoon surrounding Venice, despite the improved seawall, and the prince from that period would have made his escape in the opposite direction, descending into the storm drain to a small gondola that could slip out into the Grand Canal. With a strong scent of decaying iron before her face, Francesca now took the route in reverse, climbing to what had become of the once great palace.

The prince's family had long since fallen, their holdings sold and then sold again; the palazzo into which Francesca climbed had been separated into apartments above and shops below, catering to tourists and Venetians alike. One of the largest sections, however, had been devoted to nightlife: once Francesca had wrestled the ceramic pin out of a composite, modern hasp at the top of the ladder, and flung open a trap door heavy with an area rug, she found herself crawling into the storage room of a techno club.

The club was called, *La Fine del Mondo*, Francesca remembered, as the thumping bass pounded clear through the storage-room door, and when it was not closed by the health inspector, it hosted an egalitarian mixture of wealthy and not, all engaged in whatever vice appealed to them. More than one career had met its end under the pulsating lights of *La Fine del Mondo*. Francesca wondered if her name would now be added to the club's list.

She hastily kicked the rug back into place over the trapdoor, straightened her clothes, and set her AR sunglasses' light amplification to a reactive mode, to avoid being blinded when the strobe lights found her. She took a deep breath, hand on the doorknob, and hoped that no one would recognize her as she made for the exit. One phone-photo posted by a club-goer—"Mayor getting her freak on at *La Fine del Mondo*, OMG"—and Da Avolo's hacker would know right where she was.

Francesca slowly opened the door, just far enough to slip out, and was hit with the club's music as if by a physical blow. Taking it in her stride, glad of the earbuds that reduced the onslaught to an endurable level, she plunged into the crowd before a nearby barback noticed the intruder.

Keeping to the perimeter of the club's main dance floor, Francesca circumnavigated the room, struggling to catch sight of the exit while not attracting attention in the process. It could not be done: apart from her stunning looks—which had appeared on magazines and in newspapers for the last five years—Francesca was quite petite and could not see over the mob of partiers surrounding her. She would have needed to climb on a chair to see the exit sign, and avoiding notice was already an impossible task. Weaving this way and that, turning away from would-be dance partners, Francesca had almost made it to the door when a thick-necked young man in his twenties stepped away from the wall and blocked her path.

"Evening, donna," he shouted over the music, leaning down toward Francesca. "You are here looking for your daughter? Out on a school night and this is not allowed, right? Well, if she is here, she is enjoying herself. You should, too. Come, let us dance."

Francesca had tried to edge past the weightlifter in his skin-tight clothes, but he swayed into her path each time. Scowling up at him, she shouted to be heard over the music, "Get out of my way."

"Not until you show me what this little body can do," the young man shouted back, trying, no doubt, for seductive but only managing to convey a threat.

It had been years since Francesca had gone anywhere, in Italy or the EU, without a bodyguard. As Chief Prosecutor, she had a detail protecting her from criminals; as Mayor, her security had grown to three teams, each taking a rotating shift; she had not had to endure the advances of idiots in years, outside of cocktail parties thrown at political events, where a frigid look and a turned back were all that was necessary. The sudden necessity to dispose of a young fool when, outside the club, searching for her through the alleys and canals of Venice, armed thugs and turncoat guards sought to kill her for some petty revenge of Da Avolo's, struck Francesca not merely as absurd but as unendurably intrusive.

What this body can do, she thought in a split-second, offended at being reduced to her physicality, even by someone unworthy of respect, before she reacted by showing him just what she could do.

Francesca brought up the heel of her right palm, rotating her hips and shoulders under it, every muscle a coordinated spring, and struck the young man in the chin with such force that three of his teeth shot from his mouth. Instantly unconscious and tilting forward to fall, Francesca realized that she had just done what she had not wanted someone else to do: call attention to herself. In a flash of inspiration, she caught the collapsing man under his arms; he was far too tall and heavy to carry that way and so she threw him partially over her shoulder, bent her knees, and lifted him an inch off of the ground. Waddling, she brought him back to his space on the wall and let him slip to the floor, sagging in the attitude of someone who had over-indulged on the club's spirits. Glancing furtively about, to see if anyone had noticed, Francesca then pushed her way back into the crowd and finally to the exit.

Outside, the wide alleyway was a river of light, with cafes packing in the tourists and seas of people flowing wherever the night took them. Francesca plunged into the deluge of faces, recalled her next steps, and pursued her escape.

In the courtyard-turned-TAV-Landing-Zone of the Palazzo del Sindaco di Venezia, Da Avolo walked casually around the fountain, looking disinterestedly at the bodies of true guards strewn across the cobblestones, smoking his second good cigar in two years, and listening to the sounds of gunfire. Dressed in chinos and a light, horse-hide leather jacket, with his greying hair brushed straight back, he wore his sixty-two years well, looking every bit like a man in his early fifties. His thick fingers were the product of nature, but his rounded shoulders came from hours spent lifting weights each week, even in prison. Like the cigars he smoked, the way he wore his hair, and his longshoreman's language, he had taken up strength-training in his youth and would not drop it.

Da Avolo looked briefly over at Carlo Buruni, nominal leader of the assault, and sneered as he watched the taller and more heavily built man ponder confusedly the live stream playing on his phone. Da Avolo spat and turned away, sucking in a fresh lungfull of rich smoke. He had been out of prison for less than a day and his revenge was at hand: he wanted to enjoy the pleasures of fine clothes and a proper cigar as he anticipated the brief torments to come, not watch some ape in an Armani struggle with a body-cam app. The gunfire waned and Da Avolo felt certain that at any moment one of his boys or Carlo's mercenaries would drag that bitch prosecutor from her hole. One of his boys, dressed as a cheap, younger imitation of himself, ran to the railing of the second-floor balcony. Da Avolo thought: *this is it.*

"She ain't here, Mr. Da Avolo," the young thug shouted.

"What?" Da Avolo barked, years of smoking having given his voice the rasp of a file over metal. "The fuck you mean, she ain't here?

"Buruni, you dumb fuck, where is the goddamn mark?"

Carlo looked up from his phone, his desire to put a bullet through the old syndicate boss as clear as the night sky, but he said nothing.

"Mr. Da Avolo," another thug shouted down from the fourth-floor balcony. "There's an open window in the broad's bedroom."

"And?" Da Avolo growled.

"Just that the canal's right there and all," the thug explained.

"You think she jumped four stories?" Da Avolo said. "That's your idea?"

"Or climbed down," one of Carlo's mercenaries said, joining the thug at the railing; his black blazer bulged around his chest with magazines for his submachine gun in a slim LBV. "There are vines going down the wall and ripped leaves scattered over the walkway below."

Da Avolo rounded on Carlo, who had walked over to hear the report. "You see this shit?" Da Avolo said. "This is what your fancy plan got us. I told you we should've gone in, boom, heavy, no bribing guards, no hacking the air defense, just boom. But no, you and that friend of yours had to play it subtle and now she's on the lamb."

"Mr. Da Avolo," Carlo began, grinding his teeth and leaning down toward the older man.

"Shut it," Da Avolo shouted, pointing with his lit cigar so close to Carlo's face that the bigger man had to take a step back to avoid being burned. "I don't want to fucking hear it. We tried it your way and look what happened. I'm taking over.

"You," Da Avolo said, wheeling around and pointing his cigar at another of Carlo's mercenaries: "Get everyone the fuck out here, now. Now, goddamn it."

Slickly dressed mercenaries, thugs imitating Da Avolo, and the remaining guards from Francesca's detail, each wearing a black arm-band to designate them as part of the assassination attempt, then poured out of the surrounding palazzo, into a rough semicircle in front of Da Avolo.

"She made it out of this brilliantly planned caper of yours," he said, "so we're going to have to hunt her down—my way. No frills, no fucking around, just boom, right at her. Now, this is what I want: break up into groups of three, with one guard in each group to identify the bitch. One team in a boat; she may have gone into the canal, but if it wasn't into a boat, she couldn't have swum all that far, so look for signs, bits of clothes, wet footprints across the way, that sort of thing. Next, break out the airfoils: I want two teams in the sky, rooftop level: she's got a head start but probably had to make it across the canal first, so move out four blocks and start searching; look at every broad you see, down every alley you pass over, and move as quick as you can. Even if you can't find her, I want her to see you and hunker down; it'll give the rest of us time to catch up to her. And as for the rest of you, you're on foot: the airfoils will make a quick search, you follow that up looking under every fucking rock. Obviously, she's got an escape route that none of you fucks knows anything about: you need to get between her and her TAV out of here or her safehouse or whatever—before she fucking gets there. This is no time for shyness, neither: you go out there heavy, boom, knock people down, shoot first. Fuck tourism. Now go, get the hell out of here."

Francesca hurried down a medieval alleyway, barely wide enough for even her slight frame, her head on a swivel trying to see around the turns ahead, the rooftops above, and the path behind her all at once. She followed a preplanned route that would keep her, as much as possible, away from cameras, be they municipal or private. She could not know that Liying, Lester's hacker, had already penetrated every network provider in Venice and now searched for her, to isolate her as she escaped. For all Francesca knew, she was entirely alone and would only escape if she affected it herself.

Coming to one of Venice's few wider alleys, one that she would use to make up for the time lost in the twisting, narrow alleyways, Francesca oriented herself, remembering Cain's description of the area and the invisible boundaries set by cameras. There was a large hotel to her left, which must be avoided; cameras watched the lobby as well as the alley. To her right, however, was a movie theater with only a single camera mounted inside, watching the ticket booths. If she was careful, Francesca knew she could pass the theater while blocking the line-of-sight to her face. She hurried off to her right, unconsciously patting the .38 Super under her left arm before burying her hands in her jacket's pockets and her chin in its collar.

A few cafes were open, with patrons mostly inside; only the hardy sat outside to smoke as they drank. Francesca then felt her spirits rise as, ahead, the theater's doors swung open and people began pouring out. On a night where one of the worst possibilities had come true, she felt that she had finally caught a break. She burrowed into the mass of people, weaving amongst them as she passed the theater, hiding from the camera within that sea of humanity.

Three blocks, she thought, *and I'll dive back into a narrow alleyway. I'm going to make it.*

The narrow side-alleys were a two-edged sword: though safer from cameras, they were slower and all but impossible to escape if she ran into a pursuer. Regardless, making it past the danger of a camera added fresh energy to her escape and Francesca weaved through the crowd more quickly.

At the far end of the street, just as Francesca had passed the theater's entrance, three airfoils screamed in from above, like huge dragonflies carrying armed men.

One of the men swooped down to a hover, holding a spotlight in one hand, and shot a cone of white light into the darkness on the far side of the street, blinding a hooker. A second airfoil then came nearly to the ground, as its pilot peered at the disoriented woman. A moment passed before the light shut off and the three airfoils settled to the ground, blocking the line of theatergoers. The three men shrugged out of the harnesses attaching them to the airfoils and came forward, each with a long, metal flashlight.

As Francesca hunched down to remain as concealed as possible by the people in front of her, the three men pushed their way into the crowd. Each was large, aggressive, and took few pains to conceal the weapon he carried under his coat. Francesca then recognized one of them: Salvatore was his name, late thirties, one of her guards. He wore a black armband over his uniform sleeve. As she slowly approached the three men, carried forward by the momentum of the crowd, a confrontation inevitable, she saw that they were inspecting the faces of every woman they encountered. Anyone who objected was shoved against the wall or slapped aside.

Francesca felt her heartbeat in the sides of her neck and sweat coating her palms. If she turned and fought through the crowd to return to the theater or the alley beyond, they would certainly see her: if she continued forward, they would inevitably find her with their flashlights—and then their guns. Trying to think of some way to avoid them, as the crowd carried her relentless toward her assassins, Francesca was looking straight at Salvatore, over the shoulder of a woman in front of her, when his eyes, scanning the crowd for the next woman to accost, found hers. Their eyes locked. They knew one another. His expression shifted through a gamut of emotions in a single second, from surprise to shame to anger, and he raised his hand to point her out to his two fellow assassins.

In Francesca's mind, during that interminable second when her once-trusted guard became her most mortal enemy, she asked herself over and over, *can you do it, can you do it, can you do it?* In the next second, she tore open her jacket and pulled her pistol, its long suppressor extending past the head of the woman in front of her before she settled the flesh of her finger against the trigger, let out her breath, and squeezed.

There was no sound, not for Francesca. The pistol's slide opening to fling out the spent cartridge and then racking back into place was no louder than the closing of a car door, thanks to the long suppressor, but Francesca did not hear it. She did not hear the chatter of the crowd around her, nor did she hear when they all stopped talking at once. In the breathless silence of the moment when she squeezed the trigger, she could hear only her heart beat steadily on, as Salvatore's head caved in between his eyes and a red mist splattered the nacelles of the airfoil behind him.

Then they all screamed and some fell to the ground while others pressed to the theater's wall and only Francesca and the two mercenaries remained standing, like the slow players in some children's game. With the screams bringing her back to reality, Francesca took a quick breath as the mercenaries tried to claw their pistols from under their coats, and turned her fire upon them. With the same thoughtless action that she had acquired during the hours of weekly shooting practice, she traversed to one of her attackers and then the other, putting a single round through each of their heads. There was no thought to the moral implications, no thought of them-or-me: there was only the mechanical, release the trigger, traverse, sight, squeeze and hold, repeat.

A strange sense of shame tried to barge its way into Francesca's mind then, as the crowd fled from her, their expressions conveying the identity that they tried to impose upon her. There was no time for contemplation, however, and the rational side of her mind took charge, compelling her to run. She outpaced even the most fleet of those retreating from her, overtaking them before dodging down her intended alleyway, to plunge again into the Venetian night, weaving her way now more quickly than ever.

Da Avolo settled and resettled into one of the passenger recliners in the TAV that had brought the hit team to the Palazzo del Sindaco di Venezia. Airborne again, it soared over the Grand Canal and toward the spot where three of Da Avolo's hunters had just died. He rewatched the body-cam footage off of the guard's, Salvatore's, harness on one phone while shouting into another.

"No, no, not *to* the theater," Da Avolo barked: "*around* the fucking theater. Surround it, five-block perimeter, capiche? She's on foot, dark clothes, her hair's up; she's got a piece, too, with a silencer and she put a round through each of their fucking heads, so you see her, you shoot. She ain't shy or nothing.

"Now listen, she's not that far from the canal and she's moving north. Probably going to try to TAV out of here. It won't be something she's chartered or owns, otherwise that pet hacker of Carlo's would've found it. It'll probably be a regular flight that she can piggyback to cover her; something like an ambulance or a delivery TAV. So, keep an eye on the sky and if you see something coming in, you go check it out fast.

"On the other hand, she might be spooked now and instead try to lay low, catch her breath. If she hides, you'll need to look into every nook and cranny, you understand? Anywhere a tiny broad might squeeze into.

"Last thing and make sure you're the only ones can hear me say this," Da Avolo said, lowering his voice: "ice the turncoat guards.

They served their purpose and may be getting a little antsy now she looks like she might make it out of here. Kill them."

Francesca stood with her back to the cold, stone wall of an alleyway, not three feet from where it opened on a wide, irregular intersection. Stalls for selling fruits and vegetables filled the space, empty of their wares now and casting shadows. She held her breath and watched through the ethereal green of nightvision as three men stormed the meeting of ways, pistol and submachine guns up and scanning the stalls. Two of them wore black suits, one of them a thin leather jacket; the two with submachine guns had mounted flashlights beneath their muzzles, which they shined under the stalls or over them, into every corner and crevice; the one with the pistol did the same with a large, metal flashlight. As quickly as they swept the little market, they were nevertheless thorough in their search.

Francesca felt sweat form between her palm and the grip of her pistol, between her shoulder blades to run icily down her back. She could not know which exit from the intersection they would take, still less how she could hope to retreat without being heard or, if they chose the alley in which she hid, defeat her pursuers with their automatic weapons. She debated with herself whether it was better to wait, to roll the dice on them leaving by a different alleyway, or to shoot first, take out one of the submachine guns, and try to defeat all three as she had at the theater. The thought of adding three more dead men to the cobblestones of her city caused her stomach to tighten against a spasm of nausea.

"Baby, I'm here," Cain's voice then whispered in her ear and, for a moment, Francesca thought that she had imagined it, her mind creating the support she so keenly missed. But Francesca had always been someone who could look directly at any situation, no matter how dire, without flinching. If she had heard Cain's voice, then he was speaking to her.

"Be very cool," Cain said through her earbuds. "I'm coming up behind you. Nod if you can hear me. Excellent. Baby, I am so proud of you," he said and knew instantly that it was the wrong thing: he could see through his own nightvision as Francesca bit her lip and hunched forward, her stomach tightening up against a sob of relief. "Easy now, we're not out of this yet. I was there, though, at the movie theater; other end of the street, I saw you make your stand. We've got to make another one, right now: can you do it?"

Francesca swallowed the lump in her throat, stilled her breathing, and nodded slowly, distinctly. Whether a trick of the air currents in the alleyway or her imagination anticipating him, she thought she could just make out his scent as he approached.

"Good," he said, speaking sotto voce to keep his words from reaching Da Avolo's men, his voice only loud enough for his earbuds to pick up and transmit to Francesca's. "Things are going to get a little hectic, now. We're going to shoot two of these guys and let the third one run, run on back to Da Avolo. We'll follow. You take the fellow with the submachine gun to the left, I'll take the one on the right; we'll let the thug with the pistol run. He may shoot back: if he does, kneel down, hug the corner, and put rounds into the wall behind him, over his head, scare him the hell out of here. Can you do it?"

Francesca nodded again and sighted in on her designated mercenary, the sick feeling stirring in her stomach. She clenched her teeth against it: she would not let it nor Da Avolo nor even the men hunting her stop her from doing what she must.

"Good," Cain said. "When I shoot, you shoot; I'm right next to you, now, so you'll hear it."

A second like a century then passed, as Cain waited for both mercenaries to pause as they swept their flashlights into dark corners, before a thunderous report erupted from Cain's unsuppressed 10mm. Francesca's earbuds dampened the sound enough to protect her hearing, but it startled her, nevertheless. The heartbeat's delay did not save the other mercenary, however, as she squeezed her trigger in the next instant and evacuated the paid assassin's head.

The thug with the flashlight, screaming in his surprise, turned one way and then another, the echoes off the walls of the intersection making it impossible for him to gauge where his assailants hid. Cain removed all doubt by pushing to the alleyway's mouth and blazing away with his pistol. The young thug tried to raise his own pistol in return, but with rounds zipping past his ears, causing him to duck and scurry for cover, he never got off a shot. Francesca took a second to orient herself and then she, too, fired on the thug: one shot only, hitting his flashlight's blub. It was enough or, rather, it was too much for the thug: he gave up all pretense of resistance and fled down the opposite alleyway at a full sprint.

Cain spared only a second to pull Francesca to him with one arm, to kiss her below the ear. Tears rose to her eyes and she dashed them away impatiently, a rush of words rising in her mind, competing with the urgency to pursue, to which she knew they must respond.

Cain then held up his phone, close to her jacket's inside pocket, where her own phone sat, and said, "Liying, you got Francesca's phone?"

"Got it," Liying said from orbit, her digital control of Venice bouncing off of a geosynchronous satellite to Pons Sublicius. "She's on network now."

"Come on," Cain said to Francesca. "We've got to follow that asshole."

"I'm with you," Francesca managed to say around the stubborn lump in her throat.

They ran to the next intersection with Liying tuning their earbuds to detect the thug's footsteps, guiding their pursuit. Cain spoke to Francesca then, telling her that they needed to keep close enough to track the thug, but far back enough that he did not see them doing so. Cain wanted to follow the thug back to Da Avolo, to get close enough that Liying could pick up the transmissions from his phone or TAV or any other electronic device and attach a digital leash to him.

"Because he could not have orchestrated this assassination attempt himself," Francesca said, "and we will need to track him back to whoever is truly behind this. Of course. Lester took everything."

They ran as quietly as possible, dogging the thug's steps. At times, he slowed almost to a halt, trying to orient himself toward wherever it was that Da Avolo's TAV had dropped him. In those moments, Cain and Francesca came to a halt, too, to wait for the thug to again break back into a run, and their hands found each other.

Francesca came up on her toes, at one point, pulled the bud from Cain's ear, and whispered, "Dio mio, how I have missed you." She then kissed his neck and it was Cain's turn to fight back a lump in his throat.

Da Avolo paced along the canal at the foot of the Ponte degli Scalzi, several of his boys spread out around the open space, looking into alleyways and the fast-food restaurant at the stone bridge's end. Da Avolo had a fresh cigar going and listened, with increasing impatience, to someone on the other end of his phone.

"No, no, she's gone," he said. "She's in the wind; there's no catching her now. It's that goddamn African merc she's been keeping around for a playmate that's done it—which you should've fucking told me about. Yes, I do think that made the difference, you squirrely little fuck! If you had told me she had someone like that around, I would have told you to do it my way from the beginning; I'd never have gone along with this bribing-guards crap. What? Well, no shit. Yes, I can see it coming in now. Yeah, yeah, you go do that," Da Avolo snarled and then shut off the phone and jammed it into his trouser pocket.

Da Avolo whirled around, taking a stiff drag off of his cigar, when he saw the survivor from Cain and Francesca's ambush come stumbling in, rubber-legged from exhaustion. "What the fuck are you doing here?" Da Avolo asked, stamping over to glare at the young man.

"Mr. Da Avolo," the thug panted, "Mr. Da Avolo, I saw her. Well, not really, but I think she was there. *And* I think she had help. She killed a couple of Carlo's guys, too."

"No shit, genius," Da Avolo growled. "I saw the whole thing through their body-cams. What the hell did you come here for?"

The young man gulped in a breath of air before saying, "I, I don't know, I thought you'd want to know."

"You thought, huh?" Da Avolo sighed. "You probably led them right to me, you dumb fuck. Why the hell do you think you're alive? Because you're so slick, dio mio?"

Da Avolo looked over his shoulder as an all-but-silent, black TAV swooped in on its CasiDrive thrusters, to cram itself into the open space beside the canal; the rest of Da Avolo's new crew began to edge toward the vehicle, waiting for the old man's nod before they boarded.

Da Avolo sighed and took the young thug by the back of the neck, saying, "Alright, you're dumb but you're here. Get on with the rest of us. We're getting out of here. Have to whack the broad somewhere else. Come on."

A block south, just within the doorway leading out onto a building's roof, Cain sighted in with his phone's camera, as the TAV lifted off, and said, "Liying, you got him?"

A second passed as the young woman, a hundred-thousand miles away, isolated the navigation transmissions from the TAV, while it spiraled its way up, out of Venetian airspace; she then spoofed air traffic control's automated guidance, to penetrated the TAV's electronic suite, and then wormed her way into phones, laptops, even the coffee maker. "Got him," she said. "I'm putting a leash onto every device on the TAV."

"Excellent," Cain said and returned the phone to his coat pocket.

Francesca slipped past Cain and stepped out onto the roof, looking up through the enhanced vision of her AR sunglasses to watch the retreating TAV until it was out of sight. She released a deep, shuddering sigh, still feeling the adrenalin and stress, and nodded to herself. She then turned around and slipped off the sunglasses, to look into Cain's face with nothing between them. Cain did the same and they stepped into an embrace, Francesca all-but disappearing within those huge arms and enveloping coat, her head buried against his chest. Knowing as well as feeling that she was now safe, she let her grip of her emotions slip loose, slowly unclenching until the tears came and she could quietly weep. Cain rocked her in his arms, lips pressed to her hair; her relief was his relief, and not only from the dangers of that night, but also of the month that had preceded it.

When the sobs abated, Francesca raised her lips to be kissed and they stood long together, first kissing slowly, softly, then passionately. When Francesca finally slipped her hands between them, to caress her way up Cain's chest, to take his face in her hands and gaze at him again, she saw *that look* gazing back.

"God, how I have missed you," she said and put her arms back around him and pressed her cheek to his chest. "I don't ever want to part from you again."

Cain kissed her hair, hunching over to reach her temple, and said with difficulty, "Never."

As much as they wanted to spend the rest of the night in that embrace, they were both practical people at heart and knew that there was still much to do. Cain stepped back and rubbed his hands over his face and head, as if just waking from a long sleep; Francesca kept ahold of his coat.

"Okay, babe," he said, "I've got a safehouse all lined up. We just got to make it a few blocks to a TAV I stashed above a bakery and then we're out of here. We'll lay low for a while, give Lester and Liying a chance to gather us up some intel, and then keep off of radar while we hunt down whoever's really behind all this."

"No, I cannot do that," Francesca said. "I do not know who orchestrated this attack nor their reasons for doing so, but I know that if I lay low, if I hide, then they will take the next move and characterize the attack however they wish, undoubtedly to their advantage. Think what they could say: that I was involved with criminals and that this attack was the inevitable result, that I owed money from gambling and the assassins were really collectors, or that some other unsavory endeavor had turned violent. In other words, they could tell the public that their attack on me was my fault. I will not allow that.

"No, I must speak out and immediately. I will go on the offensive, otherwise I will have to fight their lies. We know that someone with immense resource is behind the assassination attempt, or they could not have arranged for Da Avolo's escape from prison. So, I will make a statement saying just that. Even though I cannot name my attacker, I will point him out in the darkness, tell the world that Da Avolo is merely a pawn and that someone else—with some other motive—is behind this abominable assault. If I get the word out first, then they will have to fight the truth."

CHAPTER 3

THE CORRIDORS OF the Santa Maria Maggiore Men's Prison echoed with the steady pace of the guard as he led Da Avolo to the interview room. Da Avolo wore the same tuxedo that he had worn the night of Francesca's inauguration as Mayor of Venice, now fraying at the cuffs from the constant wear over two years. In his cell, he had one other set of clothes, donated by a charity for poor prisoners, which he wore only when cleaning his tuxedo. Under all other circumstances, he comported himself as if he had just arrived at the prison, speaking to no one, waiting for no-one-knew-what.

The prison was over a century old but, like all grand edifices in Venice, it had been well maintained as the decades had passed and had retained its stateliness. The high ceilings of the interview room were now lined with soundproofing, and the telltale signs of discreet cameras and microphones were evident to those with experience in discovering them, and yet, the prison still conveyed the sensibilities of an age now forgotten, pristine in its ambivalence.

Da Avolo glanced around the room as the guard closed the door behind him. Seeing no one, he sighed his impatience, bounced on his heels, and then sat in one of the hard, wooden chairs. He had not been told whom he was to meet or to what purpose. After two years, even Da Avolo had learned something of patience.

When the door to the free side of the building finally opened, a man of obviously German pedigree came through, elegantly dressed for business, carrying a calfskin briefcase. Blond-haired and translucent-skinned, his blue eyes were so light that they appeared bleached. He inclined his head at Da Avolo, though he did not speak, and then turned impatiently to the guard that had led him there, giving him a curt nod to close the door.

Once alone, the German set his briefcase on the table, opened it, and fiddled with something inside. He then sat, without his back touching the chair and with his hands folded in his lap.

"Alright, slick, I'll bite," Da Avolo said: "who the fuck are you? I haven't seen a public defender since my last appeal got thrown out."

"Though I am an attorney, Mr. Da Avolo," the German said, "I am not here to represent you, but to simply ask you a question: would you like to leave this prison, to either enter a comfortable retirement or, if you should desire, to rebuild your organization?"

Da Avolo stared at the German for a moment before he snorted and looked off at the door through which he had entered. "Well, asshole, I got to say, that does sound enticing—or maybe *entrapping* is the right word. What the fuck is this? You haven't got me convicted of enough yet? You got to make up new stuff, now? With my organization dissolved, all my assets seized or stollen, I couldn't even afford to keep my lawyer—he's two cells down from me, too, you know. So, now you fucks are trying to pull this shit on me? Get the fuck out of here and stop bothering me," he sneered, making a rhythmic motion with his fist over his lap.

The German sat in the same posture throughout Da Avolo's tirade, his head slightly to one side; not fascinated, not disinterested, simply waiting for this expected process to conclude.

"One can certainly appreciate your suspicion," the German said, "and with your recent misfortunes, no one could blame you for your doubt. But please, Mr. Da Avolo, understand that I am in earnest and both of us may speak entirely freely."

The German then turned his briefcase so that the lid no longer concealed its contents: within, Da Avolo saw a Schweignkraft S-series jammer. The device used micro-aerials, lasers, ultrasound, and speech-pulse counter-emission to render surveillance devices powerless to monitor. It was top of the line, extremely expensive, and Da Avolo used to own one.

Da Avolo sat up straighter in his chair, put both feet on the ground, and then leaned over the table. Looking into the German's face, growing a little annoyed at what he was beginning to think of as smugness, he asked, "Alright, enough with the flirting: who the fuck are you?"

"My name is Hans Frank," the German said, "and I represent someone who has taken an interest in you."

Before Hans could continue, Da Avolo interrupted, waving his hand, "What's the deal? Start there. What would I have to do and what do I get out of it?"

"Ah, of course," Hans said, a grin tugging at the corners of his mouth. "The *deal*, Mr. Da Avolo, is quite simply this: we want you to exact revenge upon Francesca Pieralisi and—"

"You do, huh?" Da Avolo interrupted again. "Why?"

"Does it matter?" Hans asked back. "She put you here, orchestrated the dissolution of your entire organization, condemned you to spending the final decades of your life in a small, ill-appointed room. I see you have retained the one suit the raiders did not take from your estate—"

"You don't need to convince me, asshole," Da Avolo said. "If the chance comes along, sure, I'll kill that bitch and love every second of it. The question is why you or your boss want it done?" Hans merely shrugged at this reiteration. "No, I guess it doesn't matter. You want me to take her out because I've got a built-in motive; no one will question why I killed her. Keep them from looking at you and your boss. I can live with that—assuming I live."

"Oh, yes, you will live and quite well," Hans continued. "We are prepared to provide you with all of the resources you will need to affect the assassination, including a team of operatives, weapons, transportation, funds, and electronic support. Afterward, we will ask that you take responsibility for the assassination through some public forum; my office can draft remarks, if you should desire. Once that is completed, you will be given a spacious, elegantly appointed apartment on a sovereign orbital—to be named later— where you will be safe from extradition, arrest, or any other legal retribution. You will also be provided with a substantial cash and/ or material stipend, which you can spend as you wish, even on rebuilding your organization, if you do not wish to retire."

"You're goddamn fucking right I do not wish to retire," Da Avolo said and threw himself out of his chair.

He paced the four meters of the interview room, hands on his hips, shaking his head, as Hans watched him with a growing smirk on his face.

"I ain't retired now and I ain't retired when this thing is over," Da Avolo said and waived a finger at Hans. "Everything back to the way it was beforehand. My syndicate reformed, on the bleeding fucking edge, gather up a new crew of boys to knock heads, a few of your fucking kind to deal with the books, the courts, and then start raking in the cash. I want my fucking villa back, too, goddamn it. Everything as it was.

"That's the deal?" Da Avolo asked, turning to plant his two large hands firmly on the table, leaning down until his stubbled chin was a couple of inches from Hans' cleanly shaven one.

"That is the deal, Mr. Da Avolo," Hans said.

"Done," Da Avolo said. "When?"

"When I return, you will depart with me," Hans said and stood. "A few days' time."

"Just like that?" Da Avolo asked. "I walk out of here? No prison break?"

"Just like that," Hans said and buttoned his jacket. "We have a staging area in Austria; I'll take you there immediately, to prepare."

"I'm going to want a few of my old crew along, the ones that didn't get swept up by that bitch's raids," Da Avolo said. "Also, some new boys I can count on."

"I'll arrange it," Hans said and then raised a finger to his lips. He then shut off the Schweignkraft S-series jammer, closed his briefcase, and nodded to Da Avolo before knocking on the door for the guard to release him.

Da Avolo waited for his guard to take him out through the prison door, back to his cell, to resume his waiting. He walked along behind and to the left of the guard with a new bounce in his step, looking around himself, raising his chin to those he passed, and thought about whether he should say goodbye to his former lawyer before he left him there to rot.

CHAPTER 4

"GOOD EVENING, MY fellow citizens of Venice and to our neighbors throughout the European Union. I am Francesca Pieralisi, the Mayor of Venice and, as many of you have no doubt seen on the news in the last hours, my residence, the Palazzo del Sindaco di Venezia, was ruthlessly attacked by a well-armed and well-funded team of mercenaries, aided, it saddens me to say, by a few of my own security staff, bribed to treason. I can assure you, however, that I was able to escape the attempted assassination and am now conducting an investigation into the identity of those who would orchestrate such a despicable attack against our community, our civilization.

"The identity of those behind the assassination attempt remains shrouded, for now, in part because they went to such pains to conceal themselves: in an attempt to shift blame, they affected the escape of Vincenzo da Avolo, the former capo of the Da Avolo crime syndicate, which I had utterly dismantled at the time of my inauguration as Mayor of Venice. Mr. Da Avolo had no money, no resources, with which to free himself from the punishment assigned to him by the people of Venice, much less to hire a team of mercenaries. Therefore, we can conclude that someone or some organization with considerable means is truly behind the assassination attempt and merely using Da Avolo for camouflage. Their attempts to conceal themselves will fail.

"I am coordinating with both the Polizia di Stato and the Guardia di Finanza, as well as Interpol, to determine who hired the assassination team, how they entered Italian airspace, and to discover where they have since retreated. Given the extremes to which my attackers have gone, going so far as to bribe a few of my guards into killing those loyal to me, to Venice, I will conduct my investigation independently, for now. Do not be alarmed if you do not see me in the mayor's office; I am safe and my deputy is carrying out my instructions, seeing to the people's affairs.

"Thank you all for your well-wishes and for the flowers and gifts left at the Palazzo del Sindaco di Venezia; they have warmed my heart. Please share the same condolences with the families of the true guards, those of my security staff who gave their lives in defense of your mayor and our great city. Thank you."

After their harried escape from Venice—evading Italian air-traffic control, since they could not know how far their adversary's bribery had gone, whom had been bought and to what lengths they would go to kill Francesca—she and Cain had arrived at his safehouse in Monaco exhausted from worry as well as exertion, and had thought only of a quick morsel and then sleep. As soon as the door to the apartment had closed and they had let their jacket and coat slip to the floor, however, a new urgency had seized them. It had been a month since they had last made love, to each other or to anyone, and with the seemingly endless nights alone between then and now finally at their end, they would not wait another second.

The acute difference in their sizes, with Francesca barely over five-feet and not quite a hundred pounds compared to Cain's six-foot-four and more than two-hundred and fifty pounds, combined with Cain's prodigious strength to liberate them from the usual restraints of form or, indeed, any need of particular furniture. In a rush that nearly put Cain's hand through a wall, as he slowed them at the last second, to brace her there for pleasure and not to apply pain, Francesca found herself aloft, her limbs wrapped around her lover and, with him bringing them rapidly toward climax, free to roam over him with her hands, as she had so often done in the past. In the early morning hours, though, before Monaco awoke, Francesca did not caress the rippling muscles encircling her waist or between her thighs, to reacquaint herself with what she had gone without for too long; no, instead, she held Cain's face in her hands as they kissed, opening her eyes to see *that look* between each one.

After a short interlude on the couch, to cuddle up together and say what they needed to say and hear what they needed to hear, reaffirming with words what they had already promised with their bodies, they made love again and then showered together and then slept. For the first time in a month, for either of them, sleep came without a struggle and remained with them until their dreams aroused them to consciousness again and they began the day as they had ended the night.

Another shower was then needed, as well as the unfortunate necessity of recognizing that the vigor of their reunion was making them both sore. They giggled together at the sad and happy cause of this—thankfully temporary—misfortune, as the espresso machine bubbled and hissed. They then put their clothes into the washer, as they had only the one set and did not want to climb back into the sweaty garments after finally becoming clean themselves.

"We will need to stop somewhere, pick up new clothes," Francesca said, looking warm and happy in a bathrobe three sizes too big for her. She sat on a padded bench beneath the window in the kitchen, with her feet tucked under her, eating toast, as they waited for their laundry.

Cain peeked into the nook where the washer rumbled, seeing it had progressed to its final rinse, before saying, "Too bad, really. If we didn't have so much to do, I'd say let's just stay as we are for the rest of the day."

Francesca smiled her agreement and leaned forward for a kiss before falling back in her seat and watching Cain. He stood there nude without a trace of self-consciousness, the tiny espresso cup seemingly reduced to a child's toy in his large hand as he held it and split his attention between her and looking out the window behind her. Francesca was about to playfully voice her discontent with his distraction when she remembered why he was watching the rooftop opposite their building, the street, the airspace nearby; it was the same reason the apartment's windows were glazed to conceal the occupants, always giving the appearance of a dark room; it was to keep them safe.

Cain saw her expression change when he could no longer go without looking at her and he leaned down for another kiss. The washer's chime rang as they spoke through touch and Cain turned to move their clothes into the dryer.

"You know," he said, looking over his shoulder, "with all your servants at the palazzo, we never got to do this."

"Stand around nude in the kitchen?" she said, watching him over the rim of her cup. "I seem to remember you doing so many times."

"I bet you do, too," he said, grinning, and switched on the dryer. "I meant the laundry. Once we take care of this business with Da Avolo and whoever is paying his bills, and I start my new career as a *security consultant*, we'll be doing this sort of domestic thing together all the time."

"We will?" she asked, watching as he crossed to the espresso machine and loaded it for another cup. "You will not trust the palazzo staff to wash your clothes after this?"

Not looking over, he said innocently, "Well, you won't be mayor for much longer."

Francesca sent her cup and saucer clattering onto the little table, her back going straight, and said, "Excuse me? I will continue as mayor for as long as it pleases me, I will have you know."

Cain turned around smiling and said, "Deputy's in charge now, right?"

"Implementing my agenda, yes," she said, knowing that she was being teased and wondering, not for the first time, what it was about it that amused her when Cain did the teasing and infuriated her whenever someone else tried.

"Getting all that press coverage," he said, "*during the crisis*. You think she bankrolled Da Avolo, to topple you?"

"You are ridiculous," she said and tried to stifle her smile, looking away toward the dryer. "Have you seen my overnight approval ratings? Through the roof!"

Cain laughed proudly, nodding, retrieved his fresh espresso, and came around to sit next to Francesca. He said, "Yes, they are, baby, yes, they are," and kissed her, which she allowed without losing the skeptical look on her face. "But that's exactly why I don't figure you'll be mayor after this term: your star is on the rise. Mayor has just been your day job for the last year or so, all the time you've been putting into the seawall, lobbying parliament and the European Commission. Not that the people of Venice mind so much; they know you're doing right by them and they're proud— almost as proud as I am—of you moving all those mountains to do what we all know needs to be done. Come on, admit it," he said and nudged her gently with his elbow: "you want bigger and better. You love being mayor, I know, but it was always just a step toward what you're really after. So, come on, give: what's the next step?"

Unable to suppress her smile any longer, she waived it defiantly under his nose and said, "Shut up. You are the one who is changing

careers, not me. And I am so happy," she said, her expression softening, her hand coming up to caress his cheek, "and humbled, really,
that you would do this beautiful thing so that we could live our
lives together."

"No, it was nothing," he said. "Just needed to figure out a way
to go on being me while also being us."

"And you have," she said. "I do not know how I would have
continued my life if you had not thought of this way forward."

"And you'll never have to know that," he said and put his arm
around her, "because I'm sticking close to you. Easy now," he said
as her hands found his thigh, "we can't go getting romantic again
or it might fall off."

"No!" she cried in mock alarm.

They kissed and then snuggled close, listening to the dryer, and
he said, "Now, let's see, is it going to be the European Parliament or
the European Commission? Strasbourg or Brussels? Get ourselves
a little apartment, walking distance to your office, set up house,
doing laundry, buying groceries, living."

"Bliss," she said, returning her hand to his cheek.

"That, too," he said and they laughed.

CHAPTER 5

DA AVOLO RETURNED to the interview room of the Santa Maria Maggiore Men's Prison, still dressed in his fraying tuxedo, a few days after his first meeting with Hans. The deadened sense of waiting, waiting without end, had gone from his eyes, even as he spent every waking hour awaiting his unknown benefactor's return. The guard opened the door to the interview room and waived Da Avolo in with a small bow, drawing a glance from his prisoner. As before, Da Avolo waited for a few minutes until Hans Frank entered from the free side of the prison: unlike the last time, Hans came accompanied by two men, similarly well-dressed, similarly German in appearance, but considerably larger. Each carried a suit bag over his shoulder, which they deposited on the room's only table.

"I have brought you more suitable attire," Hans said and laid a hand on one of the suit bags. "Please dress. We can wait in the hallway, if you desire privacy."

"I give a fuck," Da Avolo mumbled as he took off his tuxedo and tossed it, piece-by-piece, into a corner. Inside the indicated bag, he found chinos, a shirt, new shoes, and a nice horse-hide

leather jacket, all from tailors or craftsmen whom he had patron-
ized before his incarceration. "Hey, hey, this is the good stuff, too."

Hans nodded his acknowledgment, waiting patiently for the
old don to dress. As Da Avolo sat to tie his shoes, the door leading back to incarceration opened and two men he recognized were
ushered in by the same strangely deferential guard.

"Leone, Teglia," Da Avolo said, shooting to his feet. "You
two bastards were here the whole time? Where the fuck were they
hiding you?"

Both men, each a smaller, younger version of Da Avolo in
appearance, accepted a kiss on the cheek and slap on the shoulder, life returning to their eyes as it had to their one-time capo's.
"Kept us in different wings, Mr. Da Avolo," Leone said. "Didn't
want us planning a break or something, you know. Is that, uh, I
don't know—"

Da Avolo made a casual slashing motion near his throat and
then turned to look at Hans.

"Gentlemen," the lawyer said to the two thugs, "you will find
fresh clothes in these bags. Please dress and then we will leave."

"And how are we doing that?" Da Avolo said, arms akimbo.

"We will walk," Hans said.

The warehouse hailed from at least a century before, a rusting hulk
that had somehow found its way onto an historical preservation list.
With fusion power and CasiDrives lifting Humanity to colonies on
the moon and Mars, no one wanted to invest in recycling the past;
it was easier—and far more profitable—to start fresh somewhere
else; and so, the rotting corpse of yesteryear's industry lie fat and
free for the scavengers of the world. Da Avolo stepped off of the
TAV that had glided in through the huge double-doors and looked
over the place, sneering at its ugliness, until he saw the improvised
armory that Hans' mercenaries had erected to one side.

"Now we're fucking talking," he mumbled and motioned for his two boys, Leone and Teglia, to follow him. He dropped a nearly spent cigar—his first since regaining his freedom—on the warehouse floor, having lit one from the humidor he had found in Hans' TAV and filled the small craft's interior with its smoke all the way from Venice.

Hans, too, disembarked, waiving the smoke from his face before quickening his step to precede Da Avolo to the score of mercenaries assembled near the three long tables and two, jet-black TAVs. The mercenaries were busy changing into a uniform consisting of a black suit over a slim LBV; their traveling garments were bagged up by an attendant. From the second of the three tables, they each drew a submachine gun, a pistol, and appropriate ammunition. From the third table, they drew phones, flashlights, identification, and currency.

"Not bad," Da Avolo said, nodding and looking over the gear. "Hell of a lot of guys, though: how big is her security detail?"

"Mr. Da Avolo," Hans said, ignoring the question, "this is Carlo Buruni, he will act as your *lieutenant*," Hans said, adding the inflection toward Carlo, who took a deep breath at the word, "for this operation. He will direct the assault team. The assault team, you will no doubt have noticed, is composed entirely of Italians, men that you might have employed yourself. We have also made several preparations to ensure the easy success of this operation. Carlo, if you would be so kind, please brief Mr. Da Avolo."

"Yes, Mr. Frank," Carlo said, his deep voice rumbling between clenched teeth. Stepping to Da Avolo's side and canting a tablet for him to see, Carlo brought up a 3D rendering of the Palazzo del Sindaco di Venezia. "As you see here, *Mr.* Da Avolo, the palazzo has anti-assault modules on the perimeter and air-defense emplacements across the roof."

"So what?" Da Avolo said, waving his hand at the screen. "Two guys with railguns could ace the modules on one side before we storm the place; infiltrate from the south, we won't even need to fly in, so who cares about the AD on the roof. We'll just turn the fuckers off once we own the place; TAV out after."

"We had another idea, Mr. Da Avolo," Carlo said and sighed. "We have assets on the inside."

"We were able to convince about a third of the mayor's security detail to accept new employment," Hans said, his usual smirk appearing.

"That's right," Carlo said. "They're in our pocket and will kill the AD, the anti-assault modules, and the surveillance system right before we hit the palazzo. You'll know them by their black armbands."

"Just like a funeral," Da Avolo said. "And they're going to help ice the remaining guards, right? I got your plan. Look, Hans, it's your money so it's your plan. I'll go along. It's not how I'd do it, but I'll go along since you're paying. Me? I don't go in for these fancy tactics and I sure as hell don't like traitors, even if they're working for me. My way is better: boom, go in heavy, knock them down, get it done. But, like I said, your money, your way—unless it goes wrong. It goes wrong on us, Hans, and I'm taking over, capiche?"

"Of course, Mr. Da Avolo," Hans said with a meaningful glance at Carlo.

"Alright, you know what?" Da Avolo said to Carlo. "Tell me the rest in the air; let's get going. I want to know, especially, what assets you have in case things don't pan out like you hope: things, people, whatever. You got someone hacking the city's cameras? We may need surveillance."

As Carlo ran through contingencies, Da Avolo helped himself to a pistol, a phone, and a silk-thin armored vest. He motioned for his boys to do the same before they climbed aboard the stealth TAV that would bring them back into Italian airspace.

CHAPTER 6

MONACO'S SMALLER STREETS and twisting alleyways dated back to the medieval period, as did Venice's;
unlike Venice, however, they often intersected wider,
contemporary streets, presenting different dangers to Cain and
Francesca as they wound their way to a meeting with one of Lester's
operatives. Getting trapped in an alleyway barely large enough for
Cain's shoulders would mean certain death, but out on the bustling streets they would be vulnerable to cars and drones. Liying
had taken control of the city's surveillance apparatus, as she had in
Venice, and had a program running to carefully edit any footage
of either Cain or Francesca as they navigated a twisting path to the
meet: the program could not, unfortunately, do a thing against
human eyes or independent drones.

Cain's response was to pursue a circular route to the rendezvous, plunging down narrow side streets and alleyways one moment
and then doubling back to a tourist-filled, shop-lined thoroughfare
the next. All the while, as they walked briskly along, both he and
Francesca had their AR sunglasses and surveillance nodes scanning
the crowd and sky, looking for any sign of danger. The smart way to

run close protection would have been for Cain to bring in a dozen more operatives, with scouts out a few blocks ahead and flankers to either side, along with an ECM module somewhere ready to crash the city, if needed, maybe a few armed drones of their own. Even as a single bodyguard, it would have been better for Cain to push out a few meters, walk into every danger area ahead of Francesca. He did not. The prospect of her being snatched off the street behind him proved more intolerable to him than the far-from-optimal method of traveling together. He had to exert an effort not to take her hand in his and did not always succeed.

On her part, Francesca did all that Cain had advised her to do, scanning her AR HUD, watching for anyone looking a little too closely, for cars driving a little too slowly, or the telltale signs of micro-drones' pulsing EM control channels. It was exhausting, to focus continuously block-after-block, despite the all-too motivating danger of impending assassination. She knew, too, that Cain did not want to let her out of his sight, even if it would have been safer for her to travel alone while he circled her, unobtrusively, but was glad that he had not clung to professionalism. Her solo flight through Venice had been enough. She took comfort from each time his focus waivered and he gripped her hand, even if he snatched his hand back a second later; she knew she needed to keep her firing hand free.

Their destination was a small hotel-turned-office-building, a few blocks north of the Boulevard Princesse Charlotte. The Art Deco edifice had somehow survived, tucked in between pink stucco housing and steel-and-glass skyscrapers, far from the palm trees and wide-open spaces closer to the sea, which would have made life too easy for snipers, assuming anyone knew they were in Monaco. They chose to assume the worst and took precautions accordingly.

Cain and Francesca moved with swift purpose while avoiding the attention it would draw if they burst into the building's lobby.

Tastefully appointed with glowing glass sconces, the lobby had no receptionist, merely a holographic directory to which visitors could enquire about a party's floor and suite number. They passed it by, already knowing their destination. They also avoided the elevator and instead climbed the four flights of stairs. The long, carpeted hallway down which they quietly passed was interspersed with little seating areas, each a potential ambush spot, each potentially concealing an explosive. The reduced danger that Francesca had hoped for within the building's walls seemed impossible to find.

At the suite, Cain waived Francesca back and stood to one side before opening the door. The tiny waiting room beyond was empty, save furniture, and so Cain entered, with Francesca a step behind. Other than a sofa, coffee table, and a receptionist's desk, the room offered nothing but a doorway to the office beyond. As soon as Francesca closed the outer door, its mechanism seeming to explode rather than click, a voice mumbled within the office followed a moment later by Lester appearing in the doorway.

"About time you two showed up," he said, grinning.

Cain drew his .45 auto, the suppressed pistol seeming to materialize in his hand, and aimed it at Lester's forehead.

"Wait," Francesca whispered to Cain, "why?"

"Draw," he said. "Cover the door."

Francesca pulled her .38 Super and turned to aim it at the doorknob-side of the outer door, as Lester heaved a sigh and, quite slowly, raised his hands to shoulder level. Only a little shorter than Cain, though not nearly as heavily built, Lester could have passed for a relative or at least an admirer. He wore a similarly long coat, studded with surveillance nodes; stuck through the open collar of his silk shirt was a pair of AR sunglasses of the wraparound variety, just like Cain's; under his arm, he carried a similarly suppressed .45 auto. His hair was longer, though, and more fashionably cut, the grey conspicuous by its absence, and where Cain could freeze a glass

of water simply by looking at it, Lester's eyes always seemed to spar-
kle with some inner amusement. Even at that moment, with Cain
pointing a gun at his head, a small smile brightened Lester's face.

"Here we go," he sighed.

Cain stared into Lester's eyes, the non-reflective black lenses of
his sunglasses offering nothing more to Lester than Lester's dancing
brown eyes gave to Cain. Cain motioned with the suppressor's tip
for Lester to back into the office. Cain followed him in, only far
enough to see that it was empty. The surveillance suite ran through
its broad-range EM sweep, looking for heat, air currents, radio
transmissions, anything that might indicate an adversary waiting
in ambush. Cain saw nothing—absolutely nothing, the room was
wired against electronic surveillance, but at least no one lurked in
the shadows, technologically or otherwise.

"I know it comes as a surprise, me being here and all," Lester
said, "and that your natural paranoia is perked to new heights with
them taking a run at Francesca, but Cain, are you satisfied enough
that I can put down my hands and we can talk business?"

"Where's your security, Lester?" Cain said, having backed out of
the office, leaving Lester within it, and glancing quickly to ensure
everything was still copacetic for Francesca.

"I can still do this myself, you know," Lester said and dropped
his hands to his hips.

"Yeah, but you don't," Cain said.

"Had to," Lester said. "If we're done with the flattery, I'll explain."

Cain waited another moment, before lowering the hammer on
his pistol and returning it to its holster. Francesca looked over at
the sound and then followed suit. Lester beckoned them into the
office, shutting its strangely heavy door behind them.

"Alright, give me a second," he said, pondering the door's several locks and keypad. "This office belongs to a lawyer; I'm renting
it. Got one of the best counter-surveillance suites in the city, but

only if you put this stupid thing in place in the right order. Here we go." Lester connected the door to the room grid, entered an access code, and the multi-vector, phased-banded ECM apparatus kicked in, with a hum so loud that the inmates could hear it from the walls. "Solid," Lester said with a smile and turned to his guests.

Francesca shook her head and came over to kiss Lester on the cheek. "I am glad to see you," she said, "but why did you come personally? And what was that all about?" she added, looking at Cain over her shoulder.

"He shouldn't be here," Cain said. "Neither one of us has enough money to warrant Lester's personal intervention. The guy that sprung Da Avolo? That guy might have the dough."

"He does," Lester said and chuckled to himself. "As to why I'm here, Francesca, it's to bring you good news, good news, and some bad news."

"Start with the bad news," Cain said.

The office was spacious, uncluttered, yet elegantly appointed. The Louis XVI furniture was accented with contemporary conveniences, such as holographic displays simulating the actual events below them on the street, since the windows had been entirely removed for security reasons. Lester remained standing in the middle of the room, while Francesca settled into one of the client chairs and Cain perched on the edge of the lawyer's desk, his folded arms bringing his hands close to both pistols' grips.

"I'd rather start with the good," Lester said, "as it might dissuade you from shooting your oldest and most trusted friend."

"What's Walker got to do with this?" Cain said deadpan.

"Funny," Lester said.

"Gentlemen," Francesca said, though she did smile. She had only seen the two of them together a few times in the last couple of years, all-but-once off planet. It was on those occasions only that she saw Cain joke with anyone but her; it was more aggressive, less considerate, than the playful teasing they gave to one another, but it was endearing to her nevertheless; it showed to her a side of Cain she otherwise never saw.

"I know—but cannot prove—the identity of the man who pay-rolled Da Avolo," Lester said: "Dietrich Hugo Stinnes."

"Shins?" Cain said.

"*Stinn-es*," Lester said.

Francesca pinched the bridge of her nose for a moment before saying, "He is a, let me think, a German industrialist, money man; a vocal proponent of the seawall, in fact, but opposed to the anti-colonization ruling. Why on earth would Dietrich Stinnes want me dead?"

"I think it all goes back to the seawall," Lester said, brushing back the fall of his trench coat to put his hands in his pockets.

"Hold on to that," Cain said. "Finish telling me why you're here personally."

"He's why," Lester said. "Billionaire, known racist, and no scruples whatever. He's never hanged for it, being smart enough to go through intermediaries, sovereign orbitals, but it's an open secret that outside of Germany, he will do absolutely anything. He's bribed politicians, judges—he bought a parliament once, some poor nation being swallowed by rising sea levels that he wanted to strip-mine. And he doesn't pay cheap. You see the problem? If I had sent any of my people, even my most trusted, I couldn't be sure that he wouldn't bribe them. Except maybe you. So, had to come myself. Me? I'm incorruptible," he added with a smile to Francesca.

A second passed, as a smirk spread across Cain's face, as well, before he pulled off his sunglasses and let out a booming laugh. Francesca looked over, pleasantly astonished.

"I see it now," Cain said. "Didn't you just tell me about how you raided Da Avolo's organization, burned that sucker right down to the ground, after Francesca locked up all his people? Now with this fool Stinnes making the worst mistake of his life, taking a run at her, you're hoping lightning will strike twice and you'll get a shot at seizing all of this asshole's assets, too. Tell me I'm wrong."

"There *may* be a financial incentive in it for me," Lester said and shrugged.

Cain and Francesca shared a look before she laughed, too, and said, "Ah, now it is less surprising to see you here. And I am sure we are all more secure with your presence. So, back to my question: why would Stinnes of all people want to kill me?"

"And how do you know it's him?" Cain added.

"The motive is just speculation," Lester said, "but I think it's the anticorruption provisions in the seawall legislation that's coming up for a vote in the European Parliament next week."

"In ten days," Francesca said absently.

"Ten days," Lester repeated. "Stinnes, though a successful businessman, is only a billionaire and not a big one. Shit, I'm worth more than Stinnes. Thing is, though, he's the de facto leader of a cabal of shady EU billionaires, every bit as criminal as Da Avolo's syndicate, but with better lawyers and a kink for playing at respectability. Racist sons-of-bitches, too: they run scores nearly as much as I do, but they won't hire me or anyone on our side of street, Cain. Hate the brothers.

"Now, individually, they're small, not *that* dangerous. Working together, though, colluding, they can make even Ruud van Hauer or Irrfan Singh take notice. The way I figure it, if they could strip the anticorruption provisions out of the legislation, they could make a bundle off of the seawall."

"And endanger the project altogether," Francesca said. She stood and began pacing the length of the room, between Cain and Lester, unconsciously biting her knuckle. "Enough graft, enough delay, enough budget overruns, and the seawall will never be built. Entire cities will then wash out to sea and the economic strain will push all of Europe toward collapse. Well," she sighed, "the money certainly is a motive. Back to his question for a moment: how do you know it is Stinnes?"

"Traced it back," Lester said. Looking over to his left, he crossed the room to the lawyer's modest liquor cart, held up a crystal decanter toward the other two, which they declined, and then poured himself a snifter of brandy. "Since Da Avolo was involved, I started at the prison. Had Liying go back a couple weeks, grab surveillance of everything from that side of the city, and guess what I found? Nothing. Someone had gone in and blacked out the prison altogether, clear across the lagoon to the mainland, too. No records of anything, including air traffic control."

"And nothing was raised to me, my office?" Francesca asked.

"The AI monitoring it had been adulterated," Lester said. "Not got to, not bribed, which would be in character for Stinnes, but physically altered. My bet is a physical intrusion of the hardware, maybe years in advance. Either way, the AI didn't know to tell anybody anything."

Francesca instinctively reached for her phone, to call her deputy and have the AI fixed, when both Cain and Lester raised their hands toward her. "No, of course I cannot call her," Francesca sighed.

"I've already sent a message," Lester said and chuckled. "They're tearing into it right now. Anyway, with the blackout gobbling up visitor logs at the prison, flight plans, and traffic cams for ground-cars crossing the bridge, I had to cast a wider net. I had to bring in my own AI, and the little bastard ain't cheap, either. You know the one."

"You still working with that thing?" Cain said. To Francesca he added, "Helped—if you want to call it that—when I pulled that score on Paradise."

Lester gestured with both hands and said, "You just tell her everything now?"

Cain shrugged.

"Is there a problem?" Francesca asked and, with her raised eyebrow, dared Lester to say something.

Lester looked at the ceiling for a moment before saying, "Anyway, I had my own AI look at everything beyond the blackout zone and, of course, it was too much, so I narrowed its focus to look only at lawyers, figuring they'd start with an offer, maybe a little haggling, and a lawyer would bring his own cover story. Not surprisingly, there are a hell of a lot of lawyers coming and going from Venice. It was enough to work with, though, and one of the names that the AI flagged was for a lawyer named Hans Frank.

"Now, Hans' name came up shady because he fronts for The Overture Group. It's mostly a law firm, handles venture capital; run off of a sovereign orbital by the same name. They handle a small group of clients and one-timers, take anything ten-mil and up, but ninety-nine percent of their revenue comes from Stinnes and his investments—through them to beat the anti-colonization laws—into their Mars development."

"Ah," Cain said gave Francesca a wink, "a rival to your Arcadia Planitia? Your interest in helping us is becoming clearer by the second."

"Please," Lester sneered. "That little, penny-ante, low-rent, backwater? *Overture Station*, as they call it, is barely three percent of what I've got going on Mars—and is unfinished. They're planning to do some kind of luxury-item manufacturing up there, but they've got no planned amenities for their workers. Good luck getting anyone to emigrate. When I take it from them, I'm going to use it as a prison."

"*You* are going to send people to prison?" Cain said and after an incredulous moment, threw his head back and laughed.

"I know, right?" Lester said and laughed just as uproariously.

Francesca shook her head, smiling at the two of them laughing together, and said, "You two are always laughing at inside jokes that you won't explain."

Lester wiped his eye and said, "Never mind. The point is, The Overture Group is a front for Stinnes and Hans Frank has stooged for him for the past ten years, to my knowledge. If they were involved with busting Da Avolo out of Santa Maria, it was Stinnes calling the shots." Lester drained the last of his brandy from the snifter and then set it aside. "Like I said: I know it, but I can't prove it."

A moment passed before Francesca resumed her pacing, talking through what she had learned as much for her own understanding as to convey her thoughts to the two men. "It makes sense," she said. "If they can pull the anticorruption provisions from the seawall legislation, their companies could reap billions, trillions even, from the EU and member states. Of course, I would not let them do any such thing; I have defeated every champion they have sent to debate the issue and I had planned to be at parliament during the vote, to ensure no last-minute interference would sabotaged the final language.

"So, what do they do? They free Da Avolo and arrange for him to assassinate me, which is perfect because it would not raise any alarms with the voters: they would see my murder as simply the revenge of a criminal whom I had ruined. Then they would bribe and threaten MPs into removing the anticorruption language from the legislation and—of course—do you see? They would remove the anticorruption provisions and tell the voters that they were forced to do so to ensure passage of the legislation, promising to pass the provisions separately, which they would never do, and— the most insidious part—they would claim that it was all to ensure that my death was not in vain, that they were ensuring the passage of the legislation to *memorialize my sacrifice.* Dio mio, they would probably change the law's name to mine!"

Francesca slapped the back of one of the client chairs so forcefully that it tipped over; Cain caught it with his foot and tilted it back into place. He said, "And then, their stooges in either Interpol or the Polizia di Stato would kill Da Avolo, tie up the loose end, or

Stinnes would ship him off to a sovereign orbital, to claim personal responsibility for killing you, keep everyone's eyes off of Stinnes and his cronies as they bled the seawall project dry."

"Which brings me to the bad news," Lester said. "Da Avolo has slipped the leash."

"What?" Francesca said.

"Lester," Cain said, his eyes narrowing.

"Hey, you know that if they want off, they'll get off," Lester said. "They went underground in Milan, to cut the signal, and must have dumped everything electronic before they came back out. That's how I'd do it."

"So, he will continue the hunt now," Francesca sighed.

"Stinnes can probably hire better," Cain said.

"He can," Lester added.

"He'll just have Da Avolo flown in for the kill, take credit," Cain continued. "We knew we'd have to be careful, already. This doesn't change that. And now that we're pretty sure this Stinnes fellow is behind it, I'll go take care of it," he said and stood.

"No, wait," Francesca said. "We cannot just kill him."

"Oh, yes I can," Cain said.

"No, listen," she said and stood directly in front of Cain, tilting her head back to look him in the eyes. "It would ruin me. If you just kill Stinnes, the support for Da Avolo will vanish; then, he will be arrested; without a lawyer from The Overture Group, since Stinnes is no longer there to pay for one, Da Avolo will reveal who helped him and why, because, with Stinnes dead, it would all point back to me. What other revenge would be available to him then?"

Cain sat back against the desk and said, "Then I'll take care of Da Avolo first. He won't tell no tales if he's dead."

"And that would certainly point back to me," Francesca said. "Who would have a more powerful motive than me?

"No, to save my career—and the seawall project—as well as

my life, we need to put Stinnes in prison. Now, I know you suspect Interpol of being corrupted by Stinnes' bribery—and you are probably right, up to a point—but Stinnes is not so wealthy that he could bribe *all* of Interpol. A few investigators, a few clerks, yes, but not everyone. If we can gather sufficient evidence to present to Interpol, implicating Stinnes with Da Avolo's escape and attempted assassination, then they can apply for the warrants that will ultimately reveal Stinnes' complicity, putting him in prison. That will save me, all of me."

"And how are we going to do that?" Cain asked. "Guy's blacked out whole cities to cover his tracks."

"Yes, he has," Francesca said, resuming her pacing. "If what we suspect of his motive is true, however, then it is a bit like insider trading—and can be investigated the same way. Consider, when someone has inside information on a new product or a crop report or a regulatory decision, to turn it to their advantage, they buy stock in the company or commodity or whatever so that when the news event comes to pass, they are already in place to take advantage, to make money."

"Right, so in Stinnes' case," Cain said, "that's what? He wants to make money off of the seawall, so he stockpiles cement?"

"Well, no, actually," Francesca said and turned to smile at Cain. "There is not enough cement in the entire world to supply the project; factories will need to be built. There are, however, specialized barges for sinking pylons, skilled workers, and small companies that have been building local seawalls in areas already ravaged by sea-level rise."

"And you're guessing that Stinnes is already gobbling them up," Lester said, nodding. "Preparing for the passage of the legislation *without* the anticorruption provisions that would stamp out his monopoly."

"Exactly," Francesca said. "With a monopoly, he and his cronies could drive up prices, fail to meet deadlines without consequence, position friends and punish rivals. This is why the provisions exist in the first place."

"And if he has gobbled up all these little companies and specialized equipment before the legislation passes?" Cain asked. "He'd be forced to sell them?"

"Yes," Francesca said, "regardless of profit. It would simply be illegal for him to own them and it would indicate an attempted monopoly, which would bar him and his companies from receiving contracts. He would be shut out.

"So, what we need to do is show that he has taken action that would cause him to lose money if the legislation passes in its current form, but would win him great profits if it passes without the anticorruption provisions. *That* will indicate motive and force Interpol to act."

Francesca spun around and looked at Cain and Lester, a pleased smile on her face.

Cain looked far less pleased as he heaved a sigh and said, "Okay, if that's what it takes, that's what it takes. How do we go about getting this *evidence*?"

"I'll look into his financials," Lester said. "Have Liying hack around, see what she can find, too. There are bound to be some tracks leading somewhere."

"Remember, it has to stand up in court," Francesca said. "So, no breaking in anywhere.

"Meanwhile," she said to Cain, "you and I will go to the places where such specialized resources are in abundance, see if he has acquired any of them."

"And try not to get killed by his assassins while we're doing it," Cain said.

Francesca nodded, saying, "That too."

CHAPTER 7

THE COASTAL CITY of Bremen, Germany, once situated around the Weser River, now hunkered down behind a limited seawall, running from Lemwerder to Oyten, with an inlet of the North Sea growing ever higher just beyond. The land that had once rolled away north, over many miles to the old shoreline, had submerged under permanent flooding, making islands of such places as Wiefelshede and Nordholz. The new archipelago swelled with internal refugees who, alongside the older residents, relied upon ferries to the mainland for access to employment, food, and even to hospitals. However difficult the adjustment had been for the people of northern Germany, leaving their low-lying towns for the hills-turned-islands beyond the wall, they at least still lived life as they had always known it. The same could not be said of the external refugees that daily poured into the city's outskirts.

Southwest of the seawall, in what had been the wealthy suburbs of Bremen, permanent flooding had condemned street after street of rowhouse and individual homes to abandonment and decay. Into these failing structures—a few of which would succumb each week to the softening earth beneath them and collapse—refugees had come to squat, surviving on whatever they had brought or could receive in charity, to wait for the passage of Francesca's law and the many jobs that it would create. At the far end of one such almost-abandoned town, an enclosed dock had been built by the company that had erected the seawall that had saved the rest of Bremen. It was toward this dock, often wading through calf-high water, that Francesca and Cain headed.

"What are we hoping to find here?" Cain asked, his dark clothes making him almost invisible in the unelectrified, if not entirely abandoned, former city. His AR sunglasses in nightvision mode detected a few meager LEDs behind otherwise darkened windows, the heat of bodies behind walls, and every so often the screen of someone's phone. His head was on a swivel as he led Francesca through the flooded street, reminded of his onetime home of Redhook, Brooklyn, and remembering what desperate people may be driven to do. He spoke sotto voce, relying on his earbuds to pick up and transmit his voice to Francesca. "What would count as evidence that Stinnes had bought this company, preparing for a law without the anticorruption provisions in it?"

"This is the largest storage area for equipment of this type in Bremen," Francesca said. Like Cain, she kept a constant lookout on the buildings that they passed, unusually aware of the pistol under her left arm. When the TAV had dropped them off a half-mile from their objective, she had first felt a new closeness to Cain, seeing him perform the work about which she had heard so many stories. As they plunged deeper into that dark, almost-abandoned city, the potential for danger—danger beyond the assassins that she knew hunted her—incited a queasy fear that she could not entirely suppress. Accepting that it was there to keep her alert, regardless of its unpleasantness, she pressed on and focused. "It is also the only such storage area that is enclosed, so satellites would not be able to detect if the company were to stockpile unnecessary equipment. If we can draw close enough to look inside, we may find new, additional machines for driving pylons and building footers, which would provide Interpol with probable cause."

"Because why would they have them," Cain said, holding up a hand for her to halt, as he passed just his shoulder, with its surveillance node, around the corner of a building that they would need to pass, "if the legislation prohibited monopolies?"

"Exactly," Francesca said as they resumed their course. "I expect to find cranes and similar devices piled onto the barges that the company already owns, so many cranes that the barges become useless. Barges are not in short supply and easy to fabricate, but the cranes, they are expensive, timely to build, and only a few suppliers could deliver them, so stockpiling them is crucial to forming the monopoly Stinnes and his cabal hope to form. Once the legislation passes without the anticorruption provisions, then they will bring in the new barges, distribute the cranes, and begin to snap up contracts. If I can take just a few photos through the windows of that enclosed dock, it should be all we need."

They came to an improvised boardwalk, which meandered through rows of houses before turning off what had been a main street and down an alleyway. Somewhere beyond, where a parallel street had once run, an argument between a shouting voice and a crying one could be heard, echoing through houses both empty and occupied. Between the row of homes, Francesca saw an outhouse and recoiled at the filth through which they would be required to walk to reach the dock. It struck her then that the flooding had not merely covered the streets, it had also swamped the utilities, the sewer lines, and electrical tunnels. The people living there now did what they had to do, lacking alternatives.

"It is sad to think," she said to Cain, briefly taking his hand as they walked along, "that the desperate people living here came from somewhere worse."

Cain squeezed her hand and then let it drop. "I know you feel for them," he said, "but let's keep our eyes open, anyway, try to keep out of their sight. They may be desperate enough to do something stupid, which we can handle, but just in case Lester is wrong about how racist Stinnes is, there could be a mole of his hiding among the squatters and I don't want them dropping a dime on us, call in a hit team."

"But why would he place a spy here?" she asked. "He would have to know our plan and that we suspect him, to think to monitor such a place."

"Best to plan for capabilities," Cain said, edging around the next corner, "rather than possibilities. Worst thing that happens if we keep out of sight, move cautious, is that we spend a little more time in this charming suburb: if we don't spend that time and Stinnes did put a lookout in among the squatters, then here come the assassins. Dig?"

"I dig," Francesca said and smiled.

They continued on, careful to move slowly enough that the sounds of their passage through the water did not reach the refugees. The few lights that the squatters had to enjoy soon faded, as Cain and Francesca left their streets, and the water began to rise to their knees. Even within the green of nightvision, the night seemed to darken as they approached the newest arm of the North Sea. Cain continued to precede Francesca by a pace ahead, checking each cross-street to which they came. Just as she was becoming accustomed to his periodic pauses, he raised his hand in signal, *freeze*, and then waved her back against a wall.

He stood leaning for a moment, with the edge of one shoulder just past the corner of the house against which they took cover, his coat's surveillance node taking in the alley and whatever it was that had alarmed him, before Cain turned to Francesca and said, "Drone."

She quickly shushed him, shocked that he would use a normal speaking voice so close to a drone.

"No, it's okay," he said. "It's an intermediate autonomous drone; probably a Prometheus power cell, but no CasiDrive. It's running on airfoils, too loud for audio detection. Turn up your earbuds' enhancement; you'll hear it."

Francesca slipped a hand into her jacket, to her new phone, and cautiously increased the auditory enhancement provided by the linked earbuds. The app running the enhancement detected what she was after and raised its volume while leaving everything else at normal levels, to avoid overloading her with inputs. It was unmistakable, afterward; a heavy drone, probably the size of a refrigerator held aloft by a Yahata EDF airfoil, patrolled the area a few blocks from the enclosed dock.

"What is it doing here?" she asked, still whispering.

"Patrolling the dock," he offered, "or looking for us or something else entirely. Can't know. Could be some other score is going down tonight, got nothing to do with us: could be Stinnes has guessed our game and has dropped a few hundred of those suckers around all his prepositioned assets, trying to find us and call in a strike. Doesn't matter, really. We have to operate under the assumption that it's our problem."

"Yes, that is sensible," she said. "So, should we simply avoid it or try to locate whoever is operating it?"

Cain looked over, a little surprised at how quickly she was taking to the possibility of airing out a drone operator hiding in a nearby building, before saying, "Probably controlled from orbit; sovereign orbital would be my guess. Stinnes has gone to a lot of trouble to keep us from tracing his scores back to him; an operator on the ground would be a risk he doesn't need to take, not until he knows where we are and can send in the assassins.

"We'll just have to avoid them, on our way to the dock.

Shouldn't be too hard, since we can hear them but they can't hear us. Just have to keep a building between us. Let's see if Liying can get their number."

Cain tapped the network icon on his phone, to relink to the session with Liying, which they had done at stages since preparing to leave Monaco. Lester's ace hacker had cleared the way for them by suppressing surveillance, forging flight plans, and generally pacifying the electronic landscape between them and their objective. She was not getting a lot of sleep up in Pons Sublicius, on call for Cain and Francesca *and* for Lester, as he poured over reams of financial data on Stinnes and The Overture Group. She answered Cain's call with a yawn.

"Yes, it is me," Liying said, a little pitifully.

"Oh, poor woman," Francesca said. "You sound so tired, Liying."

"It's okay," Liying said. "After you finish in Bremen, I'll get three hours sleep."

"That makes me feel awful," Francesca said. "Is there no one else that can help us or Lester? You need your rest."

"No, it's fine, really," Liying said, sounding a little more awake as they talked.

"If I can just interrupt here for a second," Cain said. "Liying, we've got a drone down here, intermediate autonomous. Can you take a look?"

"Yes," Liying said. "One moment." Cain and Francesca stood in the freezing water, their sodden shoes and clinging trousers growing colder with their inaction, as Liying brought several satellites into play, to gain visual and informational perception over Bremen. "There," she said. "Yes, an AugsRak Falcon. Autonomous mode, no continuous feed. Probably, they have it set to connect to a third-party satellite if it picks up anything. If you stay out of sight, it should be fine."

"How many are there?" Cain asked.

"Six," Liying said. "Algorithmic patrol pattern, so be careful. I could take them offline for you, if you want."

"No, better not to," Cain said. "If we take them out, Stinnes will know we've been here. I'd rather keep him in the dark as much as possible."

"That is wise," Liying said.

"We'll see," Cain said. "How quickly could you shut them down, though, if we need it?"

"I can force them into standby mode," Liying said, "in maybe ten seconds? But you will need at least that long to reestablish your link to the network: you cannot maintain communication or the drone will detect your signal. AugsRak Falcons have broadband EM detection."

"Wonderful," Francesca said.

"Good to know," Cain said. "Okay, Liying, thanks. We're going offline now. If I need you to crash the drones, I'll be in touch."

Cain then shut down their link to the secure network and both he and Francesca manually disabled their phones' transmitters. It made them less vulnerable to the drones' detection suite, but it also isolated them from each other. Their only solace was to run long, thin wires from their phones to their AR sunglasses, earbuds, and surveillance nodes, to retain their capabilities through hardwire rather than remote connectivity.

Cain could see Francesca take a deep breath after their comms cut out. He said, "Jack up the voice volume on your earbuds; we'll still be able to talk to each other, at a whisper, within a couple dozen feet. Now, listen, this is going to be a cakewalk. We know where they are, they don't know where we are. We just got to keep a building between us and them and we'll slip on in there, take a few pics, and then slip right on out again."

Ethos of Cain

"Simple," Francesca said and took a deep breath, smiling for a moment at her own heightened anxiety. "Let's go."

Locating the drones by sound proved more difficult than anticipated, with the whirring exhaust from their airfoils echoing eerily off of wood and water. Cain and Francesca splashed down a long alley between rows of houses, paused at an intersecting street, and then listened. They ducked down an alleyway when the nearest drone crossed behind them, waiting for the sound to modulate as it bounced off of houses farther down the street, and then took off. Every sprint to their next listening place deafened them, hiding the drones' exhaust from them under a blanket of splashing noise; then they came to a halt and the almost placid hum of their adversaries would come to them. In Francesca's mind, it was almost like living out a chess match, visualizing the positions of the drones, Stinnes' pieces, and where they would be in their next move. Almost it was exhilarating to evade them. Almost it held the fun of a childhood game.

"Wer ist da?" a voice then shouted, a block or two from them. "Ich kann Dich hören."

Francesca spoke only a little German and Cain none at all; their phones' apps, however, could render speech to text through a translator and the irate voice's words appeared in a scrolling line at the top of their AR sunglasses: *Who is there? I can hear you.*

Cain pulled Francesca to him by the lapel of her jacket and whispered into her ear, "Guard. Probably here to keep the migrants off the dock, away from their gear."

"We must be close," Francesca whispered back, coming up on her toes to reach Cain's ear as he hunched over. "But why employ a guard *and* drones? Is he not suspicious of them?"

"Wenn ich dich finde," the guard growled, "erschieße ich dich."

"We'll have to figure it out later," Cain whispered. "Fritz got

267

a gun, apparently. Listen, I'm going to lead him off that way, you continue on, get your pictures of the dock. Remember the drones."

"Remember the gun," Francesca whispered back. "Be careful."

After a quick squeeze of the hand, they separated, Cain splashing away toward the new North Sea estuary while Francesca moved more cautiously, more quietly toward the enclosed dock. The guard did not want to stray too far from his charge, however, and would not follow Cain out into the erstwhile suburb; instead, he moved along the long row of houses, peering down their alleyways, and shouting abuse. The drones, while unable to locate Cain or Francesca, did detect the guard's odd behavior and tightened their search pattern.

Francesca could hear one flying at treetop level, crossing over the top of houses rather than down streets as they had up to that point; it made them easier to hear but harder to evade. With no cross-street to duck down and a drone about to fly directly over her, a drone that may very well have been armed in addition to carrying a camera and transmitter, she had no choice but to find alternative cover. The house she passed was swamped to the windows, the sill buckling from the moisture. Knocking against it with her hip and then shaking it with both hands, Francesca separated the lock from the sodden wood, lifted it, and then stepped through—just as the drone glided overhead. She stepped down into a sunken living room, now a pool of stagnate and stinking water that came to her waist, and quickly lowered the damaged window back into place. In a moment, she was chilled to the point of chattering teeth and numbing feet. She stood rubbing her hands together as she waited for the sound of the drone to change again, for another house to block its line of sight to her, to press on.

On Cain's part, he could hear the drones swarming in toward the agitated guard and found himself all-but leaping from stride to stride, to outpace him as he sidled down an elevated walkway surrounding the dock. Judging by the taunts scrolling across the top of his sunglasses, Cain guessed that the migrants occasionally tried to sneak into the dock, to rummage for whatever food or other supplies they could find, and that the guard was not shy about deterring them with gunfire. The guard's allusions to rat's nests and eating garbage made his opinion of migrants—and of brown people in general—entirely clear. Cain had no time even to ignore such ignorance, with the drones circling ever closer; he knew the wise course was to withdraw, find a place to hunker down, but if he lost the guard's interest, the man might turn back toward where Francesca was beginning her infiltration. Cain splashed down a side street, instead, drawing closer to the dock and causing the guard to rush in that direction.

Even with his daily exercise over the last twenty-plus years, with his prodigious natural strength and athleticism, the disadvantage of sloshing through knee-deep water while the guard ran down a boardwalk eventually caught up with Cain. He found himself in an alley between two houses, the skeleton of a child's play equipment to one side and an open street to the other. From the curses and promises of death, the guard was on the other side of the house, charging to either end, erratic in his fury. Worse, a drone was speeding down the street, its turreted camera no-doubt looking down ever cross-street and alleyway: if it took a picture of Cain, even if it did not open up with a machine gun, word would reach Stinnes in seconds that Francesca's *African mercenary*, as Da Avolo had described him, was in Bremen. A hit team would be on the ground in two minutes. No time to escape.

With his options quickly expiring, Cain looked one way and then another—and then straight up. The overhanging eave of the house behind him was two-stories high: Cain braced a foot against the wall of one house and then jumped with the other, pushing off with his braced foot to fly across the alleyway; catching himself with the other foot on the other house's wall, he pushed off again, before gravity could drag him back to earth, and sailed back to the first house. Back and forth he leaped, twice more, until he reached the overhanging eave, his powerful hands digging his fingers into the wood. For a moment, he hung suspended from the roof, the drone seconds away from discovering him, and then he drew up his legs in a hanging sit-up before flinging them backward. His heels found the wood of one of the roof joists and he pressed against them with his feet as his hands pressed against the other joist from which he had hung. Friction and strength held Cain aloft, parallel to the ground, concealed by the overhanging roof as the drone roared slowly by.

On the other side of the enclosed dock, Francesca waited for the drones to depart, hunting for Cain, and then raised the window and stepped through. She closed it with numb fingers, thinking it best to leave no sign of her passage, and then hurried off toward the dock, careful not to make too much noise in the murky water. The sound of the guard shouting abuse came to her through her enhanced hearing and a little warmth found its way to her face, if not to her extremities. She knew that Cain would not grant such a little man a moment's consideration, the guard's filthy talk amounting to no more than the barking of a dog, but for Francesca, to hear insults hurled at someone she admired and loved, it was nearly too much to bear. She had to exert an effort not to discard her objective, her struggle to regain her life, and to simply stamp down the boardwalk and shoot the guard. Her self-control proved stronger than her fury and she instead circled the dock, a block out and in the other direction, before charging across a sunken lawn to the elevated boardwalk.

The enclosed dock was huge, five-stories tall to accommodate the cranes, and a full hundred-meters long. One of the first assignments for the newly formed company that had built the seawall was to drive pylons down to the bedrock beneath the rising water, upon which the dock was built. As such, Francesca had to pull herself up onto the boardwalk, which was several feet above the waterline, and the stain that she left alarmed her as soon as she stood.

"Dio mio," she growled to herself, slapping her sodden thigh.

There was no time to worry and no way to erase the sign of her being there. She leaped forward to the nearest window, instead, and drove a hand into her jacket, to her phone, and began taking photos through her AR sunglasses.

Ten minutes later, after a damp but much-needed embrace, Cain and Francesca ran along the migrants' boardwalk, out of Bremen's suburbs.

"So, did you get the pictures?" Cain asked, his head again on a swivel, wary of the stupidity of the desperate.

"I did," Francesca said, "but they are useless. If ever that dock held an unusual amount of equipment, it has been returned to a normal state. Oh, I do not know. Perhaps this simply is not one of Stinnes' holdings or he had anticipated us, as with the drones."

"Or he's keeping the cranes and all somewhere less obvious," Cain said, "somewhere we wouldn't know to look."

"It is possible," Francesca said. "It would be smarter, certainly. Regardless, we have lost this match. We have spent the time, of which we have little, and have nothing to offer Interpol in the way of probable cause."

"We only need to find something once," Cain said. "One bit of probably cause and it's all over. Anyway, maybe Lester's found something in the financials."

CHAPTER 8

FOR DAYS, CAIN and Francesca scoured the coast of the North Sea, from the Netherlands to Denmark, travelling by TAV, train, or ground-car, circling back to a country they had just investigated or jumping ahead, skipping the next country in line, and pressing their enquiries first during the day and then at night, anything to avoid a life-threatening pattern. They visited the motor pools of construction companies and the manufacturers that supplied them, looking for newly made or stockpiled vehicles: nothing, no more equipment than what they would expect to find, no heightened output of new units. They went to areas already ravaged by rising sea levels, to investigate the companies building the limited seawalls for member states, hoping to find excess labor, unofficially on standby, awaiting the passage of an easily corruptible law: what they found were labor shortages, skilled workers followed around by packs of apprentices, as their companies tried to hold back the sea, even without the support of the omnibus legislation; no one was idle. They next turned to less obvious preparations, the supporting agencies that would be needed to stand up a grinding monopoly, companies providing food services, temporary and mobile housing, and health maintenance, companies that were up and running but not operating at full capacity, awaiting the adulterated legislation: what they found was business as usual.

They were running out of time and they knew it. Every day was a resource, a resource that was quickly dwindling, as the vote in the European Parliament drew ever closer. If neither they nor Lester could uncover how Stinnes planned to take advantage of the removal of the anticorruption provisions before the vote began, Francesca could not attend, could not be there to defend the law to the last second, so that it might achieve its goal and hold back the sea—not without risking the inevitable snipers that would await her if she tried.

Bistrot Bellissima was one of the best Italian restaurants in Prague, with a view of the Manes Bridge out one set of windows and the Church of Our Lady before Týn out another, its spires rising above the city. The food was Michelin rated, the décor elegant, the clientele old-money. Da Avolo had demanded the largest table and then packed it with his newly formed crew, all well-dressed and unabashedly obnoxious. Leone and Teglia, his trusted lieutenants from the old days, glared at anyone bold enough to raise an eyebrow at their boisterousness. The other diners, those hanging on and attempting to ignore or those hurrying through their meals, looked up with undisguised hope when a severe younger man came striding across the dining room and leaned down to speak confidentially into the ringleader's ear. They thought perhaps the local gendarmerie had finally been summoned.

"Stand up when you talk to me," Da Avolo said, wrinkling his nose as he leaned away from Hans Frank, Stinnes' trusted lawyer from The Overture Group. To his crew, Da Avolo said, "Germans: it's like bringing a dog with you."

After patiently waiting for the guffaws to run their course, Hans said, "We are not pleased with this brazenly public tour you have taken, daring the authorities to apprehend you. You should be searching for your quarry."

"That's a job for an AI," Da Avolo said around a mouthful of linguini. He wiped his mouth with a napkin and shook his head at Hans. "Or it is now, anyway. You should have known about this African merc she's been playing around with. One of the turncoats told us about him: hot stuff, dangerous, a pro's pro. If you had told me about this guy, I would have guessed that he had set up some contingencies, some backup plans for if everything blew up. But no, you didn't think you needed to tell me a thing, did you, Hans? That fuck Carlo told me that you bastards thought she had thrown him out!"

"She had," Hans said, almost raising his voice. "Or so it had seemed at the time. There had been no phone traffic between them for a month. This is why we had timed the intrusion when we did, to avoid the unnecessary complication."

"And blew it," Da Avolo said and then told Leone to order espresso for the table. "Too fancy, that plan," he told Hans and then finished off his linguini. "You want to eat? This place ain't bad; these people are from the old country, know how to do things right. Just like me. You don't need fancy: you need good. So, you just put your resources into finding that bitch, capiche? Then you call me and I'll go in and whack her the fuck out. Nothing fancy, just straight at her and boom. Until then, I'll wait and enjoy myself while I'm waiting. This is how it's done, how men live. So, just find her and then call me. I'll do the rest."

"We have resources for that, as well," Hans mumbled and strode off.

Despite their haste and flagging confidence in finding the evidence that they needed for Interpol, Cain and Francesca still had to eat.

Which is why, whenever they stopped for a few hours' sleep, Cain would cook them a meal; safer than risking a restaurant. The natural-foods grocery store may have seemed a less-obvious place for assassins, but that is exactly why it made an attack more likely. Thus, they both took pains to keep a constant watch on their surroundings, with Liying always in the background keeping them out of the camera's eye, as they strolled the aisles, gathered ingredients, and found it increasingly difficult not to forget their circumstances and enjoy these simple moments together.

"So, this is where all of the food is kept before someone turns it into dinner," Francesca said, looking pointedly into the basket Cain carried. "Fascinating."

"You must have been to a supermarket before," he said, chuckling silently.

"Is that what this place is called?" she said innocently. "It is like the community's stockpile—the only stockpile we have managed to find, sadly."

"How is it that someone as independent as you," he said, unearthing an unwilted chard, "never learned to make dinner for herself?"

Feigning confusion, she said, "I'm not following you. The palazzo came with a cook."

"Before you were mayor," he said. "You never went to the kitchen, used that square thing, gets hot when you turn the knobs, colloquially known as an oven?"

"Why would I need an oven," she said, "when I have all of these food delivery apps on my phone?"

Cain ducked his head and tried to laugh softly enough to avoid alarming the entire store, as Francesca leaned over to look him in the face, enjoying the rare sight of him smiling. "Fair enough," he said. "I guess once this is all over and your career takes you to Brussels—"

"You are *so* sure," she said, coming up on her toes to smile ruefully an inch from his lips.

"—I better move in, too, just to make sure you're eating something that didn't come out of a cardboard box, once in a while," he continued.

Francesca smiled with pleasure, now, and took his arm in hers, wrapping the limb wider than her waist in a cuddling embrace, before saying, "Oh are we—what is the American phrase? *Shacking up?*"

"If you want to," Cain said, taking his turn at looking into her smiling face.

"Let me taste your cooking first," she said and they both laughed. "You do not have to rush, you know? Not on my account. Of course, you know that I want you with me always, at all times, never a night apart. But, it is so very much, all at once, with you stepping back from taking scores," she said, whispering the last phrase before pressing on, "starting your consulting business; it is all change, a great deal of change. If you wanted to keep your apartment and then visit me in mine—if this thing you think is so certain should happen—well, I could stand it. I would not want you to be unhappy and there is time. We will make sure there is time."

Cain leaned over to kiss the top of her head and then said, "Probably won't be able to afford Achilles Orbital once I'm consulting. No way it pays that good. Anyway, change doesn't bother me. I see no reason for us to go on living apart, if you want me around night and day."

"I do," she said.

"So, we'll do it," he said. "Change is good, but this is hardly change at all, anyway. Just choosing the right tool for the job and executing."

"Oh, very nice," she said and stepped away in a faux huff. "So, I am a *job* now?"

"Boy, are you ever," he said and then chuckled and held an arm out for her to slap when she came back to him.

"Such affectionate conversation for me," she said, unable to restrain her smile, "before lavishing me with this romantic dinner you are preparing. I am so lucky."

"A job," he said and put his arm around her, "at which I intend to work very hard, day and night, for the rest of my life."

CHAPTER 9

ESBJERG, DENMARK, WAS a port town that had largely adapted to rising sea levels, raising the height of their facilities with the tide. Seawalls had been built, as well, to stave off the water encroaching on the town's business sector and much, though not all, of the residential sectors. It was like many towns along the North Sea coast, in that respect, separating the *Haves* and *Have-nots* by the possession of a wall. What interested Francesca about Esbjerg was less its looming social crisis or successful climate adaption, but its company, Skjoldmur Inc., which had built the limited seawalls now protecting part of the town. She had a new idea about how Stinnes might orchestrate his monopoly and needed to interrogate Skjoldmur's CEO, Lars Sørensen.

The train up from Hamburg would take hours longer than a quick buzz over in a TAV, which Cain hoped would make it a less likely target for Stinnes' spies. Or Da Avolo. They used a stateroom, as much for concealment as for comfort, while Liying followed them from orbit, turning cameras at the last second and erasing any possible electronic track that they may have left during their journey. At Esbjerg, they waited until the station was as full as it would be with departing passengers, before blending into the crowd, eyes darting over every face, peering into every corner of the stately old brick station.

"An assassin could be two feet from me and I would not know it," Francesca growled, sotto voce, her earbuds transmitting her voice to Cain.

"I would," he said absently, appearing to take no notice of the crowd as he noticed each individual, ruling them in or out as possibilities and directing his and Francesca's course accordingly.

Once outside, with the last vestiges of daylight slipping into the sea, Cain and Francesca slipped off to one side, away from the crowd, to orient themselves before moving toward their destination.

"Huh," Cain said. "There are no skyscrapers—there are no buildings over four stories. These people afraid of heights or something?"

Francesca stifled a laugh and gave him a gentle shove with her shoulder, saying, "You are so cosmopolitan. There is a whole world outside of your mega-cities, much of it beautiful or quaint like this place."

"It's no Venice, huh?" he said, glancing at her self-satisfied smile for a moment. "Anyway, I like skyscrapers. They tend to have windows that don't open and are hard to cut through; makes life harder for any would-be snipers. These low buildings? Might as well be walking through a damn jungle, much as we'll be able to see."

"They would have to know that we were coming here," Francesca said as they headed off, both inconspicuously looking at the rooftops and doorways they passed, eyes and AR overlays alert for open windows on that cool night, "in order to send assassins in ahead of us."

"Like Bremen," Cain said, "and the three other places where we narrowly avoided opposition."

"But there were just as many places where we saw no one," she said.

"Yeah, but in those places," he said, "you hadn't *called ahead* before we arrived."

"Because simply looking at equipment and personnel has not worked," she said, feigning to look into a shop window, eying the sidewalk behind them before moving on. "So, we will talk to the head of this company, see if any overtures have been made to him. And, anyway, I made the appointment for *Wednesday*, this is *Monday*."

"It was me?" Cain said. "I'd have put a spotter on this Lars dude the moment the call lit up, follow him around, see if my opponent puts any assets in play that I might need to eliminate before the hit."

"That assumes that they were even tapping Sørensen's phone," she said. "Speaking of which, Liying, are you there?"

Liying was there, in Pons Sublicius, weary and a little dazed from living on nothing but caffeine and inari; she kept the volume on Cain's network set low enough so it would not distract her from the financial sifting she did for Lester, until either Cain or Francesca said her name, at which point the program would automatically raise the volume and ping an alert to her screen.

"Yes, I am here," Liying said.

"Is Lars Sørensen at his home?" Francesca asked. "Can you send us directions?"

"He is, let me see," Liying said, "not at home. He is in an apartment on the other side of town. I am sending you waypoints now." The address then crawled along the top of both Cain and Francesca's AR sunglasses, while a small map populated in their peripheral vision, with a red line leading to the apartment building. "Hmm, it is very open in this city, little concealment, dangerous."

"I know," Cain said, liking it less and less.

"And this side of town will flood at high tide, too," Liying continued, "so, be careful."

The quaintness Francesca had noticed upon their arrival faded as they walked, leaving the bustling business sector and passing through an invisible barrier into the have-not side of town. At first, it was only a feeling that something had changed, then there was a smell. A mark could soon be seen on the sides of buildings, as they came closer to the sea, a mark made by the tide when it flooded the streets. In a dying bush, Francesca saw seaweed tangled in its limbs; on the walls of that otherwise immaculate town, Cain saw a flash of graffiti, in Danish, more than a tagger's mark, a slogan of some sort. Their neighborhood was rotting to death and they knew it.

"Reminds me of Redhook," Cain mumbled.

"Where you grew up?" Francesca asked, eyes darting down every side-street they passed.

"Yeah," he said. "It started out like this: tide kept rising, flooding the streets, leaving a stink behind when it ran back out. People started rushing out, grab up the fish and jellyfish that got caught; some people even put out nets. Probably got cancer, eating that fish. Then the buildings started to collapse and pretty soon, whole neighborhoods were abandoned. Just about all of Redhook is underwater now. This place will be, too, if we don't get your law passed and wall built."

"Yes," she said. "Though, the town could wall off this neighborhood, too, like they have done for their port. Why haven't they?"

"Five letters," he said.

"Five letters?" she repeated. "Oh, in English. M-O-N-E-Y."

The apartment building where Liying had located Sørensen was a squat, wide brick edifice, with a tiny garden filled with dead plants and a loam-green ring running around the entire building. Cain steered them down an adjacent street, to avoid the front door and its lobby; one less camera for Liying to disable. Instead, they went through a rear entrance, used primarily for maintenance workers and furniture movers. Cain found no alarm on the steel double-doors and so he bypassed the lock with an old B&E trick, slipping a knife blade between the doors and prying them slightly apart, creating enough space to slip a second knife blade in behind the door ward, to trip it from the other side. That accomplished and the two small knives back in their hiding places, Cain and Francesca ascended the back stairs up to the apartment Sørensen was visiting.

Cautiously opening the door to the fourth-floor corridor, they found the interior simple but clean, with no one waiting for them or hanging around unnecessarily. The building felt half-empty, as they walked softly through, only hearing music coming from a single apartment. At the door behind which they expected to find Lars Sørensen, Cain put his back to the wall, keeping out of the sight of anyone looking through the peephole and keeping an eye on the corridor back to the stairwell. Francesca waited until he was in position before knocking.

At first, there was no answer and no sound of anyone on the other side of the door.

"Liying, is he in there?" Francesca asked sotto voce.

"He is," Liying said. "Or at least his phone is."

Francesca knocked again and this time she and Cain heard the rustling of fabric coming from within the apartment. A woman's voice then called out, asking who it was and saying she needed a moment. Cain turned back to Francesca, smiling wolfishly.

"We interrupting," he said. "I'm guessing ol'Lars ain't visiting *with his wife.*"

"Oh my," Francesca said.

The door then opened a crack, catching against its chain, and a tall, pale-skinned and fair-haired woman appeared, wearing a dressing gown and a perturbed expression. "I do not know you," she said. "What do you want?"

"My name is Francesca," Francesca said, keeping her voice low enough not to carry down the hallway, "and I am here to speak with Lars Sørensen. He is expecting me, only not today. Please, I know it is an inconvenient hour, but it is important. I would appreciate your *discretion*," she added pointedly. "May I come in?"

The woman bit her lip for a moment, clearly understanding what was surmised and what was offered. Finally, she nodded and closed the door enough to slip off the chain. As soon as Cain heard that unmistakable sound, he pushed past Francesca and into the apartment, his silenced .45 auto coming up. He pushed the woman against the wall, firmly but without hurting her, and held the muzzle an inch from her forehead; her eyes sprung open and she gaped silently at the sudden intrusion of a huge, armed man.

"Gun out," he said softly to Francesca. "Cover her."

Francesca, also wide-eyed, did as she was asked, entering the apartment, closing the door, and pulling her pistol. To the woman, she said, "I am so sorry; this is a necessary security precaution and will be over momentarily. Please accept my apology."

Cain had already stormed the front room, cleared the kitchenette, and then burst into the bedroom. Lars Sørensen possessed enough composure not to cry out, though he did freeze in the act of buckling his belt, when Cain rushed in carrying a gun.

"Oh, I, uh," Sørensen stammered, "who are you? What do you want?"

Cain lifted the bed with one hand and then slid open the closet door, before holstering his pistol and turning to Sørensen: "I'm, uh, the mayor's security," he said. Waiving toward the front room, he said, "Let's go."

"Clear," Cain said to Francesca, seemingly unaffected by her or the woman's shocked expressions, as he left the bedroom and walked over to the window overlooking the street, to stand a foot away from it, in a shadow cast by the streetlights below.

Francesca holstered her pistol and turned to Sørensen, her pale skin blushing pink right up to her hairline. "I am terribly sorry, Mr. Sørensen. I am Francesca Pieralisi."

"The Mayor of Venice," Lars cried, "of course. We were scheduled to meet this Wednesday; what is the meaning of this?"

"I can only apologize for what must be a disconcerting intrusion," Francesca said as the woman who had answered the door slipped around her, giving her as much space as the small apartment allowed, and ran over to stand behind Sørensen. "As you have probably seen in the news, there was an attempt on my life last week—"

"Oh god!" the woman gasped.

"—and I thought it would be safer to arrive unexpectedly," Francesca concluded. "I did not intend to intrude upon your engagement, it just seemed the safest course of action for all of us."

Lars looked briefly at the woman behind him, blushing a bit himself and not knowing quite what to do with the clothes he had carried in from the bedroom. He nodded and said, "Yes, of course. I understand. Quite sensible. This is my friend, Brigitte. Please," he said and motioned toward a chair before he and Brigitte sat on the sofa opposite.

"Thank you for understanding," Francesca said. "I know this question will sound strange, but have you agreed or been approached about an agreement to either sell your company or bind it to an exclusive, unpublished contract, to come into effect upon the passage of the omnibus seawall legislation?"

"I beg your pardon?" Lars said. "Mayor Pieralisi, I agreed to speak with you about Esbjerg's seawall situation, not delve into the particulars of my company's contracts—particularly anything confidential."

"Mr. Sørensen, please," Francesca said. "We think that the attempt on my life is linked to a secret campaign to weaken the anticorruption provisions in the upcoming omnibus seawall legislation. If someone were to preposition assets to take advantage of the legislation passing *without* those provisions, assets such as your company, it would indicate motive, that they knew the provisions would be stripped before passage."

"I see," Lars said, seeming to notice the bundle of clothes in his arms and impatiently setting them aside before sitting back.

"Of course," Brigitte said, crossing her legs so that they no longer touched Lars's. "The wealthy and the corporations want to squeeze more money out of people like me, while I live here and the waves come in ever higher, year after year."

"Brigitte," Lars said, glancing over at her, a longstanding argument recapitulated with a look, before returning to Francesca. "I understand now, and I am very sorry for your predicament, but no such contract exists. At least, not for Skjoldmur, Inc."

"Were you ever approached to form such an exclusive deal?" Francesca asked. "Or, perhaps, to sell a large portion of your equipment? Maybe under certain economic triggers?"

"No, nothing like that," Lars said. "I am rarely approached for anything other than building seawalls, these days. And as for equipment, I have all that I need and have no immediate plans to expand. I admit to having reached out to the company that built our cranes, to see about costs for buying additional units, but I imagine everyone remotely connected to construction is doing that now, awaiting your law's passage. It will be such a boon for business!"

"Yes, for business," Brigette said. "You will become even wealthier than you are now."

"Oh, Brigette," Lars sighed impatiently. "When Mayor Pieralisi's law passes, a seawall will be built to finally protect this side of town. Your neighborhood will return. Things are about to improve. Smile."

"Assuming the law passes intact," Francesca said. "To return to my original questions, what about your company's debt? Has it been purchased lately—or the banks that hold it?"

"No, not that I know of," Lars said.

Francesca shook her head and then looked over at Cain, to ask, "What is going on here?"

"At the moment," Cain said, "we're about to get hit."

Across the street, a TAV swooped down to the opposite rooftop, its side cargo door open, and two men, one armed with a long, suppressed rifle, jumped out. On the street below, a black ground-car, a van without windows, came screeching to a halt, blocking the road, and a half-dozen men piled out. All appeared to be Italian, none appeared overly concerned with concealing the shotguns and submachine guns that they carried under their long coats.

"Hit team just arrived," Cain said. "Stay below the window and let's get out of here. You two should come with us," he said to Lars and Brigette, as he led the way to the door: "they find you here, they may kill you to avoid witnesses—or to scare MPs ahead of the vote."

They needed no more convincing than the pistols that appeared in both of their guests' hands and the memory of the news coverage of the massacre at Francesca's palazzo in Venice. Out in the corridor, Cain led them at a run to the stairwell down to the rear entrance; as they entered, they could hear the elevators rumbling up in the adjacent shaft. Cain took the stairs three-at-a-time, pulling ahead of the others and forcing them into a gallop to catch up; he wanted to reach the exit door first.

At the ground floor, Cain hit the double-doors with his shoulder, hard enough to break the ward holding them together, and sailed through, rolling as he did to land on his back. His aggressive exit startled the man who had been sent around back to cover the possible escape route, buying Cain enough time to evacuate his skull with a single shot. By the time Francesca led the other two out of the building, Cain had come up on a knee and swept the parking lot: no one.

"Oh my god," Brigette cried when she saw the dead man

sprawled against the wall, a short, black shotgun an inch from his hand. Lars's already white skin bleached to nearly transparent as the blood ran out of it.

"Shut up," Cain demanded in a harsh growl. "We don't want them to hear us. Now, come on."

Crossing the parking lot as quickly as Brigette's slippers allowed, they turned down the wide, vehicle-accessible alleyway that ran between rows of buildings, which provided no cover at all. They cleared the first block and found no one on the other side; Cain waived Francesca to the front of their meager line.

"Take the lead," he said, "and move west, toward the marina. I'm right behind you.

"Liying, you got eyes on these clowns?"

"Yes," Liying said as Cain let Francesca and the other two get a block ahead of him. "The TAV is shielded, I can't interdict it. The sniper team it dropped is using Duos, so be careful; they're sticking to the rooftops. One man has returned to the van and four more are running after you on foot."

"Perfect," Cain muttered and sprinted off.

Duos were limited exoskeletons, originally created for paraplegics, with souped-up models now being employed by the abled to give extraordinary leaping abilities. Even with the wide spaces between buildings in Esbjerg, the sniper team leaped from rooftop to rooftop as it began its search.

Cain tuned his earbuds to pick up the sounds of running feet and the pneumatic grunt of the Duos firing and displayed them in his AR feed. Their pursuers were closing in fast, so Cain turned down a side street, sliding like a baseball player to dump his momentum, and then sprang to his feet and returned to the brick-building's corner. He blew the air out of his lungs, to make his shooting form predictable, edged around the corner only far enough to bring the muzzle of his unsuppressed 10mm into the alley, and then squeezed off a single round. Fifty meters away, the foremost assassin, sprinting with a submachine gun held in one hand, took the round in the middle of his chest and collapsed backwards, as if his legs had been taken out from under him by a hit-and-run driver. The three men following him dived either to the ground or into adjacent side-streets, one of them letting off two quick blasts from his shotgun. Cain felt a buckshot pellet impact the concealed armor covering his right arm, but barely paid it any notice: the assassin he had shot just rolled to his feet and scrambled behind cover.

"Wonderful," Cain muttered and then took off at a sprint, heading north, away from Francesca's line of march. Loud enough to transmit, he said, "Francesca, their wearing chest armor, at least; head shots only, over."

"Yes, okay," came her response, "um, roger."

"Take them a block south," Cain said as he ran, "and then turn back west again. I'm leading them a little north."

"Yes, roger," Francesca said and ushered her terrified charges down a treacherously wide street, which would offer no cover at all if the sniper team guessed their location.

The four men on foot recovered quickly, racing to the corner Cain had used for cover and then firing blindly around it before dashing into the open to continue their pursuit. A safer method, perhaps, than charging directly into possible fire, but it warned Cain that they were about to enter the street down which he fled, with little or no hope of hitting him. He again ducked down an intersecting street, his eyes and AR sweeping the rooftops for the sniper team. He gave it one second, for his pursuers to clear cover, and then edged back around the corner and took a shot, this time aiming at one of the shotgunners' heads. The mess that had been the dead assassin's head splattered backward at those who followed him, but it did not deter them: they dropped to the ground and returned fire immediately, peppering the brick corner that Cain had just fled.

"One down," Cain said, running west. "Liying, where's that van?"

"It is turning around," Liying said, her voice growing a little frantic with the firefight taking place before her eyes on the huge screens in Pons Sublicius' Command Center. "It had gone the wrong way, but it is coming back on that street; get off it. No, not that way! The sniper team is heading west along those rooftops. You have to go south."

Francesca was south and Cain did not want to bring the dismounted assassins any closer to her. But what Cain wanted and what circumstances allowed often did not agree: no choice.

Cain sprinted a block west before doubling back south, to come to another of the wide-open alleys between rows of houses and wait for the assassins to pass on their way to his last position: when they did, Cain dropped one of the submachine gunners with another headshot.

"Two down," he said and risked their fire again, this time by not pulling back behind cover, which would have taken him north, but by crossing the alley to head south. A round from one of the remaining submachine guns hit him under the armpit, staggering him into the brick wall. The armor prevented penetration, but did little to dissipate the kinetic energy. He grunted, "That'll leave a bruise."

The two remaining assassins were again after him, firing blindly around the corner before risking the open space. This time, however, Cain pulled his other pistol and fired back as he ran, before ducking into a side street, suppressing them, and then leapfrogging down to another corner. Bound after bound, he and the two assassins continued south.

"Francesca," Cain said over the sound of his own shooting: "you at that last corner before the marina?"

"Yes, I am here," Francesca said; having squeezed Lars and Brigette into a small space between a restaurant and a dumpster, she knelt covering the eastward approach, .38 Super in hand.

"In about fifteen seconds," Cain said, "I'm going to run past you, a block east. A few seconds later, the two assholes following me are going to run by. Can you shoot at least one of them? It's got to be in the head."

A second past and then Francesca said in a voice firm with anger, "Yes, I will shoot them."

A block east, Cain fired with one pistol while reloading the other (returning it to its holster to swap out magazines, one-handed). The two remaining assassins had grown cautious, covering each other with suppressive fire as the other bound forward, alleyway-by-alleyway. Cain had to fire at both sides of the alley as he ran backwards to the next block south, quickly depleting his remaining ammunition. Both guns ran dry before he made it to the next corner, forcing him to turn and sprint. He took a round in the back, which staggered him, but he made it, diving behind cover as the submachine gunner opened up with full cyclic fire.

Francesca watched as first Cain ran past, causing her heart to race, and then as her AR sunglasses highlighted the passing rounds and buckshot. She found herself breathing harder and harder and, remembering all those hours spent in practice, on the guards' range, she forced her lungs to quiet, preparing to expel her breath and steady her form. Then, in a split second that elongated into what felt like hours, one of the assassins, firing his submachine gun from the hip as he ran, hove into view. He would only be visible for a second and yet, to Francesca, there was a conscious moment that she had not anticipated, expecting that training and necessity would take over: instead, it was her choice to kill this man who hunted her lover and herself or to let him pass. She put a single round through his temple at twenty meters.

The last of the dismounted assassins backpedaled as he ran, slowing enough to take cover behind the brick-building's corner and orient his shotgun toward the dumpster behind which Francesca crouched. She swung her pistol around toward the second attacker, but it was too late—Cain had already reloaded and returned, putting a round through the shotgunner's head, catching him in a hasty crossfire.

"That's three and four," Cain said as he raced back up the alleyway toward the two dead assassins. "Liying, where's that van?"

Francesca heard Cain's voice and heard Liying say that the van was on the pier, circling behind her; she heard Cain tell her that he would be in view in a second and to not shoot him; she heard her own voice say that she would not, but her mind returned to her choice and, almost, she expected it to affect her as some great, life-altering moment and was shocked that it did not. There was no time to wonder at her own willingness to kill, regardless of the defense of herself and others, not with the last assassin on his way and a sniper team roaming the rooftops somewhere. She motioned to the two Danes to stay put and then joined Cain as he raced down the street toward her.

He waved her back, swapping out magazines for his .45 auto; his 10mm was dry and he was out of magazines for it. Passing Francesca, resisting the urge to reach for her, he came to the edge of the restaurant, his AR indicating the roaring engine of the van approaching from the north. Swaying out just for a moment, Cain put a single round through the windscreen, through the driver's head, and then pulled back behind cover. The van smashed into the opposite corner of the restaurant, flinging glass across the pier that led to the marina.

"Liying," Cain said, walking back to Francesca, "SITREP?"

Cain took Francesca's non-firing hand with his and leaned down to kiss her lips. She returned the kiss and then turned away briefly, steadying herself so the sudden drop in stress would not usher in a bout of tears; she gulped air and then turned back, to finish the kiss as Liying reported.

"The TAV has returned," Liying said, her own relief apparent in her voice; "it is picking up the sniper team."

Francesca returned her pistol to its holster, took a deep breath, and then lifted the unexpected tears, which she suddenly noticed clinging to her eyelashes, with her fingernail. Flinging them away, she turned back to Lars and Brigette and motioned for them to come out.

"It is over," she told them. "The sniper team has evacuated."

"Probably over," Cain said. "We can't hang around."

"I know," Francesca said to him and patted his arm. To the Danes, she said, "I am so sorry to have dragged you into this, to endanger your lives all for the sake of questions that have become pointless."

"No, I am sorry," Lars said, still bone white to the hairline, his voice and hands shaking, though that may have been his state of undress in the cold night, with his jacket around Brigette's shoulders. "I am sorry that this is happening to you, you who have tried to better the lives of all by championing the seawall project. You have defeated its opponents with words, time after time, and so now they send men with guns? It is preposterous. It is wrong. It is not how our society should work."

"We need to go," Cain said. "Now."

"I am sorry to delay you," Lars said. "Of course, go. If there is anything that I can do—that we can do—tell me. I will do it."

"Yes, I will help, too," Brigette said, stepping from behind Lars, shivering in the cold night. "Our city is drowning and no one will help. Except you! And they want to kill you, to stop you? It is insane. Give me a gun: I will shoot them, too."

"I hope it will not come to that," Francesca said. "I think you will be safe once I have left. It may, however, be wise to hire a bodyguard, Mr. Sørensen, until the legislation passes. Goodbye."

Cain and Francesca then hurried away south before turning east, giving Brigette's apartment building a wide berth as they returned to the train station. Using a different escape route from their infiltration would normally have made sense, but Cain did not think that they had been discovered until they had reached Brigette's: attacking them on the train would have been far easier and less likely to fail, if Stinnes' assassins had known that they were there. And so, after more than an hour, he and Francesca returned to the train station, to stand out of the way and watch every direction at once, and wait for the next train to depart, going anywhere.

"Of course," Francesca sighed, reading a text message scrolling across her AR sunglasses. "Did you see this from Lester?"

"Yeah," Cain said, looking over her head as she looked around his shoulder, each watching a different direction, "I read it. Another nothing in the financials."

"And our time to gather evidence against Stinnes," Francesca said, "for Interpol is nearly depleted. The vote is almost here."

"Yeah," Cain repeated. "This tactic ain't working. It may be time for us to choose another one."

"I know," Francesca said, "and I have been thinking, their plot hinges upon Da Avolo killing me, yes? They want him to kill me because of the story afterward, to avoid the backlash that they would face if the public thought that I had been assassinated because of the seawall legislation."

"Da Avolo doing it," Cain said, "would just be revenge, unrelated to the seawall."

"Exactly," Francesca said. "So, what if we remove him from the equation? If Da Avolo is not available to play the—oh, what is the English phrase? The patsy! Yes, if Da Avolo is not available to play the patsy, then they cannot openly kill me without risking a public backlash. The anticorruption provisions might even be strengthened, if Stinnes' plot were discovered."

"Maybe," Cain said, "but how do you figure we can remove Da Avolo from the equation?"

"By staying here," Francesca said. "By staying in Esbjerg and staying visible. They will come back and try again and, this time, Da Avolo will come himself. I know him. He does not value subtlety, guile; he is no more than a thug in a fifty-thousand-dollar suit."

"Easy," Cain said, momentarily glaring at her in mock annoyance.

Francesca laughed soundlessly and squeezed his non-firing hand with hers, saying, "An *unattractive* thug in a fifty-thousand-dollar suit. He will not wait for an opportune time or advantageous place: if he sees an opening, he will charge right in. He will want to kill me himself, as much for revenge as for Stinnes' plan. So, we let him try—and then we kill him. With Da Avolo then out of the equation, Stinnes' plan falls apart. Well? What do you think?"

"I think you're trouble," Cain said.

"What?" Francesca said, smiling uncertainly.

"It wasn't a week ago," Cain said, still watching the train station, "that you burned your first thug and then shook like a leaf in my arms the whole night."

"And I'm shaking now," Francesca said, stepping closer, raising her chin and standing arms akimbo, "after having *burned* another man tonight. And so what? This is not about bloodthirstiness: this is about practicality. Without Da Avolo, their plan will not work. It will prevent them from assassinating me prior to the vote, buying us the time we need to find evidence against Stinnes."

"Or they could just bomb parliament," Cain said, trying to keep the smile off his face and pay attention to what he should be doing, "and claim Da Avolo had planted it before we got him, as a failsafe."

"Dio mio," Francesca said and turned away, crossing her arms.

"But that's not what I'm talking about," Cain said. "You're trouble. Eventually, we'll put Da Avolo and Stinnes in prison, the ground, or the river and, afterward, you'll go right on out and find someone new to antagonize, won't you? Someone new to provoke. Some new trouble to start."

"Me?" Francesca said, turning back to smile under his chin. "Diplomatic, prudent, unimpeachable me?"

"Troublemaker," Cain said.

Francesca laughed and had to cover her mouth to stifle the sound, before saying, "Are you surprised?"

"Now that I say it out loud," Cain said, "it actually makes perfect sense. But, I feel like I should have appreciated this aspect of your personality before now."

Coming up on her toes and pulling him down by the coat collar, Francesca kissed Cain on the lips before saying, "Yes, you should have."

CHAPTER 10

AFTER A SERIES of trains, ground-cars, and TAVs, Cain and Francesca returned to Monaco, to the safehouse apartment they had used more than a week before. The tighter quarters and the bustling crowds, though rife with potential danger, imparted a feeling of anonymity and, with it, almost safety, after the broad streets and lack of cover in Denmark. Almost safety. Each of their attempts to discover Stinnes prepositioning assets to take advantage of the seawall legislation passing without anticorruption provisions had failed: no staged equipment, no idle workforce, no secret agreements. After a brief rest and a change of clothes, they returned the lawyer's office where they had met Lester, last time, to meet him again and hear the particulars of what he had also failed to discover.

Francesca sat in a large wingback chair, with her feet tucked under her and a cup of tea steaming in her hands, as she listened to Lester catalogue all of the purchases, accounts, and agreements he and Liying had not found, when sifting through Stinnes' financial data. Lester, impeccable in a new Italian suit—one of six he had picked up, since he was on Earth—seemed untroubled by their collective setbacks, almost amused by them, an artist admiring another artist's brushstrokes. Cain stood with his arms crossed, on the opposite side of the room, and gazed at Francesca, thinking about how much larger she made the chair appear, just by sitting in it, and wondering how he would convince her of what must be done.

"So, the way I see it," Lester concluded, "either we got it all wrong and Stinnes ain't trying to kill you over the anticorruption provisions or he's running everything through The Overture Group, which we can't hack into and which doesn't need to report anything, being sovereign and all."

"Or through another sovereign entity," Francesca said absently.

"Maybe," Lester said and shrugged, "but it's the only one we've found. He's funneling a ton of currency up to Overture, ostensibly to fund his Mars project. It could be that some of that money came back down to buy up resources to build a monopoly, if the legislation goes through un-anti-corrupted. But I doubt it. I know every euro he's spent on Mars—nothing happens there without my hearing about it—and it jives with what we've been able to find going up to Overture."

"Perhaps it is quid pro quo, then?" Francesca said, looking up. "With the other billionaires you mentioned last time."

"You mean, he creates corruption opportunities on Earth and they pay him back by investing in his Mars operation?" Lester said. "Maybe, but there's no sign of it."

"Well, of course not," Francesca said and leaned forward to set her tea on the lawyer's desk. "He has yet to deliver his end, my death."

"Either way," Cain said, "no evidence."

"True," Francesca sighed. She slipped out of the chair and began to pace the length of the room. After a moment, her exasperation rising, she said, "There has to be a trail! I have seen it too often as a prosecutor not to know that: there is no way to orchestrate something like this without leaving a trace."

Lester shrugged and took a pull from his snifter of brandy, before saying, "If you're good enough, there is."

"Or bad enough," Cain said and they both grinned. "Either way, we're out of time. We tried to gather evidence the legit way, Francesca, to get Interpol to do its thing. No dice. I think we got to cross over to my side of the street and find it any way we can. Or I go pay Stinnes a visit, put an end to him and be done."

"Be done with me," Francesca muttered. "Everyone would know I was behind it, even if it could not be proven."

"How?" Cain said. "Apart from Liying, we're the only three people in the world that know Stinnes is behind this."

"For now," Francesca said and stopped in her pacing, looked Cain in the eyes. "But if you kill him, there will be an investigation and an investigation will uncover his role in freeing Da Avolo. Then the questions will begin, about why I suddenly came out of hiding after Stinnes' assassination, did I order it, know about it, and with each question, which I will not be able to answer, my credibility will suffer, my reputation degrade until I cannot remain in public life—until I can no longer defend the seawall project in the years to come. I'll be finished."

"You'll be alive," Cain said and stepped away from the wall, "and we'll be together."

They stood in tableau, eyes locked in a shared expression of affection and contest, their physical forms, so starkly different when viewed together, accentuating how similar they were in will.

"There may be a middle way," Lester offered, clearing his throat and trying not to openly laugh at them. He was fond of them both, in his own way, but his dispassionate nature forever took amusement from the sentimental motivations of others. "We can cross the street without crossing the line. Our problem is that we can't find the evidence we need: so, let's solve that problem. If we can figure out where to look, we can figure out a legitimate way to have found it, a story to tell Interpol afterward that won't taint the evidence."

Dragging her eyes away from Cain, Francesca turned to Lester and said, "We would still need to know where to look, even if we were to break the law in looking. We do not."

"Well, maybe we don't *know*," Lester said, "but we can guess. Like you said, lesser men always leave a trail."

"Is that what I said?" Francesca said, smiling in spite of herself.

"That's what you meant," Lester said. "Now, Stinnes may enjoy reminding every person he talks to that he hails from Prussian royalty, but he don't live in Prussia: he lives right here in Monaco. Maybe we pop over to his mansion and *take a look around.*"

"I do not like it," Francesca sighed. "It creates a vulnerability for us. What if someday, someone finds out about our having broken into this place?"

"Then we're back to your career being over," Cain said. "But this way, at least there's a chance." He watched her until she, very subtly, nodded her head, before he continued. "Thing is, if we do it this way, we can't leave any witnesses. We run into anyone, they got to die. Can you do it?"

"I will not kill innocent people," Francesca said. "And that includes bodyguards simply doing their jobs. Especially not while *I am* breaking the law."

She looked over and watched Cain until he nodded his head, though it was not clear if he was accepting her decision or merely acknowledging her statement.

"We do this right," Lester said, "ain't no one going to know we were ever there. I had a feeling it might come to this, soon as I saw Stinnes was involved, so I had a few goodies sent down from Pons Sublicius: Yahata Suterusu infiltration suits. Got you a small, little lady."

"Charming," Francesca said, crossing her arms. "What do they do?"

"Photonic camouflage," Cain said. "It basically wraps light around you, so you blend in better with your surroundings. They only sort of work if you're standing still; you move and it looks like the bad special effects from a movie."

"That's a side benefit," Lester said, waving his hand, "for what we need. We'll keep out of sight the old fashion way. What the Suterusus will do for us is keep us from leaving behind any DNA. They're fully enclosed and filtered. We won't even leave breath moisture behind. And, if anyone sees us and we need to skedaddle, all they'll see are three people looking like blobs of paint; no way they trace that back to us."

Francesca stood biting her thumb for a moment before finally nodding her head and, looking between the two men she had had to rely on for her life more than once, she said, "Alright, we will go in and see if there is anything in his mansion that might direct us to real evidence. *But*, no shooting anyone. Can you promise me that?"

"Sure," Lester said and grinned.

"No, I can't promise you that, Trouble," Cain said and watched as Francesca turned toward him and failed to stifle a smile, despite the anxiety she felt, "but I will try."

CHAPTER 11

S TINNES' RESIDENCE IN Monaco was a portion of a newly constructed über-row, mere blocks from Le Palais des Princes de Monaco, not far from the Rue Colonel Bellando de Castro, on the edge of the cliffs overlooking Port de Fontvielle. It was estimated to be the most expensive real estate in the world, at nearly one-million euros per square meter, and had required bribes of unprecedented breadth to pass the city zoning commission. Despite the expense, however, and the grand Art Deco styling of the edifice, the three "mansions" that constituted the property were little more than lavish row houses; thirty-five room rowhouses, it was true, replete with grand staircases, balconies, and every convenience, but physically connected, nevertheless. Which is why, once Lester had Liying look for opportunities in the area, they saw their chance in an exclusive party taking place in the mansion next door, that night.

They spent the day arranging rooms in a nearby hotel, to use as a staging area, and buying the necessary clothes for the party. Sneaking the Yahata Suterusus into the mansion seemed a tall order to Francesca, as her dress afforded only barely enough room for herself, let alone for a sealed-environment, photonic camouflage suit. Lester merely smiled and said no one would suspect a man of his coloring attending the party with a briefcase in hand: certain stereotypes seemed never to go out of style and the elite of Monaco needed their party favors. And so, at just after nine PM that evening, Cain and Lester, wearing tuxedos—Cain with a classic black bowtie and white display handkerchief, while Lester went with a daring crimson shirt and onyx collar stone—and Francesca in a subtly glittering, form-fitting, strapless gown, brushed past the security guarding the entrance to Stinnes' neighbor's home, two beefy men who had inexplicably received orders through their earbuds to let them pass. Liying, in orbit, then sat back, a little sulky at not attending the party, too, and consoled herself with inari as she monitored the mansion's security center.

What Liying could not monitor, however, was the interior of either mansion: though both sported cameras pointing in every direction externally, and had counter-assault modules on their roofs (thus preventing any attempts at an air insertion), neither had even hidden cameras inside. While most of the world's regular people had grown wearily accustomed to a total lack of privacy, their every electronic device recording them at all times and under all circumstances, the obscenely wealthy had taken to expressing their exclusivity in the only truly exclusive way left: privacy. Internal ECM also prohibited the recording devices of guests from transmitting beyond the property, while EM sensors could be used to detect active devices of any kind, if the owners needed to exclude any possibility of someone leaving with blackmail material.

The party into which Cain, Francesca, and Lester walked teetered on the edge of the abandon it had been designed to elicit. Despite the minefield of social, economic, and etiquette missteps that each guest had carefully avoided to secure an invitation—to this and every other important event that season—as soon as the protective cloak of privacy enveloped them, they indulged in a bacchanalian debauch every bit as predictable as that of an American high school student whose parents were out of town. The music had begun to inch toward deafening, spouses had begun to look around for that evening's diversion, and the trays of passed hors d'oeuvres had become obsolete. More than one guest smiled to a companion when they saw Lester's briefcase.

The three weaved their way through the dancers and minglers, Cain's size and mien clearing a path before them as they headed for the sweeping staircase up to the top floor. Down the hallway, following a floorplan ripped from the city archives, they went to a guest bedroom and bypassed the simple, mechanical lock with a flexible sheet of plastic with a half-millimeter-wide roller on the leading edge. Cain cleared the room, to ensure no shy partygoers had retired within, while Lester watched the corridor. Satisfied, they locked the door and secured it with the oldest of old-school technology: Lester withdrew a wooden doorstop from his briefcase and kicked it into position.

"How long before someone comes to the door," Francesca asked, turning her back and lifting her hair for Cain to unzip her dress, "in search of whatever drugs they think you are carrying, Lester?"

"All the doors are locked," Lester said, setting his briefcase on a writing desk and carefully keeping his back turned as he handed a Suterusu over his shoulder. "The hosts don't want people getting busy in all their guest rooms. Any freaks come by and find this door locked and no one answering, they'll move on to the next. Besides, even if someone does kick their way in, what are they going to find? An empty briefcase and three sets of clothes."

"Think we're having a party of our own," Cain said, unbuttoning his shirt, "somewhere nearby."

"A ménage à trois?" Francesca said, as she carefully spread her gown across the bed and smoothed out the wrinkles. She looked teasingly back at Cain before adding, "How intriguing."

"Easy," he said, noticing the silent bouncing of Lester's shoulders.

The three quickly donned their Suterusu suits, which not only covered them head to foot, but entirely enclosed their heads. Every inch was concealed and a sophisticated microfilter captured the moisture of their breath, so that they left nothing behind. Lester then passed a hand-vacuum over each of them, to eliminate the possibility of a hair or even a single skin cell from clinging unintentionally to their suits. Their preparations finished, Cain opened the door to the balcony and edged slowly out.

The Port de Fontvielle, protected by its seawall and locks, stretched out below, with the grand city just beyond and the Mediterranean under moonlight glistening off to their left. Cain could hear Francesca draw breath when she joined him on the small balcony and knew that it was not due to pleasure taken from the view: to gain access to Stinnes' mansion, they would need to cross from their balcony to one of his, across several feet of open space with a drop of dozens of meters to the jagged rocks fronting upon the port below.

Cain gave his legs a quick stretch and then raised his foot to the balcony railing, when Francesca whispered, "Wait."

Both Cain and Lester ducked, reacting to the sound, and then held their fingers in front of their air filters. Cain pointedly used the keypad mounted on the arm of the Suterusu, typing in a message that ran scrolling across the top of the suits' integrated AR lenses.

No sound, he typed. *We can't know if there are passives in place, recording.*

Fine, Francesca typed back, huffing a sigh. *But why do we not use a Duo or something, instead of you trying to jump five meters?*

Duos? Lester typed before taking three lengths of rope from his briefcase.

They had them in Denmark, Cain wrote. To Francesca, he typed, *Too late, now, and they're loud as hell. Even with that racket below, the guards over there would hear us. Anyway, don't worry. I got this.*

Not comforted in the least, Francesca ran a hand over Cain's shoulder, just in case it was their last moment, and stood silently by as he mounted the balcony railing. Even with his native athleticism and prodigious strength, balancing on the thin railing was not easy. Cain took a moment to get the feel of the thin metal beneath his feet, standing and squatting several times to see how his center of gravity would shift, and then began swinging his arms in preparation. The camouflage of his suit attempted to keep pace with his movements, adopting the green of the vines cultivated on their host's balcony one moment and then the dappled marble of the building in the next; regardless, the way he moved, the set of his shoulders and the focus evident in his gaze all declared his identity, his calm certainty, to Francesca, every bit as if he still wore his tuxedo or nothing at all.

And then he leaped. Leaning forward until he was nearly parallel with the ground one-hundred-meters below, Cain pushed off of the balcony railing with such force that the metal bent momentarily in the opposite direction; he flung out his arms as he sailed across the defensive expanse, doubtlessly designed to thwart just such an attempt, and descended, inch-by-inch, as the microseconds passed; at the last possible moment, his gloved fingers met steel. Cain swung for a moment from the lowest bar of Stinnes' balcony railing, as Francesca let out the breath she had not realized she had held, steadying herself against the opposite railing. Cain then pulled himself up, like a wrestler exercising on a peg board, until he could raise his legs high enough to assist. In the next instant, he was on Stinnes' balcony, his posture clearly transmitting how pleased he was. Francesca wanted to throw something at him.

Instead, Lester did. First one end of one rope, then the ends of the other two: Cain fastened one of the three ropes to the bottom of Stinnes' balcony, as a footbridge, and the other two to either side of the top, to be used as handrails. As bridges went, the rope-bridge was not especially stable nor safe, but it was enough. Francesca had grown somewhat accustomed to heights from her wall-climbing and, combined with her own natural athleticism, she quickly crossed the bridge, though she did not object to Cain seizing her by the arm as soon as she was close enough to reach; even if she did not need the physical assistance, it was still a comfort. Cain did not extend the same gesture to Lester, however, when he made the crossing.

Now unsafely within Stinnes' mansion, keenly aware of the cameras mounted nearby on the roof, watching the port below for attempts to scale the cliffs, the three cloaked people set about gaining entry to the guest bedroom beyond the double French doors. The glass was bulletproof and laser-reflective, to defeat both assassination and eavesdropping attempts; with the counter-assault modules on the roof and the seemingly impossible climb up the cliffs below, however, the lock was little more than a defense against the wind. Lester bypassed it using a thin metal hook, after awaiting Liying's message that there was no alarm wire strung across the entrance.

Inside, the guest bedroom was sleek, elegant, cold, and uninviting. It would have impressed visitors with its costs, just as it advised them against a long stay. The three new guests had no intention of staying longer than necessary and crossed quickly to the hall door. Cain withdrew a small probe from the thigh pocket of his suit, uncoiled a stiff wire from the black-metal box, and slipped it under the door: the probe was a fiberoptic camera, which transmitted what it saw to an AR overlay within each of their suit's visors. The hallway was not a hallway, but another balcony, this time an internal balcony that ran in a sweeping arc from one side of the front wall to the other, off of which were bedrooms, offices, and other rooms; at either end of the balcony, a grand staircase led down to the lower floors and, eventually, the entryway. Cain saw an open door, off to the right of the guest bedroom, through which a flickering light came. No other sign of life could be seen from that angle.

Satisfied that he could open the door without bumping it into someone, Cain stowed the fiberoptic probe, withdrew his silenced .45 auto, and opened the door—and immediately pulled back out of sight. Francesca and Lester did likewise, slipping out of the rhombus of light spilling through the open doorway. What they heard sounded initially like fighting, until the rhythm and occasional words mingled with the grunting raised another possibility. Cain looked over his shoulder at the other two and, by the cant of his head, though his features were all but invisible, Francesca knew that he was grinning.

Someone having a very good time, Lester typed, his shoulders again bouncing in silent amusement.

The possibility of Stinnes being home during their visit had occurred to them while planning; while the new possibility of him being occupied seemed encouraging, the five-story ceiling off the main room in the mansion echoed and reechoed the sounds of passion until it was impossible to locate their source. Cain did not want the three of them to stumble into Stinnes mid-coitus and so waved the other two back before heading out to scout on his own. In a crouch, he padded down the balcony, visually confirming that there were no internal cameras, counting the doorways, and looking for people. At last, he reached to the room from which the flickering light came and gently swayed in front of the doorway until he could see inside.

Within what turned out to be a living room, two men, probably bodyguards, sat on a sofa watching a World Cup match. Both had their jackets off and wore shoulder holsters, glasses of beer ran with moisture on the table before them, and both snacked on nuts from a large bowl. Cain backed away slowly, wondering how long they had before the match ended and the bodyguards returned to what they should have been doing. Either way, if things got out of hand, he would have at least these two to deal with.

Clearly not the source of the sounds of passion, nor a likely source of intelligence about Stinnes' operation, Cain returned the way he had come, slipping his fiberoptic probe under doors as he went. There were other bedrooms, a library, and a billiard room before he returned to the guest bedroom where Francesca and Lester peered through the doorway. Cain waived them back and then continued on, searching for the something that would help them.

Even with the echoes, Cain found that he drew closer to the sounds of lovemaking, the farther he traveled in that direction. No use of the fiberoptic probe was necessary, once he was within a few feet of what appeared to be the master bedroom: it was certainly the source. Backtracking, Cain slipped his probe under the next door over and discovered a study, complete with a computer, VR conferencing suite, and the usual accoutrements of a successful capitalist raider. He stowed the probe and then motioned with his gun and, it not being camouflaged like the rest of him, Lester and Francesca could easily see it and came softly down the carpeted balcony.

Inside the study, with the door closed and the lights off, relying on their suits' visual enhancement and other devices, they split up, looking for that which they did not know to find. Lester and Francesca withdrew remote readers, small black boxes that could scan a computer's memory without interacting with the operating system, thus leaving no trace that data had been accessed. They combed through both the computer and the VR conferencing suite's hard drives, looking at correspondence, calendars, saved searches, frequently used applications, call logs, and then scanned for keywords related to the seawall, Venice, The Overture Group, and Francesca. Nothing.

This is taking forever and is proving useless, Francesca wrote. *Clearly, this is just a public computer, something official for auditors or investigators to inspect.*

Agreed, Lester wrote back. *The volume of correspondence and VR conferences wouldn't cover half of the business I know he's up to. There must be a second office or computer or something, somewhere.*

While the two of them had searched the electronics, Cain had looked around manually, inspecting the art, the furniture, liquor cabinet, and moldings, certain that there must be a safe hidden within the room. While he searched and the other two read, the sounds of passion from the other room grew in pace and volume until the rhythmic grunts of a man climaxing preceded a sudden silence. Within the study, everyone turned toward the connecting doorway. The unspoken question became, would Stinnes stay to cuddle his paramour, fall asleep, or, having sated his physical needs, return to his true passion, business, and enter the adjoining office? The answer seemed to come a moment later when footsteps creaked across the floor.

Everyone froze. A moment passed and then the footsteps started again, deliberate and clearly crossing the bedroom. Francesca and Lester stowed their readers back within the camouflaged thigh pockets of their suits and then retreated to the far wall, opposite the bedroom door, and stood as motionlessly as possible. If Stinnes entered and only switched on the multicolored Tiffany lamp, rising gracefully from one side of the desk, its delicate light would not reveal them: if, instead, he flipped on the overhead recessed lighting, even the suits' photonic camouflage would not entirely conceal them. Francesca found herself trying not to breathe.

A moment stretched out for what felt like weeks until, barely audible through the heavy wooden doors, the sound of running water reached them. Francesca stifled a sigh and Lester edged out from behind the copper screen, which he had used for cover. Cain, however, had held his position behind the desk, upon hearing the footsteps, and continued to look over the objets d'art and vintage liquors mingling together on an antique sideboard. If Stinnes had walked in, Cain would have broken the man's jaw, at a minimum, consequences be damned, and so saw no reason to hide; also, there was something about the collection of little artworks that did not sit right with him, demanding his continued attention.

Stinnes' decorator had taken the Art Deco style of the mansion to heart, when decorating the place. One of the objects on the sideboard was a replica of *Spirit of the Wind*, which was a glass head with hair like wings flowing straight back; though originally created as a hood ornament, the figurine had become a standard example of the Art Deco period. Cain had seen replicas of the little head on many occasions, rendered in the original glass as well as other materials; some were cheap knockoffs, others were new works, borrowing only the general form and baroque sense of movement. Stinnes' copy bothered him. Off to one side, flanked by a bottle of Napoleon Brandy, the piece was overshadowed in material by the other works of gold, jade, and ivory; where they were originals, it was a reproduction; while they would have been sourced from an antique dealer, it could have been ordered online.

Cain, playing a hunch, reached out and rotated the little head—and was rewarded with a click that made all three of them duck before the wall behind the sideboard lifted on hidden pneumatics to reveal an alcove three-feet deep, filled with currency of various sorts, little boxes of precious stones, vials of designer drugs, and a computer. Francesca and Lester rushed over, squeezing in beside Cain; Lester produced his reader and the three of them watched as it fed line after line of text to the overlays in their AR vision. Lester quickly dumped everything that they found onto the reader's internal memory, but slowed when they came across a series of documents and correspondence related to something called, *The Madagascar Plan*. It took only a few seconds to see that Stinnes' motivations had nothing to do with the seawall and were far more despicable than mere corruption. Then the hallway door behind them creaked open and a slash of light split the room in half.

Cain slipped away to one side, while Francesca and Lester withdrew in the other. Silhouetted in the doorway, one of the bodyguards stood, his jacket still off and his pistol visible under his arm. By the tilt of his head, he was listening for something. With cautious steps, he crossed the carpeted room, relying only on the thin bar of light from the doorway to guide him to the desk. If he saw that the alcove was open, it did not bother him, though Cain doubted that he saw it at all. The guard carefully raised the lid of Stinnes' humidor, helped himself to a couple cigars, trimmed them, and then slipped back out of the office.

Well, that just cost me a year of my life, Francesca typed. She wanted to pinch the bridge of her nose, feeling the stress of the moment building up tension there, but her suit prevented her. *In any event, we have found what we sought and have learned that Stinnes is not here; his itinerary said that he is attending a meeting tonight. Let us go.*

Lester agreed and led the way to the hallway door, but Cain, propelled by either caution or curiosity, crept to the bedroom door and slipped his fiberoptic probe under it. There, on the bed, having just sipped from their glasses of water, lie what appeared to be one of the bodyguards—by his shoulder holster—and one of the maids, seemingly taking advantage of their employer's late night out.

Leaving the two to their own devices and careful not to alert the other bodyguards, no doubt enjoying their cigars as their match concluded, Lester, Francesca, and Cain returned to the guest bedroom, the rope bridge, and finally to the party. After a quick change and stowing their Suterusus and the ropes in Lester's briefcase, they left the mansion and walked quickly back to their hotel staging area.

"I was expecting corruption," Francesca said. "I could have accepted corruption, having seen it my entire professional career. But this? I am equally furious and sickened."

CHAPTER 12

THE *MADAGASCAR PLAN* proposal document had been distributed to Stinnes' cabal of European billionaires on printed hardcopy, the correspondence revealed, and no electronic copy had ever left the concealed laptop that Cain had discovered in Stinnes' Monaco residence. Even a cursory read of the cover letter revealed the necessity for such fanatic secrecy. *The Madagascar Plan* envisioned a European Parliament swept to the far right after an unspecified event that would sway voters to embrace conservative, reactionary candidates; with the new MPs' voting power, the plan would come into effect. The goal was simple: to forcibly expel all citizens, registered guests, migrants, and asylum seekers from the European Union who were not of what the plan considered *European ancestry*, though the definition in the plan's appendix made it clear that what the author meant was, *not white*. The specific means outlined in the execution section detailed the mass emigration of targeted people to Stinnes' Mars colony, to work in its factories producing luxury items for the European market; anyone who refused to work would be allowed to starve to death as an example. The plan also called for regular documentaries to be created and broadcast, detailing the harsh conditions and lack of legal recourse in the sovereign colony, to ensure that potential migrants knew what awaited them if they dared to enter fortress Europe.

Francesca slammed her reader down on the hotel suit's coffee table and strode to the windows overlooking Port Hercule, wiping tears from the corners of her eyes.

"Now that I read it," Lester said, thumbing through the text on his phone, reclining with his feet up on the couch, "it doesn't surprise me at all. Should have guest a racist fuck like Stinnes—pardon my language—would have concocted such a lunatic idea. Never hid his hatred for the brown people. Would say shitty things right to a brother's face and then rely on his army of bodyguards to back it up. And there were no exceptions with him, either: if he found anyone not white enough for him holding too much stock or sitting on a Board of Directors, he'd back out of a deal or set them up to take a fall or just have them shot.

"What I don't get, though," he said and dropped his phone on the couch, "is why he named it *The Madagascar Plan*. Does he think we all came from Madagascar?"

Francesca turned around, her arms crossed so tight that she appeared to hug herself, and said, "Your school system was a disgrace."

"Yeah, I imagine it was," Lester said, his usual amusement reappearing. "On my side of LA, though, it was under water before I had a chance to attend."

"You poor man," Francesca said.

"Not anymore," Lester said, smiling and waving his diamond-adorned pinky at her.

Francesca smiled sadly back before saying, "The original *Madagascar Plan* was created by the Nazis, around the time that they had conquered France. They intended to forcibly expel all

European Jews to Madagascar, which had been a French colony at the time, before they abandoned the idea in favor of genocide." A moment passed and Cain could see the muscles in Francesca's jaw clenching, before she said, "This. This was the inspiration for Stinnes' plan, his guiding principle. Hatred. Of all our history, hatred. Not the ideals of democracy, not the art of the Renaissance, nor even the century of peace our union has created, no. Hatred."

"It all kind of falls into place now," Cain said, slipping his phone back into his inside jacket pocket. He had, like the others, returned to his usual attire. "It never was about business and the anticorruption provisions in the seawall legislation. That's why we didn't find any evidence. He didn't want to kill you to keep you from preventing their removal: he wanted to you dead so you couldn't fight him on this."

"By why her?" Lester said. "There must be dozens of MPs, national leaders, whoever that would have—or will—fight him when he tries to move the EU Parliament to the right, start shipping people off to his Mars ghetto."

"Yeah, but none of them have succeeded the way Francesca has," Cain said, "and damn sure not as fast. She hammered through the seawall project in, what, two years? People been calling for it for at least the last fifty. And, if I'm remembering this right, when the budget hawks tried to stop the legislation from reaching a vote, they teamed up with the pro-colony faction, saying Mars was a better investment than the seawall. Francesca then orchestrated the EU Commission's ruling that existing anti-colonialism laws extended to Mars, severely limiting the kinds of investments the EU could make in Mars or anywhere else."

"Yes," Francesca sighed and again wiped her eyes, "making it that much harder for this awful plan to come into effect, as they will now have to seize the commission as well as parliament."

"Why are you crying?" Cain gently asked.

"Because I did not stop the colonization effort because it was wrong," Francesca said. "I stopped it to protect the seawall project. And now I find that it was at least as important, but to me it was merely tactics."

"I sure do love a rich, white, liberal up on her horse," Lester said, laughing silently. To Cain's hardening expression, he raised his hands and said, "Easy now. I'm just saying, Francesca, you did the right thing and you are hated by the right people: maybe that's good enough, dig?"

"I dig," she said and, becoming frustrated with her own response, flung the tears from her eyelashes with an impatient gesture. "I am just feeling sorry for myself. I should have known this was happening, that this creature was plotting such a despicable act. Well, now I know and now I *will* stop him.

"His itinerary said that he is attending a secret meeting with others that support this, this *plan*. Given that it violates a dozen statutes *and* explains why he wants to assassinate me, I suggest we hurry there and join them, record their little meeting and then deliver the recording to Interpol. It will certainly provide enough probable cause to search every facet of his business and every inch of his property. Then they will find that damning laptop and all it contains."

"Now you're talking," Cain said, smiling at the pride and strength that always swelled within Francesca, whenever anything difficult appeared. "Okay, where is this place?"

"It's here," Lester said, grinning with him and pointing toward the windows behind Francesca. "Right here, in Monaco. They've rented out an enclosed dock, down in the port. Nice and private for their morally upstanding plan to defend all Europe from the brown people."

"Let's go get them," Cain said and stood.

CHAPTER 13

PORT HERCULE WAS Monaco's larger, deep-water port, capable of berthing the world's mega-yachts, like Stinnes'. Along with much of Monaco's coast, it had been encased within a seawall, employing specialized locks for ships to pass into and out of the port. It was far more costly than simply walling the land behind the port and raising the facilities with the ever-rising Mediterranean tide, but the locals liked their port the way it was and had the money to keep it that way. The result was a port out of time, hardly changed in more than a century, catering exclusively to the yachts of the carriage trade.

The boathouse that Stinnes had rented was primarily for yacht maintenance, but doubled as a function space by covering the watery hole in the floor with a giant wooden plank. Sealed and plush, with a polished wooden floor suitable for dancing, the boat-house had become an uncommonly posh venue, known only to the yachting set. At the far end of the dock, with a hundred meters of boat slips and anchorage between it and the pier connecting it to Monaco proper, it was sufficiently secluded for a confidential rendezvous—and frustrated attempts at a clandestine approach.

"There it is," Francesca said, back in the clothes that she had first donned in the ancient escape route under Venice, her .38 Super under her arm. She, Cain, and Lester stood together on the pier, away from the closest light source, watching the boathouse through the nightvision of their AR sunglasses.

"Indeed," Lester said, stroking his chin, feeling the day's growth of stubble forming. "Liying, talk to me."

From Pons Sublicius' Command Center, Liying stood inches from the touch-screen wall, zooming in and out of the feed from the geosynchronous satellite above Monaco. "They have ECM active inside the boathouse," she said. "I cannot get through without making enough noise to warn them. I assume you do not want that."

"No, I don't," Lester said.

"The only thing I can pick up," Liying continued, "is the transmissions to the four sentries, standing outside at the corners of the boathouse. Someone inside—I assume, again, it is Mr. Stinnes' Chief of Security—asked for a status update, four minutes ago, but nothing since. A last guest had arrived. He also said that they would begin the meeting shortly and expect it to run for only twenty minutes. You will have to hurry, if you plan to record anything."

"I must join them inside immediately, then," Francesca said. "How do we bypass the sentries?"

"Wait, *you're* going inside?" Cain said. "I don't think so."

"Oh, you don't?" Francesca said, turning to him, arms akimbo. "And whom would you prefer? Which of you two, as Lester puts it, *brown people*, would like to join this clandestine meeting of European racists?" Lester covered his eyes as his shoulders bounced, managing, at least, to keep from laughing audibly. "No," Francesca continued, "it must be me."

"They might recognize you," Cain said. "They are hunting for *you*, after all."

"They might," Francesca said. "But if this is a meeting of sorts, and if I know this Stinnes person's type, he will want to make a speech. They will all look to him, pay close attention, and leave the security to the sentries. I will slip in unobtrusively, record what they say, and then slip back out. Please, my friend, my love," she said and, seeing Cain's features harden as he prepared for the final resistance, came up on her toes to kiss him, "it is the only way."

"She's right," Lester said, a last snicker escaping. "If they've got ECM active, probably the walls are too thick or shielded for us to record from the outside. We'll be standing by, though, little lady, in case they do notice."

"Fine," Cain said, "but there are two doors to the place: Lester and I will stand at both, keeping them open a crack—which would be a great opportunity to record the audio from safety—"

"We need video of who is speaking," Francesca insisted.

"—and we'll come in shooting, if it plays out that way," Cain finished.

"Fine," Francesca said. "Now, what about these sentries?"

"You leave them to me and Lester," Cain said. "One thing, though: if you want to be able to turn whatever you record over to Interpol, we have to have a legit reason for being here. What is it?"

"Liying?" Lester said, a satisfied smirk parting his lips.

"I reestablished my surveillance of Hans Frank, over the weekend," Liying said. "He arrived in Monaco a couple hours ago."

"Hans Frank?" Francesca said. "Stinnes' lawyer, whom we believe may have arranged Da Avolo's escape? Then Da Avolo may be here, as well."

Cain nodded before saying, "Alright. Stakes getting higher all the time. So, we're here following Hans Frank; cool. Lester, let's do this thing."

After a moment's conferring and a couple implements from Lester's briefcase, Cain strolled off to one side of the dock while

Lester went to the other. The dock—and other docks throughout the port—had rows of yachts of various sizes lined up, most ready for the next day's leisure or next season's races, while some hosted parties ranging from liaison to bash. Music of various sorts played in the distance, candles, spots, and strobe lights flickered in the darkness, and everywhere it appeared that the rich really did live differently. Naturally, none of them noticed as Cain and Lester helped themselves to a couple dinghies.

Most of the yachts had some sort of small craft tied nearby for a variety of purposes. Cain's purpose was to approach the sentries at the boathouse without giving them one-hundred meters of open space to prepare for his attack. As such, he left the oars for the dinghy where they were and, instead, pushed the little boat along with his arms, first passing around the yacht to which it had been tied and then under the dock. Pushing from pylon to pylon, Cain quietly passed the hundred meters of the dock's length, underneath, slowing as he came to the boathouse, and looking around to make sure that Lester had kept pace on the other side of the dock, in his own borrowed dinghy. Avoiding the sound of even speaking sotto voce, Cain motioned for Lester to follow him past the boathouse, to its north side. They then tied off their small boats and climbed carefully up the pylons.

The sentries stood at the four corners of the boathouse, eyes constantly in motion, sweeping the nearby yachts and sky, their own AR sunglasses employing drone-detection software, despite the port prohibiting their use (the wealthy not wanting photos of their nude sunbathing appearing in the tabloids). As such, they oriented outward, their backs to the boathouse: with Cain and Lester coming up the pylons between the north and southside sentries, they were no more than shadows and all-but out of sight.

"Okay, you are both in position," Francesca said, watching them from the far end of the dock, coordinating since neither would want to speak while inches away from his target. "Ready and three, two, one—now!"

Both Cain and Lester shot the sentry standing a foot before them, using one of the little electro-stun devices Lester had brought along. About the size of a pen, the pneumatic device quietly propelled two needles through the sentries' clothing before running fifty-thousand volts into their bodies. The amperage was such that it rendered them helpless, though not—as was commonly thought—unconscious; on rare occasion, it would stop the heart. Using their left hands for the stunners, both Cain and Lester immediately wrapped their rights around the sentries' bodies and dragged them around the corner, in case the southside sentries heard something; they then lowered the two men's bodies to the dock and bound and gagged them with duct tape. From either end of the boathouse, squatting over their trussed-up prey, Cain and Lester grinned at each other before turning south.

Following the same course, Cain and Lester dropped and bound the southside sentries; Francesca sprinted down the dock as soon as the men fell. Knowing that they had already lost much of the little time that they had available to record anything incriminating, Lester slipped around to the northside door, cracking it only far enough to hear the speech, while Cain drew his pistols and stood with his back to the wall beside the southside door. Francesca gave him a nod and then slipped into the boathouse.

Rather than the greasy garage of an auto-repair shop, the yacht-maintenance building was surprisingly plush, paneled in walnut, with an open, vaulted ceiling; the machinery for lifting yachts had been discreetly covered and a wide bandstand installed along the north wall. No chairs had been brought in, however, and so the crowd of three-dozen stood, still in their jackets or coats, as they listened to Stinnes address them on the need for European purity.

Stinnes, in his early sixties, wearing a Milan suit, could have passed for a man of forty, with little grey in his russet hair and few lines etching his pale skin. Despite his less than six-feet of height and slim, fencer's build, he held his audience captivated, speaking to the crowd of Germans, Italians, French, Dutch, and Danes in English—their only common language—his methane-blue eyes smoldering as he railed against the forces aligned against them, pounding his fist again and again on the podium. The crowd murmured their agreement, at times, and did not notice the slight, darkly clad woman slip into the boathouse, to stand near the refreshments table and watch the speech through sunglasses.

"And every day it grows worse," Stinnes bellowed, pausing for the murmur. "Every day we find that the rising tide of dark invaders have seeped through another trickle of their kind, another boatload of sickly refugees to live off of our garbage, to pollute our streets with their hovels, and demand—in their gall, *demand*—that we expend our capital to improve their lives.

"Why should we? Did we ask them to come here?" Stinnes asked, not having to wait long for the shouts of *no* from the audience. "Did we invite them to steal, to practice their dirty religions in our cities, to steal jobs from our countrymen, slaves that they are, settling for a slave's wages? No! We did not invite them and we do not want them.

"Droughts have destroyed their agriculture, they say: to this I reply, what is that to us? If they had prepared, as we have, they would have mastered this violent planet, forcing it to bear fruit, as we have, and gone beyond, to master other planets, as well. They have not. *Their* failure to prepare is not *my* emergency. *My* emergency is their unwarranted invasion!"

More cheers interrupted Stinnes and he stood nodding to his audience, waiting for their enthusiasm to cool sufficiently for him to continue. "Yes, yes, my friends," he said, "an invasion it is. And we must confront it on those terms. The shortsighted, the soft, the foolish would have us house these mongrels, pauperize ourselves through pampering them, diluting our storied bloodlines with a most unnatural mingling of the races. No! No, again I say, no!"

More applause. Francesca panned the audience, recording their faces when one turned to another to ensure that his enthusiasm was appropriate; and it was always a *he*, for there were no women in the boathouse-auditorium.

"And so, what is to be done?" Stinnes continued. "Day-by-day, more mongrels gather at our doors: should we allow them to destroy our homes as they have destroyed their own? No. No, we will now allow that. However, we will also not commit the same mistakes of the past. We, the white race, who have brought our beloved Europe to its glorious present, have learned from past failures, as the mongrel peoples cannot. And so, we shall not exterminate them, as they deserve." A polite applause greeted this news, with one or two shouting that they should. "No, no, my friends, I understand your just fury, but there is another way, a way that will rid us of this most unwelcome guest, preserving our way of life, and will also create economic opportunity, rather than expending our resources. We will send them to Mars."

The applause came hesitantly at first, but Stinnes glared at them as the three men standing behind him, all facsimiles of himself, clapped thunderously in example, until the crowd gave its approval.

"Yes, we will expel the mongrels," Stinnes said, "to a facility that awaits them, there to labor in the creation of needed merchandise. There, they will find the jobs that the left have shed so many tears to gain for them," he said, pouting facetiously to the crowd's amusement. "Now, there are a few unfortunate laws that prevent us from doing so at present, but we shall remove these laws. Yes, we shall remove them and also we shall replace the Members of Parliament that would labor against the righteousness of our cause. And when we have succeeded, when we have purified our beloved Europe, restoring the sanctity of the white race, and reaffirming our destiny to rule the lesser peoples of the Earth, then, yes, even those who in their foolishness strive against us, yes, even they will breathe a sigh of relief, knowing that they have been preserved along with us."

Clapping and nodding ensued, as the crowd assumed the appearance of benevolence.

"However," Stinnes said, his features hardening, "though we will grant clemency to those who have struggled against us and the righteousness of *The Madagascar Plan*, there are those to whom we will not offer our leniency. There are those, my brothers, whose perversity is beyond forgiveness, who have set back our plans and delayed our future; those of such despicable personal choices that we simply cannot withhold our wrath. To these race-traitors, we will give only death."

All restraint and propriety were then shed, as the applause rose to an overwhelming volume. Stinnes stood proudly smiling, nodding along for a moment before motioning to the crowd to listen again.

"Francesca Pieralisi is one such traitor," Stinnes said. "She has lied to the European Commission about colonization, stymying our efforts to expel the mongrels; she has had the gall to seek high office; and she has engaged in a level of personal perversity that I will not offend you by detailing. To move forward, we must elimi-nate this threat, so cunning in her speeches that she can convince the stupid masses of nearly anything. And that is where you come in, Mr. Da Avolo—Hans, bring him up here."

From the far side of the boathouse, Hans Frank motioned to two of his beefy security men to propel an uncertain Da Avolo toward the bandstand. Still in his leather jacket and chinos, he stumbled the last few steps, having been shoved from behind, and stood trying to moisten his lips and teeth, as the crowd murmured and Stinnes glared.

"Mr. Da Avolo," Stinnes said, both hands on the podium, turning to his left to address Da Avolo without yielding the stage, "you have been brought here tonight because of your repeated failures. You have been brought here tonight to see for yourself that your mission to destroy this woman is not, as you seem to believe, a *piece of business*. I am a far more successful businessman than you have ever or will ever be, as is true of each of these gentlemen gathered here this evening. This is not business. This is war. For us, this is the defense of our homeland, our race, and for us there is nothing more sacred. So, when you fail to deliver us the death of one *woman*, you are not failing a business deal, you are failing your race, our race. Do you understand? You have the resources of every man here at your disposal. There is no excuse for failure and so you will be given only one more chance to succeed. Do you understand the consequences that await you, if you should fail again, Mr. Da Avolo?"

Da Avolo, understanding perfectly well, tore his eyes away from Stinnes, and looked out over the crowd, realizing, finally, the true nature of the deal he had made. Francesca had escaped time and again, popping up all over northern Europe and then disappearing again, before he could reach her. Da Avolo understood now that if he could not kill her, these men would certainly order his death in retribution.

And then, the luck upon which Da Avolo had always relied, came through for him once more: there, at the back of the auditorium, disguised but recognizable nevertheless, stood Francesca Pieralisi.

"Yeah, Mr. Stinnes," Da Avolo said, grinning and taking a few steps in place, "yeah, I understand just fine: you want that bitch and you want her right now. Okay, you got it. She's standing right there."

Stinnes, taken aback, swung around as the crowd turned to follow the line of Da Avolo's outstretched arm, following it back to a slight woman at the back of the room, wearing sunglasses despite the late hour.

"That is her?" Stinnes blurted. "She is recording us, you idiot. Shoot her! Shoot her and bring me those glasses."

Francesca tore open her jacket and drew her pistol as, across the room, Da Avolo and the three men behind Stinnes did likewise. Around the perimeter of the room, the half-dozen other guards Stinnes and Hans had brought also fumbled weapons out of their jackets or from under long coats. The odds were awful; they were beyond awful and there was no other play to make for Francesca than to stand and fight, hopeless though it was that even the concealed armor under her blouse could absorb the onslaught from so many weapons at once.

And then came Cain. The crowd of racists crying out in panic and dropping to the floor bought him the half-second he needed to burst through the door and stride toward the bandstand. Caught between their order to kill Francesca and the sudden appearance of that which they feared most—a huge, armed, black man—Stinnes' bodyguards hesitated one vital second and Cain opened fire on them. There was no chance to avoid their return fire, but that was what Cain counted upon: with the impossibility of dragging Francesca behind cover, the only other option to preserve her life was to take the rounds intended for her. He therefore made himself the largest, most pressing target in the room.

The only one on the bandstand to not fire upon Cain was Da Avolo. He, too, turned his pistol toward the charging mercenary, when Cain entered the boathouse, but he did not fire: he was not motivated by racial hatred, but rather by revenge. He swung back in the next instant to kill Francesca. Francesca, however, though caught off guard by Cain's entrance along with the others, saw the flash of movement and raised her pistol in response. On one side, more than thirty-years' experience, beginning with muggings in alleyways and winding through a lifetime of murders, turf wars, and extrajudicial executions: on the other, a few months of dedicated practice and three gunbattles, saving her own life. Francesca shot Da Avolo through the left eye, blowing out the back of his skull and dropping his corpse into an ever-widening pool of his own blood. Da Avolo's shot shattered the coffee urn behind Francesca.

In the point-blank gunbattle that lasted five seconds, Cain was shot seventeen times, mostly in the chest and arms, his armor—thicker and heavier than Francesca's—absorbed the rounds, though not all of their energy. He staggered to a halt under the barrage, firing with both pistols, sweeping the bandstand before turning his fire on the left side of the boathouse. He did not concern himself with the right side. The moment that Cain had burst into the room, Lester had slid open the northside door and—wisely remaining behind the, admittedly, dubious cover of the boathouse wall—opened fire first on the bodyguards near Hans and then turned to catch the remaining shooters on the bandstand in a hopeless crossfire with Cain and Francesca.

A silence, broken only by the unconscious moaning of a couple wounded bodyguards and the terrified crowd members, then took the boathouse, as Cain, Francesca, and Lester passed their pistols over the dead and the cowering. Cain then holstered one pistol and rushed over to Francesca.

"Are you alright?" they both demanded of each other.

Cain then patted Francesca's chest and arms, looking carefully under her jacket.

"What are you doing?" she said, slapping his hand away.

"Checking for blood," he said. "In case anything made it through your armor."

"I am fine," she said. Leaning in closer and speaking softly, she added, "I was hit in the right bosom; the armor defeated the round but it is now *throbbing*."

Cain grinned and said, "Yeah, you have a hell of a bruise to look forward to."

"And you?" she asked, returning his searching caresses. "Are you alright? Look at your coat, your shirt!"

"I'm fine," he said and raised her chin to look away from his torn clothes and at his grinning face. He then looked over his shoulder at the cowering Stinnes, who had ducked behind his podium and not moved since: to him, Cain said, "*Black* and blue all over, no doubt, tomorrow, but a lot better off than these punks."

Cain and Francesca then walked through the prostrate crowd of racists, indicating with their pistols that everyone should remain on the ground, and came finally to the bandstand and Stinnes. Cain grabbed Stinnes by the back of his collar and lifted him off the ground, to dangle there with his toes scrapping the wood beneath him.

"Herr Stinnes," Francesca said in her most authoritative, prosecutor's voice, "you will now accompany me to Strasbourg. There is just enough time for us to attend tomorrow's session, where I will play for them the recording of what has happened here tonight and *you* will explain *The Madagascar Plan* and the steps you have taken to affect my assassination. Then I will deliver you to Interpol."

"Release me at once," Stinnes cried, his voice going up an octave. "I am not going anywhere with you—I have not broken any EU laws!"

"You have just ordered this man," Francesca said incredulously, pointing her .38 Super at Da Avolo's corpse, "to assassinate me in front of a room full of people."

"This is Monaco," Stinnes shouted, "not an EU state."

"Ah," Lester chuckled from where he covered the crowd, "I think he may have bribed a magistrate or two in the principality."

"Meaningless," Francesca said. "You have also admitted to funding Da Avolo's attempt on my life in *Venice*."

Stinnes, looking around wildly, finally shouted, "You cannot do this! You cannot remove me from Monaco—it would be kidnapping!"

"Oh, can't I?" Cain said and shook Stinnes until he cried out.

TAVs touched down on the dock and pier within minutes of the firefight's end, disgorging armed teams from Pons Sublicius, accompanied by lawyers; after a few minutes, the TAVs were followed by ground cars from Monaco's police department. Lester took command as the boathouse filled with his people, including a sleepy Liying (dressed in combat attire, but with the unaccountable addition of pink, fuzzy slippers).

"Pat down everybody," Lester told his lieutenant, "give first aid to anyone not dead, and then cuff all the rest of them. Ah, Francois!"

The Chief of the Monaco PD looked around, largely unconcerned, as Lester's people carried out his orders; Monaco police officers observed and provided assistance as needed, though it was largely unnecessary. Francois wore his uniform elegantly, having had it custom made by the same tailor that made Lester's new suit; his pencil-thin mustache and neatly parted hair gave the fair-skinned gentleman the appearance of an old-time aviator; his perpetual smirk was nearly a match for Lester's.

"Ah, Lester, my friend," Francois said and strode forward to take the other man's hand. "So much excitement for so beautiful an evening—I am glad you put a stop to it. We had begun to receive noise complaints."

"Oh, it was my pleasure, Francois," Lester said, chuckling. "We had a whole lot of terrorism going on up in here. The leader is right there, dangling from my large friend's fist, and, of course, you know the Mayor of Venice."

Francois bowed to Francesca, saying, "Of course! It is a pleasure to make your acquaintance, your Excellency. I have a young daughter and she tells me of all your exploits. You are quite a hero to her."

"Thank you, Francois," Francesca said. "That is very flattering. Please send her my regards."

"With pleasure, your Excellency," Francois said and bowed again.

"Yeah, fantastic," Lester said and turned Francois back around by the shoulder. "Francesca needs to take this guy, the terrorist chief, up to Strasbourg, show him to the EU Parliament, play the recording of what went down here tonight. That's no problem for you, I take it?"

"No, none at all," Francois said; Stinnes choked at this news. "Simply furnish me a receipt and return him when you are finished. Unless, of course, you intend to give him to Interpol? Yes? If so, have them contact my office so that we may coordinate joint prosecutions."

"Thank you, Francois," Francesca said, favoring him with a smile. "And thank you, Lester, for everything."

"It was my pleasure," Lester said, the purr of coming spoils in his voice. "Cain, your TAV awaits you, through the northside door."

CHAPTER 14

WITHIN THE CABIN of Cain's AugsRak TAV, he and Francesca sat holding hands, across the small space between the swivel chairs, eyes only for one another, and ignored the forward view screen's image of Switzerland passing beneath them. In the rear cabin, Stinnes struggled fruitlessly against his restraints, standing in the soundproof cell next to the shower. Since they had not broken Earth's gravity, Cain and Francesca had chosen to celebrate their victory with champagne.

"Well, Trouble," Cain said, touching his glass to hers, "you did it."

Beaming a smile filled with pleasure and satisfaction, heightened by relief, Francesca touched her glass to his and they sipped their wine before she said, "Thank you. And, do you see, there is no more trouble now."

"Oh, I think Trouble has always been there," Cain said, to Francesca's delight, "and always will be. Twenty years from now, when that old seawall is built and safe and no longer needs such strenuous defending, my guess is that you'll go right on out and find some new person to pick a fight with."

Francesca took another sip of wine and sat pensively for a moment before asking, "Do you really think I will wait that long?"

Cain laughed as the smile returned to her face and said, "No, now that you mention it, no, I don't. And I'd never ask you to. I'd never ask you to give up that dangerous lifestyle of yours, even though I feel like it's my life hanging in the balance, only less in my control."

Francesca's smile turned a little rueful then and she set her glass aside, taking Cain's hand in both of hers. "If that was revenge," she said, "it was sweetly done. Seriously, though, no, I could not give up this life I lead. I would feel purposeless, that I had failed not only myself but everyone, anyone I could have helped. Which is why I can so fully understand and admire the choice you have made to step away from *your* dangerous lifestyle. It makes my heart race to ask this, but are you having second thoughts?"

"Yes," Cain said, trying—and failing—to entirely stifle his grin. "I am. I don't think I can go into security consulting, like I was thinking."

"Oh, you do not think so?" Francesca said, also failing to stifle a grin; she knew she was being teased but could not quite see how or to what end, and would not cede the contest to Cain so easily. Matching his conversational tone, instead of slapping his hand as she wanted to, she said, "And what will you do instead?"

"Well, with you out there causing all this trouble," Cain said, "I figure you're going to need one hell of a new Chief of Security."

Francesca caught her breath and then shot to her feet and fell into Cain's lap, throwing her arm around his neck and kissing him. "Yes, yes, I agree," she said, her other hand caressing his cheek. They kissed again, long and slow, savoring as much the time that they knew they would spend together, which seemed to stretch out before them, as the time they enjoyed in that moment. Francesca pressed her forehead to his and, in the same intimate tones, said, "I suppose this means, then, that you are my employee."

"Excuse me?" Cain said, pulling back far enough to look into her taunting smile. "It does not."

"Yes, yes it does," Francesca said, laughing and touching his lips as he protested. "If you are my Chief of Security, then that means that you work for me."

"You think you could afford my rates?" Cain said.

Francesca tossed her head back and laughed before saying, "Well, no, probably not. I am merely a public servant, you know."

"Alright then," Cain said and settled back into his chair. "Let's consider this a kind of partnership, then."

"Yes, alright," Francesca said and kissed him again. "I will get us into trouble and you will get us out of it."

Cain kissed her back before saying, "Deal."

The End

Made in the USA
Middletown, DE
03 July 2024

56793354R00201